Niagara Squadron

The Eighth Carlisle & Holbrooke Naval Adventure

Chris Durbin

Chris Durbin

To Ellworth and Wendy Beckmann

Who took Lucia and me on a tour of Fort Niagara and the Great Lakes

'Not another fort!'

Niagara Squadron

Editor: Lucia Durbin

Cover Artwork 'Schooner Mohawk on Lake Ontario' by Bob Payne

Cover Design: Book Beaver

Visit my website at:

www.chris-durbin.com

First Edition: October 2020

Chris Durbin

CONTENTS

Chris Durbin

LIST OF CHARTS

NAUTICAL TERMS

Throughout the centuries, sailors have created their own language to describe the highly technical equipment and processes that they use to live and work at sea. This holds true in the twenty-first century.

While counting the number of nautical terms that I've used in this series of novels, it became evident that a printed book wasn't the best place for them. I've therefore created a glossary of nautical terms on my website:

www.chris-durbin.com/bibliography/

My glossary of nautical terms is limited to those that I've mentioned in this series of novels as they were used in the middle of the eighteenth century. It's intended as a work of reference to accompany the Carlisle & Holbrooke series of naval adventure novels.

Some of the usages of these terms have changed over the years, so this glossary should be used with caution when referring to periods before 1740 or after 1780.

The glossary isn't exhaustive; Falconer's Universal Dictionary of the Marine, first published in 1769, contains a more comprehensive list. I haven't counted the number of terms that Falconer has defined, but he fills 328 pages with English language terms, followed by an additional eighty-three pages of French translations. It is a monumental work.

There is an online version of the 1780 edition of The Universal Dictionary (which unfortunately does not include all the excellent diagrams that are in the print version) at this website:

https://archive.org/details/universaldiction00falc/

PRINCIPAL CHARACTERS

Fictional

Commander George Holbrooke: Commanding Officer, Naval Party, Niagara Expedition

Lieutenant Charles Lynton: First Lieutenant, Naval Party, Niagara Expedition

Reverend John (David) Chalmers: Chaplain, Naval Party, Niagara Expedition

Jackson: Bosun, Naval Party, Niagara Expedition

Jacques Serviteur: Captain's Servant, Naval Party, Niagara Expedition

Abraham Sutton: Carpenter, Naval Party, Niagara Expedition

Kanatase: Mohawk Warrior

Martin Featherstone: Corn Merchant in Wickham

Sophie Featherstone: Martin Featherstone's Wife; stepmother to Ann

Ann Featherstone: Martin Featherstone's Daughter

***

Historical

William Pitt: Leader of the House of Commons

Lord George Anson: First Lord of the Admiralty

Admiral George Forbes: Lord Commissioner of the Admiralty

John Clevland: Secretary to the Admiralty Board

Brigadier General John Prideaux: Commander of the Niagara Expedition

Sir William Johnson: Indian Agent, known as *Warraghiyagey* to the Mohawks

Lieutenant Colonel Eyre Massey: Commanding Officer, Forty-Sixth Regiment of Foot

Captain Joshua Loring: Commander of naval vessels on Lake Ontario

Pierre François de Rigaud Vaudreuil: Governor of New France

Louis-Joseph de Montcalm: Military Commander in North America

Captain Pierre Pouchot: Commanding Officer, Fort Niagara, known as *Sategariouan* to the Indians

***

Chris Durbin

1759 American Campaign

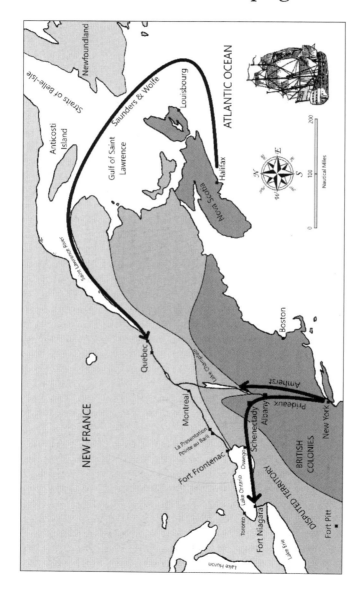

Fort Stanwix to Oswego

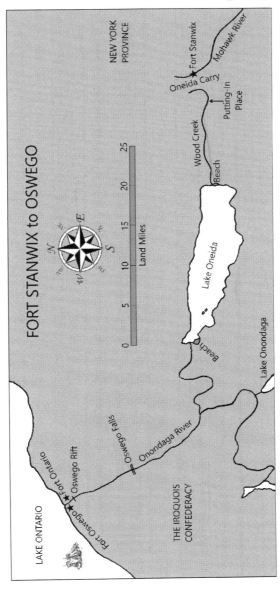

Chris Durbin

Lake Ontario

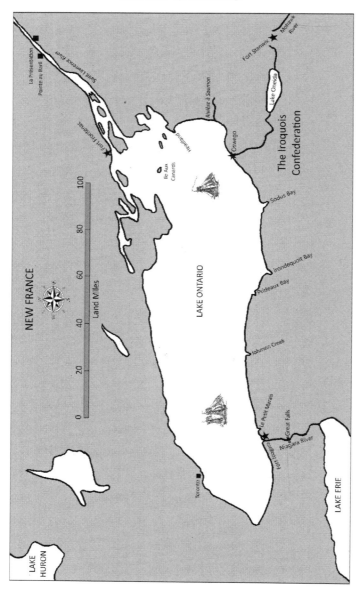

Fort Niagara and La Belle Famille

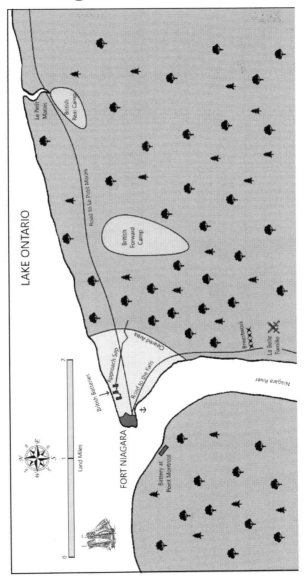

'The great importance of this fort will sufficiently appear, when it is considered that by this pass alone the French can pass to the river Ohio, Fort du Quesne, Detroit and the Mississippi... Thus, by being masters of this pass, we may for-ever prevent any incroachments of the French, and confine them within the proper limits of Canada'

***

Account of an English Prisoner at Fort Niagara (presumed Captain Jonathan Carver, of Roger's Rangers) 1758

***

INTRODUCTION

The War in North America

William Pitt had planned that the end of 1758 would leave him in command of the Ohio Valley, Lake Champlain and the Saint Lawrence as far as Quebec, so that in 1759 he could squeeze Montreal and force the surrender of all New France. However, the year didn't turn out as well as he had expected.

The campaign season started with a defeat as a powerful force led by General Abercromby failed to capture Fort Carillon at the southern end of Lake Champlain and suffered heavy casualties at the hands of Montcalm's troops. As a result, Abercromby was replaced as Commander-in-Chief North America by General Amherst. To Pitt's frustration, the French would hold Lake Champlain for another year.

Further west there was a surprise victory when Fort Frontenac, located at the point where Lake Ontario empties into the Saint Lawrence, was taken and destroyed, briefly disrupting French communications between Montreal and Quebec and their western territories.

In November, a mixed force of British regulars and colonial militia advanced on Fort Duquesne. They had learned the lessons of wilderness warfare in the disastrous 1755 attempt and, after an initial repulse, they took possession when the French destroyed the fort and withdrew to the north. The British rebuilt it and named the new structure Fort Pitt.

However, the best news was the taking of Louisbourg which fell to General Amherst and Admiral Boscawen in August 1758. It was welcome news indeed, but it fell so late in the year that the army couldn't push on up the Saint Lawrence River to lay siege to Quebec, as Pitt had intended, before the end of the campaign season. Amherst left a garrison at Louisbourg and Boscawen left a squadron at Halifax, and the remainder of the British forces withdrew until the next year, (see the seventh novel in this series, *Rocks and Shoals*.)

***

While 1758 wasn't an unqualified success for William Pitt's strategy, it did lay the foundations for 1759. This time there would be no mistakes. General Wolfe and Admiral Saunders were to sail up the Saint Lawrence and take Quebec. Amherst was to advance up Lake Champlain while a separate force was to cross the wilderness to attack Fort Niagara. If the strategy worked, then Montreal would be isolated, unable to communicate with France and unable to support its western possessions.

***

Carlisle and Holbrooke

In 1758 *Medina* had been part of Admiral Boscawen's fleet at the siege of Louisbourg, where Carlisle gained renown for his leadership in cutting-out two French ships-of-the-line. When the fortress fell, *Medina* was sent south with a convoy and Carlisle reached Williamsburg just hours after the birth of his son. In early 1759 *Medina* was ordered to join Admiral Saunders' fleet for the attack on Quebec.

Meanwhile, in 1758, Holbrooke's *Kestrel* joined the Inshore Squadron of the Channel Fleet under Commodore Howe to take part in Pitt's strategy of descents on the French coast. His hopes of being made post-captain – and with them his prospects of marrying Ann Featherstone – were dashed when he was captured on the beach at Saint-Cast, as he was covering the withdrawal of the army. When he was exchanged and returned to England, he found that *Kestrel* had been given to another commander. There was no ship for him, and at the end of 1758 he was sent to North America to command the small naval party that would manage the boats for the advance on the French fort at

Niagara, and confront the French navy on Lake Ontario.

**

PROLOGUE

The Promotion Board

Monday, Fifteenth of January 1759.
The Admiralty, London.

Edward Boscawen lowered himself into the chair at the head of the boardroom table. Lord Anson was absent, commanding the Channel Fleet during the period of Hawke's disgrace, and it fell upon Boscawen as the senior naval lord to chair the meetings of the Board of Admiralty. That was particularly so when the subject under discussion was a purely naval matter, if anything could be so described in the hot-house political atmosphere of the middle years of the eighteenth century.

Boscawen looked around as the other members took their seats. John Forbes was there, of course, the only other naval lord, and the three civilians: Hay, Hunter and Elliott. John Clevland sat on Boscawen's right hand side. Clevland wasn't a member of the board, he was the secretary – the only permanent member among them – and he wielded enormous power. Boscawen would rather that the civilian members had given their excuses for this session, but with patronage to be dispensed, he could hardly have hoped that they would forego the opportunity to have their say. Boscawen understood the role of patronage; it was what kept the votes coming and the money rolling in, and it maintained the government's war aims, but still he regretted it.

Anson had made his views clear before he sailed with the fleet: there were to be no promotions without merit. That didn't exclude the consideration of political and personal patronage, but it did mean that an officer couldn't achieve promotion on those grounds alone. He had to have proved his worth, preferably in action against the enemy, but if he had not had the good fortune to be engaged, then through the solid reports of his superiors. The days when the King's commissions were handed out without any regard to the needs of the service were over, swept away eight years before on the wind of change when Anson became the first lord.

Boscawen took a quick glance at the wind dial over the mantlepiece. It had been installed at the time of the Dutch wars and was a good indicator of the ability of the fleet to sail from the Thames. It was less useful for the winds to the west of London, but with an intelligent understanding of the weather patterns it gave at least some idea of what the Channel Squadron was facing off Ushant. East-nor'east, he noticed. The inshore squadron – the most weatherly of the ships – would be patrolling in the approaches to Brest, perhaps pushing as far as the Blackstone, if the tide permitted. Anson with the main body of the fleet would be hard on the wind, tack upon tack to avoid being swept away into the Atlantic. This was the perfect situation for the French fleet to sail and Anson would be on his guard, trying with all his might to keep his station and deny the enemy the freedom of the seas. God, he wished he were on a quarterdeck instead of sitting in a stuffy boardroom.

'You've seen the lists, gentlemen. We have eight vacancies for sloops and six to be made post. I don't have to remind you of Lord Anson's criteria for making these promotions.'

Hunter and Elliott exchanged glances. They were political animals and all that mattered to them was the arithmetic of votes in the House. The navy was by far the most expensive institution in Britain; it sailed on a sea of money that could only be obtained by marshalling enough votes to get the appropriations through parliament. These naval lords could proselytise all they liked about merit, but the arithmetic couldn't be denied.

'We'll start with the lieutenants to be made commander. Mister Clevland, be so good as to outline the candidates from the short list.'

There were twelve on the list. All were officers who, by their demonstrated capability and experience, had a good claim by their merit to that vital step to commander. It didn't take long to determine those that also had the backing of powerful men in the House and in government. There was a balance of sorts: five of them had both merit and sufficient interest and they made the cut with little discussion, the other seven had varying degrees of merit but little or no interest, and that was where the horse-trading took place. Three of them would be made master and commander and each given a sloop, the others would be placed on the next list, unless they should be promoted on a foreign station by a commander-in-chief or so distinguish themselves that they were plucked out of the lieutenant's ranks without the need to go before a board. It took half an hour but, in the end, it was done. Eight new commanders had been created, six of them to fill the places of officers to be made post and two of them destined for the new sloops that were being added to the fleet month by month.

By comparison, the list of candidates for post-captain was considerably more difficult. A master and commander was rightly regarded as little more than an elevated type of lieutenant, while a post-captain was a different class of officer entirely. Post-captains had tenure. Their half-pay when they didn't have a ship was enough to live on and they only had to continue to exist to be made admiral in the fullness of time. If their Lordships came to regret the promotion of a man to the rank of commander, then they could cast him ashore after a short time in a sloop, to rot on the meagre half-pay and never bother the councils of the mighty again. That was decidedly not the case for post-captains and Boscawen knew that this would be a harder-fought discussion.

'The first three, I think, will cause us little difficulty. They are all capable and experienced officers, and all have influential friends.'

'Indeed. We certainly can't pass over Jefferson. The

Duke of Devonshire mentioned his name in the clearest terms when he wrote to me about the naval vote,' said Hunter, 'and the other two are similar cases.'

'Then are we all agreed?' asked Boscawen, looking around the faces at the table. 'You may put your mark against Jefferson, Palmer and Scruton, Mister Clevland.'

They continued down the list, marking two more for promotion and placing a question against another two. Forbes was curiously silent until they came to the eighth name.

'George Holbrooke,' said Clevland, 'lately of *Kestrel* and now seconded to the expedition to Fort Niagara.'

Hay, Hunter and Elliott exchanged glances. They had only the vaguest awareness of Fort Niagara and, if asked, couldn't have said why a sea officer should be involved in an expedition to capture it. Clevland hadn't mentioned any influence that Holbrooke may wield.

'I confess that the name means nothing to me. Does anyone know Mister Holbrooke?' Boscawen asked.

Forbes paused for a few seconds. He was an old hand at these boards, and he knew that it required finesses to achieve the result that he wanted.

'I know Holbrooke,' he said calmly.

All eyes were on him. Don't rush, state his credentials before expressing support for him.

'He commanded *Medina* at Cape François while Carlisle was injured, and he drove a French frigate aground in the Caicos Passage.'

One item at a time, keep it simple.

Boscawen nodded. Every sea officer knew about Cape François, the first naval victory of the war and a much needed boost after the debacle at Minorca. He was starting to look interested.

'He was promoted by Cotes on the Jamaica Station and given *Kestrel*, which incidentally he had personally captured from a Dutch pirate.'

Positive evidence of his zeal, that always struck home.

'And he was with Holmes at Emden. By some accounts he took Emden before Holmes arrived.'

Experience of a higher level of decision-making.

'Then he was with Howe on the French coast and commanded a division of flatboats at Saint-Cast.'

'Now I remember the name. He was captured, wasn't he, and wounded?' Boscawen asked.

'That's correct, sir,' Forbes replied. 'but sadly, by the time he was exchanged his sloop had been given to Rickets who was on the last list.'

'Mister Holbrooke is a most deserving officer, I take it,' said Boscawen.

Forbes inclined his head in agreement.

'But without interest,' Elliott interjected, 'while Perrin, the next on the list, is a friend of Viscount Barrington.'

Hay and Hunter nodded vigorously. Barrington was the Second Lord of the Treasury and it was vital that his wishes should be honoured.

Forbes knew that he had lost as soon as Elliott spoke. Boscawen still looked thoughtful, but it was clear that the stark arithmetic of influence was against Holbrooke.

'I agree that Holbrooke is a deserving candidate,' Boscawen said slowly and carefully, 'However, he is out of reach for months to come and the army won't thank us for recalling him in the middle of a campaign. I take the point about Barrington…'

'It is most essential that he is satisfied, sir,' Hay said, interrupting.

Boscawen looked up in irritation.

'…I take the point about Barrington,' he repeated. 'We will bear Holbrooke in mind for the next board, or the first that sits after his return. Make a note, will you, Clevland?'

***

CHAPTER ONE

The Mohawk

Sunday, Third of June 1759.
Bateau No. 79, Mohawk River, New York Province.

The river was narrow here and the trees crowded in on either side, their canopies overhanging and almost meeting above the dark, shadowed water. Last year's fallen leaves had all been swept away downstream but there were still plenty of snags where fallen boughs hadn't been cleared by the working parties sent down from the fort. They had rowed where the water was deep enough and the current sluggish, but for most of the time they had used long poles to push the boats upstream, employing the least scientific method of waterborne travel ever known. Now at last they were just a mile from their first destination, and the bend that carried the river north to Fort Stanwix was in sight ahead. They had been travelling for seven days from Schenectady where the portage – the overland passage between bodies of water – from the Hudson River met the Mohawk. Now the mixed group of soldiers, American bateau-men and the handful of sailors were looking forward to landing the two precious eighteen-pound siege guns and resting for a day or two before the next leg of their journey.

Commander George Holbrooke had spent three wearying spring months at Schenectady attempting to bring some order into the provision of waterborne transport for this small army. The task had been completed, but only just in time and with the providential arrival of five-hundred or so boatmen from Albany and thirty additional boats, fresh from the yard. Eventually, six hundred boats had been dispatched on the long passage up the river. The majority were the ubiquitous bateaux, the work-horses of the American inland waterways, but there were also a hundred or so whaleboats, lighter and faster than the bateaux but without their phenomenal carrying capacity. All this was needed to bring Brigadier General Prideaux and his army of five thousand British regulars and American provincials to Lake Ontario and thence to within striking distance of Fort Niagara. It was no job for a sea officer, he reflected, but it gave a certain satisfaction to see the boats on their way.

The Forty-Sixth regiment was already at Fort Stanwix, but the remainder of the army was spread along the hundred twisting miles of the Mohawk. This was Iroquois territory, or more specifically the hunting grounds of the Mohawk tribe, one of the six nations that made up the Iroquois confederacy. The Iroquois were at least nominally allied to King George and the Mohawks had been friends to the British for generations. From here to Lake Ontario they would be travelling in safe territory as the passed through the lands of the Mohawk, the Oneida, and the Onondaga. Holbrooke, however, had listened attentively to the advice of Sir William Johnson, the Indian agent for the province, and knew that the native tribes didn't have the same concept of fixed borders that the Europeans understood. The boundaries were constantly shifting, and bands of hunters moved from one area to another, sometimes having to fight for the right to do so.

***

Holbrooke's whaleboat was rowed by four brawny bateau-men from Connecticut. They had caught the slack water on the inside of a bend and for a short while at least they could pull the boat using the four oars, rather than poling it. Holbrooke looked eagerly upstream in the hope of catching the first glimpse of the fort, but all that he could see were the encroaching trees. Then something caught his eye on the far bank. Was that the stern of a bateau just showing from under the overhanging foliage?

'What do you make of that, Jackson?' he said to his bosun. 'Is that a bateau?'

Jackson narrowed his eyes against the slanting afternoon sun.

'I thought I saw something, sir, but the angle's wrong now.'

Holbrooke had been groping in his bag for his telescope, but it was too late. Whatever he'd seen was only visible from a point that was now twenty yards downstream of the whaleboat. And one thing that Holbrooke had learned on this long haul up the Mohawk was that upstream distance was as jealously hoarded by a river traveller as the windward position was by a seafarer. He would need a powerful incentive to return and look again, and an even more powerful incentive to cross the river into the full force of the current. Probably he'd seen nothing.

'Mister Lynton's signalling, sir. He's seen something as well,' said Jackson, looking astern at the second whaleboat.

It must be just at the place where Holbrooke thought that he had seen a bateau.

'Ahoy there, Captain Holbrooke!'

Lynton was pointing to the shore but sensibly keeping the bateau moving towards its destination.

'Easy on the oars,' growled Jackson.

Holbrooke twisted himself around on the thwart. These whaleboats didn't take well to people standing in them.

'What do you see, Mister Lynton?' he shouted through cupped hands.

'A bateau, maybe two, right under the trees,' he replied, pointing again.

Holbrooke had published the orders for the passage of the Mohawk, and they'd been counter-signed by Brigadier Prideaux. Nobody was to set foot ashore except at the regular camps along the way and nobody was to stray beyond the pickets. It was just possible that those boats were from the fort on some other errand, but it didn't seem likely. Most probably they were a couple of the bateaux carrying supplies that had become separated, and the crews had decided to rest before they arrived at the fort. It was a risk, but in principle they were in friendly territory and there had been no sign of an enemy, either French or Indian, on the long haul up from Schenectady.

'Corporal!' he said sharply to the man in charge of the four infantrymen in the boat. 'Stand-to in case there are any problems. Coxswain, take us over to those boats.'

The New Englander at the helm looked for a moment as though he would object, but over the past week he'd learned something of naval discipline, so he held his tongue and pushed the tiller over to starboard. He fervently wished that this English sea officer would go to the devil; they would be at the fort in only an hour or so, and he didn't want anything to delay their arrival.

'There's a canoe coming down towards us, sir,' said Jackson.

Holbrooke had seen it at the same moment. He'd heard about these interesting craft but not yet seen one. It was a small canoe made of tree-bark, large enough to carry two men. However, there was only one man in this boat, an Indian whom Holbrooke thought he recognised as having been in Sir William's company back in Schenectady.

'Hold our position here, coxswain, and let the bateau pull past us.'

They waited in the stream as the slow bateau moved ahead and the canoe came towards them. He was certain now that he'd seen this man before. A mental image came back to him. The Indian's upper body was lean and well-muscled, and he had a shaven head except for a tuft of hair from the top running down the back. He remembered with a shudder that it was called a scalp-lock. The lock was decorated with red yarns and a single eagle's feather that sloped down onto the Indian's neck and he had a black disc inserted into each ear-lobe. He was bare-chested with a plain silver gorget at his throat, and much of his body was painted in dark blue and red. Now he could see that the Indian had a belt slung over his shoulder carrying a powder-horn and a row of cartridges. All that Holbrooke could remember of him was that he was a Mohawk, one of the Iroquois who had attached themselves to Sir William as part of the alliance agreement. Holbrooke had never yet spoken to an Indian, and he was unsure how to begin.

'That's Kanatase, sir,' said Jackson. 'I've met him.'

'Does he speak English?'

'Quite well, sir, quite well. Better than many men I've met on the deck of His Majesty's war canoes,' he replied, smiling at his own joke.

'Then hail him if you'd be so kind.'

Jackson had no inhibitions about the protocol of speaking to another nation. He just raised his hands to his mouth and shouted in a three-reef bellow.

'Ahoy Kanatase. It's good to see you!'

The only sign the Indian showed of having heard him was a thin smile as he sat back on his heels and let the current of the river take him down to the whaleboat.

'Jackson. Greetings,' he said as with a deft stroke of his paddle he brought the canoe alongside the whaleboat. 'This must be Captain Holbrooke. We have not met, sir.'

Holbrooke took a moment to recover. Kanatase's English was not at all what he'd expected. It wasn't quite grammatical, and he had a strong accent, but certainly Holbrooke had known many men both forrard and aft who were less intelligible. Of course, Kanatase's tribe had been in close contact with the colonials for generations, and Sir William wasn't known as the *Mohawk Baronet* for nothing.

'I'm glad to meet you, Kanatase,' Holbrooke replied. He restrained himself from offering his hand, believing that it wouldn't be welcomed, and was surprised when Kanatase thrust out his own. They shook and smiled at each other.

'I've come down from the fort to find two bateaux that haven't arrived. They were last seen a mile downstream from here.'

'Then I believe we can be of service. They're over there,' he said pointing at the dense line of trees on the shore, 'but you can't see them from here. We were just about to investigate.'

Kanatase steadied his canoe with one hand on the

bateau's gunwale and stood to get a better view. Holbrooke could see now that he wore a plain deerskin breech-clout and leggings with moccasins, and at his belt he carried a tomahawk and a scalping-knife. In the canoe beside him was a flintlock musket, of a type that was lighter than the infantry weapons, and a short spear or lance decorated with a few coloured feathers near the blade.

'A Seneca scouting party was seen yesterday, just a day's march from the fort,' the Mohawk said, studying the line of trees where they met the river.

'I had understood that the whole Iroquois nation was with us,' said Holbrooke, thinking about his conversation with Sir William.

Kanatase gave him a strange, almost paternal glance.

'You have much to learn of the Iroquois, Captain. The council speaks for the tribes, and yet the tribes do not speak for all their members. The Frenchman Captain Pouchot, whom the Seneca call *Sategariouan* – that's something like *the centre of fair dealing* in your language – has returned to Fort Niagara, and the Seneca have a long history of friendship with him. There are Seneca warriors who will speak kind words to both sides until it is clear who will win. Seneca, Cayuga, Onondaga, Tuscarora, Oneida, their allegiance to your King diminishes the further west their hunting grounds lie.' He shaded his eyes again and stared at the shore. 'Only the warriors of the rising sun can be fully trusted,' he added. 'It's too quiet over there, if the crews of two boats were ashore, we would hear or see them.'

Holbrooke looked thoughtful. He didn't know how far he could trust this Indian, despite his assurance of faith. If the Seneca could be sitting on the fence, why not the Mohawks? He looked at his two whaleboats. Besides his first lieutenant, his bosun, his servant and the chaplain, he had eight soldiers of the Forty-Fourth regiment, led by a corporal. These were cast from a different mould to the hapless line infantry that had been cut to pieces at Monongahela four years before. They'd learned about fighting in the wilderness and they were better trained and equipped than the men who had followed General Braddock to ruin. There was no sign of the bright regimental coats and they wore sleeveless waistcoats of browns and greens. They carried the handier carbines, and each had a tomahawk tucked into his belt. Kanatase was waiting patiently – politely even – to see what this English sea-captain would do.

'We'll stay together; I'll not have the force split when we don't know what we're up against. Mister Lynton, you stay close on my left. We'll approach slowly and when I give the signal pull like your life depends upon it.'

Kanatase gave a barely-perceptible nod of approval, cautious endorsement from a born forest fighter.

'Corporal. As soon as you can, jump ashore and take your men twenty paces forward, no more than twenty paces, mark you, and establish a perimeter where your men can see each other. Mister Lynton, Mister Chalmers, Mister Jackson, Serviteur, stay with me close to the boats. Boatmen stay in your boats and be ready to move quickly if needed. Kanatase, will you join me?'

The Mohawk nodded soundlessly and caught a stern painter thrown from the whaleboat's transom. With his canoe secured he stepped into the whaleboat.

Holbrooke noticed the soldiers adjusting their equipment, checking their flints and easing the tomahawks in their belts. The corporal was talking to them now, brutal advice and cruel jests, pumping up their courage before they jumped ashore into the unknown. They looked nervous, but not yet terrified. Holbrooke reflected that however many times they did this, the act of throwing themselves into the dense forest against a people born to the wilderness was a singularly courageous act.

'Captain Holbrooke, a word if I may, sir.'

That was Captain Strachey, commander of the Royal Artillery detachment. He was with one of his eighteen-pounders in a cumbersome bateau. Holbrooke had made it quite clear that whatever the two escorting whaleboats did, the bateaux with their irreplaceable cast-iron cargoes were to press on upstream; Strachey was not invited to join the two whaleboats.

'Be careful with the savage,' Strachey whispered, 'they can't be trusted.'

It was certain that Kanatase had heard him, but he chose to ignore the remark, turning his back pointedly and scanning the shore. Holbrooke inclined his head in reply. He'd already decided how far he could trust the Mohawk and didn't care to be advised on the matter. He was irritated that Strachey should have made such a clumsy remark. If this was an example of the way that the regular army treated their Indian allies, then Holbrooke could foresee trouble in the future. It was comforting to know that Sir William took a different approach

The coxswain of Holbrooke's whaler shifted his quid from one cheek to the other and spat a black stream of tobacco-juice into the river.

'Give way easy lads,' he said to his oarsmen, 'and stand by to stretch out when I give the word.'

'Half-cocked and ready, sir,' the corporal said.

Holbrooke looked over his shoulder and beckoned to Charles Lynton, his first lieutenant in this odd little command, who waved in acknowledgement. Soon both whaleboats were pulling steadily towards the southern bank of the river. The rest of the convoy continued its way towards the fort. Strachey gave a heavy shrug of resignation.

It was a hard pull across a current that increased rapidly in strength as they passed over towards the outside of the bend. Something was amiss, but whether it was a minor disciplinary matter or a bloody end to the bateaux crews, he didn't yet know. At the very least the bateau-men were disobeying his standing orders that nobody was to set foot ashore without an armed guard; those bateaux carrying the army's supplies had no soldiers on board and the crew were not well-unarmed. It was very strange, and ominously none of them were in sight.

The still air hung heavily over the river. There was a feeling of thunder, and the hairs on the back of Holbrooke's neck were prickling, telling him that all was not well. There was still no sign of life on the two boats. Now that they were closer, Holbrooke could see that it was not such a bad landing place. From downstream it looked as though the forest came right down to the river, but now he could see a cleared space on the bank. The two bateaux nestled under the trees, apparently abandoned, although it would have been impossible to see their crews if they'd ventured as little as ten yards into the forest.

'Magazine boats, sir,' Jackson said with certainty. 'I can see the powder barrels.'

Holbrooke stared again. Jackson had good eyes; they could as easily be barrels of flour as far as he could tell.

***

'Now!' Holbrooke said in a low growl. 'Pull for all you're worth, straight at the bank. Brace yourself, men.'

He waved at Lynton, an imperative forward motion of his extended arm.

Was he nervous himself? In a way, yes, but he was already experienced at putting a force of soldiers onto a hostile shore. He'd spent months of the previous year engaged in doing so on the coast of Brittany and Normandy. He'd paid for it as well, being wounded and nearly killed before being taken prisoner in that disastrous retreat at Saint-Cast. And yet this was different. The terrain was close and wooded whereas in France he could always see the enemy. And the French were more like the English, civilised if that was the right word. In any case, he hadn't run the risk of scalping or being carried away to slow torture. No, he wasn't nervous, he told himself, suppressing a shudder. He wasn't nervous...

The banks of the Mohawk River were in no place neatly tended, and often there was a marginal zone of wooded debris and weed that stretched some yards from the hard, true bank. And it was fortunate that it was so because it slowed the whaleboats before their prows hit the bank, and the occupants merely swayed forward against each other rather than tumbling onto the bottom-boards.

The soldiers were ashore before Holbrooke could collect his wits. Their actions bore little resemblance to the ponderous drills of the line infantry in Europe. Even the grenadiers that Holbrooke had put ashore had moved slowly by comparison. They threw themselves onto the bank and in seconds had vanished into the forest. Twenty yards, Holbrooke had said, but they may as well have been a mile away for all that he could see of them. But he heard them calling softly to each other, with the louder voice of the corporal issuing orders. Their discipline, their sense of self-preservation had impelled them to run straight over the scene of horror that was waiting for them on the bank.

Kanatase was the next to jump ashore, with his musket in his left hand and his spear in his right. He moved stealthily to the edge of the tiny clearing and crouched low, waiting.

Holbrooke was rooted to the boat for a moment, immobilized by the horrific scene in front of him. The clearing was no more than ten paces deep and perhaps fifteen paces wide, and yet at a quick count there were seven bodies lying scattered around. Chalmers moved quickly from one body to the next. Each had been scalped, that much was obvious, and most had deep gashes across their throats. They lay in pools of their own congealing blood.

Kanatase dipped his finger in the blood of the body closest to him and held it briefly to his lip.

'They are not far away,' he said in a low voice. 'This was done less than less than twenty minutes ago.'

Holbrooke hefted his pistol and forced himself to look at the bodies. He'd never seen the victim of a scalping before and he recoiled from the brutal reality. Yet he was the leader of this small group and knew that he had to keep his nerve.

'Will they attack again?' he asked.

'Perhaps,' said Kanatase, 'but they are few, no more than twelve, and they've taken their scalps.' He looked thoughtful for a moment and stared into the forest.

'Here's one still alive,' said Chalmers. 'The cut to his throat was a shoddy affair, not deep enough to reach the artery, nor the windpipe. He's lost a little blood and a portion of his scalp, but he may yet live. Ah, he's awake.'

Holbrooke left Chalmers to deal with the man. Surely he couldn't live with a hand's breadth of skin ripped from the top of his skull. Yet he'd heard that it was not unlikely.

'Mister Jackson, Serviteur. Help Mister Chalmers load those bodies into one of the bateaux. The wounded man can go in the other, the three of you will stay with him, if you please. We'll take them in tow to the fort.'

He looked at the bateau-men and saw that they agreed with him. These were their own friends, and they deserved a decent burial.

Chalmers was listening intently to the wounded man. His voice was too weak to reach Holbrooke, so it was from Chalmers that he heard the news. The Indian war-party had carried off one of their number, the youngest of them, a boy of fourteen, Holbrooke looked questioningly at Kanatase.

'He's safe,' he said. 'They will take him into the tribe to increase their numbers. All of these,' he swept his hand around the pathetic bodies and the wounded man, 'are too old. They only want young men.'

Holbrooke nodded. He had heard about this Indian custom. All the tribes had a perpetual problem with maintaining their numbers in the face of warfare, disease, harsh winters and famine, and they had no qualms about kidnapping to bolster their ranks. Probably Kanatase was right, and the boy was as safe as he could be anywhere.

'All quiet, sir.'

That was the corporal coming to report.

'Ssss.' Kanatase let out a sharp sibilant and held up his hand for silence. He cocked his ear to the west.

Now Holbrooke could hear it, faint and far-off, the whooping of a war party, strangely impersonal and benign at that distance, considering the gory scene that surrounded them.

'Stand to!' the corporal shouted, breaking the stillness, and he ran back to his men at the perimeter.

Kanatase grunted dismissively and stood erect.

'They're only taunting us, Captain. They are far away now and won't stop until they reach their own lands. They're Seneca, I'm sure, and they have four days of hard travel before they can display their scalps in their villages. Seven scalps and a captive! They have much to celebrate.'

Kanatase continued to listen intently, as though the sounds meant something more to him, something personal perhaps. Then he nodded as if in recognition of a particular voice. He smiled grimly and nodded to himself.

Holbrooke looked carefully around. There was no doubting Kanatase's sincerity. All that remained now was to carry their grizzly cargo to Fort Stanwick. And to try to erase the memory of that bloody clearing beside the Mohawk River.

***

CHAPTER TWO

Fort Stanwix

Friday, Fifteenth of June 1759.
Fort Stanwix, Head of the Mohawk River, New York Province.

Fort Stanwix had been hastily built the previous year and a generous heart would agree that it was at best a work in progress. Earth and logs from the forest were the staple building materials, and sods to keep the earth in place during the cold, wet winters. Its shape – a four-pointed star – paid a sort of modest homage to the great military engineers of the time, but it was tiny by comparison to the massive stone forts being built in Europe.

The fort's sole purpose was to guard the Oneida Carry. This strategic portage crossed the watershed that separated the Mohawk River, flowing eastwards to the Hudson and the Atlantic, from Wood Creek, Lake Oneida and the Onondaga River that drained into Lake Ontario and thence into the mighty Saint Lawrence River. The portage itself was of no great length, between one and four miles depending on the height of the water in Wood Creek and whether its upper reaches had been cleared of debris. And yet the Oneida Carry was vital to Pitt's plans, as the only route available for an army to take on its march to Lake Ontario and thence to Fort Niagara. For in the eighteenth century the only practical way for a large body of men and supplies to cross the wilderness of North America was by its rivers and lakes, with the occasional stretch of dry land between one waterway and another. The forests were impassable without a huge effort to clear the trees, fill the swamps and build roads.

The structure of the fort sat some five hundred yards west of the Mohawk River where a bend marked the point where a traveller heading for the frontier lands would otherwise be forced to turn north, away from his destination. If well-manned, it could survive an attack by Indians and it could hold out for some time against an attack by French infantry, if they weren't supported by field guns. Fort Stanwix could be described as adequate for its limited purpose, but no more than adequate. It was usually a quiet spot, manned by a couple of companies whose principal purpose was to keep the portage road clear.

However, an army was now gathered in and around the fort, the army that Brigadier Prideaux had brought up the Mohawk from Schenectady. There were three regular infantry battalions, drawn from the Forty-Fourth and the Forty-Sixth regiments and a battalion of the Sixtieth, the Royal Americans. The New York Provincials had also provided two battalions that included a unit from Rhode Island, and there was a detachment of gunners from the Royal Artillery. Some five thousand British and colonial fighting men made up the force, and they were supported by another thousand men of the Bateau and Transport service, each of whom was armed, though principally for defence. The Iroquois warriors made up the remainder of army. They were led by Sir William Johnson, the British Superintendent of Indian Affairs for the northern colonies, and they were arriving in small bands every day. It wasn't a huge force, and arguably it was light for its intended task, but it was the largest army that had yet been seen at the Oneida Carry, and its huts, tents, wagons and boats filled the area between the fort and the river.

***

The brigadier's headquarters at Fort Stanwix was nothing more than a one-room clapperboard cabin with a shingle roof. There was no chimney and the windows, entirely innocent of glazing, were closed by rough wooden shutters when needed. It must have been uncomfortable in the extreme when the snows came but in high summer it let the cooling breeze blow through while shading its occupants from the sun.

'We march from the fort within the next few days,

gentlemen,' said Prideaux, sweeping his eyes across his senior officers who were sweltering in their heavy regimentals for this most formal yet.

A tall, strongly-built man wearing the type of austere wig that was becoming rare on campaigns was the first to respond. Prideaux' second-in-command, Frederick Haldimand, was a Swiss in British service, in command of the Royal Americans.

'May I ask, sir, have the six nations agreed to the posts on Lake Oneida? I wouldn't like to move forward to Lake Ontario without securing our lines of communication.'

'Sir William? Perhaps you can offer the true word from the Iroquois.' Prideaux replied, turning his head to look directly at Johnson.

Sir William Johnson had been resident in the Mohawk valley for over twenty years and he was well known – even respected – by the Iroquois. He was a good choice to command these important allies and he was an experienced soldier. He'd earned his baronetcy leading the British forces at the Battle of Lake George four years earlier and although he had no formal rank in the regular army – his commission as a colonel was a provincial rank – his reputation gave him an imposing status.

'These things move slowly, but I believe we'll have permission before we reach the lake. The Iroquois are impatient for us to take Fort Niagara and open up the trade routes for them, so it's only a matter of formality. I should hear tomorrow, but we can move forward with the vanguard in anticipation of agreement.'

Prideaux nodded. It was irritating to be so dependent on a single man, but he had little experience with the Indians and was relying on Sir William to manage these important allies. In this tree-encumbered wilderness where horses were nothing but an encumbrance, the Iroquois filled the role of light cavalry. They were his scouts and his screening force, his skirmishers and his pursuers.

'Mister Holbrooke. How soon can you be ready to move

the boats?'

Holbrooke looked quickly at Captain Allan MacLean to his right. MacLean was a company commander from the New York Provincials and had a special knowledge of the use of boats in these northern waterways. He was responsible for the management of the bateau-men and as such was Holbrooke's right-hand man. Maclean nodded covertly. They hadn't had a chance to speak before the meeting, and Holbrooke had therefore not had a recent report on the readiness of the boats. That nod told him all that he needed to know.

'There are just a few stragglers to come up the Mohawk, sir. Otherwise all the bateaux and whaleboats are ashore, and the wagons are being assembled. I expect to be ready for the portage on Sunday.'

'Tomorrow would have been better, Mister Holbrooke, but Sunday will do. See that they are all ready to move at daybreak.'

No what was all that about? Holbrooke wondered. They all knew that both ends of the Carry had to be secured against attack, and the road had to be improved before the vulnerable boats and supplies could start to be moved across. The vital eighteen-pounders could not be lightly exposed to enemy attack. Certainly, the earlier they started moving they better; there were far fewer wagons than there were loads to be moved and Holbrooke guessed that each wagon would need to make between six and eight trips to move everything to Wood Creek. It had been a wet winter and spring and the rivers were above their normal summer height but still it was a three-mile haul from the fort to the closest navigable part of the creek. Nevertheless, he couldn't see how the road could be made ready and secured before Sunday, so why was the brigadier implying that it was he, the sole sea officer on the expedition, that was holding up the army?

He watched the faces of the other land officers in the room. He'd been aware of a certain tension, a silent competition that ran in multiple directions through the army. On the one hand, the experienced commanders of regular line battalions, William Farquhar of the Forty-Fourth and Eyre Massey of the Forty-Sixth, tended to dismiss the value of the colonial officers. The colonial officers, Sir William who led the Indians, and John Johnston of the New York Provincials, thought the British regulars unsuited to this kind of frontier warfare. Sir William believed that he should have been given command of the expedition, and Massey thought that he should be the second-in-command. Haldimand of the Royal Americans occupied the middle ground, being neither British nor Colonial, and nobody trusted him.

It was clear that Prideaux felt himself surrounded by shifting alliances and he was lashing out in the direction that he thought safest. It showed in his expression and the way he squarely faced Holbrooke while his eyes flickered from one to another of his turbulent commanders, testing their reactions. Holbrooke noticed that he looked tired, as though he hadn't slept well for weeks. Henry IV, that most troubled monarch whose reign was defined by intrigue and rebellion, described the condition most neatly: *uneasy lies the head that wears a crown.*

Nevertheless, Holbrooke couldn't leave it there. He had to deal as an equal with these lieutenant colonels and to show weakness at this, their first formal gathering, just wouldn't do.

'I cannot answer for the safe delivery of the boats and supplies until the road is cleared and secured, sir, and that is a matter for the army,' he said firmly, holding the brigadier's eye. 'Even then, it will take four days for the last boat to reach Wood Creek, and a further two days to the head of Lake Oneida. I can stand by that schedule, sir, *if* the road is ready for the wagons and *if* it is made safe from attack.'

The silence in the cabin was intense. The sounds from outside; the shouted orders of a company being drilled, the creak of wagon wheels on their axles, the babble of six or seven thousand men crammed into a single square mile, went unnoticed. Prideaux looked for a moment as though he would explode, then the moment passed.

'Very well, then,' he said, backing down from the confrontation. 'You'll have your orders within the hour, gentlemen,' he added, breaking Holbrooke's gaze. 'Meanwhile, one company from each battalion is to be ready to march in two hours to secure the road as far as the put-in at Wood Creek; Colonel Farquhar, you'll command. Another company from each battalion for road clearance; Colonel Massey if you please. Colonel Haldimand will retain two companies to hold the fort until the last of the army has left. Colonel Johnston will command the remainder of the men to bring the boats and supplies to Wood Creek.'

None of this was a surprise to the men in the cabin, it had all been agreed before.

'Mister Holbrooke. The open water being your domain, I wish you to draw up an order of sailing for the passage of the Lakes. I've heard no word of the French coming this far east, but they command Lake Ontario and from there it's an easy ascent to Lake Oneida, and I have no desire to be surprised. I particularly wish that the guns are protected. When can you have those orders in draft?'

'Before the evening muster, sir,' Holbrooke replied.

He blessed the guardian angel that had whispered to him in Schenectady that he should prepare such orders against the need. Chalmers, who had taken upon himself the duties of clerk in advance of a navy board order to that effect, had carried them in his writing-box the length of the Mohawk River. They only needed amending for the latest returns of strength from each battalion.

Prideaux inclined his head gracefully. It appeared that even brigadiers had a conscience, and he was silently acknowledging the injustice of his earlier comments.

'When will you leave for your reconnaissance, Sir William?' Prideaux asked.

'At dawn, sir. I'll take a party of my Mohawks and

descend the creek as far as the head of the lake. It would be best if I can take some of the whaleboats,' he replied, 'and perhaps Mister Holbrooke could accompany me, or at least lend me his lieutenant to make the best assessment of the navigation of the creek and the landing places.'

Holbrooke had not been expecting this request, but he was starting to learn the army way of doing things, this off-the-cuff planning and insistent testing for their colleagues' weak points.

'I'll be honoured to join you, Sir William,' he replied.

***

Holbrooke left the cabin feeling as though he'd been subjected to an intense scrutiny. His passing examination for lieutenant had been easier than this. Massey joined him as he walked across the cleared centre of the fort and through the gate towards where his tent had been pitched among the bateau-men and the boats. He had a moment to notice two things: first that Massey was walking away from the direct path to his own battalion's lines, and secondly that Kanatase had been waiting outside the cabin and was now talking to Sir William, and they were both looking at him.

'I regret that we've hardly been able to become acquainted, sir,' Massey said as an introduction. 'On campaign I'm afraid we get into rather lax habits and don't stand too much on formality. I'm Eyre Massey, commanding the Forty-Fourth of Foot.'

'I'm pleased to meet you, sir,' replied Holbrooke with a smile of relief. At least here was a man who was prepared to extend the hand of friendship to a sailor far from his element. 'George Holbrooke, commanding the naval detachment and the bateau-men, and of course the boats.'

They walked together in silence for a few steps, but it was evident that Massey was not a man to whom this was a natural state. He was of middling height and slender build with a restless energy that showed in the quick movements and abrupt gestures.

'What do you think of this endeavour, Holbrooke? This

is a strange place to find a sea officer, although I know that you have some experience of land affairs. You were at Cherbourg and Saint-Cast, weren't you?'

Holbrooke grimaced at the memory.

'Yes, I had the honour to command a division of flat-boats on each occasion, and I had a section of the beach for the withdrawal.' He moved on quickly from that evil memory. He still occasionally woke up in a sweat remembering those French bayonets thrusting towards him as he struggled helplessly in the surf, and even now the ribs on his right side ached if exposed to a draught.

'But as for this enterprise, I can hardly offer an opinion. I understand that Niagara is a great fortification for these parts, much more formidable than this,' he said as he waved an arm at the earth palisades that were now behind them. 'Whether we have sufficient forces to take the place is a question beyond my competence.'

'Ah, but that's not quite what I meant. We mere soldiers can manage that business and just so that you understand me, I believe we have a perfectly adequate force for the task. The fort is, in a way, the easy part. Before that we have to bring this army to the walls of Niagara, and that can only be achieved by traversing Lake Ontario, which as the brigadier pointed out, is commanded by the French. That is where I would value your opinion.'

Holbrooke considered for a moment. He'd already had a brief discussion with Prideaux on this subject, and it was clear that the brigadier considered it to be Holbrooke's responsibility to ensure that the army passed safely through the lake.

'There are at least three, possibly four French vessels on the lake. The Indian reports are contradictory and probably wildly exaggerated; they may be first or second rates and have anything up to a hundred guns apiece.'

They both laughed at this patent absurdity.

'I suspect that in reality they are schooners or brigs with around ten guns, that seems more likely. But the number of guns is immaterial. With no British ships on the lake, either of them alone could destroy this army if they catch us.'

'Could such small ships really sink five-hundred boats? I ask in all ignorance.'

'No, not even all four of them – if there are four – could sink more than a handful before the rest ran for the shore. But once forced ashore, and with an alerted enemy cruising within sight, would we be able to continue? It's some hundred-and-thirty miles from Oswego to Niagara. Could the army march that distance with no road or bridge building materials, no draught animals, no proper wagons and with an artillery train to be carried?'

Massey looked thoughtful. He was clearly an intelligent man who considered all the possibilities.

'If we were cast ashore more than thirty miles from Niagara, we would be forced to turn back, that's my opinion,' he said. 'Much of the success of this expedition rests on your shoulders, it appears, Captain Holbrooke.'

Holbrooke nodded. He'd known that from the first moment that he'd looked at a map of the route that the army would take and heard of the French ships that patrolled the lake.

'Well, I must see to my men and issue my orders for tomorrow. I wish you luck, Captain Holbrooke.'

Now that was a strange conversation, Holbrooke thought. He had no wish to take part in the squabble that he saw developing in this army, and it did appear that Massey was attempting to recruit him. But perhaps he was misunderstanding the soldier, possibly this was just Massey's way of offering friendship and getting some early insight to the problems that the army would face on Lake Ontario.

***

'Serviteur, would you tell the officers that I'd like to see them in my tent in half an hour?'

Holbrooke's servant was a freed slave from Saint Domingue in the Caribbean. He'd joined Holbrooke two years before, coming aboard the frigate that Holbrooke was temporarily commanding just before the bottom dropped out of his little fishing boat off Cape François. He was a very superior sort of officer's servant, having been major-domo of a large French plantation house, and his English had become excellent.

Serviteur bowed.

'They've been waiting for you, sir, expecting orders, I believe. Shall I call them now?'

'Yes, please do, and ask Mister Chalmers to bring his writing case. And you should join us too, Serviteur.'

This strange little command of his demanded a different leadership style to a frigate or even the sloop that he had so recently commanded. With two commission officers, a chaplain-cum-clerk, a bosun, a carpenter and but one servant, it just wouldn't do to maintain the sort of distance that shipboard organisation would normally require. In any case, his servant had saved his life once and had been with him when he had scouted the French positions on the dunes at Cancale Bay on the French coast. He was far too valuable to be left out of the planning, and none of his officers expected that he would be.

Jackson arrived first. He was Holbrooke's bosun from his previous command and he'd volunteered to follow Holbrooke on this expedition. Next came Charles Lynton, the first lieutenant, then Abraham Sutton, a warranted carpenter from Plymouth Dock, and finally David Chalmers, unbeneficed clergyman and now temporarily rated captain's clerk for the purposes of pay and rations. A small command indeed mustering two commissions, two warrants, a nominal petty officer and a nominal servant.

***

CHAPTER THREE

A Black Humour

Friday, Fifteenth of June 1759.
Fort Stanwix, Head of the Mohawk River, New York Province.

The meeting was over, and his officers left the tent to make their preparations for the following day. Chalmers lingered behind. He had an ambiguous relationship with Holbrooke; one the one hand they were good friends and even used Christian names when the others weren't around. But Chalmers was also under Holbrooke's orders. He had been signed on to the strength of the expedition as an able seaman, but his real role was as Holbrooke's clerk.

'A messenger followed us up the Mohawk, George, with dispatches mostly for the brigadier. There's only one official letter for you; it's from the navy board and it formally appoints me as your clerk, which is useful for the extra pay alone.'

Holbrooke laughed. They had both made substantial sums in prize money and head money during Holbrooke's time in command of the sloop *Kestrel.* Neither of them was short of funds, and with no homes in England to maintain and nothing – absolutely nothing – to spend any money on in this wilderness, the question of pay seemed like a concern from a remote and exotic world.

'There are two personal letters,' Chalmers added in an expressionless voice.

He laid the envelopes on the writing desk.

'I didn't mention this before the meeting to avoid disturbing your train of thought. I'll leave you for a while, George.'

***

Holbrooke should have been warned by Chalmers' cautious manner, but it still came as a shock. He'd been in bubbling high spirits after the meeting; he liked all the people in his crew, and it was a delight to give orders in the certain knowledge that they would be promptly and competently fulfilled. Now he was faced with a situation that he could neither predict nor control.

The first letter was innocuous enough. The sailcloth wrapping tied with tarred small-stuff was a sure sign of a letter from his father, and the archaic address confirmed it: *Mister George Holbrooke, Master and Commander.* It was the second letter that caused the immediate descent into despair. The identity of the sender was clearly written on the back: *Mister Martin Featherstone, Esquire. Bere Forest House, The Square, Wickham.* He held the letter gingerly as though it carried a charge of black powder.

Holbrooke had written to Featherstone in November while they were off Ushant and the letter had been entrusted to a snow, *Hazard's Prize,* to be taken back to Plymouth. He had received no reply from Featherstone these last seven months, and he had concluded that either the letter had never reached its recipient, or the content had been so disagreeable that Martin Featherstone had not deigned to reply. Of course, he knew very well that there were a hundred things that could go wrong in such a fragile chain of communications. The snow may never have made Plymouth – the hazards of the sea and the enemy were quite sufficient to make that a possibility – and even then, the letter may have miscarried on its way to Wickham. Even if the letter had arrived quickly and safely, he could not have reasonably expected a reply until January or February at the earliest and by then he was on his way from Williamsburg to New York and Schenectady, and he had not stayed in one place for more than a few days in all that time. No, considered objectively, this was not an unreasonable time to receive a reply.

He opened the writing case and taking out his clasp knife, he sliced through the thick parchment of the covering. It was a short letter and it took no more than a few seconds to absorb its meaning. Martin Featherstone had been polite but firm, and the letter left no room for misunderstanding. Regardless of Holbrooke's new-found wealth – that was a bit much coming from a corn merchant – he was determined that his daughter, his only child, would marry into a higher stratum of society than a naval commander could offer. He had nothing against Holbrooke personally, and certainly nothing against the King's sea officers. He did not go so far as to say *you may re-apply for my daughter's hand when you are posted*, but that was the implication of the letter. Furthermore, it appeared that Martin Featherstone had little expectation of Holbrooke's advancement, as he had been a commander for a whole year at a time when commanders rarely served so long in the rank.

Holbrooke looked again at the date. The letter had been sent at the end of December, and if Martin Featherstone had written shortly after receiving Holbrooke's letter, then it must have taken an unconscionable length of time for *Hazard's Prize* to make Plymouth. Had the letter been received in Wickham in November, then Holbrooke could have received this reply while he was still in Williamsburg for Christmas. But what good would that have done? It would have tarnished the last few days with Edward Carlisle's family, and it would have brought a resolution no closer. For to Holbrooke, this letter solved nothing... unless, of course, Ann's father had found her a suitor already. It wasn't impossible. It was even quite likely, that his letter had stirred the ambitious corn merchant into action. Ann could already be married for all he knew. That thought brought on a black despair.

The shadows lengthened outside the tent as Holbrooke sat contemplating how he could have acted differently, how he could have made himself more agreeable to Martin Featherstone. But it appeared that only promotion would achieve that, and he had tried – was trying still – as hard as he could to make their Lordships take notice of him. What made it worse was the certainty that he had been forgotten, sent on this awkward mission to the far ends of the earth, and other commanders who had been lieutenants while he had command of *Kestrel*, were being posted ahead of him.

***

With a start, Holbrooke realised that he would need to read his father's letter immediately if he were not to have to call Serviteur for a lantern, with all the inconvenience that would cause in a tented camp.

It required rather more effort to penetrate his father's letter. The old man was a superannuated sailing master, now supplementing his pension by teaching navigation at the naval academy in Portsmouth, and the old habits of sealing a letter against the elements had not been lost. He cut through the wax seal and spent a few minutes untying the twine, dirtying his fingers with the tar as he did so. Then he carefully unpicked the sewn seam of the sailcloth pouch. Was this an unconscious delaying action while he continued to chew over the putrid carcass of Featherstone's letter? Probably.

At last he broke through the letter's final defences. Inside was a loose sheet densely packed with his father's economical writing, and an envelope, a much more feminine item of smooth, cream paper. Holbrooke's heart was racing, then he looked more closely at the address and saw that while it was undoubtedly a lady's hand, it was not Ann's. He turned the envelope over; there was no sender's address on the back. Disappointed, he picked up the loose note from his father.

Well, George. Time passes and the tide turns, but it exposes the same ground each time.

Holbrooke smiled. He had never known his father in a poetical mood before.

Not six months have passed, and I am again importuned (is that the right word? I mean no disrespect) by Mrs Featherstone. You will see enclosed a letter that she asked me to send to you, knowing that I understand the dispatch system better than she did – or so she said. I'll say now that the letter is from Mrs Featherstone, not Miss, to avoid disappointment on your part. I have not seen the letter, but Mrs Featherstone stayed some time with me explaining the situation, and she swore me to secrecy about her visit. I must say that I found that a little uncomfortable and do not know what I will say if challenged by Mister Featherstone, but I will cross that bridge when I come to it. Mrs Featherstone's character makes it difficult to sustain a disagreement. I have no experience in writing on these matters, so I will allow the letter to bear you the news. I will just say that all is not lost if you truly are still interested in Miss Featherstone, even if you should be unlucky in promotion (which I do not expect!).

All is well and life continues as usual. The stream is frozen today, and I tremble for the poor trout hiding under the alder roots. But spring will bring new hope as always.

Send me news of the campaign when you have a chance.

Holbrooke realised that he was straining to read the letter, it had grown so dark. The flap of the tent moved aside and Serviteur's massive shoulders came into view, carrying a shielded lantern.

'Mister Chalmers said that you would want this, sir,' he said and disappeared without another word.

Then it was known among his crew that he had letters. Would Chalmers have said where they came from? Unlikely; he was the very soul of discretion and would have revealed nothing more than that the captain needed to read after dark.

Dear Captain Holbrooke, the letter started.

Sophie Featherstone was Ann's stepmother and, in many ways, more like an older sister than a mother. If ever Holbrooke had an ally in his wooing of Ann, then it was Mrs Featherstone. She was of quite a different temperament to her husband. While Martin was a forthright, self-made man of business for whom a marriage was closely akin to a commercial transaction, Sophie had high notions of romance and marriage for love. While naturally respectful of her husband's views, Sophie worked diligently to frustrate his plans for his daughter's future. She had intervened twice before, to Holbrooke's knowledge. Once to send an illicit letter from Ann to George, using the same means as she now employed for her own letter, and again to have Ann wave to Holbrooke's ship from the Round Tower at Portsmouth as he sailed for the French coast. She was now saying in as direct language as she dared that Holbrooke should not despair, that Ann would wait for him, and that she would throw any objections that she could find in the way of other suitors.

Did Sophie Featherstone know that her husband had written in most discouraging, nay dismissive, terms to Holbrooke? Probably, he decided. He felt sure that she could wheedle any information that she chose out of her husband, but apparently her influence stopped short of changing his mind on the suitability of Holbrooke as a son-in-law. That was probably the difference between being a wife and being the mother of her husband's child; perhaps there was a lingering suspicion in Featherstone's mind that his wife didn't care so much for his daughter's future as he did. Be that as it may, Sophie's letter had indeed given Holbrooke new heart. He needed to walk, to think this through, and in this campaign tent – he had the luxury of not sharing it with another person – he couldn't even stand straight, more less pace up and down as he was accustomed to doing on his quarterdeck.

***

The sky was almost completely black when Holbrooke stepped out into the night. There were a few glimmers of light from nearby tents where officers were reading, or composing their orders or playing cards, but otherwise it was only the stars that illuminated the cleared space outside Fort Stanwix. The moon wouldn't rise for another thirty minutes as Holbrooke knew well, and it would be another half-glass before it came clear of the forest canopy across the Mohawk River. That was the seaman in him; he could tell the times of sunrise and sunset, moonrise and moonset, and the bearings of the celestial bodies, without even thinking. If he'd been within smelling distance of salt water, he could have told the state of the tide as well.

Despite the dark, Holbrooke knew the layout of the camp well enough. The great thing to bear in mind was to avoid wandering towards the picket lines. He didn't want to be the first officer on this campaign to be shot by a jumpy sentry, ready to see an Indian raid in every rustling in the bushes. He felt uncomfortable wearing his sword within the camp, but the brigadier had ordered that officers should always be armed, and a sword was the least encumbering weapon that he could reasonably wear. He strolled towards the where the boats were drawn up in neat rows ready to be sent to the portage.

'Good evening, George.'

Holbrooke jumped at the sound, then relaxed when he recognised the stocky figure who had come alongside him noiselessly and unseen in the dark.

'Oh, it's you, David. It's late to be out walking.'

'I could say the same for you.'

They walked on quietly. The last of the tents was behind them now and only the starlight guided their steps.

'You'll have seen the letter, I suppose,' said Holbrooke, at last breaking the silence.

'I noticed that you had a letter from Mister Featherstone, the long awaited reply to yours, I imagine.'

Chalmers knew Holbrooke well, perhaps better than he knew himself, and he had learned that it was no use pushing the young man. If he was going to open up it would be in his own good time.

'Yes, and it's much as I feared.'

Silence again as the two men reached the first of the boats and naturally started back towards the tents, turning inwards, of course, as they had learned to do on endless walks on small quarterdecks where it was important not to interrupt the conversation every ten paces.

'He'll not countenance a match with a sea officer of less than post-captain's rank. Do you know, he as good as said that he doubted whether I will ever be posted! He's been talking to that cursed half-pay captain up in Soberton I expect. I can just imagine what he said, he'd have trotted out the old story about commanders getting one shot, and how I've had mine and been shuffled off to the colonies.'

Chalmers nodded in understanding as he walked.

'And you know, he's probably right! My name will have been long forgotten in Whitehall. They'll be considering all the new commanders who were given their sloops after me. Yes, that old scoundrel in Soberton is probably advising him well.'

'Is this not an important appointment though? I know you have no ship, and I understand the importance of success at sea, but you were sent here through no fault of your own. Surely, in all justice, their Lordships will remember your sacrifice at Saint-Cast.'

'Perhaps they will,' Holbrooke replied. 'I don't say that there is no hope, just that the longer I stay here the further that hope recedes. I heard from Prideaux' secretary, by the way, that there is a post-captain to succeed me at the end of next month. There's no name mentioned, but he's already over here, with Amherst on Lake Champlain. There was a hint that I could remain under his command. If there's no hope for me at home, I may just do that and make a new life here. There'll be nothing for me back in Hampshire.'

Chalmers recognised that his friend was slipping into a black humour. There were many things that he could say to refute Holbrooke's pessimism – being succeeded by a post-captain must surely be a compliment, for example – but he knew they would do no good. Better to let the fit work itself out.

'I tell you one thing, David; I'll stop at nothing to make

my name on this expedition. There's no enemy I won't dare to come to grips with, and if I perish in the attempt? Well, it will be no great loss. You can have no idea how much I hope to find a French ship on the lake. I nice schooner or brig with perhaps half a dozen guns will be perfect.'

***

CHAPTER FOUR

The Oneida Carry

Saturday, Sixteenth of June 1759.
Fort Stanwix, Head of the Mohawk River.

Dawn came early this close to midsummer, and the sun burst over the treetops beyond the infant Mohawk River, shining brazenly from a cloudless sky and intensifying the already stifling heat.

'Now then, sir, you'll look after my whaleboats?' said Sutton as he fussed around the carriages that were to take them the three miles to the putting-in place at Wood Creek.

There were six whaleboats to carry the reconnaissance party, and four bateau-men to each boat with a larger gang to provide the muscle-power to move them swiftly over the portage. Sir William had brought forty Indians, all Mohawks, his most trusted tribe of the six nations. Holbrooke could see Kanatase close to Sir William. He was dressed much as Holbrooke remembered from two days before and appeared to carry nothing but his weapons of war and a single blanket that he had wrapped diagonally across his shoulder.

The whaleboats lay upon their carriages ready for the journey and the bateau-men stood around, ready for the massive effort of propelling them along the road to the creek. Sutton wasn't coming on the reconnaissance, but he was checking the carriages before they set off. This was the first time they'd been used for any great journey and Sutton didn't want anything to go wrong. He'd supervised the construction to a new design of his own that allowed the carriages to be broken down and carried in the bateaux or whaleboats when they were afloat. They looked ungainly at first sight: two stout axles joined by a flimsy-looking pole that didn't appear to be capable of taking any weight. But that was the beauty of the design: the keel of the boat provided the rigidity for the whole structure and the two axles merely supported the keel. The wheels on the forward axle were noticeably smaller than those on the rear, to accommodate the robust swivel arrangement that allowed the carriage to be steered. A shaft was attached to the forward axle, with two cross-pieces for the apparatus to be dragged by men, or by draught animals in the unlikely event of them being available. The sternpost of the boats – both the whaleboats and the bateaux were double-ended with no transom – offered a solid place for a man to push against when the going was rough. It was a good design, light in weight and easy to assemble and break down, and the same carriage worked equally well for the whaleboats or the much heavier bateaux.

This was why Sutton had been brought all the way from Devon. The New England craftsmen could build good boats, they could build good carriages, and they could produce them in great quantities. However, they lacked the experience to build to a standard design, a discipline that was by now second nature to the carpenters of the King's yards in England. Sutton had demanded standard sizes for the boats and a carriage made to a single pattern, so that there would be no delays while the boats were married up with the correct means of transport over land. The result was two sizes of bateau: one of thirty-eight feet and another of twenty-nine feet, and all the whaleboats were a uniform thirty feet in length. Of course it wasn't quite that simple, and at the last moment they had been gifted a flotilla of bateaux from New York that varied wildly in length, breadth, depth, weight and shape; but at least they would all fit on the standard-size carriages.

'I'd feel happier if the whaleboats could take a boat gun, Mister Sutton,' said Holbrooke, ruefully contemplating the lack of any mounted guns in his squadron.

'Couldn't be done sir, not anyway I look at it. They'll stand a pair of swivels, however. Now the bateaux, they'll take a four-pounder in the bows as well as a pair of swivels alright and I'll fit the first few with sockets for the crutches before you're back.'

That was the advantage of having an intelligent carpenter under his direct orders. They'd carried two four-pound boat guns and six half-pound swivel guns all the way from the ordnance yard at New York against just this need. It was all part of the plan to deal with the French on Lake Ontario that they'd worked out the previous evening, before the weariness and lack of light had driven them to bed. The clinker-built whaleboats were too flimsy to take much strain, but with a solid oak pad clenched to the outboard side, their gunwales could take a swivel gun each side. The bateaux were much stronger and their white oak sides could easily take the rotating crutch that gave the swivel-guns their name, and the bow thwart could be built up to take a four-pounder on a campaign carriage with the wheels locked to the keelson. Holbrooke wanted two bateaux and a whaleboat fitted out as gunboats; that was what the remainder of his party would be working on while he was away.

***

'Ready my lads? Then heave!'

The sergeant of the bateau-men, a great brute of a fellow, arched his back against the stern-post of the first boat while a gang of men strained at the cross-pieces and hauled at the spokes of the wheels. It took a dozen strong bateau-men to get the first whaleboat moving but then it was an easy matter for the four men of the crew to keep it rolling along on this flat, hard, dry ground. The big, spoked wheels helped; they didn't seem to notice the smaller stones so long as the carriage maintained some momentum. The secret was, as Holbrooke noted, to have a reserve of manpower for starting the carriages moving and to add muscle-power over the rough places and up the inclines.

During these early stages of the journey the men had time to laugh and joke as they pulled the boats along because at this end of the portage the road had been maintained, after a fashion. He could see working parties levelling the road ahead with shovels and pick-axes while pickets patrolled in the tree-line, guarding against surprise.

The road trended gently uphill – nothing to the brawny bateau-men – but he could see that at the top of the rise the trees pressed in and the road became vaguer, less well-kept. That must be the top of the watershed. When they were on the downhill run, they would cross from the land that drained into the Hudson to the hinterland of the continent where all rivers flowed towards the Great Lakes and the Saint Lawrence basin. With a gulp he realised that it symbolically took him from King George's domain to the lands claimed by King Louis. They were thrusting a blade into the soft underbelly of New France, while his friend Edward Carlisle was with the main attack some four hundred miles or so to the northeast, presumably at this moment ascending the Saint Lawrence towards Quebec. And that was not all. General Amherst was taking yet another force onto Lake Champlain to strike at the very heart, the capitol of the French American empire, Montreal. Did Montcalm have enough men and resources to guard against all three strokes? He had shown brilliant generalship so far. Constantly outnumbered and outgunned, he had not been content to wait for the British to come to him, but he had struck hard and often. In the Ohio Valley, on Lake Ontario and on Lake George, he had faced and defeated half a dozen British armies. Nevertheless, time was running out for the French. Unless they could parry two of these three thrusts, they couldn't last another year. Which would Montcalm deem least dangerous? Probably this one, Holbrooke thought. The loss of Niagara would certainly be a disaster and would herald the end of French ambitions for the Ohio Valley and the western Great Lakes, but it would be nothing compared to the loss of Quebec or Montreal. Would he commit any resources to defend the fort, or would he just abandon it and accept the inevitability of losing control of the West?

They paused at the top of the rise, while the bateau-men attached drag ropes to the rear axles of the boats. Now the purpose of the light poles that joined the axles together became apparent. Without them there was a very real danger of pulling the axles apart as the rear one was retarded in its way downhill.

The headwaters of Wood Creek were only half a mile ahead, marked out by a line of taller trees that took advantage of its moisture. The road that Holbrooke saw before him was dramatically different to the one they had ascended. Whether it was policy or a natural reaction to the change in the topography and the change of ownership, from the crest of the rise to the creek the road clearly hadn't been touched since the previous summer. It had become scrubland with the occasional fallen tree across the path and the winter's frost had broken the ground into ridges and small chasms. As far ahead as he could see, fatigue parties were clearing the worst of the obstructions and filling the deepest holes, but it was going to be a difficult task to get the boats down there.

'Ready again, lads?' shouted the sergeant.

Rough and ill-disciplined they may be, these New Englanders and New Yorkers certainly knew how to apply their muscles to a task. There was just one man at the cross-pieces to steer the carriage and the remainder were at the drag ropes and wheels. A rational man would expect that it would be easier moving these ponderous loads downhill than it had been to haul them uphill, but in this case he would have been wrong. The men at the drag ropes had to dig in their heels to stop the boats running away from them, while the reserve gangs ran ahead with ponderous great baulks of timber to thrust in front of the wheel if the carriages started to run away. Uphill, all the boats could move at once, but downhill it had to be done in two groups of three boats; there just weren't enough men to manage all six at once.

The road bumped and twisted gently downhill to the

head of the creek, then ran along the left bank close to the water. Here the ground was tormented by tree-roots and rocks, but it too had to be negotiated. Had they started two months earlier they could have taken advantage of the flood water and put the boats in at the first point that they came to on the creek. One look told Holbrooke why they hadn't even paused there; the creek here was a mere trickle, there wasn't enough depth to float even an unladen whaleboat. They scrambled and cursed another whole mile until they came to the first usable put-in. It could have been worse; in another month they would have had another two miles of portage before they could take to the water.

The sergeant knew his business. He hadn't let the boats get too close to each other to reduce the risk that they would collide when the first one stopped.

'Lean back, men!' he shouted, suiting his actions to the words as he threw his weight onto the wheel of the first carriage.

The man at the cross-piece hauled the shaft over to the left and the forward wheel ran into the brush and came to a halt. The next boat pulled in neatly alongside and so did the third. Like hackney carriages drawn up in neat rows on Whitehall, Holbrooke thought.

'Get a breather, then it's back up the hill for the others.'

Even the sergeant was blowing now, and his shout came with less force than before. It was a long mile uphill to where the other three whaleboats had been left and then he and his men would have to repeat the harrowing descent.

***

They were at the limit of the area that Farquhar's companies had secured; the land beyond had been scouted by Sir William's Indians, but it was by no means safe. If the Seneca, a nominally friendly tribe, could be raiding as far as the Mohawk, then they or some of the Indians from beyond the Six Nations' territory could easily be probing Lake Oneida and Wood Creek.

The Mohawks had not helped with moving the carriages

and boats, and now Holbrooke could see that Sir William was giving instructions for about half of them – some twenty warriors – to move down the creek on the left bank beyond Farquhar's most advanced picket. Having given those instructions he exchanged a few words with Kanatase and walked back to where Holbrooke and Serviteur were examining the bank of the creek, checking its strength for the heavy boats that would soon be launched.

'Those carriages are fine affairs, Captain Holbrooke,' he said looking closely at the swivel arrangement on the front axle of one nearest to him.

'My carpenter, Mister Sutton, is immensely proud of them, Sir William. There's nothing special about the design, it's just that he's brought his skills for producing a great many of them to a standard design. We have spare axles, wheels and shafts that will fit any one of them, and that may be a great advantage where we are going.'

'Well, this reconnaissance is at least partly for your benefit,' said Sir William. 'I take it that you are not familiar with this frontier land and its people, is that correct?'

Holbrooke smiled ruefully.

'I could hardly be less familiar, Sir William. Ships and the sea are my calling although I have some experience of putting armies ashore on hostile coasts. This endless forest, however,' he swept his arm around the enclosing trees, 'is a new environment to me.'

'And yet Kanatase tells me that you managed that gruesome affair with the two bateaux on the river like a seasoned forest fighter.'

'That's kind of him to say so,' Holbrooke replied, bowing towards where the Indian waited twenty paces away. He really wasn't sure how much the Mohawk understood of the English language. He certainly understood enough to hold his place alongside Sir William, but did he understand the subtleties of phrases such as he had just used? Holbrooke imagined that he should feel superior in some way to this savage, and if he were in Hampshire or on the deck of a ship, perhaps he would. Here however, in the stifling forest of North America and a hundred winding river-miles from the nearest proper town, he felt at a decided disadvantage.

'That affair on the river was nothing compared with the difficulties we may face on this expedition, Holbrooke, and Kanatase has represented to me that you should have a personal guide. I tend to agree with him. I'd hate to lose you before you've dealt with those French ships on Lake Ontario. He's volunteered his services; will you take him?'

It was strange how Sir William's thoughts had paralleled Holbrooke's. He'd just been considering whether he should ask for an Indian guide, but he'd imagined it would be someone of a lowlier status than Kanatase, who was clearly a valuable man. He'd expected that Sir William would want to keep Kanatase close to him.

'I really would recommend it, Captain Holbrooke,' Sir William prompted when the silence stretched to a few seconds. 'I'll be sorry to lose him, but he seems to have taken a liking to you, and he's as loyal as they come.'

Holbrooke shook himself out of his reverie. Of course, there was no real question, it was a gift from heaven to be offered the services of this impressive Mohawk.

'I'd be delighted, Sir William,' and he smiled across at Kanatase and was favoured with a rare smile in return.

***

'I've brought some breakfast, sir,' said Serviteur, offering Holbrooke and Kanatase bread and cold meat from a canvas bag.

They made an unlikely trio, stood on the banks of the infant Wood Creek, surrounded by the virgin forest. Holbrooke was not a short man, but Kanatase was tall for a Mohawk and his scalp-lock stood a good inch above Holbrooke's tricorn hat. Serviteur was taller and bigger-built than either of them, a massive presence in shirt and breeches with a broad-brimmed felt hat that towered above them both. Holbrooke was surprised to see that Kanatase and Serviteur already knew each other very well. Of course, the Indians were quite used to inducting new blood into their tribes, most often forcibly. They lived such a precarious life in this harsh land, that they welcomed any strong men and the fact of Serviteur's colour didn't appear to be of interest to the Mohawk. They must have spoken in the camp after they had met on the river. However it was, they were friends, and that made Kanatase's induction into Holbrooke's crew so much easier.

The last three carriages were coming down the road now. Holbrooke looked at his watch. It was only two hours since they had left Fort Stanwix and already they had brought the six boats, the stores for two days and the band of Indians to the headwaters of Wood Creek. The fine, sensitive point of the blade was inching deep into the French King's territory.

***

CHAPTER FIVE

Lake Oneida

Saturday, Sixteenth of June 1759.
Wood Creek, New York Province.

The waters of Wood Creek were dark yellowish brown, stained to the colour of tannin by the rotting of the forest leaves that decomposed slowly in its fetid margins, a continuous process that didn't end before the autumn's fall brought a fresh crop of fallen vegetation. The stream crept tortuously through the silent forest, rarely seeing the light for the canopy of trees that met above it like the roof of some ruined and abandoned cathedral. And yet there were signs that humans had attempted to improve the waterway. The Iroquois had used it for generations and when the Dutch, then the English came, they had built small forts and even a short canal to bypass a particularly difficult meander. All that industry had been abandoned in this present war and the Iroquois felt it keenly. This was the eastern end of their vital route for the beaver fur trade, and its regeneration by English labour was one of the conditions – negotiated by Sir William – under which Prideaux was permitted to move his army through their lands. It was a key factor that the Iroquois had considered in deciding which of the European factions to back: the British or the French.

The whaleboats, lightly burdened though they were, rarely travelled further than a few hundred yards before the occupants were forced to push and pull them over a shallow patch or through the wooded debris left behind after the winter's floods. It was only seven miles as the crow flies from the put-in to the head of Lake Oneida, but the route that the creek took was at least twice that far, and even with the aid of the sluggish flow it took the little flotilla eight soul-destroying hours. It was backbreaking work for all hands and within an hour Sir William and Holbrooke were as tired and filthy as the bateau-men.

By the time they issued out onto the lake the sun was well past its zenith and was inching down towards the nor'-western horizon. But what a sight! It was like coming out of a darkened room into the bright daylight, and the analogy was hardly exaggerated. There was barely a cloud in the sky, just a few wisps high up and far away being spawned by the Green Mountains a hundred miles to the east. The lake shone in azure splendour with barely a ripple upon its sparkling surface, and its turquoise blue was set off by the green of the forest that came right down onto its pristine shores. It took a few minutes before the travellers could bear to look directly to the west, such was the contrast from the gloom of the creek. As they left the cover of the trees, the creek became magically free of obstructions and although it was shallow, there was enough depth for free rowing. The bateau-men joyfully took up their oars as a novelty after so long pushing and pulling through a tangle of shoals, reeds and fallen tree boughs.

'On this side,' said Kanatase pointing to the left, 'is the Mohawk camping ground that I told you about. We use it in the autumn for fishing and hunting.'

Holbrooke looked to the south side of the estuary. There was a cleared area of perhaps half a mile with a wide sandy shore dotted with old washed-up tree roots and branches; it was spacious enough to encamp the army and pull out all six hundred boats. The site was indeed just as Kanatase had described and in fact it was the only place in view that was even remotely suitable, the whole of the rest of the shore being encumbered by trees. Holbrooke knew all about those trees now, and he knew how impossible it was to land unless there was a beach or a forest clearing that extended to the shore. It looked pretty, certainly, but in reality, it was a green hell of rotting trunks and tangled undergrowth. This beach of Kanatase's was a paradise by comparison.

'Well, this is as far as we are to go, Kanatase. I believe Sir William intends that we'll camp here and ascend the creek again tomorrow.'

And may God help us, he said to himself, inwardly shuddering at the prospect of hauling the boats *up* Wood Creek. It would be a matter of poling most of the way because there were so few places with sufficient water for oars. He was comforted – a little – by the memory of how sluggishly the creek had moved.

Sir William shouted from the lead boat and pointed to the sandy shore. The bateau-man who was steering pushed his oar over to the starboard side of the boat and it described a graceful curve to larboard. With twenty yards to go the oarsmen put on a burst of speed to run the boat up onto the shore under its own momentum, not unlike the flatboats that Holbrooke had become so familiar with on the coast of France. There, however, the similarity ended, because unlike the massive flatboats, there was no need to lay out a kedge anchor; the whaleboats could be easily pushed back into the lake and there was no rise and fall of the tide to consider.

***

'What do you make of it?' asked Sir William. 'I've been here many, many times before in my dealings with the Iroquois. We've used it for meetings of the tribes, so to me it's a familiar sight, but it is beautiful is it not?'

Holbrooke could see that his companion was deeply affected by the view. This, after all, was just a day or two of light marching from his home ground of the Mohawk Valley, and he had a proprietorial interest in it. He was probably eying it with a speculator's instinct, assessing what it would be worth when the settlers came this far, and whether he could secure title from the Indians before that happened. But perhaps that was unfair.

'The Mohawks only use the lake seasonally. The forest isn't rich hunting ground, it's too dense, and the fishing is only moderately good, but they value it for its glory, I believe.'

Sir William continued to study the lake. Whether he was

looking for signs of the enemy or just revelling in the sight, Holbrooke couldn't say.

'It's strange, isn't it? There's not a canoe to be seen, no smoke from fires, no people on the shore except our Mohawks. It's as if we are in a place set apart. You see how enormous the sky appears? It's the same sky, with the same dimensions as we see from our cities, and yet it achieves a fresh grandeur in this setting. But I forget; you're used to this being a seafarer.'

Holbrooke covertly studied the man. He had the reputation of a tough diplomat, a fearsome fighting soldier and an unscrupulous man of business. He'd successfully combined his duties as superintendent of Indian affairs with the expansion of his personal wealth, and he now owned tens of thousands of acres of what had once been Indian land. And yet he was known as a friend of the Iroquois nation, and the Mohawk tribe in particular. Holbrooke had expected that Sir William would have become hardened and cynical, but here he was expounding on the sublime beauty of lake and sky, forest and mountain. The man was an enigma, which was perhaps how he had survived – and indeed thrived – for so long in this unforgiving land.

'I can't imagine a fairer spot in the world,' Holbrooke replied, and he meant it.

'You have land in England, Captain Holbrooke?'

'No, sir. My father is a naval warrant officer, retired.'

That said it all to a man such as Sir William. Holbrooke had no family influence, but it didn't seem to change his attitude.

'We have a cottage on a beautiful stream in Hampshire where the trout rise freely. I hope to set up my own home in the nearby town, when this campaign is over.'

'You wouldn't think of staying here? The opportunities for a man of your sort are limitless. I came here at the behest of my uncle, Admiral Warren, but he was really trying to put me aside, to close his obligation to my father. A man can make his own fortune here.'

Holbrooke recognised that Sir William was trying to make a connection, offering a version of his own personal story that was comparable to Holbrooke's.

'No, it's England for me, Sir William.'

'A woman, I expect,' he said with a smile, 'but that's your business, not mine, and I wish you well. Of course, this is nothing compared with the lakes beyond,' he continued hastily. 'This one is only some twenty miles long, but Ontario is ten times that length. I've been as far as Lake Erie, and that's only a little larger than Ontario, but the lakes further west are true inland seas, by all accounts, and they have all the temperament of the oceans.'

'Then you've seen Fort Niagara?'

'Sadly not. The French were not exactly welcoming, and I had to give it a wide berth.'

He was staring west now, shielding his eyes as though he could pierce the leagues that separated them from the Great Lakes that few Englishmen had seen, but French trappers and explorers knew so well.

'That's our destiny, Holbrooke, out there, and this is the critical moment. Perhaps it matters less to you, being a settled Englishman, but for those of us whose futures are tied up with these lands, it's vital that we don't let the French cut us off from the great continent to the west. That's what this war means to us, you know. We have little interest in the sugar islands and none whatsoever in the sovereignty of land and people in Germany. For us, this place *is* the war and all else is hopelessly remote.'

They stayed a while, gazing out at the lake as the sun crept inexorably towards the horizon. Behind them the bateau-men were securing the whaleboats and the Mohawks that hadn't been sent out to patrol along the southern lake shore were making camp. It was hard to imagine that the world was at war and that they were trespassing on the disputed zone that was claimed by two great empires and a lusty indigenous people.

***

The Mohawks may have left the hardest work of navigating Wood Creek to the bateau-men, but now the New Englanders were taking their ease around the fires while the Indians had melted into the surrounding forest providing a screen of warriors to secure the site. It was extraordinarily peaceful as the loom of the setting sun cast its gentle glow while the fireflies set the surrounding trees a-sparkle. Kanatase was telling tales of the lake that he had been told by his grandparents: tales of war and love, of feasts and famines, shamans and spirits. Holbrooke was entranced; he had never heard anything like this before and he was learning to respect the reverence that the Mohawks had for their land.

Kanatase paused in the middle of a story. As if from far away Holbrooke heard voices whooping. It wasn't the wild yell of a war party, nor the triumphant, mocking voices of the Seneca at the bloody clearing beside the Mohawk River. This was a much softer sound and at first, he thought it was part of Kanatase's dream-like tale.

'That's a party of Mohawks announcing their arrival,' said Sir William.

Kanatase solemnly inclined his head in agreement.

'I know those men,' he said, 'they promised they would answer the call to the warpath, and now they are here. This is perhaps all new to you, Holbrooke,' he said.

Holbrooke knew his features would be indistinct in this gathering gloom, but he smiled in response.

'It's all new, Kanatase, and I'm happy to learn how your people conduct their affairs.'

Kanatase looked at Sir William who almost imperceptibly nodded in his direction. *Warraghiyagey* had given permission for Holbrooke to learn something of the Mohawks.

'In the forest, it's dangerous to approach a camp without announcing who you are and why you are coming. We have lost many warriors through misunderstandings. That call you heard said that it is a party of Mohawks approaching peacefully. We are a small tribe now, and we can all recognise each other's call, so we know that we are not being deceived. This is the last of the men that *Warraghiyagey* summoned. They are late because they have been to Oswego to observe the lake. They may have news of your French ships, Holbrooke.'

They sat in silence waiting for the party of warriors to arrive. Holbrooke wasn't sure what he should do, what part he should take in the arrival. He was faintly disappointed that Kanatase's stories had ended, but he was eager to hear news of the French.

***

Holbrooke had to compose himself in patience. It appeared that the scouting party spoke little English, and Kanatase and Sir William had to get the story from them in their own language. It involved a lot of talk, fuelled by large amounts of the rations that had been brought down from the fort; salt beef and biscuit appeared to be the favourite, while they pulled faces at the hard ration-cheese. Eventually Sir William and Kanatase broke away and joined Holbrooke.

'Well, as I hoped but hardly dared expect, Oswego is deserted. There's not a Frenchman in sight and no war parties in the neighbourhood. It seems like the land between here and Lake Ontario is holding its breath, waiting for a great event; that's the way they saw it, do you agree, Kanatase?'

'Yes, *Warraghiyagey*. It is like the feeling in the forest before a storm. Everything is quiet, even the leaves are stilled. That is how they described it.'

'These are good men, and I trust them,' Sir William added. 'We'll make Oswego unopposed. However, I can't say the same for our passage of the lake. They saw two ships – great ships, they said – but that is a relative expression, and anything larger than a canoe for ten paddles could be called *great*. They did, however, count the gun ports. The larger one had five ports on each side and the smaller had three. My impression was that the first may be a brig and the second a schooner.'

Sir William and Kanatase spoke rapidly to each other in what Holbrooke assumed was the Mohawk language with its long compound descriptive words.

'Excuse me Captain Holbrooke, I was just checking my understanding with Kanatase, and we can best do that in the language in which the reports were made to us. The first ship had square sails on both masts,' he sketched an oblong in the sand, and Kanatase nodded in agreement, 'and the second had fore-and-aft sails. They each had two masts and the first was much larger than the second. They had seen the smaller one before, but the larger was new to them.'

'That makes sense, Sir William, a ten-gun brig or snow and a six-gun schooner. There should be a second brig somewhere as well and possibly another schooner.'

'Just so,' Sir William agreed. 'We'd heard that Captain Pouchot saw to the completion of two vessels on his way from Montreal to Fort Niagara in the spring. If this is one of them then there's another of a similar size somewhere, only a few months off the stocks.'

'It's about what I had expected, although it wasn't certain that the brigs had been completed. That's a powerful little navy for a lake.'

'Then you know your challenge. I imagine you've done this kind of thing before; can you deal with a brig and a schooner? I ask in mere curiosity because it is Brigadier Prideaux to whom you must answer.'

Holbrooke stared at the embers of the fire. It was dying down now that the food had been consumed. It was amazing how these soldiers had such blind faith in his ability to see them safely across the lake to Niagara, but perhaps Sir William was different. Really, he had no idea how he would defeat two vessels of such force with a scratch squadron of bateaux and whaleboats armed with boat-guns and swivels, but he wasn't going to let Sir William know that. He would have to assess the situation as he found it and without knowing where the French ships were at that moment, it was futile making plans. He sensed that Sir William understood that. After all, he couldn't have made his way in this country without extemporising. Nevertheless, it was difficult to phrase a response without sounding pompous.

'I'll discuss that with the brigadier as soon as we return,' he said, trying to look like a man who didn't care to discuss his business.

***

CHAPTER SIX

A Silk Purse from a Sow's Ear

Sunday, Seventeenth of June 1759.
Fort Stanwix, Head of the Mohawk River, New York Province.

'Well, at least we'll have surprise on our side,' said Lynton, 'The French captains can't possibly be expecting us to oppose two brigs and a schooner with a pair of bateaux and a whaleboat!'

Holbrooke grinned to see his second-in-command in such high spirits. With such a willing mind, he knew that they could achieve wonders. It had been a tedious journey back up Wood Creek and across the portage. The army had done well; the Oneida Carry had been cleared of trees and bushes, the ground levelled, and the larger obstructions moved aside. It was fit to transport Prideaux' force, and that was just as well as the brigadier intended to depart Fort Stanwix in just two days. There was great activity with parties of Indians and light infantry patrolling as far as Lake Oneida which Holbrooke had just left. The land was quiet, they all reported, panting gently in the early summer heat and breathlessly waiting for the next move. For it was clear by now that the French were on the defensive. In the great war of movement over the vast American wilderness, it was Britain's armies that held the initiative this year.

'Where do we stand with the masts and sails, Mister Jackson?' he asked the bosun. This was a real clear lower deck of a meeting. Every man in his small naval command was present because each could offer something to this critical question of how to ensure the army's safe passage of Lake Ontario in the face of the established French presence. Kanatase sat silently beside Chalmers and Serviteur. He was listening intently to every word. How much of the technical naval language did he understand? Not much, presumably, but then few landsmen would be able to follow it.

'Two bateaux, as you ordered, sir. They're too flat-bottomed to have any realistic chance of sailing to windward, so I've given them each a free-standing mast, but for a pair of backstays, and Chips has reinforced the thwart to serve as partners. They'll need to be handled with care, though, and the sail's only for fair weather and at least ten points off the wind. There's no jib, of course.'

'Very well, Mister Jackson. You couldn't fit a forestay and shrouds, I suppose?'

'The forestay would have fouled the arcs for the boat-gun, sir,' he replied confidently, 'and without a forestay there's not much point in rigging shrouds. There's not enough beam to have the guns mounted broadside, and not enough depth in the forefoot to have the gun over the stem. The masts are plenty strong enough with the wind anywhere from two points abaft the beam to the stern. The beauty of it is that it leaves the whole forrard third – the fo'c'sle if you like – clear for the four-pounder and two swivels. We'll have a regular gundeck.'

Holbrooke looked thoughtful. Jackson had also caught the mood of optimism, although God knew where it came from; they had a pitiful force to oppose the French brigs and schooners.

The converted bateaux were as he had expected, but disappointing, nevertheless. His gunboats – his ships-of-the-line in this strange squadron – would have to labour into position with the oars alone unless they could establish themselves to windward of the enemy. It was reassuring to remember the stout muscles of the New England bateau-men; he'd pick the best for his gunboat crews, the best and most willing. Still, having his capital ships unable to sail to windward was a huge constraint on his tactical freedom.

'The whaleboat, Mister Jackson?'

'Ah, now that's a different story, sir,' he said. 'I've rigged her out as a regular small longboat, a single mast with stays and shrouds for the lugsail and a jib on an unstayed bowsprit. At least it has some sort of a keel and I hope she'll lie perhaps six points off, but any schooner will eat the wind out of her.'

'Mister Sutton, are the boats sound?'

This was not such a rhetorical question as it sounded. The original design of the bateaux included a short, stumpy mast to raise a primitive sail when the wind was fortuitously abaft the beam, Jackson had merely reinforced it to take a larger sail. However, the whaleboat had no such provision, being purely propelled by oars. Any modifications would have involved compromising some other element of the boats' capabilities.

'Ship-shape and sound, sir,' Sutton replied. 'Your sow's ears are regular silk purses now,' he added grinning broadly.

There was something very un-naval about Sutton, and it showed in the casual way that he addressed Holbrooke. In fact, he had spent precious little time at sea; he was a dockyard carpenter with just enough time on ships' books – although not necessarily spent at sea – to persuade the navy board that he was worthy of a warrant. But on the other hand, that sea-time may have been no less real than many young gentlemen who presented themselves for their lieutenant's examination. Nevertheless, he was a competent carpenter and had shown himself entirely capable of organising the colonial shipwrights in Schenectady.

'I've made some new clamps of my own design for the four-pounders in their field carriages, and I'll answer for their security, but the bateaux are much heavier now.'

'Surely not as heavy as when they're loaded with stores, Chips?'

'No, sir, not quite although with the masts and sails, the guns and the powder and shot they're not far off. No, it's their weight on the carriages that worries me. They're made to take empty bateaux, not full ones, and the weight of the extra timber has meant that I've had to adapt two of the carriages specially. The whaleboat is much the same though.'

Well, that was a concern for getting across the Oneida

Carry, after that he hoped that the boats would float all the way to the lake.

'Mister Lynton, you inspected the work?'

It did no harm to remind his warrant officers that their work was subject to scrutiny, even this far from any normal naval routine.

'Yes sir, all is sound as the bosun and Chips have said. We have as neat a fighting squadron as you'll see this side of the Hudson River...'

It was clear that Lynton has something more to say.

'...but may I ask, sir, why we are not fitting out more boats? There are plenty of willing subalterns in the regiments and the bateau-men are all competent in boats of this size. We could take the swivels out of the bateaux and arm two more whaleboats; and the army has four-pounders aplenty for more bateaux.'

Holbrooke had thought this through during the tedious return passage up wood creek. The thought of having a larger striking force was attractive and – whisper it softly – involving the soldiers would share the blame if it all went wrong. But he knew – he was certain – that he would achieve nothing with brute force. If they were to achieve anything, then it would be by guile, and for that he needed the boats to be commanded by men who thought as he did. Holbrooke shook his head.

'The soldiers may be willing, but they know nothing of a sea-fight. I want each boat to be commanded by a sea officer who can act on their own initiative. This is perhaps the best time to tell you all where you'll be serving.'

He looked around his men and saw the eager anticipation.

'I've been promised two artillerymen for each of the four-pounders and there'll be six bateau-men in each boat. That should be sufficient for a crew. There will be two squadrons. The frigate squadron, if you like,' he said with a wry smile, 'will consist of the whaleboat and will be commanded by Mister Lynton. Chips, you will be his second-in-command.'

Lynton smiled broadly. He didn't yet know the plan, but he was being given the kind of responsibility that he craved.

'The line-of-battle ships will be commanded by me in one of the bateaux, and Mister Jackson will command the other. Mister Chalmers, you'll be my first lieutenant and Mister Serviteur, you'll second Mister Jackson.'

That use of Mister for Serviteur had just slipped out; Holbrooke hadn't intended it, but it seemed somehow appropriate in these circumstances. He was giving his servant the status that he needed to lead the artillerymen and bateau-men in his boat. He knew very well that neither the colonials nor the Englishmen would normally take kindly to being commanded by a freed slave, but he was relying on the novelty of the situation to reconcile them to the unique arrangements. In any case, he didn't care what they thought. Serviteur was the best man for this job; he was a competent seaman and naval gunner, and he had the intelligence and the physical presence to carry off this new responsibility. He could rely on Jackson to clear up any misunderstandings in his boat, by force if necessary.

'Now gentlemen, the latest information suggests that the French have at least three vessels on the lake, two brigs of ten guns each and one or two smaller schooners. You'll see immediately that we cannot lie broadside-to-broadside with even one of those vessels, so we must even the odds. I can't tell how things will look when we get to the lake, so we must be ready to adapt our tactics to the situation. That's one of the reasons why I don't want any soldiers commanding boats in this squadron. If I could give them definite orders before we set sail onto the lake, then it would be a different story.'

'It's a big lake, sir. Do we have any information on the disposition of the enemy?'

'That's a good point Mister Lynton. I have a few observations to make. First, you're correct, it's a big lake. They must by now have heard of the army advancing on them, and they must know that we are marching to Oswego or some point on the shore to the east of Fort Niagara. That's a hundred-and-thirty miles that they must cover with only three or four vessels. Then, of course, they'll be concerned about the security of their positions at the head of the Saint Lawrence. It's only last year that Colonel Bradstreet sacked Fort Frontenac, and they'll probably keep one of the brigs and a schooner to protect that area. That will leave a brig and a schooner to cover the south side of the lake. They'll be stretched, and without good intelligence they'll be unsure where to concentrate their force. If we're lucky – and I say *if* – we'll only have a brig or a schooner to deal with.'

'Then perhaps the whaleboat can be the bait to draw the brig to leeward,' said Lynton.

Holbrooke smiled. It was good to hear his second-in-command thinking along the right lines, but he lacked ambition.

'Draw them to leeward, aye, Mister Lynton, but I have in mind to take a prize or two. I'm not sure how it can be achieved yet, but when the opportunity arises, we must be ready to grasp it!'

***

'And is this possible, Holbrooke?' asked Kanatase. 'Can you really sink these three French ships with a handful of boats?'

Holbrooke was quick to notice the customs of others, and the Mohawk tendency to long pauses for reflection fitted perfectly with his own temperament. They were sitting together outside Holbrooke's tent, or rather Kanatase was squatting in the Indian style, but Holbrooke just couldn't get his hip and knee joints to bend that far, so he was hunched European-style on a log. The sounds of the camp were trailing off into a whisper punctuated by the occasional challenge and reply of the sentries. An officer – a subaltern of the Forty-Fourth – greeted them and passed on to his rounds of the pickets.

'Yes, we have a good chance of success,' he replied at length. 'The main factor in our favour is that the French must patrol all of the southern and eastern shores of the lake; it's a huge area. They may guess that we'll come to the lake at Oswego, but they won't be certain, and the whole of the lake shore from Fort Niagara to the Great River must be guarded. They'll keep a ship close to Frontenac because that guards their supply and repair base. Then they'll need to hold open the communications between Niagara and Montreal, and the commander at Fort Niagara will want to keep a vessel close. That means they'll only have one ship to patrol the south shore.'

Holbrooke paused to let Kanatase digest this information. He wasn't certain how much English the Indian understood; these long silent spells could either be for reflection or for translation.

'Then only one ship,' Kanatase replied, 'that's good.'

'Yes,' Holbrooke replied. 'One ship, and it could be either one of the brigs or the schooner. If I were the commander at Niagara, and if I had authority over the ships, I'd send the schooner to scout along the shore and keep a brig at the fort.'

Kanatase sat again in silence. Somewhere he'd developed a taste for coffee, and he took a sip from the mug that Serviteur had given him. Holbrooke couldn't see his face clearly in the darkness, but it looked as though he was frowning.

'The schooner has six guns and the boats have only two smaller guns,' he held up his fingers in the gloom. 'That's not the Mohawk way of fighting,' he said. 'How can you win?'

Holbrooke drank his coffee slowly. He'd intended this to be a casual chat, but it was turning into an interrogation. He realised now that Kanatase was asserting his independence, his ability to choose his battles. If he wasn't satisfied that Holbrooke could win, would he decline to join the crew of the boats? On one level, it didn't matter.

Holbrooke had no need of an Indian guide for this fight. And yet... he regarded Kanatase as part of his crew. It would be disappointing if he couldn't explain how he would win in a sufficiently persuasive manner to satisfy Kanatase's caution. Perhaps it was the best test of his plan. He knew that his own people were too willing to accept anything he said, but that didn't apply to Kanatase, who hadn't experienced the string of naval successes that had brought him this far.

'Fighting at sea shares this with fighting on land: the winner will be the commander who brings the greater force to bear on the enemy's weaker point.'

He could see Kanatase nodding in the darkness, yet still he frowned at this apparent admission that Holbrooke's flotilla of boats couldn't win against the French naval superiority on the lake.

'The French commander will be using his lightest and fastest ship – the schooner – to find us and then use its speed to bring up one or both of the brigs. If we allow that to happen, we will have given away the fight before it's started, and the army will never reach Fort Niagara. The brigadier cannot possibly commit his boats to the lake until something has been done to neutralize the French squadron.'

Holbrooke let Kanatase digest the impact of this statement. A minute passed in silence.

'My advantage is that I can guess the French schooner captain's orders, and if I'm right, then I know what he'll do. As soon as he's made an estimate of the size of the army at Oswego, he'll hurry back to Niagara to report.'

God, I hope so, Holbrooke thought. There are a hundred variations to the situation, and then of course there's the weather.

'I'll set a trap. My three boats will be the first at Oswego and we'll be waiting for him. When I've taken the schooner, I'll have blinded the commander of Fort Niagara. He'll have no idea that we're coming. And with a schooner I can tackle a brig, if necessary.'

They sat in profound silence for perhaps five minutes. It was fully dark by now and the soldiers' fires had almost all been extinguished.

Kanatase's voice came as a surprise to Holbrooke, who was deep into the details of how he would capture a schooner with only three boats and two guns.

'I will fight with you, Holbrooke,' he said, 'if you will have me.'

***

CHAPTER SEVEN

The Silver Lake

Saturday, Twenty-Third of June 1759.
Head of Lake Oneida, New York Province.

It's an easy thing to say *six hundred boats*, and in an academic way Holbrooke had been contemplating how to manage an armada of that size for the past month. Yet he was unprepared for the sheer grandeur of the sight as the whole fleet set out on the lake. Thus far, the army had travelled piecemeal. It had mustered at Schenectady in May and had ascended the Mohawk in small groups. It had crossed the Oneida Carry by battalions and companies and never, at any point, was the whole force within the compass of a single observer. Now, however, it was different. The screen of Iroquois and light infantry that had been thrown forward a week before had only ventured as far as the headwaters of Lake Oneida. The lake and the river beyond had not been scouted, and from here they must travel in a battle formation. Lake Oneida, the Onondaga River and Oswego on Lake Ontario were presumed hostile territory and the army was disposed accordingly.

'Well, I can't say whether they're all here, sir, but the beach looks empty.'

Jackson was squinting into the rising sun, attempting to see past the columns and rows of boats to the sandy strand beside the estuary of Wood Creek. All the boats were under oars, their blades dipping and lifting rhythmically, shedding sparkling drops of water in the dawn light. For now, Holbrooke's whaleboat was also under oars as it led the fleet onto the lake, and the bateau-men looked ruefully at the mast and sails that lay along the thwarts. They could be taking their ease now, while the southerly breeze wafted them westward, if it weren't for the ungainly bateaux.

The light infantry and grenadiers of the Forty-Fourth

and Forty-Sixth formed the vanguard in the sleek and speedy whaleboats. They were ready to screen the main force and fall back when pressed. The main body of the army followed in three columns, all embarked in the squat, ungainly, heavy but oh-so-useful bateaux. The guns of the artillery travelled in the centre, where they were closely protected by eight regular companies of the Forty-Sixth. Sixteen companies of the Forty-Fourth and the Royal Americans guarded the right flank, the side closest to a bold French sally from Montreal or the Upper Saint Lawrence while the New York Regiment guarded the left flank, the side that should be held by the friendly Iroquois tribes. The rearguard was mounted by the light infantry and grenadiers of the Royal Americans. In all, the six hundred boats carried over six thousand men and all the supplies and material that they needed to lay siege to a modest Vauban-style fortress.

'Keep a half a cable ahead of the brigadier, Mister Jackson. You'll need to pull easy.'

Lynton was back among the main body, temporarily commanding one of the bateaux fitted out as a gunboat. Holbrooke needed the speed of a whaleboat today on the relatively safe Lake Oneida; he couldn't be held back by a pair of heavily-laden bateaux.

'Aye-aye sir,' the bosun replied. The traditional naval response came easily now that they were afloat, although it had an odd ring in an army encampment. Kanatase had asked the meaning of the words when he first heard them and had repeated the strange vowels; so far it was the only time that Holbrooke had heard the solemn Mohawk laugh.

Lake Oneida was twenty miles from east to west, and they hoped to make the journey in the fifteen hours of daylight that they enjoyed this close to the longest day of the year. Twenty miles in fifteen hours with a beam wind and no tides or currents; it should have been easy, but the whole fleet was constrained to the pace that the heavily-laden artillery bateaux could row.

'What speed do you think we're making, Mister

Jackson?'

The bosun looked at the water flowing past the stem. He took a chip of wood from the stash in his pocket – trust him to have thought of that – and threw it into the water, counting the seconds solemnly. This was the oldest method of determining speed at sea, the most ancient origin of the word *log*, and yet it was still useful, occasionally.

'Six, seven, eight…'

The chip passed the stern and was soon lost in the glare of the low morning sun.

'Eight seconds, sir, I make that two knots and a fathom,' he reported, just as though they were on the quarterdeck of a real ship. Way back on the Mohawk River he'd worked out the arithmetic for a boat of thirty feet from stem to stern.

Holbrooke nodded; at that pace, the fleet would make the head of the Onondaga River before sunset. The orders that he'd drafted for the brigadier insisted that the boats should be propelled in two watches by mixed crews of bateau-men and soldiers. The soldiers would be much less efficient, but if it allowed the boats to keep moving without a pause to rest the bateau-men, then it would be worth the slight reduction in speed.

Holbrooke watched as the fleet settled down into some sort of order. He had to admit that it wasn't at all badly done. The columns weren't straight, and the Royal Americans' boats tended to sag to leeward towards the artillery and supply divisions, but otherwise the fleet looked in good shape. He breathed in the clean, cool air, knowing that it would soon be heated almost beyond bearing.

They were leaving the biting insects behind as they moved steadily away from the shore, and that was a great relief. Yet even here and so early in the morning there was a hatch of aquatic flies. He could see sporadic dimples in the water caused by creatures that looked very much like the mayfly that he knew so well from his own River Meon in Hampshire. Whatever they were, they spent little time on the surface, just a few seconds to stretch their new wings then they were off. He saw one launch itself into the blue just in advance of the jaws of a rising fish. Was it a trout? He didn't know whether there were trout in Lake Oneida, and he didn't know the right words to ask Kanatase. When they were next ashore, he'd draw one and emphasise the adipose, the fatty fin between the dorsal and the tail that identified the trout and salmon tribes. He was sure that the Mohawk, with his keen interest in the natural world, would recognise it if it had been seen on the lake.

***

'Mister Jackson! You may drop back now into hailing range of the brigadier.'

They were well out onto the lake now, and Holbrooke had fulfilled the first part of his duties.

'Rest on your oars,' Jackson said in a conversational tone. He'd learned that it did no good to bark at these independent-minded New Englanders.

'What do you think of the wind,' Holbrooke asked. 'Will she carry the lugsail and jib?'

Jackson carefully watched the wind-lines on the placid lake. The sails had not yet been tested on the water, and it was only his years at sea that gave him an insight into how a whaleboat with this makeshift rig would lie.

'The map shows the head of the river lying west-by-north of us, sir,' he said casting a glance at the boat compass, a provident purchase in a New York chandlery that they had carried the whole length of the Hudson and Mohawk Rivers. 'In which case I reckon she'll sail two points free, so long as this wind holds.'

The brigadier's boat moved slowly towards them. Holbrooke saw him stand up in the stern, expecting a hail from his naval adviser.

'With your permission, sir, I'll push on to the end of the lake. Kanatase knows the place and we can mark the landing site.'

'Very well, Captain Holbrooke. But don't take any risks. At the first sign of trouble you are to retreat. I need you to tell me if we are opposed, not leave me to guess, you understand?'

'Yes, sir. I understand.'

He didn't want this to become a protracted conversation. Prideaux had a way of handing out unwanted advice, particularly to Holbrooke whom he suspected of being unable to look after himself so far from salt water.

It took only seconds for Jackson to rig the mast and set the sails, and to the infinite satisfaction of the bateau-men the whaleboat heeled to the sparse breeze and with barely a ripple at its forefoot clove the brilliant blue waters of the lake. Jackson had the tiller and was clearly enjoying himself as the vast fleet of lumbering boats receded in the distance behind them.

'Give me one of those chips, would you Mister Jackson?'

Holbrooke clambered forward, stepping over the bateau-men and the six light infantrymen who encumbered the boat.

'Ready?'

'Aye, ready, sir,' Jackson replied.

Holbrooke tossed the chip well ahead, beyond the miniscule bow-wave. He watched as the ripples from the chip advanced to meet the whaleboat.

'Mark!' Holbrooke said as the chip passed the stem.

This time the chip moved much faster down the side of the boat.

'Three seconds, sir, near enough. I make that six knots.'

They both watched the wake that slanted at an acute angle away from the stern and to windward.

'Leeway's not too bad, sir. I've seen worse on a longboat.'

Then they should make the landing place by noon if the wind didn't veer into the east. Holbrooke checked that the soldiers were keeping a proper lookout then clambered back into the stern sheets. It was spacious compared with many boats and there was ample room for himself, Jackson and Kanatese. He had little to do for the next few hours and he sat contentedly watching the silver lake slip by. The sun climbed inexorably into the cloudless sky astern, and the busy mayfly continued their struggles to be free of their natural environment and to engage in the procreation of the next generation. He had never seen a more beautiful place.

***

'There's the landing,' Kanatase murmured in a low voice.

Holbrooke woke with a start and knew instantly that he'd been asleep. He felt guilt, then embarrassment when he realised that everyone in the boat must have been whispering for the last two hours, to avoid waking him. The sun was high in the sky and his shirt was clinging to his chest, his whole body was sticky with sweat.

'Where away, Kanatese?' he replied. It was no use trying to pretend he hadn't been asleep; it was far better to assume the air of a man who had intended to take a few hours break. He could see that others of the crew had been taking the opportunity to rest their eyes. Jackson, he could tell, hadn't slept and probably hadn't relinquished the tiller since the sails had been set. That meant that at least the watch had been kept; Jackson would never allow a lookout to fall asleep.

Kanatase pointed right ahead. Holbrooke could see nothing to distinguish the place from anywhere else on the lake. The trees that girdled the shore were no different and at this distance he couldn't see the promised river that drained towards Lake Ontario. However, the signs were encouraging. It looked like they were sailing into the mouth of a funnel; the sides of the lake were closing in towards the west and even here it looked like the north and south shores were only three miles apart. There were two small islands to larboard, both apparently devoid of life. Holbrooke had seen them on the brigadier's map, but they had no names. He remembered that Kanatase had said that his people only used the lake in the autumn, when the leaves started to turn. That was when the fishing was best. Still, it was eerily quiet. The fleet was out of sight astern and as far as the eye could see there was no sign of human activity, not a boat, not a hut, not even the curl of smoke from a cooking fire. It was as though he was looking upon the world at the dawn of creation.

They continued in silence until Kanatase again spoke.

'There, Holbrooke. Do you see where the trees become smaller?'

The sun was high enough that he needed to shade his eyes to look to the west. Yes, he could see how the line of trees dipped towards a point on the bow, then rose again on the other side. That could certainly be the tail of the lake.

'The landing place is on this side,' Kanatase said, motioning to the larboard bow.

Holbrooke already knew that. They'd discussed the best place to pull out six hundred boats and prepare them for the long journey down the river. The best estimate was thirty-five miles, but the river was bedevilled by meanders and rapids and there would be a considerable amount of portage to be done. That's where Sutton's carriages would come into their own.

In that magical way that a shoreline gradually gives up its secrets to an approaching mariner, the details of the shore ahead of them became clearer as each minute passed. Now it was certain, even if Kanatase hadn't asserted it, that this was the true tail of the lake. With the islands astern of them, the shorelines abruptly closed in to only half a mile on either side. Now they had need of caution because a well-handled canoe could shoot out from the shore and be upon them in five minutes. If the French, or just their few remaining Indian allies, were waiting for them, this would be the time to attack, with the fleet out of sight and with the room for manoeuvre reducing minute-by-minute.

Up ahead the lake was splitting. Kanatase gestured firmly to larboard.

'That's just a bay on the other side,' he said. 'Good fishing,' he added with the ghost of a smile.

Without being told, Jackson pushed the tiller slightly to starboard and the bows of the whaleboat moved across until they were pointing right down into the spout of the funnel. Everyone was awake now. In the bows the light infantrymen were checking the priming on their muskets and easing the tomahawks in their belts. Not one of them looked like the line infantry at the start of the war. Now they dressed and acted as the seasoned frontier fighters that they were.

They had passed the blind bay to starboard and the channel narrowed even more to less than half a mile wide. To starboard the trees held dominion right down to the water's edge, while to larboard – the south side of the lake – a gleaming white beach was starting to become visible. Its pristine sands were punctuated by the debris from the winter's floods, with whole uprooted trees cluttering the shore in some places. As the whaleboat penetrated further towards the head of the river, it became clear that there was ample space for six hundred boats to be pulled out. This was critical to the planning. After the formation sail across the lake the deficiencies in the loading plan would become evident. It was at the western end of Lake Oneida, before the fleet embarked upon the difficult Onondaga River, that the boats would be re-organised.

'Steer for the centre of the beach, Mister Jackson, beside that slight mound looks good.'

The corporal of light infantry nodded slightly. He was looking at the tactical situation. He had only six soldiers to guard the beach until the fleet should arrive in perhaps six hours, and he wanted to have as much space between him and the tree-line as possible. Here he had perhaps a quarter of a mile each side and a hundred-and-fifty yards in front. It was as good a place as any.

'Strike the mast now, Mister Jackson. You men take to the oars.'

Jackson swung the bows into the wind and at a word the corporal hauled down the jib and cast off the hitch that secured the forestay to the stem-post. He lowered the mast towards Jackson's waiting arms without any of the formality of dropping the lugsail and its yard. Now it was ready to be rigged in an instant if they needed a speedy retreat. The whole mass of mast, yard, sails and rigging joined the two long flagpoles on the thwarts.

With a few last strong pulls, the bateau-men ran the whaleboat's forefoot up onto the sandy beach. The corporal and his men were over the side and running up the beach long before the boat ground to a halt. There weren't enough of them to secure the whole beach and their task was merely to protect the whaleboat while Holbrooke and Kanatase surveyed the landing area. Holbrooke tried not to think of other times that he'd landed soldiers on unknown shores. Most certainly he didn't want to think about last year's landings on the coast of Brittany. That had led to his wounding and capture and the loss of his first command, his beloved *Kestrel*, given to another commander when it was deemed by their Lordships that he was either dead or imprisoned.

***

After the sounds of the wind in the whaleboat's sails and the constant movement of the boat, the sandy beach that stretched to their left and right appeared eerie in its silence. There was a hint of thunder in the still, close air and the clear blue of the sky was starting to be obscured by a thin layer of grey cloud. Kanatase stood still and quiet on the sand, searching the line of the forest for who-knew-what signs. He pointed towards the west, where the start of the Onondaga River could be guessed at from the way that the trees closed in again.

Holbrooke could see nothing but then he heard the Iroquois whoop. He was becoming wise in the ways of the Iroquois. Even after this short time in the wilderness he could tell the difference between a war-whoop and a

75

warning that friendly Indians were coming in. Kanatase nodded approvingly at Holbrooke's lack of concern.

'Keep your men in sight this side of the trees, Corporal, there'll be no hostiles today,' he shouted.

The bateau-men weren't so certain and still hung around the whaleboat. Their leader was testing how quickly they could get the boat back into the water by tentatively pushing on the stem.

Another whoop, a different sound this time.

'They are telling me that they'll break through the tree-line now,' said Kanatase. 'They are Onondaga and friends to the English.'

'Corporal! Look to your right. The Indians coming through the trees are friendly. Hold your fire.'

***

CHAPTER EIGHT

Trust and Understanding

Saturday, Twenty-Third of June 1759.
Head of Onondaga River, Territory of the Iroquois Confederacy.

The sun was still a hand's-breadth above the western forest when the flotilla came in sight around the tree-clad headland. Boat after boat, their oars catching the rays of the sun and returning them from each scintillating drop of water that ran back into the lake. Not a sail was set and not a mast was stepped. It gave them a lean and predatory look, so low in the water and never a lick of paint among them.

Holbrooke had used the party of Onondagas to secure the perimeter, to their great amusement, as they knew very well that there were no enemies within a day's march. The corporal and his small band of light infantry clustered around the two flagpoles marking the extent of the landing area. Holbrooke had not yet fully grasped how the Iroquois federation conducted its internal politics. These Indians knew which of their cousins sided with the French, and they knew the number and intentions of every hostile war party. Nevertheless, the Onondagas were joining the British force for the advance on Niagara and expected payment and plunder for doing so. For today, they were happy to demonstrate their loyalty by noisily beating the undergrowth where the forest met the sandy beach.

'How many warriors will join us at Oswego, Kanatase?' Holbrooke asked. He had heard the lengthy conversation between his friend and the leader of the Onondagas but had understood nothing.

'They say there will be two thousand warriors, Holbrooke,' Kanatase replied. He looked back at the Indians at the tree-line and shook his head. 'You must understand that this man,' he nodded towards the leader of the Onondagas, 'hasn't seen all two thousand. Each of the tribes will have stated how many warriors they will muster, but if the Onondagas say they will have a hundred, then the Oneida will say that they will have two-hundred, and the Seneca will say three hundred. When this party left Oswego there were only a few hundred gathered there. I would expect a thousand by the time we reach the lake, certainly no more. *Warraghiyagey* understands and he will give a realistic estimate to Prideaux.' The Indian's normally solemn face cracked into the ghost of a smile.

Holbrooke looked sharply at Kanatase; was he being mocked?

'You have much to learn about my people, Holbrooke. I can teach you, but it will be much easier if you trust me.'

Holbrooke studied Kanatase's face. It gave nothing away, yet its very immobility was reassuring. He was used to European manners where friendship was reinforced by constant smiling and winning ways. Clearly that didn't apply to the Mohawks. He had a choice; he could treat Kanatase with suspicion or he could give him his trust. If the former, then he could see that life would be difficult for the duration of this campaign. From what he already knew, the Indians didn't respond well to an assumption of superiority. The right to lead them had to be earned; starting with a lack of trust would only end in a lack of co-operation. Trust it must be, and if so, it must be whole-hearted. As soon as he'd made that decision, he knew it was the right one. There was something about Kanatase that he liked – and yes, trusted.

'Then we are bound together, Kanatase,' he said, looking the Indian in the eye. 'I'm proud to go to war with you.'

***

The bateaux and whaleboats slid smoothly up the shallow incline of the white sand and the soldiers and boat crews hauled them well up away from the water. By the time the sun had dipped below the trees the army was ashore, the pickets and sentries were positioned, and the once quiet beach took on the aspect of a military camp with all the attendant sights, sounds and smells. There was no point in trying to hide their presence; Sir William had laughed at the very idea. If the Indians that were already with them knew their location, then all the tribes in the eastern half of the federation knew. An army of six thousand with artillery, ammunition and provisions is a difficult thing to hide, even in the North American wilderness.

The soldiers had quickly learned that an upturned boat made a useful overnight shelter, and if supplemented by a few branches from the forest, it could keep its crew and passengers dry and out of the immediate reach of biting insects. Soon a thin trail of smoke started to curl its way skywards from beside each boat, and to the casual observer it looked like a town of dwarfs had been established on this western corner of Lake Oneida.

'How are you getting along with Kanatase?' asked Sir William as he and Holbrooke walked together along the shore. It wouldn't do to be shot by a jumpy sentry, so they were staying far away from the edge of the forest on this dark night.

'Well enough, sir,' Holbrooke replied, 'well enough, although I have no idea what he's thinking. He's so different to a European.'

Sir William laughed softly and turned towards Holbrooke.

'If you ever know what a Mohawk is thinking, be sure to let me know!' he said. 'I've lived with them most of my life and I've learned to interpret what they say, but never what they really think. It's not merely a matter of understanding their language, you know, you must understand the context. Things that to us are unimportant – such as when the leaves will be falling from the trees – are vital to their survival.'

Holbrooke looked quizzically at Sir William.

'Ah, I see you really do have a long journey ahead of you. When the leaves turn, the hunting will for a time be impossible. All the game will still be well-fed but now the deer will see their approach. Only when the weather turns cold and food is scarce will the hunting become good again.'

'Is that why they fish in the autumn?' Holbrooke asked. 'I had always associated the best fishing with the spring.'

'It is. Well done Captain. Until you understand what's important to them, you won't understand how they value information.'

'Then this business of the number of Iroquois warriors that will be waiting for us at Oswego. It seems incredible to me that the discrepancy in reported numbers – is it one thousand or two thousand? – is taken so casually. Surely their plans must be affected by that difference.'

They walked a few steps in silence as Sir William prepared his answer.

'Why do we need to know the number of our troops? Well, the first reason is that we can achieve greater military outcomes with one thousand than we can with two thousand. But that assumes that we can rely upon that number of soldiers going into battle. For the Indians in this part of the country, the concept of military discipline hardly exists. A thousand warriors may turn up to a fight, but perhaps two-thirds of them will decide on the day that the battle isn't for them. Because each tribe will come to its own decision, and each warrior within the tribe will also have his own views, it hardly matters how many they nominally have available, only how many take up the lance on the day.'

Holbrooke nodded slowly. He'd started to expect something of the sort.

'The other reason that knowing the size of our army is so important is that we have to feed it and supply it with ammunition. An Iroquois chief has no such duty. Each man will bring his own ammunition and shift for himself as far as victuals are concerned. They have no artillery, no engineers and no supply wagons; a warrior carries everything that he needs on his back and lives off the land, and whatever food he can plunder. No, numbers are not so significant to the Indians, and of course that leads them to exaggerations. I know many men who have dismissed the Indians as mere savages because they don't understand how they think.'

'And trust, Sir William,' Holbrooke asked, 'How am I to know when I can trust them?'

'You'll be thinking of Kanatase, of course. Well, they don't have the same hierarchical networks as we do; they are much more locally loyal. You can expect a Mohawk warrior, to give an example, to fight and die for his family or his tribe, but for the Iroquois Confederation? Certainly not! They see that as a political convenience and no more, so you can imagine their views of the government of King George. They'll be loyal only if it serves the interests of the tribe. This year, they see three great English armies on the march, and the French retreating everywhere; for that reason and for no other, they are allied with us. Two years ago, when the French were boldly pressing towards the Ohio, it was a quite different story. I wouldn't have trusted an Iroquois warrior as far as I could have thrown him in 1757.'

Sir William stopped abruptly and turned towards Holbrooke.

'And yet, Kanatase is different, you know. He's been with me on-and-off for ten years and his loyalty hasn't wavered in that time. He's more far-sighted than any Indian I've known, and he's been waiting for the sleeping monster – as he sees us English – to awaken. He can read maps and he understands numbers. He can envision the whole of this part of the continent and he knows the weakness of the French position. For the Mohawk, it's all about the trade routes through the Mohawk valley and down to Lake Ontario; the very route that we are taking from Schenectady to Oswego. He knows that we English can secure those routes and offer a market for the furs that the Iroquois gather in the winter. The French would send them north to Montreal and Quebec, leaving the Iroquois – and more pertinently, the Mohawks – marginalized and impoverished. Kanatase can be trusted, at least one more step than any other Iroquois that I have known. He can be trusted even if we lose a battle, but if he senses that we may lose a war, then think again, Captain Holbrooke, think again. He's a Mohawk first, an Iroquois second and an ally of King George a distant third!'

***

'I request permission to go ahead with my three boats, sir,' said Holbrooke.

Prideaux looked at him quizzically. He'd just stated that the army would stay a whole day on the beach at the end of Lake Oneida, and wouldn't attempt the Onondaga River until the twenty-fifth, the Monday. They would spend the Sunday making the boats ready for the difficult descent, re-stowing the loads after their experience of the lake. He had been assured that friendly Iroquois held the mouth of the Onondaga River, where it reached Lake Ontario at Fort Oswego, and there appeared no need for a scouting party.

'I don't require a reconnaissance of the river, Mister Holbrooke,' he said flatly, 'The Indians that we met here came that way only a day ago, the French cannot be there yet and the Iroquois tribes are all accounted for. Why do you see the need to go ahead of the army?'

'Not for the river, sir. I accept that we know enough about the rapids and the portages, and as you say there is no enemy this side of Fort Niagara; no enemy on land, that is. However, I can be at Lake Ontario two days ahead of the army if I leave immediately, and that will allow me to start scouting for the French ships. It's certain that they'll be told to watch Oswego, it's the obvious place for us to embark on the lake.'

'You still believe that you can attempt something against a regular French ship with your three small boats?'

'Certainly, sir,' Holbrooke replied with an outward display of confidence that wasn't matched internally.

It was astonishing, really. How did Prideaux believe he would take his flotilla of six hundred unarmed rowing-boats onto a great lake with two-or-three French ships opposing him? His force would be decimated, and he would never reach the Niagara River. Holbrooke may have been dispatched by the Admiralty to bring some order to the building of the bateaux and whaleboats, but he could see with a sailor's eye, and what he saw said that something must be done to neutralise the French ships. Whether that was to defeat them in battle, or draw them away from Oswego, or some other stratagem wasn't clear, but he knew that he needed to see this Lake Ontario and the French ships as soon as possible.

'I must represent to you the importance of assessing the naval position as soon as possible. I have never seen Lake Ontario and the reports of the strength of the French ships are sketchy at best...'

'And what is the consequence of my refusal, Mister Holbrooke,' Prideaux interrupted, 'what are you suggesting; threatening, even?'

Holbrooke was taken aback by the hostility. He knew that Prideaux had his hands full with dissenting colonels and a force that he considered barely adequate to the task, even if they came withing range of their objective, but this really was unbelievable.

'I hope my words can't be taken to be a threat, sir. I'm merely pointing out that, as your naval adviser, I believe it's vital to destroy or deflect the French ships for long enough to allow your army to make its passage of the lake. It will be too late by the time we all reach Oswego. The scale of our undertaking will become obvious and they'll bring their whole force down upon us. I intend to catch them while they are still scouting, to deal with them piecemeal.'

There was silence among the gathered staff officers. They were crowded into one of the tents that had been brought on from Fort Stanwix and it at least gave them some illusion of privacy for their discussion. Prideaux stared hard at Holbrooke. In that instant, Holbrooke could see that Prideaux knew himself to be wrong. He'd been so taken up with the logistical problems of bringing his army through the wilderness that the consideration of how he would deal with the enemy had been lost. In a flash of intuition,

Holbrooke knew that he needed to make this easy for the brigadier.

'Sir, perhaps I haven't made the situation clear before. There are at least three, possibly four French ships on the lake, and no British ships. Between them, they deploy thirty or forty guns, many of them twelve-pounders. Each will carry over twenty rounds of ball for each cannon, with some canister and grape besides. When they find us, they will close to perhaps fifty yards before opening fire, and at that range hardly a shot will miss. Muskets fired from the boats will be lucky to hit a ship at that range, more less a naval gunner sighting from behind a gunwale. You will be forced to make for the shore to preserve your army. If you don't, in an hour they will have sunk so many of your boats and drowned so many of your soldiers that you will be unable to continue.'

The silence had become profound. Most of the soldiers were visibly moved, not only by what Holbrooke was saying, but by the utter certainty with which he was delivering the message.

'Give me two days at Oswego and I can surprise the French. I'll either even the odds or destroy them.'

Prideaux swept his gaze around his colonels, and what he saw shocked him. They were all, to a man, on Holbrooke's side. Yes, let the sailors go ahead and clear the way. If they succeed, then all is well. If they should fail and the army is forced to retire, then they would do so in the face of a threat to which they had no answer, and the navy could be blamed.

'Very well, Mister Holbrooke. Take your three boats and whatever else you need. That fellow Kanatase will go with you, I presume.' He raised an eyebrow at Sir William, who nodded judiciously.

'Thank you, sir. I'll leave at dawn, and I will see you at Oswego.'

***

'We have our marching orders, Mister Lynton. I want to

be underway by six bells tomorrow morning.'

When it came to giving naval orders, ship's timekeeping came naturally.

'Aye-aye sir,' Lynton replied, removing his tricorn as he hurried off to get his men moving.

'Kanatase, could I have your advice, please?' asked Holbrooke. It was a curious fact that the Mohawk was always to hand when he was needed. Now Holbrooke urgently needed to know about the descent of the Onondaga River. He knew that it was some thirty miles, but he'd heard about the rapids and the marshy stretches. 'How long will it take us to reach Oswego?'

Kanatase considered for a moment. He looked up at the sky and felt the wind.

'It will be clear tonight, Holbrooke, and perhaps we can expect the same tomorrow. There is no need to stop, and we can be there before midnight.'

Holbrooke looks surprised. He'd expected to have to camp overnight, but Kanatase looked certain.

'Good, then will you travel in my boat?'

'That would be best, Holbrooke. My brothers in the Iroquois tribes do not know you.'

***

CHAPTER NINE

Oswego

Sunday, Twenty-Fourth of June 1759.
Lower Onondaga River, Territory of the Iroquois Confederacy.

The barest sliver of a moon had set two hours before and now the cloudless sky was ablaze with starlight as the boats approached the twin forts of Oswego and Ontario. On board ship it would have been seven bells in the first watch and the decks would be hushed as tired men looked forward to their turn below. It was equally peaceful on the Onondaga River. Holbrooke and his crew had been lucky in their descent of the river and had passed the last obstacle, the Oswego Falls, before it had grown dark, wheeling the boats over the portage on the Sutton Carriages and rejoining the river below the torrent for the easy last stretch.

There were two forts at Oswego, one on each side of the estuary, and both lay in ruins. Before the war it had been a thriving trading post and the British colony's only permanent foothold on the lake. Then, in 1756, Montcalm had landed in bateaux and after some skirmishes with Bradstreet's men, had lain siege to Fort Ontario on the eastern shore. The fort was made of logs and piled earth and it held out for only a few days. As soon as Montcalm took control of it, he turned its guns on Fort Oswego across the river. Fort Oswego was mostly stone-built, but it was on lower ground and despite an intense artillery duel, it didn't hold out much longer than Fort Ontario. Montcalm didn't stay long; he destroyed the boats and provisions and partly destroyed the forts before moving on. Since then there had been an intermittent British presence, and Oswego had been used as a jumping-off point for Bradstreet's raid on Fort Frontenac in 1758. Otherwise it had become a ghost town under constant threat of re-occupation by the French. It was avoided by the Indians and only occasionally visited by the colonials. The Indians told tales of the ghosts of butchered British soldiers that passed through the ruins as the fogs drifted in from the lakes.

'That is where the British ships used to lie,' said Kanatase, pointing to a wide, shallow harbour on the left bank of the river.

It was abandoned now. All that was left of the colonial trading fleet were the charred bones of a few small vessels – schooners probably – and the spectral presence of Fort Oswego looming over the harbour.

Kanatase stood and, cupping his hands, let out a whoop. It was returned from the darkness of the shore and Holbrooke saw several figures illuminated by the starlight.

'They are friends, Holbrooke. Those closest to the shore are of my tribe, they are Mohawks. We can safely land here.'

The beach here was stones rather than sand and there was no jetty or wharf. The bateau-men had to lower themselves carefully into a foot-or-so of water and haul the bows the last few yards to prevent damage to the boats. Holbrooke let Kanatase go ahead and waited in the boat. In fifteen minutes, the Mohawk returned.

'All is well, Holbrooke. There are eight hundred warriors here from all the tribes of the Iroquois. More are expected in the next two days. They want to know when the army will arrive because Sir William promised them provisions. I told them it would be in three days and they are content with that; they can tighten their belts until then.'

Out of the corner of his eye, Holbrooke saw two of the bateau-men starting to wander off towards the fort.

'Keep the crews beside the boats, Mister Lynton,' he said sharply. 'They can sleep on the thwarts tonight.'

In the dim light Jackson could be seen rounding up the strays and organising the boats.

'Have they seen anything of the French?' Holbrooke asked.

'A French ship comes every morning, Holbrooke. They say that it is searching the shore. The chief is a clever man.

He knows that he can't hide all his warriors if the French come ashore, so he lets a small band – twenty or so – show themselves whenever the ship comes past. They yell and threaten the French, which prevents them landing. He believes that the French know nothing of the great gathering of the tribes.'

'Should I speak to this chief, Kanatase?'

'In the morning, Holbrooke. His name is Okwaho, it means wolf in our language. Many years ago, long before I was born, he came to us as a boy from the tribe that the French call *Loup*, so we named him for the wolf, in honour of his birth tribe. He speaks little English but would be glad to meet you. I have told him that you are a great sea-warrior!'

Kanatase's smile flashed in the darkness.

***

The night was short and yet Holbrooke felt refreshed after only a few hours' sleep on a hard oak thwart. By the time that the first glow of dawn was showing in the northeast, Holbrooke, Kanatase and Jackson were squatting among the ruins of Fort Ontario, staring eagerly to the west – to windward – where the French vessel was said to have been seen each morning. They waited among the rotting logs and tumbled soil as the sun rose higher and the air became more heated; soon the insects found them, and they were covering their heads with their neck-cloths.

'The French must have a different view of when the morning starts,' Jackson grumbled. 'It must be four bells by now and still no sign.'

Holbrooke made no reply but adjusted his telescope to study the lake and the shore. There wasn't much to see. The lake looked more like an ocean than Holbrooke had anticipated and the westerly breeze that had increased in force with the rising of the sun still created nothing that could rightly be called a wave. As far as the eye could see the shore was covered in thick forest that didn't quite meet the water's edge. In this respect it differed from Lake

Oneida where, except for a few beaches such as those they had camped at, there was no discernible strand between the trees and the water. In some places on Lake Ontario the shore of was rocky, in others the bright gleam of yellow sand showed and here and there the sun reflected off mud flats. That was what made it look more like the sea; there was a clear influence of waves on the shore and if what Holbrooke had learned was correct, at times the waves were mighty indeed.

He was looking for something that he could use as a tactical advantage. An island or a shoal patch, but there was nothing. Between the strand and the horizon there was no break in the eternal blue of the lake's waters.

'The warriors are ready with their usual greeting?' Holbrooke asked for at least the third time.

'Yes,' Kanatase replied tersely.

Jackson walked a few yards towards the lake, embarrassed at the tense atmosphere. He shielded his eyes looking now to the northeast. Holbrooke ignored him and concentrated on the west, towards Fort Niagara. The sun rose higher in the sky and the flies became more voracious.

'Sail ho!' shouted Jackson, pointing along the shore to their right, directly into the track of the sun.

Holbrooke spun around and levelled his telescope, cursing himself for his foolishness. The Indians had said that the French ship came always from the west, and the implication was that it patrolled between Fort Niagara and Oswego, the only likely threat direction. But of course, Pierre Pouchot at Niagara reported to Montcalm, who was either at Montreal or Quebec. In either case he was some way down the Saint Lawrence, in the opposite direction to Niagara. Pouchot must have a need to communicate with his commanders and one of his brigs or schooners was the obvious means. Kanatase turned away hiding his face. His advice had been wrong.

'Tops'l schooner, sir,' said Jackson, 'although she's not carrying her tops'ls today. As pretty a little lake cruiser as you could wish.'

Holbrooke put aside his telescope. It was no use when looking right into the sun. He was horrified to see how close the schooner had approached without being seen – she was less than three miles away on the larboard tack, heading nor'-nor'west. Soon she'd be able to come about and fetch Oswego on the starboard tack. He'd been juggling with the idea of tackling whichever ship came today, but it was too late now, there was no time at all to prepare a trap and in any case he wanted to know more about how this Frenchman handled his schooner.

'He's coming about, sir,' said Jackson.

Without her tops'ls the schooner tacked neatly; fore and mains'l, jib and stays'l swinging easily across the centreline as her bows passed through the eye of the wind. Now her bowsprit was pointing slightly to the west of the forts. With no tide or current, no waves to speak of, she'd fetch the river entrance easily.

'How close will he dare to come?' asked Jackson.

'He won't see our boats and he'll know that the Iroquois have nothing heavier than a musket. I expect the river has carved a gully here. Look, there he goes, he's paying off a point for the channel!'

Now the bowsprit was pointing right at them. The schooner was sailing a point free and there was a fine, white bone in her teeth.

'She doesn't look French, sir,' Jackson offered tentatively. 'Look at the steeve of that bowsprit, and the beakhead. I do believe she's British-built.'

Holbrooke looked closely. Jackson was right, there was something altogether homely about the build of the schooner. He searched through his memory. Yes, there was a schooner built here at Oswego back in 'fifty-six. She was named *Mohawk*. She must have been brought into French service when Montcalm took the place.

'Six gunports, sir,' Jackson reported.

Yes, she'd been armed with British four-pounders.

Probably the French had replaced them with their standard three-pounders.

Holbrooke heard a yelling from across the water. A band of about twenty warriors were taunting the Frenchman, daring him to come ashore. They were being quite properly ignored, but it didn't look as though the captain of the schooner saw anything untoward. There he was. Holbrooke could see him quite plainly now that the sun wasn't in his eyes. A young man, possibly a little older than Holbrooke himself. He was studying the shore through a telescope. He watched as the telescope settled on Fort Oswego, then it swung left and moved towards their observation post at Fort Ontario.

'Keep low Jackson, we don't want him to start looking in this direction and seeing Europeans.'

Holbrooke lowered his telescope to avoid the sun glinting from it. He cursed himself for a fool for not thinking of that earlier. Any flash in this wilderness would suggest the presence of Europeans.

Holbrooke watched the French captain through a chink between two rotting palisades. He appeared to suspect nothing. He was just going through his normal routine: Fort Oswego, the normal small band of savages, the harbour, no boats, Fort Ontario, deserted as usual.

The Frenchman closed his telescope with an air of lofty disdain for the Iroquois warriors calling to him from just beyond musket range. Holbrooke saw him say something to the steersman and dimly across the water he heard the orders to bring the schooner about. The bows swung to starboard and the schooner tacked handily in the constricted space. That was useful information; this captain was perfectly comfortable coming this close to the river mouth. The germ of an idea started to form in Holbrooke's mind.

***

They watched the schooner until it was almost out of sight, still hard on the wind, presumably making his way to

Fort Niagara. What was the pattern? The round trip from Fort Niagara to Fort Frontenac then southwest to Oswego and back to Fort Niagara could decently be accomplished in two or three days. They wouldn't go to Frontenac more than once a week, he guessed, but Pouchot would want to have this coast under surveillance every day. Fort Niagara was a hundred-and-thirty miles from Oswego, so that was perfectly achievable by just one schooner or brig. There must be two vessels running that routine. Then tomorrow it was likely that they would be visited again, either by this same schooner or by a brig, if the Indians' description was anywhere near accurate.

'Holbrooke, you know this ship?' asked Kanatase.

He'd recovered from his shame at not predicting from which direction the schooner would appear.

'I know that one like this was built here by the British and captured by the French. She was called *Mohawk*.'

'Yes, it was an honour to my people. The French have named her *Huron*.'

He looked angry for a moment then mastered himself. Holbrooke had gathered enough about relations between the Indian nations to know that the Mohawks and Hurons had a long-standing disagreement over trading rights and hunting grounds.

'When the French named the ship *Huron*, it is a direct insult to my people,' he said and stared angrily after the schooner.

'Are you sure that is the correct schooner?' Holbrooke asked, being careful not to name it.

'Yes, Holbrooke, I am certain. It is smaller than the other two ships and its sails lie differently.'

He made a pantomime motion to describe the difference between a fore-and-aft rig and a square rig.

'Then it's certain, Jackson,' said Holbrooke. 'We have to deal with two brigs and at least this small schooner.'

'Well, best we deal with the tiddler first, sir, and then have a crack at the brigs. A worm to catch a sprat, a sprat to catch a mackerel.'

It was reassuring to hear Jackson so confident. It was all very well, and he had a worm in mind, but the sprat may not be so accommodating, and the mackerel, well...

They slid down the ruined earth ramparts of the fort and back to the whaleboat that was hidden in the tiny boat creek on this eastern side of the estuary. There was no need for secrecy now, the schooner was out of sight and there were no other Frenchmen within fifty miles.

***

'So, Mister Lynton, you are to be the worm.'

Holbrooke had agreed that Okwaho should attend the meeting and he sat there now, staring intently at Holbrooke and occasionally nodding as Kanatase interpreted the key points. Kanatase appeared to have an easy relationship with his chief, a casual sort of respect for the man. But he was old, and long past his fighting days. He wasn't planning to join the expedition to Niagara but would remain behind at Oswego.

Okwaho held up his hand for Holbrooke to pause, then he spoke at length in his own language to Kanatase.

'The chief wants to know what you will do with the ship, Holbrooke. Will you sink it, or will you keep it?'

Holbrooke thought for a moment. He knew how difficult it was to sink a schooner of that size, and his two four-pounders would have to hammer away at the hull for hours to achieve anything. He'd always known that he'd have to fight it out on the deck. What then was the point of the question? Did Okwaho want the schooner to be gifted to him? That was unlikely. Was it something to do with the insult of its name, *Huron*? That was probably it.

'I plan to capture the schooner and use her to destroy the other French ships,' Holbrooke replied.

There was another conversation between the two Indians.

'Is it your custom to give new names to captured ships, Holbrooke? The chief wishes to know.'

So he was right.

'You may tell Okwaho that when I capture the French schooner,' he was careful not to name it, 'on behalf of King George, I will call her *Mohawk*, in compliment to our great allies.'

The chief was listening intently, and he caught the name of the King and the reference to *Mohawk*, but he waited until Kanatase had carefully translated for him. He said a few more words to Kanatase, then smiled at Holbrooke, shook his hand vigorously and departed.

Lynton was looking curiously at Holbrooke. He knew that his captain had overstepped his authority. Only the Admiralty or local commanders-in-chief could rename prizes. But Holbrooke didn't care. First, he had to secure the schooner then he would worry about the limits of his authority. This far from civilisation, he reasoned, he *was* the naval commander-in-chief. Certainly, there was nobody else in Prideaux' army who would be able to quote Admiralty regulations. Then he gulped, hoping he hadn't actually turned pale. Committing himself to naming a prize was nothing compared to the temptation of fate that he had committed by assuming that he would win the prize. Two four-pounders and a handful of swivel guns against six three-pounders behind stout wooden gunwales. Even with surprise and luck it was a tall order.

***

Holbrooke and Kanatase sat beside the last embers of the fire as the sun set. There was no moon again tonight and the Milky Way stretched across the vault of the heavens as though some celestial being had cast a net of silver, studded with pearls and diamonds. Kanatase was silent for long minutes. When he spoke, it was evidently a speech that he had been carefully preparing, to avoid giving offence by clumsy words.

'You are very certain that you will be able to capture the schooner, Holbrooke. It appears to me a great undertaking. How can you be so sure of winning?'

And that was just the question that Holbrooke had been asking himself. It was a feeling, nothing more. He'd lost his last command through evil chance and had been sent across the world to this howling wilderness. He'd endured forests and swamps, and mosquitoes by the million, and now he was back in his element. Lake Ontario may not be the great salt sea that girded the world, but it was the nearest that he'd seen for months. He'd been presented with a quite straightforward task for which he felt himself well-suited. He had a good crew and sound boats, and he had the element of surprise. He knew the French captain; he was as certain of his capabilities as he would have been if they had served together. The man was a confident seaman, but he was cautious and a little timid where fighting was concerned. He should certainly have sent a few balls into the Iroquois who were taunting him from the shore, even if it risked a volley of musket shots in return. For the honour of the flag if for no other reason. A dozen fights at sea had taught him boldness and caution and how to tread the fine line between them. Chalmers had once quoted Shakespeare at him: *there comes a tide in the affairs of men*... Well he was wrong that time, but Holbrooke could sense that flood tide under his keel today. It was now or never. He sensed that this was his last chance to stake a claim to be made post. No other opportunity would present itself for months, and by that time it would be too late.

'I cannot easily answer you, Kanatase,' he said. 'I watched that French captain today, and I saw the way that he conducted his reconnaissance. It was just another routine patrol for him. He didn't expect to see anything and therefore he saw nothing. He's forgotten that he's a fighting man. I just know that if I can get a boat alongside him, he's ours!'

***

CHAPTER TEN

A Worm for a Sprat

Wednesday, Twenty-Seventh of June 1759.
Oswego, Lake Ontario.

Holbrooke's three boats lay silently in the tiny inlet, hidden beneath leafy branches newly cut from the forest. Above them the ground rose steeply towards the wreckage of Fort Ontario, and across the river was a glimpse of the shattered stonework of Fort Oswego. They had lain there all the previous day also, waiting for the French schooner or one of the brigs, but nothing came. Okwaho, the Mohawk chief, was visibly upset. He'd told Holbrooke that they came every day, usually alternating between the smaller schooner and a larger square-rigged brig. He'd staked much of his reputation on his certainty that they would come again, but when noon passed and there was still no sighting, he had come personally to assure Holbrooke that the French would arrive tomorrow. Nevertheless, the boats had stayed in hiding until the sun had dipped in its golden glory across the lake, and after a short night's sleep they were back before dawn the next day.

'This is good,' said Holbrooke. 'If the brig didn't come yesterday, then it should be the turn of the schooner today. I'd rather tackle the schooner first; that's our sprat.'

He hoped he was sounding confident; he was trying to raise morale in his little command. His own crew, Lynton, Jackson, Chalmers, Serviteur and even Sutton, needed no encouragement. They had each absorbed the stoicism of the fighting sailor and were prepared to wait for days on end without a sight of the enemy. The bateau-men, however, were fidgety. They had all volunteered for Holbrooke's command, lured by a small bounty and the prospect of less labour in getting the heavily laden supply bateaux down the Onondaga River. Did they really understand the risks that they would be taking when they tackled the French? He'd outlined the plan to them, he'd armed them all with pistols and cutlasses, and he'd tried to explain the sheer ferocity of a boarding, but he wasn't certain that they had really grasped it. As it happened, two of them had been with Bradstreet's expedition to Fort Frontenac the previous year, so they had at least seen some fighting, but to Holbrooke, they appeared altogether too placid. Yet it was the Mohawks that gave Holbrooke the most concern. He had no doubt that they would fight, but would they fight to his plan? It was impossible to keep them in the boats and whenever his back was turned, they would be wandering off to speak to their friends, or to find a quiet spot to sleep. Kanatase shrugged his shoulders and pointed out that his people were different to Europeans. Holbrooke just had to trust that they would be with him when needed.

Holbrooke watched the lake as the first dim loom of the sun extinguished the stars. Soon it would rise and then at any time they could expect the French.

'I'll be away then sir,' said Lynton, picking himself off the thwart where he had been sleeping soundly.

The whaleboat was the bait – the worm – that was to draw the French ship in. All the previous day Lynton had tacked backwards and forwards off the river mouth where he would easily be seen by the French, from whichever direction they came. It was important that the whaleboat looked unthreatening, so the two swivels had been struck down below the thwarts and the crew – Sutton, two bateaumen and four Mohawks – had likewise hidden their arms. What would the French captain see? Holbrooke had spent hours with Chalmers talking it through. Until now, they had observed only a small band of Iroquois on the shore. The French captains may suspect that they were the precursor to the anticipated British expedition, but he wouldn't be certain. The sight of a whaleboat under sail would be an important change from the routine. It could still be explained in many ways, just a few traders perhaps, and their

Indian clients, but they would surely want to investigate. They would want to capture the whaleboat if they could do it without setting foot ashore. Lynton's task was to draw the Frenchman in so close that he couldn't retreat before Holbrooke could spring the trap.

***

They waited. The sun rose in the clear sky and the westerly breeze gradually increased so that the ripples on the lake became tiny waves that burst over the whaleboat's stem. Holbrooke leaned his telescope on the familiar broken palisade and scanned the horizon from nor'east to sou'west and back again. He had a good clear view in both directions and would see anything that was standing out into the lake, but any vessel clinging to the shore would be upon them with no notice. That was partly why Lynton was standing so far off, so that he could cover that gap in the surveillance, as well as give the Frenchman a hope of cutting him off from the shore.

Holbrooke looked at his watch. Seven o'clock and he'd had no breakfast. How far away was Prideaux? He desperately wanted to have a chance at the French before the army arrived at Oswego. He knew that six thousand men and their arms and stores, to say nothing of six hundred boats, couldn't remain hidden from a cruiser on the lake. As soon as Prideaux arrived his advantage of surprise would be lost.

An insect landed on his hand and bit him before he could swat it. It died with a squelch and left a bloody mass to cover its parting gift of a rising lump that would surely itch within five minutes.

'Whaleboat's setting its jib, sir,' Jackson said calmly.

Holbrooke looked quickly out over the palisade. He didn't need a telescope to confirm what the bosun had said. That was the signal; his heart started to race. They'd discussed at length what the whaleboat could do to indicate the presence of the enemy without advertising the fact that they were signalling to someone ashore. What could be more natural than that the whaleboat would increase sail on sighting another vessel? Lynton was telling him that the French were approaching. From his vantage point on the hill, Holbrooke could see further out onto the lake than Lynton, so the vessel could only be coasting along close to the shore. But which shore? The sou'west from Fort Niagara or the nor'east from Fort Frontenac? It hardly mattered, but the schooner had departed three days ago towards Niagara, so if it was from the west than it was more likely the schooner.

'Go back to your boat, Mister Jackson, and make sure the Indians are onboard. I'll stay to see what we're up against.'

The whaleboat had started its reach back towards Oswego. This was the critical point. The Frenchman had to believe that he had a chance of cutting off the whaleboat's retreat without raising his suspicions that he was running into a trap. Still no sight of the Frenchman. Holbrooke crawled a few paces to where the hill dropped steeply towards the water. He looked to the left; nothing but the empty lake. To the right it was also clear. Whichever direction the French were coming from, they were hugging the shore.

Holbrooke lay flat on the ground and crawled forward a few more yards. Now he could see it, the unmistakable bowsprit of the schooner that he had watched so carefully two days before, and it was coming from the west, directly from Fort Niagara. Good God, it was going to be close! He caught a glimpse of the tops'ls being shaken out then he crawled back to the shelter of the ruined fort and ran down the hill, out of sight of the schooner, to where his two bateaux lay waiting.

'Keep under cover,' he shouted as he came into sight.

It looked like Lynton would draw the French right into the channel, closer than they'd come the other day. But now he was concerned for the whaleboat; it didn't seem possible that Lynton could reach the channel ahead of the schooner. Had Lynton left it too late in his eagerness to deceive the enemy?

'Is everyone ready? Good, then take those branches in hand but don't move them yet. You'll see the schooner in a moment.'

But would he see the whaleboat ahead of the schooner? If Lynton should be cut off from the shore, then the schooner would not need to come any closer. The French captain could make his capture, or if Lynton tried to run, he could sink him with those six three-pounders. Holbrooke had a narrow field of view from this tiny cleft in the rocks. He could see down the channel, but the whaleboat was out of sight to the right and the schooner likewise invisible to the left.

'There's the whaleboat!' Chalmers exclaimed just before Holbrooke saw it. Lynton's boat was sailing hard for the safety of the river. It was a convincing display as his gunwales dipped to the lake and showers of spray burst over the boat's bows. He could only guess what Lynton's Mohawks made of this; they had presumably only had experience of native canoes until now, and a slim whaleboat under full sail in a rising breeze must be terrifying.

Holbrooke watched in fascination as the schooner started to appear to the left of his tunnel of vision. Just as the whole vessel came into view, a puff of smoke erupted from her larboard bow, followed by the sharp crack of a small cannon. A three-pounder for sure. What would the Frenchman be thinking? He wouldn't want to put people ashore to find out what was going on, it was too dangerous with the Iroquois obviously in the area. He would be keen to take prisoners, to gain intelligence of the British army that surely was heading for Fort Niagara. That would mean that he'd keep up these warning shots for a while yet. There was another shot, clearly aimed ahead of the whaleboat. Now Holbrooke could see that the schooner was going to win the race. She was flying along with the wind dead astern, probably travelling twice as fast as the whaleboat. But the point where they would meet was too far out.

With a sick feeling Holbrooke realised that he had put Lynton at risk. Lynton and Sutton, the two bateau-men and the Mohawks. He'd underestimated the speed of the schooner sailing large, with those big tops'ls pushing her along at seven or eight knots even in this moderate breeze. It was that old enemy of his, hubris. Overconfidence leading inevitably to a fall. He'd have to admit to Prideaux that not only had he lost a whaleboat and its crew, but he'd thrown away the army's advantage of surprise, giving Pouchot at Niagara a day or perhaps two of gratuitous notice that the British were on their way.

'Stand by, Mister Jackson.'

All he could do now was to attempt to rescue Lynton and the others.

'Away with the camouflage.'

'Wait, sir, wait! Look at Mister Lynton.'

Holbrooke looked again at the whaleboat. He'd expected to see her hove-to, with the sails flapping listlessly as Lynton surrendered to the overwhelming force arrayed against him. But the whaleboat was tacking to get under the schooner's stern. He could see puffs of gunfire from the boat, as the Mohawks and bateau-men fired their muskets and pistols.

The whaleboat tacked again. Now it was beam-on to the schooner and racing for the estuary, drawing the Frenchman in pursuit. Someone was hoisting an ensign at the stern of the schooner; the white of the Bourbon dynasty broke out, flying free in the breeze.

'Hold the branches, Mister Jackson. I do believe they are coming to us.'

Holbrooke smiled savagely, perhaps this was still possible. The schooner had handed its tops'ls and was hard on the wind trying to make the harbour entrance. She was no more than half a mile away. Could it be done? Yes, by God, it could.

'Let's go,' Holbrooke shouted.

The two bateaux shot out from the little cove, scattering the protective branches as they went. They'd been stripped down to the bare essentials for this race and each now had eight powerful New England bateau-men to propel them. They had the advantage for a few minutes as the schooner's concentration was all on the whaleboat, and they were sheltered from the wind that was tending to come from the sou'west.

'Pull!' shouted Jackson. 'Heave for all you're worth.'

Jackson's boat was a little ahead now and he could see that Serviteur had taken up an oar. It was no use asking Chalmers to do likewise in Holbrooke's boat, he had no experience of rowing. Nor did the Mohawk warriors, who could paddle well enough facing ahead in a canoe but had never pulled an oar and found the idea of facing the stern amusing.

The schooner wasn't firing warning shots anymore, those were broadsides – all three of her guns were firing together – with the intention of sinking the whaleboat. Holbrooke gulped as a broadside straddled the frail craft. He saw splinters flying from where at least one shot had hit. But still the whaleboat came on, leading the schooner deeper into the trap.

'He's seen us,' said Chalmers breathlessly. Even he had been affected by this contest, this race for the life of his friend.

Sure enough, the schooner was tacking, offering her stern to the whaleboat as she tried to manoeuvre in the narrow channel. The bateaux would never reach her before she had completed the manoeuvre.

'Pull like the devil!' Holbrooke shouted.

There were seconds in it. Once the schooner caught the wind in her mains'l and fores'l there'd be no stopping her. The Mohawks in the bateaux were aiming their muskets, willing the range to close.

Then Holbrooke heard a new sound. Sharper than the crash of the French three-pounders, it was the swivel guns in the whaleboat. Lynton must have shipped them as soon as it was clear that the trap was sprung – as soon as he no longer needed to play the innocent lake trader.

The whaleboat still had all its sails drawing, and Lynton had tacked to follow the Frenchman. He was trading broadsides with his single half-pound swivel gun against the three three-pounders on the Frenchman's starboard side. The muskets and pistols were still popping away, but now the schooner was starting to draw clear. Men were racing up the masts to set the tops'ls again, and when those square sails were drawing, she'd be running faster than the whaleboat could sail, and far faster than the bateaux could pull. Holbrooke knew that he needed a miracle.

Then it happened. The whaleboat's swivel belched another load of cannister, and the schooner's forestay parted, bringing the stays'l down in a rush. The mast didn't follow it; with the wind astern, there was enough support from the backstays, but the jib was in tatters. The Frenchmen were making frantic efforts to lower the schooner's mains'l, but the halyard appeared to be jammed. The bows of the schooner swung around, despite the efforts of the man at the tiller, and her way came off. She was helpless, caught in irons with two gunboats closing in on her.

'Fire when you are ready,' Holbrooke said to the artillerymen. 'Mister Chalmers. Steer directly for the schooner.'

The four-pounders were still in their campaign carriages, with all non-essentials stripped out. The only way to aim them was to point the boat at the target. The elevation was the business of the men of the Royal Artillery.

The first shot missed, it was good for line, but the ball flew high, making a neat hole in the schooner's mains'l.

Jackson's boat had also started firing and was making better practice as his first shot slammed into the gunwale sending a shower of splinters over the deck.

Lynton was moving away now, giving space for the gunboats to do their lethal business. It was an even match, two four-pounders against a broadside of three three-pounders, for the schooner couldn't manoeuvre yet, and only its starboard battery was engaged. The weight of metal was broadly even, but the Frenchman still had the advantage. It would only take one well-aimed shot to sink a bateau whereas the schooner could absorb ten, twenty times that amount of punishment.

***

'When will you board her?' asked Chalmers, looking keenly at the men on her fo'c'sle rigging a new forestay while he steered the boat. Even he knew what those men where about. As soon as the forestay was rigged they'd be able to hang a sail on it and get their head off the wind. They could almost do it now with what was left of the jib, and he could see the mains'l being laboriously hauled down. It would be only a few minutes.

Holbrooke ignored the chaplain. He had only asked what Holbrooke was already considering. He was just waiting for the last factor to be resolved, the fitness of his bateau-men. They had pulled hard for ten minutes – pulled like their lives depended upon it – and now they were blown. He needed one more superhuman effort on the oars and then they could board. He keenly watched the man at stroke. He was breathing hard and staring fixedly at the stern-post as his body moved forward and back in a rhythmic motion, hauling the heavy oar through the resisting water. Then he looked up and nodded grimly.

'Give way!' Holbrooke shouted, so that Jackson would hear him. 'Give me your last effort men, and then it's up for the prize!'

Even in the remotest parts of New York, Massachusetts and Rhode Island they knew about prize money, and the mere mention of it could call forth extremes of effort. Prize money, that great, unearned, almost illicit cascade of gold. It was almost piracy, but with the advantage of being completely legal; twice as attractive as money earned by their honest sweat. The bateau-men made the oars bend and the guns spoke their last as the bateaux closed on the wounded but still dangerous enemy.

***

Crash! Holbrooke was thrown forward as his bateau smashed against the side of the schooner. It was no distance up the gunwale to board her, but already one of the bateau-men had fallen, groaning and staring at the blood spreading across his shirt. The schooner's gunwale was lined with men, some with the distinctive red caps of the French sailors, some wearing deerskin or beaver. Thankfully, few of them had muskets but each wielded a weapon, whether it was a tomahawk, a cutlass, a pike or merely a belaying-pin.

Holbrooke had no time to think, he just grabbed hold of the sill of a gunport and hauled himself up, slashing with his sword at the arms and legs and torsos lined up before him. He could see on either side that his crew was following him. There was Kanatase, his tomahawk and lance in his hands, and the other Mohawks behind him. One dropped over the side as a musket ball caught him in the shoulder, but the others pressed on. The bateau-men came up with a mighty roar, wielding their cutlasses and firing their pistols. And yet the advantage of numbers was with the French. Jackson and his crew were boarding over the bow. He could see the mighty figure of Serviteur, his cutlass looking more like a butcher's knife in those huge fists.

All order quickly left the fight and it degenerated into frantic personal battles all over the deck of the schooner. Holbrooke tried to reach the French captain but there were too many in the way. He looked desperately around. All the crewmen of the bateaux were on the Frenchman's deck now, and yet still they hadn't won the day. And now they were being pushed back, back towards the schooner's side, and the bateaux. Then he saw with horror that the boats weren't there! They were twenty yards away, drifting down to leeward. Holbrooke turned back to face the enemy and fight to the end.

'*Kestrel, Kestrel!*'

Holbrooke heard the familiar, blessed sound and saw the commotion on the larboard side of the schooner. Lynton had boarded over the quarter and had taken the enemy in the rear with his miniscule force. The French captain turned to face the new danger and fell from sight as a blade flashed down on him. Now the French were in disarray. 'Charge!' shouted Holbrooke, for want of a better word of encouragement. The corporal of artillery beside him took up the shout, and now the whole mass of Englishmen, colonials and Mohawks was herding the French crew towards the larboard side of the waist. There were bodies on the deck and Holbrooke skidded in a pool of blood, but they were winning!

'She's struck!' He heard the magical cry and knew instantly that it wasn't quite true. No Frenchman had touched the halyard, but Lynton had slashed it with his sword and the white of France had come floating onto the deck. The symbolism of it was irresistible, and one by one the Frenchmen dropped their weapons and turned their sullen and frightened faces to the victors.

***

CHAPTER ELEVEN

A Prize for King George

Wednesday, Twenty-Seventh of June 1759.
Oswego, Lake Ontario.

Holbrooke always felt a wave of depression after a battle. This time it was worse. He'd been able to prevent the slaughter of the Frenchmen who had surrendered, and he had stopped the scalping after the first two, when he saw what was happening. And yet he should have been prepared; he'd seen the bodies on the banks of the Mohawk River, and he knew that this was the custom of the Iroquois. And he'd been unprepared for the way that the bateau-men joined in so enthusiastically, with an unseemly scramble over the still-warm bodies. It had taken all his authority and the amused support of Kanatase to save the remainder. The Mohawk just couldn't see the value in sparing the lives of Frenchmen who as prisoners would only become heavy burdens to their captors.

There were six dead Frenchmen and three more who would undoubtedly join them. He handed them all over to the care of the French surgeon's mate – a schooner couldn't muster a full surgeon – and the unwounded prisoners, now utterly demoralized, he locked below decks. And there were deaths and injuries among the British and Mohawks; One dead bateau-man and the Indian who had been shot and had fallen over the side during the battle. He tried hard to shake off the sense of futility. He knew that he alone felt like that and he could see the elation in all the rest of his crew. He made an excuse about interrogating the schooner's captain and examining its papers to stay below out of sight.

Lynton worked the schooner into the harbour beside Fort Oswego and anchored in just two fathoms of water. It has taken an hour to rig a stays'l and re-set the mains'l. Luckily, Sutton had secured the whaleboat to the quarterdeck rail, which simplified the recovery of the two drifting bateaux. Perhaps that was why Sutton was the only one among them who didn't look as though he'd come through a desperate battle. As a skilled shipwright and carpenter, he didn't feel that fighting was his business. He'd probably assigned himself the task of boat-keeper for the few minutes that it took to overpower the schooner's crew.

While the schooner tacked to and fro making her way into the harbour, the sun rose higher and the crowd of Iroquois on the shoreline grew larger. There was no need to hide their numbers now and this was a celebration. First blood to the British and the Iroquois!

***

'Do you have a damage report, Mister Lynton?' asked Holbrooke when he came back on deck. He was followed by the French captain who had a livid bruise to the head but was otherwise unhurt. The Frenchman looked nervously at the raucous crowd of Iroquois on the shore, hardly sparing a glance for the vessel that he had so lately commanded.

Lynton and Sutton were deep in conversation on the quarterdeck. Lynton broke off and removed his hat, a curiously formal gesture amidst the shambles of the schooner's upperworks.

'Two shot holes above the waterline on the larboard side, sir, and some damage in the waist.' He pointed forward to where a four-pound ball had ploughed its way through the gunwale capping. 'Mister Jackson is just finishing off the repair to the forestay and the mains'l halyard has already been freed. Other than that, the decks need a thorough swabbing and she'll be as good as new. The boat's a wreck though. Sutton says he could make her seaworthy, but not in less than three days, her side's all stove in.'

'Thank you, Mister Lynton. Ask Mister Jackson to hoist the whaleboat inboard.'

He looked appraisingly at the yards.

'They'll take the weight, and then at least we'll have a boat. Are the prisoners secure?'

'I've put Serviteur in charge. He has the four artillerymen and the bateau-men,' Lynton pointed at the sentries on the hatches, each with a musket and apparently mindful of their duty. 'There is no other way out of the lower decks, and I expect the Frenchies are happy to be locked away with so many Iroquois around.'

That was profoundly true, Holbrooke thought. The crew were all Frenchmen or Canadians and they had no illusions as to their fate if they came into the hands of the Indians. It was far better to stay under the custody of the British, particularly as there appeared to be regular sea officers in command.

'Mister Sutton, you have the rest of the day and tomorrow to make this schooner look as though it hasn't been in battle. On Friday I want her to look as though she's just been about her normal business.'

Sutton knuckled his forehead. That was a different task to merely making the schooner seaworthy and it would take more work, but two of the bateau-men had been jobbing shipwrights before and all of them could handle tools.

'Ah, Mister Jackson,' Holbrooke said as the bosun came aft with a coil of two-inch rope across his shoulder. 'The French captain,' he indicated the disconsolate figure behind him, 'tells me there's a spare suit of sails below, so you can replace the jib and stays'l. I can see some holes in the fore tops'l as well, so bend on the new one if you please. Take him to the hatch and let him talk to his men below so that you're not molested. There's no time to lose.'

The French captain had been unusually helpful. Perhaps it was the sight of hundreds of Iroquois warriors on the shore and the complete absence of the British-led army that he had expected to see. He was wholly convinced of the need for him and his crew to remain under the custody of this British officer. He'd freely informed Holbrooke about the rest of the French force on the lake, adding as much detail as Holbrooke could absorb. There was another schooner and two powerful new brigs that were only completed in April, each carrying ten twelve-pound cannon. One of them, *L'Outaouaise,* had been damaged in a storm and was refitting at Pointe au Baril, fifty miles down the Saint Lawrence from Fort Frontenac. The other, *L'Iroquois,* was at Fort Niagara and was expected to come down the coast in three days' time. It was *L'Iroquois* that must be deceived into thinking that the schooner was still in French hands.

***

'Mister Lynton, a word with you, if you please.'

The furthest aft twelve feet of deck was unstained by battle and the taffrail was the only place on the small schooner with any pretence to privacy. She lay with her head to the nor'westerly wind and by looking astern up the river, they could almost imagine that this little vessel hadn't been in action only an hour before. The view was exquisite, with the Onondaga River advancing placidly towards them broken only by the Rift, where it tumbled over a submerged outcrop of rock that stretched across the river.

'You did well, Mister Lynton, and you can be sure that I'll mention you in my report to the Admiralty. That boarding over the quarterdeck saved the day.'

Lynton smiled broadly. It was no secret that although Holbrooke was under Brigadier Prideaux' command, he sent his reports directly back to their Lordships. His name would come to the fore at just this critical point in his career. Who knew? Perhaps he'd even be promoted to commander!

'Thank you, sir. Does it remind you of something?' he asked with a strangely familiar grin.

Holbrooke looked confused for a moment until he remembered the fight against the French frigate *Vulcain* in the Mediterranean back in 'fifty-six. He'd been just a master's mate then, and he'd turned the tide of the battle by boarding the frigate from his little prize barca-longa. That was the pivotal point in his career, from there had come his lieutenancy, and then his promotion to commander. Was that the way it would go with Lynton? He hoped so.

'Yes, indeed. Let's hope their Lordships take notice, Mister Lynton. God knows, you deserve it.'

They stood in silence for a moment watching the sun glint off the river.

'However, back to the present. I'm renaming the schooner *Mohawk*, in compliment to Kanatase, and I'm giving you command of her.'

Lynton looked startled and his face went pale. He'd dreamed of an opportunity like this but had dismissed the possibility on this occasion. There was only one British man-o'-war on the lake, and he'd been certain that Holbrooke would reserve the command to himself.

'Let me explain, Mister Lynton,' he said smiling at his friend's confusion. 'We still have to take this army a hundred and thirty miles along the lake to Niagara. My place must be with the flotilla until the soldiers and the siege train are safely ashore. There's a French brig at Niagara with ten twelve-pounders and she cannot be allowed to get among the boats. *Mohawk* is no match for her in a fight, but I have in mind that you will lure her away. You've been the bait once, you can do it again, and you're as capable as I am of commanding a schooner. I'll not ask the brigadier's permission. He's unsure of his authority over me and I'm going to present him with a *fait accompli*. As soon as he arrives, I'll give him your acting commission to sign. Of course, you'll be under my command still.'

Lynton brought himself back to reality. This was a real step forward. He wasn't being given temporary command of a prize to bring her into port, he was to be the legal captain of a man-o'-war; a commissioned ship in King George's navy from the moment that the brigadier signed the commission. Of course, it would have to be confirmed by their Lordships, but that would take many months and what else could they do? A schooner was too small for a commander, and he was the only lieutenant within hundreds of miles. He looked furtively around for Chalmers who he knew would have to write out his commission.

'You'll have Jackson of course, and Serviteur can stand a watch on the lake. Sutton will be under your command for the next two days until the repairs are complete, but I'll want him back to keep an eye on the boats. I'll make up your complement from the bateau-men and soldiers when I've spoken to the brigadier. Twenty should be adequate, I don't expect you to be doing any fighting.'

'I… I don't know how to thank you, sir…'

'You can start by having an ensign hoisted. I expect there's enough bunting in the flag locker to make up something. If I'm not mistaken that's the advance party of the army that I can see coming over the Rift, and I expect the brigadier will be here in a couple of hours. I wouldn't want him to mistake you for the enemy!'

***

It was a very cordial interview with Brigadier Prideaux. After all, this was the first success of the expedition, and it was a real, tangible achievement. The dispatches that he would send back up the river tonight would tell of an army advancing upon the enemy and taking a French man-o'-war along the way. They would hint that the process of achieving naval superiority had at least been started, while acknowledging that the French navy still posed a threat. The brigadier was happy to sign the acting commission. In truth, he had no idea of the limits of his authority in naval matters but consoled himself with the knowledge that the Admiralty had no power over him. In any case, it was an eminently sensible proposal. He would retain the services of Holbrooke – whom he had reluctantly come to respect and rely upon – while the schooner would be commanded by a man of the appropriate rank. It was too small to be rated a sloop, therefore a lieutenant it must be. He wouldn't have to worry about the details because Lynton would report through Holbrooke. It was only the new name that caused him to frown.

'But look here, Captain Holbrooke. I don't see why we must give her a new name. I recall that most captured

French ships retain their old name. Why the change?'

Holbrooke stifled an exasperated sigh. If Prideaux hadn't yet grasped the need to deal generously with his Indian allies, then this was going to be difficult.

'The schooner was launched here at Oswego in 'fifty-six and christened *Mohawk*, sir. It was the French who renamed her *Huron* in honour of their own Indian allies. It was done as a calculated insult to the Mohawks who favoured the British...'

'But still, I understand their Lordships reserve the right to name their ships, and there's no hurry. You can suggest the change in your dispatches and if they agree then you can rename her when we hear from them.'

Holbrooke started to reply. He wasn't going to let this go easily. Perhaps he'd been too quick to tell Okwaho and Kanatase of the new name, but he was damned if he would go back on his word without a fight. If necessary, he'd defy Prideaux. He opened his mouth to reply when he saw Sir William striding towards them.

'My congratulations, Captain Holbrooke,' he said, pumping his hand. 'A brilliant action and may I say it was a master stroke to compliment our allies with the new name? Oh dear, if we had kept the name *Huron*, I can't imagine what effect it would have on the Iroquois; they've been deadly enemies for generations. I expect they would have refused to set foot aboard and half of them would have left us. Okwaho is delighted and has asked if he could visit the schooner. When would that be convenient? Perhaps you could accompany him, Brigadier. Can you arrange some naval ceremonial, Holbrooke? What would be appropriate?'

Sir William's energetic interruption rode right over the brigadier's objections which were forgotten in the bustle of arranging for a visit to King George's newest schooner. Holbrooke was marvelling at how conveniently it had all turned out when he saw Sir William covertly wink at him. He must have heard Prideaux' objection – he wasn't a quiet man – and decide to take direct action to avoid what would certainly have been an insult to the Indians.

***

Holbrooke had resisted the temptation to base himself aboard the schooner. It was Lynton's ship now, and he would only inhibit the lieutenant at a time when he needed to be focussed on getting the schooner ready to sail, rather than worrying about his superior. Yet he was more comfortable ashore than he had expected. A party of Mohawks had made his regulation tent more comfortable with the addition of deerskins and scented brushwood to keep the insects away and offer shade from the sun. The Mohawks knew very well who they should honour for the naming of the schooner.

Holbrooke and Chalmers sat in front of the tent after sunset, watching the stars light up the sky. They heard soft footsteps approaching and by now they knew that no European walked that quietly.

'Holbrooke, Chalmers, good evening,' said Kanatase.

He waited to be invited to join them and then folded up his limbs and sat cross-legged beside Chalmers. Holbrooke watched enviously. He'd tried over the past week but still he couldn't sit in that fashion, his joints creaked even as was sitting now, with his back against a log. He had also noticed that Kanatase rarely faced the person he was talking to but stood or sat beside them facing the same way. It had the interesting effect of making conversations less adversarial, as though with each of them looking at the same thing, it was easier to come to a mutual understanding. They sat in silence for a few minutes before Kanatase spoke.

'You did me a great service today, Holbrooke,' he said. 'Okwaho has stated before all the warriors that the new name for the schooner is both an honour to the tribe and a personal honour to me.'

'You deserve it, Kanatase. I am ready to reward loyalty and bravery. Also, you have taught me all that I know of this place,' he swept his arm around the horizon in a gesture that he had seen the Mohawks use to encompass all the lands around.

Kanatase stared into the darkness while Holbrooke waited. He was starting to understand the rhythms of conversation with the Mohawks.

'I am your man, Holbrooke,' he said, still looking at the river that gleamed softly in the starlight. 'I am your man and will fight alongside you until you leave this land.'

There was a sound of heavier steps as a man passed by in the darkness. It was Sir William, observing as always, and watching over his Indians. Holbrooke wondered how he had gained such an ascendancy. The Mohawks certainly revered him and to a lesser extent all the Iroquois nation did likewise. It appeared to be something deep-rooted in the Indians' culture, a generosity of spirit that allowed them to ignore a man's origins and see him only for what he was at that moment. Perhaps it was a result of the precarious life that the tribes led, constantly on the verge of starvation and permanently at war with someone. They needed to adopt new members wherever they were found, and they absorbed all sorts of people into their ranks: Englishmen, Frenchmen, Indians from other nations and tribes. It was all grist to the mill for them.

***

CHAPTER TWELVE

A Sprat for a Mackerel

Monday, Second of July 1759.
Schooner Mohawk, Off Irondequoit Bay, Lake Ontario.

The westerly wind was blowing keenly as Lieutenant Lynton scanned the windward horizon. This was his third day at sea – should he call it *at sea?* It felt like the sea, but perhaps *on the lake* would be better – and his third day in command of King George's latest prize. She was a beautiful creature, almost alive as she sliced through the sparkling waters of Lake Ontario.

'Good morning, sir,' Serviteur said, raising his tricorn, just as though Lynton was the captain of a frigate and as though Serviteur was the officer of the morning watch. He felt that they were both play-acting.

'There's nothing in sight, sir. The wind's freshening as usual and we're in for a good day, I believe.'

'Thank you, Mister Serviteur,' Lynton replied, unable to repress a smile.

Lynton looked up and saw that there was a lookout at the main topmast head. It wasn't an onerous duty on a day like today. They were tacking to windward and with the tops'ls furled he should have been sitting comfortably on the crosstrees where the main topmast joined the mainmast. Perhaps it was sheer high spirits, but the soldier, one of the rank-and-file of the Forty-Fourth, had climbed as high as he could and would give an additional five minutes notice of anything coming down from Fort Niagara. The soldier waved cheerfully with his free hand and Serviteur acknowledged with an answering wave. There was nothing wrong with the morale in his command, Lynton reflected.

Yes, he had a good schooner under his feet and his crew, although some of them were no seamen, were at least all volunteers, eager for the variety and excitement that was offered. Jackson had used the three days well, and now every man of the crew could at least haul on the correct line and half of them could hand and reef too. As for steersmen, there were plenty of those available from the bateau-men. Leaning on the great tiller of a schooner was little different in principle to steering a bateau or a whaleboat.

He'd been on the lake for three days now. His orders were quite clear: he was to stay a day's passage ahead of the army and intercept the brig *L'Iroquois* that was expected at any time. If all had gone to plan, the flotilla would have spent the last night at Sodus Bay, thirty miles to leeward of *Mohawk's* present position, and would be moving up to Irondequoit Bay through the day.

Everything depended upon the brig. The captured French captain had said that it should have been expected yesterday, but Lynton could swear that no brig had passed him. Apparently, the normal routine was for the French brig to sail slowly along the coast, looking into all the creeks and bays, and then lie-to or anchor overnight so that it didn't miss anything in the dark. Lynton had done likewise, tacking to windward through the daylight hours then reducing sail overnight and letting the prevailing westerlies drift him back down the coast. No, he hadn't missed the brig unless it had stood far out into the lake, and why would it do that?

So far, so good. Now he just had to sight the enemy, and then… well, it all depended on what the French captain did.

***

'I'm relieving the watch, sir,' said Jackson, touching his hat.

How had the time flown so fast? He must have been on the deck for three hours. Lynton suddenly realised that he was hungry. He could smell the breakfast cooking below. Bacon, perhaps, with hard-tack and pease pudding. Not a bad breakfast, all things considered, and there'd be coffee, Serviteur had made sure of that.

'Put her about now, Mister Jackson, if you please. We'll stand out into the lake for an hour.'

The schooner was handy in stays and tacking was easy with the tops'ls furled. Nevertheless, the novelty of commanding his own ship was still new to Lynton and he stayed on deck to see the manoeuvre completed.

'Stand by the sheets,' Jackson called. Two men rushed to the lee sheets ready to cast them off while four more took hold of the weather sheets.

'Helm a'lee,' he shouted.

The steersman pushed the tiller away from himself, not too far, taking care to judge how quickly the schooner swung into the wind. There was a jolt and a burst of spray over the fo'c'sle as the forefoot dropped onto its own bow wave, and then she was through the eye of the wind.

'Down helm, meet her,' Jackson called. 'Haul on the sheets, another fathom there on the staysail.'

The schooner settled onto the larboard tack and started her short beat out into the lake. Lynton nodded at Jackson and turned for the ladder and his breakfast.

'Sail Ho! Sail on the larboard bow!'

That was the new lookout, one of the bateau-men. There was no need to confirm the sighting and no need to identify the newcomer. Any sail on Lake Ontario was necessarily French, and a sail bringing the wind down from Fort Niagara was almost certainly *L'Iroquois*.

'Call the hands to quarters, Mister Jackson, clear for action.'

There was no drummer, no bugler and the men didn't understand the bosun's call, so for the first time in his life Lynton saw a ship go into action on the shouted command alone. There was a rush of men to the guns. He had the same four Royal Artillery gunners who had been with him and Holbrooke when they had taken this schooner, was it only two days ago? They were at least efficient in clearing away the guns that he hoped not to use.

Jackson was at the masthead now.

'That's a brig all right, sir. She's under easy sail close into the shore, just where we expected her.'

Jackson flung out his arm about eight points off the beam.

'I think she's seen us, sir, she's come a few points to larboard.'

'Very well, Mister Jackson. Stay up there and report her movements.'

So far, so good, Lynton thought. Now he just had to make sure that the brig recognised her fellow man-o'-war, the *Huron* as she had been known.

'Spill the wind, there, on the main and foresail.'

That should knock a knot or so off their speed. But he had to be careful to keep far enough from the brig so that the whaleboat on his deck couldn't be seen.

Lynton stared hard at the shore on their beam. At some point, just to the right of where the tree-line merged into the lake, he should see her. Ah, there! A topmast, and now a hint of a tops'l.

'Steady on this course, steersman.'

Lynton's orders were to lure the brig away from the flotilla. He relied upon the brig recognising the schooner and following her out of curiosity. He had the simple signal book that the French captain had been unable to throw overboard, and he had prepared the signal that he wanted. A blue swallowtail over a red flag: chasing to leeward.

'Hoist the signal, Mister Serviteur.'

There was no need for a French ensign; there had been no need for the schooner to fly one for three years until that fateful day off Oswego. All ships on the lake were French, until now, and it may look artificial to fly one, as though the schooner was trying too hard to be taken as French.

'Give him a gun, Corporal, and repeat that every half-glass.'

That should keep him interested, Lynton thought. A gun was a universal reminder to pay attention to signals.

'The brig's gaining on us, sir,' shouted Jackson, 'and she's come further to larboard as though she's trying to intercept us.'

And so she should. The brig was holding the weather-gage and would be sailing six miles to the schooner's four. The trick now was to look as though he was in hot pursuit of an enemy and not to let the brig get close enough to suspect that the schooner was no longer in French hands.

'Bring her three points to starboard, ease the sheets.'

'You're sure she's seen us, Mister Jackson?'

'I'm certain, sir. She's cracking on for all she's worth. She's setting some sort of stuns'l on the main... oh, it's carried away; what a mess.'

'Very well, come on deck now and let's get the tops'ls set. Send up a lookout to keep an eye on her.'

That would give them the speed to keep ahead of the brig and further reinforce the impression that the schooner had a chase in sight. They were probably evenly matched on this beam reach, though perhaps the brig would have a marginal advantage.

What would the French captain be thinking? He'd come along the coast on his normal routine and had seen nothing until the schooner came into sight. He would have expected to see her and to get the latest news of what was happening at Oswego. When the schooner reported a chase in sight, what then? What Lynton hoped and what in a sober assessment was most likely, was that the Frenchman would follow to support the schooner. He cannot have any idea what nature of vessel the schooner was chasing; no foreign men-o'-war had been seen on the lake for over two years, but Bradstreet's raid was fresh in their minds. Yes, the brig would keep following – at least Lynton hoped so. He would assume that the chase – whatever its identity – was still over his horizon.

But at some point, the brig would guess that something was amiss. What would he do then? That was the important question. If he believed the schooner was in enemy hands, would he continue chasing it or would he realise that it was a ruse to draw him away from the coast. At all costs, he couldn't be allowed to turn back.

'You have the deck, Mister Jackson,' said Lynton. 'I'm going below to look at the chart.'

The schooner had a just a few charts; one of the entire lake with soundings around the shores and two others – just sketches really – showing the approaches to Fort Niagara and Toronto. There was a more elaborate chart of Fort Frontenac and the Saint Lawrence River as far as La Présentation; evidently the schooner never went further downstream towards Montreal.

As he had thought, he could only sail a little over thirty miles on this course before he came to the north shore of the lake. At this speed they'd be there before noon, and then what? Probably the brig would smell a rat long before then. After all, there was nothing of importance on the north shore. Frontenac was twice that distance and would take up most of the day to get there. More importantly, it was to leeward. For every hour that he lured the brig in that direction, it would take four hours to beat back to windward. Lynton paused to consider. Assuming he could draw the brig to within sight of Fort Frontenac, and if this wind held, it would be unable to beat back up the lake to catch the flotilla before it reached Niagara. Holbrooke would by then have led the bateaux and whaleboats to their destination keeping one step ahead of the labouring brig.

He looked again at the chart. It was a bold ploy certainly. There was room to manoeuvre out here on the lake, but as soon as he was past the island that sat squarely in the approaches to the Saint Lawrence – it had no name on the map, or perhaps that crabbed scratching beside it was its name, *Ile Aux Canards*, Island of Ducks – he'd be caught in a trap of his own making. It wasn't an attractive proposition. He stood considering for a moment. Perhaps the whole expedition would stand or fall on the decision he made now. That was certainly a consideration, but really, deep down, he knew that there was only one opinion that mattered, and that was Holbrooke's. He'd been given this task to distract the French brig, and by God that was what he would do.

Lynton walked purposefully back onto the quarterdeck.

'Mister Jackson, we'll steer for Fort Frontenac, the course is nor'east-by east, but I want to make it look as though we are altering to follow a chase. Bring the schooner a point to starboard every half-glass until you're on the course.'

'Aye-aye sir,' Jackson replied, studying the younger man carefully. He knew very well what this new course meant; he had also studied the charts. 'I'll have the corporal drill the men on the guns again.'

***

All that day the schooner and the brig ran to the nor'east, bringing the wind with them. The brig was the faster with the wind astern, and yard-by-yard she closed on the schooner. Lynton barely moved from the taffrail. He could see the brig's sails clearly now and with the signal card in hand he hung out a series of flags to reinforce the idea that he was chasing an enemy. Luckily, the card was limited to statements and orders, and there was no hoist for questions such as *where is the enemy*? or *how many*? That allowed him to be creative and feed the brig information that would support the subterfuge.

'Land ho! Land on the larboard bow!'

The lookout was obeying his orders to watch ahead rather more frequently than astern.

'That'll be the southernmost point of the mainland,' said Lynton.

It was just past noon and the sun was high in the sky. The wind was fading, and a mist was rising from the lake's surface. The land to the north was only just discernible at four miles.

'Come a point to starboard, Mister Jackson. The land trends east-nor'east here.'

He studied the faint outline of the land through his telescope. It was no use. There were no distinguishing features and in any case the chart showed nothing but an outline of the shore. He had no idea whether the country was flat or mountainous, and the vague shapes that came and went in the thin mist gave no clues.

'Mind your course! You'll gybe and the French will be upon us!'

Jackson gave the tiller a nudge to leeward to correct the steering.

'Beg pardon, Bosun, but I was looking at the sun,' said the bateau-man. 'There'll be a fog tonight or my name's not Ezekiel Fullerton.'

Jackson craned his neck back to look at the sun. It was high in the blue sky. The mist was lying low on the water and didn't obscure the sun at all. Or did it?

'You see that, Bosun. The sun is starting to look... I don't know, watery perhaps. I've seen that before. I was with Bradstreet last year in these waters when we chased a Frenchie along the coast. The mist came with a fading westerly, just like this, then the sun lost its heat and before dark we were in a thick fog.'

Lynton was listening carefully. A fog! That would change things. It brought its own dangers, of course. They had no pilot for these waters and the schooner's charts hardly helped. But they had a lead-line and a compass. What more did they need?

Lynton knew that Jackson and Serviteur were looking at him, waiting for a decision. The seamanlike thing would be to put the schooner hard on the wind and head south before they were embayed in the fog. Lynton looked at his pocket-watch. Too soon. If he could tack out of this then so too could the brig, albeit more laboriously with her square rig, and then the flotilla would be endangered.

'Stand on,' said Lynton tersely. This was not the time to be discussing his decisions.

He strode the few paces up and down the quarterdeck, lost in thought.

'Who are the best leadsmen, Mister Jackson?'

'Why I do believe Mister Serviteur and me,' he replied, 'but I'll check with the bateau-men.'

'I can cast a lead and sing out the marks,' said the steersman. 'I sailed on the Guinea run a time or two and you don't get far up those rivers without a lead line.'

'I'll need you on the con, Mister Jackson, so it'll be Serviteur and Fullerton on the leads. We do have two leads?'

'Aye, sir, we do, in the lazaretto,' Jackson replied. He'd modified them himself, substituting the English marks for the French.

'Can't see the land anymore, sir.'

That was the lookout. The brig was still visible, but only as an indistinct shape. But she was closer now and nearly hull-up to the men on the schooner's quarterdeck.

'Let's have a cast of the lead,' Lynton said.

Fullerton was relieved on the tiller and he and Serviteur went forward to hunt out the lead-lines. Only five minutes later the first sounding came floating aft. By now the mist had thickened perceptibly, the sun could barely be seen behind its opaque cloak and the brig was lost to sight. The air was growing cold. Lynton held up his wetted finger to test the breeze and looked all around the horizon. Nothing. *Mohawk* was alone in her two-mile wide arena, hemmed in by a soft, wispy, white curtain.

***

'No bottom, no bottom on this line.'

That was Fullerton's voice, his clipped New England accent coming through clearly even though he was affecting a stage whisper. It didn't matter how far away the enemy was, the fog caused everyone to speak in hushed tones.

Lynton looked again at the chart that he had tacked to the binnacle cover. He was past caring if it was spoiled by the moist air. There were no soundings beyond three miles from the shore, but he knew that the lake was deep. He'd heard that depths of two hundred fathoms had been found no great distance offshore, and the hand leads were only twenty fathoms long. If he had correctly estimated his position, about half-way along the southern coast of the big island, then he could be just a mile offshore before he struck soundings.

'No bottom, nothing on this line.'

The schooner was still moving fast through the now-calm water. It was becoming important to know how fast.

'A cast of the log, if you please, Mister Jackson.'

He was acutely aware that the bosun was being loaded with an unfair share of the work, but he was the only truly competent seaman on board, the only one he could trust to handle the log. He heard the splash behind him as the triangular wooden log hit the water, and he heard the hissing sound as the line snaked through Jackson's hands and over the taffrail.

'Four knots and five fathoms, sir,' Jackson reported.

There was one thing to be said for these lakes: the navigation was easy. There were no tides and no currents worth speaking of. He could say with some confidence that if the wind held, he'd be abreast Duck Island in four hours. Now, how to amuse the brig in the meantime. If he was really chasing an enemy – another schooner perhaps, carried in sections down the Onondaga River and launched by the British at Oswego – what would he do now that the fog had come down?

'Corporal, a gun to leeward every five minutes if you please.'

That should persuade the Frenchman that he was still chasing in earnest.

***

The dull boom of the three-pounder sounded monotonously as the schooner groped its way deeper into the funnel that would end at the head of the Saint Lawrence River. It wasn't the sharper crack of a shotted gun with a full charge, this was intended as a signal gun. After all, no captain would throw away either shot or powder when a half charge blank would do.

The wind had shifted from sou'west to west and had slackened further. The log showed three knots now and *Mohawk* had the wind broad on her larboard quarter. There was still no bottom to be found on the hand lead, but Lynton was confident that he'd strike sounding long before he strayed too close to the big island to windward.

'Mister Jackson, Mister Serviteur, a moment of your time if you please.'

They huddled together around the binnacle as Lynton smoothed the creases out of the damp chart.

'By dead reckoning we are here,' he said, pointing to a spot three miles off the coast and level with the end of the peninsula that thrust east-nor'east from the big island. As Jackson and Serviteur looked intently at the chart, they could see how little information it offered. 'I trust that our friend is sailing at the same pace as us, perhaps just a little faster, but in any case, he must still be a couple of miles astern.'

'I heard a signal gun ten minutes ago,' said Serviteur.

'Yes,' Lynton replied. That gun had heartened him. If he were the French captain, he would be doing just that, a gun every hour or so to reassure the schooner that he was still there. It was the schooner – still perhaps in contact with the supposed enemy – that needed to fire a gun every five minutes for the brig to follow.

'Every mile that we can draw the brig on is an hour more for the army to move towards Fort Niagara. I intend to stand on until we pass this island, then I'll wear and bring us out southwards through this passage,' he pointed at Duck Island that should now be ten miles on their starboard bow. 'I'll give it a wide berth to be safe, but from the moment we wear ship the guns will stop and there'll be dead silence. I want the lead cast constantly and the log streamed every glass.'

Jackson looked doubtfully at the chart. It would take no great error in estimation of the speed of the schooner, or the amount of leeway that she made, to cast them ashore on any of half-a-dozen islands.

'Is there a current there, sir?' he asked. 'We are almost at the head of the Saint Lawrence.'

'Now that I don't know. It's still quite wide until Frontenac, but I expect there'll be some current carrying us nor'east.'

Jackson nodded. It stood to reason that there would be a flow into the head of such a great river.

'The guns are to remain cleared away. Make sure that the priming is kept dry in this fog and all hands are to be on deck. I aim to leave the brig feeling its way down to Frontenac while we escape back to the southern shore.'

It sounded so simple, but Lynton knew that it wasn't. As soon as they started manoeuvering it would be easy to lose track of their dead reckoning, and with the sides of the lake so steep, they could hit an island or a pinnacle between two casts of the lead.

'No bottom on this line.'

The cry had become monotonous, but it reminded Lynton of the precariousness of their navigation. They had no reference to the shore or the lake bottom and had not had any for two hours. They were in an unfamiliar schooner whose propensity for leeway wasn't known, and God only knew when the log and glass had last been calibrated. This was navigation at its most primitive.

***

Boom! The three-pounder spoke. Now the sound was flattened by the ever-thickening fog – they had long ceased calling it mist – and the flash showed as an orange bloom in the thick, white air.

'That will be the last signal gun, Corporal,' said Lynton softly. 'Now load with full charges and ball. When I give the word, I want four broadsides as fast as you can fire them.'

'Aye-aye sir.' Even the artillerymen were picking up the naval language.

'Mister Serviteur, you have your muskets ready?'

'Ready, aye, ready,' Serviteur reported, grinning happily in the gloom. Ranged on the foredeck were all the firearms that the schooner could muster: a dozen muskets and twenty pistols.

'As soon as the fourth broadside has been fired, you're to start up the musketry, reloading as fast as you can. Ten minutes should be adequate.'

Serviteur nodded and strode to the foredeck.

'Mister Jackson, hand the tops'ls and prepare to wear ship. As soon as that's done, we'll fire the broadsides.'

There was a rush of feet up the ratlines and the tugging, thumping sounds of thick canvas being drawn up to the yards.

'Ready to wear ship,' Jackson reported.

'Commence firing, Corporal.'

The silence of the fog was shattered by the four broadsides. The loaded guns made a perceptibly different sound to the blank signals that had been fired up to now, but even those sharper cracks were absorbed by the fog and the echoes came back in fragments from all points of the compass.

Then the muskets started. Serviteur had five men firing and another five loading as fast as they could. It made a fine cacophony of sound.

'One more gun from each side, Corporal, just for variety.'

He was trying to imitate the chaos of a night engagement between small vessels. A steady roll of broadsides would sound too artificial.

The guns ceased. Lynton could see the artillerymen panting after running the guns out and the bateau-men laughing and joking after the fun of firing the muskets.

'Silence on deck!' he said in a voice calculated to carry to the foredeck.

'Wear ship, Mister Jackson, make your heading sou'east.'

The booms made a horrible sound as they swung across the deck and to Lynton's ear even the sheets running through the blocks and cleats must be heard a mile away. And a mile was where he calculated that the brig would be by now. The last gun that he had heard from her seemed to suggest that he was correct, although sound played strange tricks in the fog.

'Sou'east it is, sir,' said Jackson softly.

'Very well, well stay on this course for an hour then turn to the south, that should bring us clear of the island.'

The deck was silent now. Dimly in the distance they heard a single gun from the brig, otherwise there was not a sound except the wind in the rigging and the waters of the lake bubbling under the schooner's forefoot.

'By the mark, seventeen.'

Their first sounding.

'That should put us a mile or so to the north of Duck Island.'

Lynton crossed his fingers covertly behind his back. He had no real idea what soundings he should expect, he was working on the assumption that there was something of a tail of shallow water behind the island, as the current swept the silt down from the lakes into the Saint Lawrence.

'Deep fourteen.'

'Two points to larboard, Mister Jackson,'

Better safe than sorry, he'd just give this island a few more cables of clearance. Was it his imagination, or could he feel its presence to windward, just out of sight? Damn this fog, he couldn't even tell how far he could see, whether he would recognise a danger at a mile or at half a cable.

'By the mark, seven.'

Shoaling fast! Lynton opened his mouth to order the helm put up when he felt the contact under his feet. The schooner staggered, there was an awful rending sound, and then it seemed to break free. He looked at Jackson.

'I'll go below and look, sir.'

Jackson seemed to be gone a long time. Was it his imagination, or was the schooner sailing more sluggishly? Was she a little down by the head? Better not to speculate, better to wait for the report.

In a few minutes Jackson was back on deck. He looked unperturbed; then all was well. He beckoned to Lynton to move aft to the taffrail. Now that was not Jackson's usual respectful manner.

'She's holed on the starboard side of the stem. Five planks have been started and the water's pouring in. We've got a bare few minutes I would say, sir.'

Lynton took only seconds to recover from his shock.

'You're certain, Jackson? There's no hope?'

'None, sir. She'll founder in thirty minutes at most. We should get the whaleboat over the side while we can. It'll take us all.'

***

CHAPTER THIRTEEN

A Long Pull

Monday, Second of July 1759.
Sodus Bay, Lake Ontario.

They broke camp at first light and soon the five hundred boats were heading out of Sodus bay and back onto the lake. A hundred boats had been left behind at Oswego with Colonel Haldimand, who was securing the expedition's supply line. The five thousand men that Holbrooke had taken onto the lake were the striking force. They would be the ones to lay siege to Fort Niagara.

It had been a long pull the day before and it looked like being a long pull today. Twenty five miles was hard but achievable, Holbrooke had noted with relief. His plan for the advance on Fort Niagara was predicated on making that distance in a day, and a few miles more for the last leg of the journey. He had a chart, of course, and it showed two good bays or creeks where they could bring the whole flotilla into safety for the night. However, the detail on the chart became vaguer the further west he looked. This Sodus Bay was known to Sir William, as was their next destination, Irondequoit Bay, but beyond that they relied upon the testimony of the Iroquois. Bays and creeks there certainly were, but at what distances and how suitable to harbour the flotilla would have to be seen.

'You, sir! Yes, you! Get your boat back in line! You are supposed to be leading the column. If your oarsmen are tired already you can put them ashore to find their own way home.'

The guilty boat veered to larboard, the subaltern at the tiller reddening at the rebuke while the oarsmen philosophically pulled a longer stroke, staring aft as though nothing had happened.

The frustrations of the day had started even before the

last boat had nosed out onto the lake. It was vital to keep all the boats moving and there was no time for breaks in the rowing. Holbrooke blessed his insistence that everyone in each boat took a turn with the oar. There was no doubt that the bateau-men were the strongest and best oarsmen, but they could only row for a couple of hours and then the boat would either have to drift or a new draft of less-able oarsman must take their place. They needed to make a constant four knots to reach their next campsite before they were benighted. At that rate the passage to Niagara was only five days with four overnight camps.

Holbrooke was irritated. It wasn't just the huge task of keeping all five hundred boats moving, but he was starting to have misgivings about sending Lynton away with the schooner. The lieutenant should be cruising off Irondequoit Bay now, and if the French captain had told the truth he would meet the brig *L'Iroquois* either today or further west tomorrow. He knew that he'd given his friend a daunting task, perhaps an impossible one, but if he was successful it would preserve the lives of a good proportion of the men in the army and perhaps save the expedition. He had no doubt that Prideaux and his colonels would try to press on even if the brig picked off a proportion of the boats, but how many could they stand to lose? The soldiers just didn't understand how much damage a well-handled vessel with ten twelve-pound guns could achieve against essentially unarmed boats. He still had his two gunboats, of course, but the brig would surely deal with them first. Then the French captain could manoeuvre into a range where his grape shot and canister could hardly miss, and still he'd be beyond the effective range of the soldiers' muskets. A couple of hours – in Holbrooke's opinion – would see the end of the expedition. He'd come under intense pressure to keep *Mohawk* close to the flotilla, and that would certainly have reassured the soldiers, but it would have been a false comfort. Three-pounders against twelve-pounders could only have one result, and then the boats would be as vulnerable as they always had been. It didn't help that Holbrooke knew that he was right. If Lynton failed to lure the brig away and the army was decimated, he knew that much of the blame would fall on his own shoulders.

***

As Holbrooke's whaleboat sailed up and down the long columns of boats, he could see that the men were cheerful enough, and seemed to be making the four knots that he had ordered. Each boat had two watches of oarsmen, with a mix of soldiers and bateau-men in each watch. The off-watch had quickly adopted the ways of the sea, and despite having a full night's sleep behind them, were mostly lying stretched out in any spare space they could find. Some of them were in fantastic positions with their shoulders lolling over the gunwales and more than one man had used an oarsman's knee to cradle his unconscious head, lulled to sleep by the rhythmic motion of rowing. The westerly breeze was steadily in their teeth, but the oarsmen hardly seemed to notice it as they kept up their monotonous stroke hour after hour.

'How far would you say our next camp is, George,' asked Chalmers, who had appropriated the tiller to himself. Those long hours with Jackson had at last born fruit, and the sometime chaplain, sometime clerk, had become a competent helmsman.

'Thirty miles from our last and we must have come five miles already, so perhaps twenty-five from here,' he replied. 'Of course, those are land miles, they're about two-tenths less than nautical miles.'

Chalmers nodded distractedly. It was all the same to him. He was well aware that the two were different, but as far as he could see, with the influence of the westerly wind, and the uncertain accuracy of their charts, the difference wasn't significant.

They were pressing ahead now, scouting for any dangers. The visibility was good, and Holbrooke had decided to make a bold board out into the bay before tacking back to the coast. So long as he stayed within ten miles, no brig could slip between him and the shore and he'd be covering the widest area possible. By standing on the stern seat and holding the backstay, he could see the flotilla right astern, the green shores of the virgin forest to larboard and the wide expanse of Lake Ontario ahead and to starboard. He didn't expect to see *Mohawk*. In fact, he'd be disappointed if he did. His orders to Lynton were to stay a day's pull ahead of the flotilla and lie-to overnight.

It was peaceful out here. The noises of the five hundred boats of the flotilla had been left behind and the whaleboat made hardly a whisper as it slipped through the short waves.

'Did I hear thunder?' asked Chalmers, looking over the larboard bow of the boat.

Holbrooke had heard it too, so had the whole boat's crew. Their faces took on distracted expressions as they strained their ears to windward.

'There's no sign of a storm,' Holbrooke said, scanning the horizon, 'and that sound was too sharp, don't you think?'

Nobody said what they were all thinking, that single peal of thunder had sounded more like a light cannon, a three-pounder perhaps.

The wind was still westerly, although it was just starting to show signs of backing. There wasn't a cloud in the sky to indicate a thunderstorm although they were all-too common on the lake in summer. Perhaps it was nothing, just a trick of the wind.

'I can only just see the flotilla now,' said the New Englander who was taking his trick as lookout.

'Very well, bring her about, Mister Chalmers,' Holbrooke said formally.

Only part of his attention was on the whaleboat as Chalmers eased her head through the wind, his mind was away to windward. It could be *Mohawk*, firing a gun to attract the French brig perhaps, but Lynton should be far ahead of them, beyond hearing range. And yet, the day had heated up fast, and that played strange tricks with sound over water.

There it was again, more of a crack than a boom, and coming from somewhere to windward, and fifteen minutes later they heard another. There was no denying it. Ahead of them, towards Fort Niagara, some vessel was firing a light cannon at regular intervals to signal to another.

Holbrooke knew the worst agony of command in those next few hours, as the sound came whipping over the lake. It was too high-pitched for the French brig's twelve-pounder, more like a three-or-four-pounder, and therefore in all probability coming from Lynton's schooner. And the direction of the sound was drawing off to starboard, away towards the northern shore of the lake, which was just what Lynton had been ordered to do. Could Lynton manage this delicate affair? Could he keep ahead of the brig and persuade the Frenchman that he was still their loyal consort and chasing an enemy towards the Canadian shore? His instinct said he should follow, but his reason was insistent; he should continue back towards the southern shore. If he read it correctly, then his plan was working, and he must let Lynton carry out his part without interruption. In any case, he couldn't catch them now, and the sounds were getting less distinct as each quarter-hour passed. Nevertheless, his anguish was plain to see.

'You will find that Charles is quite a capable officer, you know,' Chalmers said quietly.

'Eh? Oh yes, of course.'

Holbrooke was startled out of his reverie.

'You show all the signs of an anxious parent when his offspring first sets off to school alone. You do yourself and Charles an injustice. You've taught him well, and he has a better chance of fooling the French than any man I know.'

'You're right, of course, David. But it's still worrying. There are so many things that could go wrong. If the brig is faster than I believe, or if the schooner is slower, then Charles will be fighting for his life before the dog watches.'

Chalmers nodded slowly.

'You're concerned for his safety…'

'And for Jackson and Serviteur, and the soldiers and bateau-men, David.'

'Of course, but consider. If he were not out there luring the Frenchman away – and I contend that he's the best man for the job – then he'd be here waiting for a twelve-pounder brig to come among us like a fox in a chicken-coop. He's safer where he is, and we'll probably see him tomorrow morning.'

Holbrooke knew that Chalmers was right, but it didn't ease his mental anguish.

'I doubt that we'll see him tomorrow, unless the wind changes, but Wednesday or Thursday is quite possible. In any case, I haven't heard the gun for a while now, so he's beyond my help. With any luck he's leading the brig along towards the northern shore, and if I'm reading the signs right, that halo over the sun says that we'll be in fog or at least a good mist before the dog watches, and that should make it easier.'

Holbrooke was right. The same mist that was giving Charles Lynton hope of losing the brig in the approaches to Fort Frontenac was sweeping down towards the whaleboat. The flotilla was only in sight because the whaleboat was sailing two points free and was steadily converging with the head of the columns. But as the distance decreased, so the visibility became less and less. It was still no more than a mist here, off the south shore of the lake, but it was a thick mist, and the tail of the flotilla was lost to sight when Chalmers brought the whaleboat alongside the brigadier's bateau.

***

The east and west shores of Irondequoit Bay were barely visible as the flotilla nosed its way into the calm waters between the enclosing reed beds. The air was stilled inside, the water was flat calm, and the wide beaches offered plenty of space to draw up the boats. Holbrooke leapt ashore as soon as the forefoot slid up the soft sand and strode off to find the brigadier.

'We'll stay here tomorrow, Captain Holbrooke,' Prideaux said flatly.

Holbrooke looked for support. It was clear that there was a division of opinion that had worked through before he arrived. Perhaps it had been brewing on the lake as the brigadier's boat had moved from column to column, discussing the campaign with the colonels. Holbrooke had discovered that Prideaux was not an impulsive person. He did things in a measured way and was of the firm opinion that battles were won more by logistics than by dash and elan. It showed in his determination to keep a strong force in his rear at Oswego and it was manifesting itself now in this decision to hold up the advance for a day.

Inevitably, when the force was split at Oswego, the loading of the boats had been affected. Stores were taken from here and there to sustain Haldimand and it was only when the boats were on the lake and nothing could be transferred that the problems started to show. Some units had been separated from their ammunition or their stores tents. Engineering tools weren't concentrated, and boats weren't evenly loaded with soldiers. Prideaux wanted a day in the peace of Irondequoit Bay to put all in order before they neared their objective. Holbrooke could see his point, and had read enough about the campaigns in North America to know that most of the disasters had their roots in poor logistical plans, but they were only three day's march – he was falling into the army terminology – from Niagara and there was a ten-gun enemy brig on the loose somewhere on the lake.

'Sir, every day we are on the lake is dangerous, the French brig…'

'I thought you had dealt with that, Captain Holbrooke,' Prideaux interrupted, his face showing his irritation at being contradicted.

'…the brig, I hope, has been drawn away to the

northeast, but it's only a temporary reprieve, sir. When the French captain grasps that he's been duped he'll either return to Fort Niagara or he'll go south to investigate Oswego. If it's Oswego, then we can only hope that he'll hurry back to Niagara with the news that it's in enemy hands. Whether he does that or decides to scout the southern shore, he is certain to see us unless we are fortunate, and he passes us in the night. I believe I've outlined the consequences if we are found out on the lake.'

'Nevertheless, we will remain here tomorrow. It's imperative that the loading of the boats should be correct so that there is no delay when we reach Niagara.'

The colonels nodded their agreement. Then there was no more to be said.

'Look here, Captain Holbrooke. Your stratagem appears to have been successful, and I congratulate you for it. The naval elements of my command are in good hands. The Frenchman is far away – to leeward as you say – and what he does next, we cannot say. Now you must bow to the needs of the army. The landing place that I have in mind is just three miles from the fort. If Monsieur Pouchot is the enterprising gentleman that we are led to believe he is, then a sortie against us as we are trying to match up our guns with our ammunition and putting the companies in fighting order could be disastrous. We need this day to stow the boats correctly. We will sail from here at first light on Wednesday.'

***

'Do you know this creek that is said to be three miles from the fort, Kanatase?'

The evening was drawing in and the heavy lifting was finished. Holbrooke had to admit that the expedition looked in much better order for the extra day they had spent at Irondequoit Bay. Now the boats were drawn up in company groups, with the artillery and stores separated and with a regular guard on each boat. When they came to leave the bay in the morning, it would be easy to get the flotilla into its proper order.

'I know it, Holbrooke. A warrior could walk to the fort in an hour; he could run the distance in twenty minutes.'

'And is there space to bring all the boats in, like this?'

Holbrooke waved his arm around the wide expanse of the bay. Kanatase considered for a moment.

'The creek is smaller than this, but there is space for the boats. There is good ground close by for the stores and ammunition.'

Perhaps he had been too pessimistic. They would be at Niagara in three days and so far, there had been no sign of either the French brig or Lynton's schooner. As each day went by it seemed more likely that they would reach their destination unopposed.

'The French had four ships on the lake, I believe,' said Chalmers.

Holbrooke looked blankly at him.

'We have captured one,' he said, making a mark in the sand with his finger, 'and according to the schooner's former captain one of the brigs – *L'Outaouaise* – is at Pointe au Baril being repaired and is not expected back on duty for a week. That's half of the French navy on Lake Ontario accounted for.'

'Perhaps, if this talk of the second brig being out of action is true.'

Chalmers bowed his acknowledgement but didn't adjust his arithmetic.

'Then there are two left to concern us. To our best knowledge *L'Iroquois* is far to leeward and may even decide to put into Frontenac before he comes back this way. The second schooner we know stays close to the head of the Saint Lawrence.'

Holbrooke had to admit that Chalmers' estimate was probably correct, although he was suspicious of such a favourable estimate of the enemy's actions.

'Wouldn't you say that, in pure naval terms – I cannot answer for the army – we are in as good a position as we could be?'

Kanatase was following the conversation with what looked like a keen interest. He was showing himself to be a man who absorbed new concepts quickly. His grasp of naval strategy would soon put most soldiers to shame.

'You're right of course, David. I just have an uneasy feeling that it's gone too well. Yes, *L'Iroquois* may not even come this way before we reach the fort, any one of a dozen things could detain it. And then I'm concerned about Lynton and his people. The whole of this lake is hostile territory, apart from Oswego, and he may be in need of a safe harbour. I'll feel better when I see his tops'ls on the horizon.'

***

The flotilla made two more overnight stops at unnamed indentations in the otherwise featureless southern lake shore. The first was just a morning's pull from Irondequoit Bay because the soldiers were still not satisfied with the loading of the boats. They named it Prideaux Bay and spent an uninterrupted night, showing no fires in case the French brig should pass by in the dark. By the time they pushed out into the lake, the oarsmen were fresh and ready for two long days of labour.

They named the second pull-out *Johnson Creek*, and they left it before dawn on the Friday. On this last day of their journey the wind at last fell and the glassy-smooth lake offered no resistance to the rowers. The flotilla sped towards its destination, and by four o'clock in the afternoon, the leading boats were being hauled up the shores of the creek. *La Petite Marais*, the French called it, *The Little Swamp*, but its name was a slander on this pleasant spot. There were swampy patches, certainly, but mostly the shores were sand with some reed beds, and only a hundred yards from the water the ground was firm and dry. It was protected by a bar at its mouth and on each side of the entrance the ground rose to shield those inside from the frequent summer storms and from direct bombardment by vessels on the lake. Holbrooke had to agree that it was perfectly situated to start a regular siege of the fort that was now less than four miles to the west.

Prideaux' determination to have his men and equipment stowed correctly bore fruit. It was quite likely that the French would have fortified this obvious landing site, so close to the fort. The grenadier and light infantry companies rushed out of the first boats and formed skirmishing lines to guard against surprise, while the musketeers gathered in their companies and marched forward, forming an ever-expanding perimeter. However, they were pleasantly surprised. There was no sign of the French or their Indian allies, and the tranquility of a pleasant summer afternoon lay over the creek.

***

CHAPTER FOURTEEN

The Whaleboat

Tuesday, Third of July 1759.
Off Ile Canard, Lake Ontario.

Lynton issued the orders to get the whaleboat over the side.
It would be done by brute force – there was no time to set
up the tackles on the yards.

'Let the men do that, Jackson. You stay with me. Let's
have a look at the chart.'

He pulled the disintegrating paper chart out of his
pocket.

'The hole's on the starboard side?'

'Yes, sir, right forrard.'

'Then we must be here, to leeward of Duck Island. I
misjudged the current. I thought the flow into the Saint
Lawrence would be greater this close to its head. I see I have
a lot to learn about navigation on the lakes.'

They both studied the faintly marked coastline of the
island with its outlying islet to the sou'east.

'Don't touch those sheets or halyards,' Lynton called as
loudly as he dared.

Jackson glanced at him questioningly.

'There's sure to be shallow water here to the east of this
island and I want the wind to take us out into deep water.
The schooner must sink completely to keep the French
guessing. They'll see nothing until the morning and by then
any flotsam will be dispersed and we'll be gone.'

Jackson looked with new respect at Lynton. He hadn't
thought of the mission from the moment that the schooner
had touched the rock, his only thought was to get into a boat
and row to safety. But he had to admit that they were in no
immediate danger. The whaleboat would be overloaded but
quite safe unless they had a severe blow, and he could see
bales of food being hauled on deck. Muskets, boxes of

cartridges, cutlasses, tomahawks and pistols were being stacked by the schooner's mainmast. At least they didn't have to worry about drinking water here on a freshwater lake.

'Heave!' shouted Serviteur, and a dozen strong arms slid the whaleboat over the gunwale with a great creaking and splintering of wood. It slid bows-first into the water and the stern followed with a huge splash. The schooner seemed to gain new buoyancy with the loss of the weight, but it only accentuated the way that the bows dipped towards the hungry water. Serviteur was busily supervising the loading of stores into the whaleboat.

'A cast of the lead, Mister Jackson.'

Jackson was back in a few minutes.

'No bottom, sir, he said. It's good and deep here.'

No bottom on a twenty-fathom line. The schooner would sink without trace, not even its topmasts would show above the surface. He had considered the need to strike the topmasts if it had been shallower, but that wouldn't be necessary.

The boat was alongside now, and the men were starting to embark. It was tight, but Lynton could see that even with the food and water there would be room for all thirty of them. Rowing would be awkward, but not impossible.

The schooner's stern was tilting up now. Not long to go. He would have liked to blow a hole in the stern to be sure that the schooner would sink, but the French brig was still somewhere out there in the fog, and he didn't want to draw them to the scene, not even after they had rowed away, not until the schooner was on the bottom and the flotsam had dispersed.

'She'll go, sir,' said Jackson. 'I was on a cutter this size that foundered in the Channel. As soon as the bows went under, the cabin windows blew out and down she went. I've taken off all the hatches. She'll be on the bottom in no time, but there'll be a lot of floating wreckage.'

'There's enough current to carry it away and he'll

probably see nothing in the dark in any case.'

And what would the French captain make of it if he did see the wreckage? Lynton wondered. He'd be unsure what had happened, and probably he'd stay at least a day trying to determine whether the schooner or whatever it had been chasing had foundered. The important thing now was to avoid being taken by the French so that they would remain in ignorance.

'Then let's get away in the whaleboat, Mister Jackson.'

Serviteur came aft at that moment and with a mighty wrench he freed the compass from the binnacle.

'You may want this, sir,' he said with a grin as he carried it to the whaleboat.

A chart, a compass and a lead-line; mariners had found their way in far greater seas than this with lesser navigation instruments.

***

They watched in silence as the schooner slipped beneath the fog-shrouded water. She was still under full sail but with her hull so deep in the water she was barely moving. First the bows dipped under, bringing the stern clear of the water so that her keel showed clear. She seemed to hang like that for an eternity, but within a minute the air pressure blew out the stern window frames with the glass still intact. Then the schooner started sliding into the water more quickly. At the last moment, the bows briefly came level with the water, then the whole thing went swiftly down on an even keel. The last that Lynton saw of his first command was the button on the top of the mainmast with the commissioning pennant – his pride and joy – flying free. Then, in an instant, that was gone also, and all that was left was a wide circle of flotsam – hatch covers, gratings and barrel-staves – floating gently away to the northeast, driven by the slight wind and the all-too-sluggish current.

A passage from the psalms came unbidden to Lynton, a familiar line from his childhood. It had chilled him even then, but only now did he properly understand its doleful significance:

For the wind passeth over it, and it is gone; and the place thereof shall know it no more.

There is no silence like the utter stillness after a vessel slips into the deep.

'What do you think, Mister Jackson? Oswego must be our destination, that's for certain. If we steer directly it's about thirty miles and with any luck, we'll be there tomorrow forenoon.'

'I don't know, sir. We're safe enough now but if the wind gets up, we may be in trouble. I'd feel happier nearer to the shore.'

He dipped his hand over the side to show how much freeboard the loaded whaleboat had.

'Eight or nine inches, no more.'

Lynton looked forrard. The eight oars were shipped and being pulled steadily by the bateau-men. They wouldn't be able to pull all night and at some time the soldiers would have to take their turn, then their speed would reduce.

'Let's have the bateau-men pull the bow and stroke oars and put soldiers on the others. That way they can keep rowing through the night if we need to.'

'Shh!' hissed Serviteur, cupping his ear to the west and holding up his hand. 'Shh!'

At first Lynton could hear nothing, then, very faintly, the sound of wind in rigging. Then voices, French voices.

The oarsmen had stopped without orders and the boat was dead quiet, drifting gently ahead with the remains of her way.

Christ, they were close. Just two or three cables. How long since the schooner went down? About twenty minutes, Lynton decided. Then there was a good chance that the debris had dispersed far enough to be undetected

145

in this appalling visibility. Every man in the boat was watching him. He held up his hand to reinforce the need for silence.

More voices from the fog. Imperative orders now, and he heard the unmistakable sounds of a vessel wearing, the jaws of the booms grinding against the mast and the dull crash as the boom swung across when she put her stern through the wind. The brig must be moving off to the northeast, he decided, towards Frontenac and the head of the river.

Not a man moved in the boat as the sounds receded astern. What would he do if he were the French Captain? Lynton tried to clear his thoughts. The brig had followed what he thought was a friendly schooner all through the day, assuming that the schooner was chasing an enemy. The French knew very well that a British army was on the way, but they probably didn't know its objective – Niagara, Frontenac, Toronto, perhaps – or from which direction it would strike. In fact, an attack on Frontenac made a lot of sense. It would complete the encirclement of the heart of New France and join up with the armies surging up the Saint Lawrence and Lake Champlain. This was the clearest information that the French had so far, and it indicated an attack on Frontenac. It would be a bold captain that now sailed away from where he believed the enemy was last seen. He'd stay at least until daylight to find the schooner, and in the meantime, he'd probably anchor nearer Frontenac. He wouldn't want to be blundering around in this fog any longer; yes, he'd anchor. How long would it take him to realise that there was nothing to be found? Not long, and he could be steering for Oswego by the start of the forenoon watch. In that case he could catch the whaleboat on the open lake where they would have no chance of either fighting or running. And that would give the game away. It wouldn't take long for the French to hear that the flotilla was on its way to Niagara, and then it would be unusual if they couldn't find it when it was at its most vulnerable. Lynton's duty suddenly became clear. He had to keep out of sight of the brig for as long as possible while making his way to the safety of Oswego.

'We'll make for the eastern shore then coast around to Oswego,' Lynton declared. 'I believe the French haven't settled in that area and we can find a place to rest for the day. East-sou'east for four or five hours should do it, Mister Jackson.'

***

Soon after midnight the fog started to lift, but a thin cloud hung over the lake, obscuring the moon and stars. The whaleboat rowed on through the gloom, changing the oarsmen every half hour but never pausing in their race for the safety of the shore.

'There's something on the larboard bow; do you see it, sir?' asked Jackson, pointing to what looked like a low headland.

'Unless this chart is far out, that must be this island here,' Lynton replied. He pointed to the chart but with no light it would have taken Jackson too long to make out the outlines. 'We must have been set somewhat to larboard. Come a point to starboard if you please.'

They watched as the ghostly land slipped by. From what they could see, it was a low island, wooded as they all were. For a moment Lynton considered heading for it, but it was too near the scene of the sinking. They'd do better to press on for the mainland.

Dawn was just starting to show a point or two forrard of the larboard beam, and by its faint illumination, a much more substantial landmass gradually became visible. It stretched from the bow all the way around to the north. This must be the headland that he'd been steering for, but they were later than he'd hoped.

'Stretch out now, men. Let's get to the shore before the sun catches us!'

The oarsmen dug long and deep and the whaleboat put on a burst of speed. Now he could see that it was a low bluff. According to the chart there was a bay just to the south, and that was what he was heading for.

The sun had still not hauled itself above the surrounding forest when the whaleboat ran hard up on the compacted shingle to the south of the headland. Lynton looked around; there wasn't a sign of humans as far as the eye could see. He knew this was Iroquois territory, but he also knew how sparsely populated it was. They hunted here, but mostly in the autumn, Kanatase had said during one of their long discussions. He didn't want to meet any of the natives; he spoke none of the language and nor did any of his men. Even if they were friendly to the English, it may be impossible to prove that they weren't French. It was a risk, but on consideration, a risk worth taking.

'Mister Jackson, drag the whaleboat up to those trees and hide it from the lake. Serviteur and I will climb up to that rock to see what we can see.'

The rock surmounted the bluff and stood out from the surrounding trees. Low though it was, barely two fathoms above the water, it offered the best view of the lake for miles around. The ashes of a fire lay on the smooth rock, but they were weeks, possibly months old. Lynton raised his telescope and methodically quartered the horizon. He was just starting his second slow sweep when Serviteur pointed to the west.

'Tops'ls, sir,' he said simply.

How had he missed that! Lynton looked in the direction that Serviteur had pointed. The smooth lake was bounded on the right by the chain of islands that they had passed in the night. Furthest away, over the horizon, was Duck Island where his schooner *Mohawk* lay in her watery grave. And there, a finger's-width to the left he could make out the briefest glimpse of white. The two men watched the white patch for a few minutes. Yes, it was growing bigger.

'Mister Jackson!' he shouted. 'The brig's on its way. Make sure everything is hidden in the trees and sweep over the marks where you dragged the boat up.'

With no tides, the marks where a heavy boat had been hauled out would last until the winter storms and would tell a tale to anyone who cared to look. The whaleboat had left a deep furrow and Jackson was busy with the bateau-men filling it in again and brushing it over to make it look like the surrounding shingle.

The brig – for it was certainly their pursuer of yesterday – was about eight miles away with the wind abaft her beam. If she held her course, she'd be here in less than two hours. Lynton silently thanked the inspiration that had made him head for shelter rather than row directly for Oswego. He'd have been caught before breakfast if he'd stayed out on the lake.

***

Lynton, Jackson and Serviteur watched the approaching brig from the shelter of the trees. There was nothing to show that a thirty-foot whaleboat had been dragged up the foreshore and into the forest. The marks had been swept clean and every one of the men was in deep cover. Nevertheless, they had prepared for a cross-country march if the French should come ashore, and each man carried four days of rations and a firearm.

'He seems to be searching the shore,' whispered Jackson. 'Look, he's spilling his wind.'

They burrowed deeper into the undergrowth and Lynton covered his telescope.

The brig was coming close inshore, but they were evidently concerned about the depth. Even without a telescope Lynton could see the rhythmic motions of a seaman heaving the lead. On it came until the crew could see around the headland and into their cove. It backed and filled for ten minutes then, evidently satisfied, it filled on the larboard tack and moved away to the nor'west, back towards Frontenac. They watched it until it was lost in the haze.

'Well,' said Lynton, 'that answers a few questions. They

are looking for something, but they've calculated that it can't have travelled further than this bay. They're right, of course, for here we are, thankfully out of sight. Now they're heading back to search again off Frontenac. We can be grateful that they're not immediately heading for Oswego or Fort Niagara, but I'm sure that will be their next goal. We have perhaps a day or two's grace.'

'Then I do believe you have fulfilled Captain Holbrooke's orders,' said Jackson. 'My congratulations, sir.'

***

CHAPTER FIFTEEN

A Schooner for a Schooner

Wednesday, Fourth of July 1759.
Schooner Mohawk's Whaleboat, Eastern Shore of Lake Ontario.

Lynton and his crew spent the rest of the daylight hours of Tuesday hidden in the undergrowth behind the headland. They lit no fires and ate their beef and bread cold. It had not been necessary to impress the need to remain hidden upon the soldiers and bateau-men, for between the threat of capture by the French and discovery and possible attack by the Indians, they had more than enough incentive to suffer the insects and heat in silence. Lynton had perhaps the worst of it, keeping a watch from the rock, subjected to the full force of the sun. Once he saw a flash of white to the northwest, just where he'd see the brig's tops'ls, but it soon disappeared again over the horizon.

'Right, let's get the boat back in the water while we still have some light.'

'I'll have the marks swept over again,' Jackson replied. 'If that brig comes this way today there's no need to tell him that we've been here.'

Amen to that, Lynton thought. He was determined to follow the coast rather than take the straight path to Oswego, and that meant a pull of over thirty miles, perhaps as much as forty, given the inaccuracy of their chart. Ten hours pulling at least, and they only had six hours of darkness. The chart showed a coast that trended due south before it swept to the west and then sou'west to Oswego. There were several coastal lagoons showing and right down at the southernmost point, deep in the bay to the east of Oswego, a pencil line indicated where a stream entered the lake. *Rivière à Saumon*, it was called, The Salmon River. There was no habitation marked on the map, just the bare fact of the estuary, and that wasn't to be relied upon. Nevertheless, that's where he would aim to spend the day on Wednesday, hidden away from eyes on the lake, as they had through Tuesday.

***

There was less wind tonight, and they made good progress along the featureless coast. The sky was clear, and they could see the little waves lapping against the sand and rocks. They never strayed more than five cables from the shore and one man was always standing in the centre of the boat watching the nor'westerly horizon. With dawn just starting to break, Lynton saw the estuary of the Salmon River. It was deserted and they again pulled the whaleboat clear of the water and hid for the day in the forest.

'Only fourteen miles tonight, Mister Jackson. We'll be at Oswego before dawn.'

'Yes, sir. Perhaps we should row easy though. Colonel Haldimand will be keeping a watch against attack and I wouldn't want to end my days with an English musket ball through my head.'

'Sunrise is about half past four, so we'll aim to arrive then. That shouldn't alarm them too much.'

He studied the chart again.

'I'm not at all convinced by these distances though, we'll start as soon as it's dark. If we're early, then we'll lie off the river mouth until it's light.'

'The men will be ready for a good night's pull, sir. We're making seamen of them; they're happy to sleep whatever the time of day and turn out when they're called. They'll be fresh by the time the sun's down.'

***

They arrived off the mouth of the Onondaga River with two hours to spare and drifted peacefully, watching for the sunrise and alert for any sign of either the French or the garrison at Oswego. The moon had already set in the southwest, and the stars were hidden by a banket of high, thin cloud. An hour ago, Jackson had thought he'd seen the hill to the east of the river mouth, with the angular remains of Fort Ontario at its crown. But since then they'd seen nothing but the faintest line of the eternal forest, outlined by the loom of the approaching sun that yet had more than an hour to its rising. The light westerly breeze barely moved the whaleboat and some of the men were already asleep, lying across the thwarts or lolling over the gunwales, oblivious to the discomfort of their positions. A few pulls on the oars every ten minutes kept them from drifting to leeward.

Lynton, however, wasn't asleep. He was thinking about how his actions of the last few days would be seen. On the one hand, he'd fulfilled his mission and drawn the French brig far to leeward of Prideaux' flotilla. On the other hand, he'd lost the schooner – his first command – and that was a hard thing to explain away. It all depended upon Holbrooke and how he viewed the incident. He knew that his captain reported directly to the Admiralty, so a mention of his name would carry weight. Would he be mentioned at all? And if he was would Holbrooke endorse his actions and justify his loss of the schooner, or would he lay the bare facts before their Lordships: the loss of the first man-o'-war in two years to fly the British flag on Lake Ontario? The uncomfortable truth was that the damned brig could have already worked its way back up the lake and could be ravaging the flotilla later today. In that case there was no hope for him. No amount of careful wording could conceal the fact that in the end his mission had failed, and he'd lost his ship.

He shook himself and brought his concentration back to the present. They were still afloat on a French lake in an open boat armed only with muskets. The here-and-now was still perilous and demanded his complete attention.

'Do you hear something, sir?'

That was Serviteur speaking softly from the bows. The boat's head was to the west, stemming the light breeze, and Serviteur was clear to windward of the noises of the boat.

'Silence in the boat!'

Lynton spoke quietly but he knew he could be heard by

all those who were awake. He saw them nudging the sleepers, bringing them to consciousness, just in case.

The silence was profound, broken only by the small waves lapping against the whaleboat's hull, and out on the lake the darkness was absolute. But yes, he could hear something. The familiar sound of wind in rigging and the creak of yards rubbing against masts. It could only be the French, coming down to investigate Oswego, and aiming to reach the river estuary with the dawn.

'Out oars,' Lynton ordered unnecessarily.

The oars were already shipped and the bateau-men, recognising the situation, had elbowed the soldiers aside to take their rightful places.

***

The whaleboat moved away to the west to be in a position from which they could either attack or retire. Still nothing could be seen in the stygian blackness and Lynton started to wonder whether he'd imagined it, but a look at the faces of his crew told him that they'd all heard the sounds.

Of course, it didn't have to be the French. Holbrooke could have taken a prize on his way to Fort Niagara, and it could be returning to Oswego now. But in that case, why was it approaching from the nor'east? It looked very much like a French reconnaissance of Oswego, or an outright attack. The timing was right, after the suspicious incident with their schooner and its subsequent disappearance. The French must be nearly certain that the British were on the lake, and Oswego was by far the most likely place to find them.

'I'm assuming that's a French vessel, or perhaps two. Probably that brig and something smaller,' Lynton said in a whisper. 'They'll be doing the same as us, waiting for the light. The question is, are they scouting or is this a determined raid on the army's line of supply?'

Jackson and Serviteur looked blank. It was a rhetorical question, of course, and in any case, they had no answer.

'Well, we're in the right place; we'll see them long before they notice us.'

'Lie down, you men,' said Jackson. 'Let's not show too much of ourselves. Load your muskets and pistols. No priming yet; I'll clout the first man that reaches for his priming-powder.'

The heavily laden boat, floating low in the water on the side of the enemy furthest from the rising sun, would indeed be hard to see. On the other hand, the sailing vessels – Lynton thought they were small, but it was only an impression based on their sounds – would be clearly visible from the whaleboat before the sun was above the hills to the nor'east.

Half an hour passed. They'd heard nothing for twenty minutes, but there was a definite glow appearing where the sun would soon pop up.

'There they are!'

That was one of the soldiers right up in the bow.

'Two of 'em I think, sir'

Lynton strained to see what the soldier was pointing at. Was that a gleam of white in the gloom? Yes, sails, although he couldn't tell what sort of sails, and there was another to the left.

'They're getting underway, sir,' said Jackson.

So they were. They'd seen the loom of the sun and knew that soon they'd be visible from Oswego. They were moving determinedly forward. And now he could see some of the details of the shore, the outline of the ruined Fort Ontario and below it the blackness where the river flowed into the lake.

Lynton stared at the enemy vessels – for he was now certain that they were enemies. Could he do anything? The thought of being a passive bystander was obnoxious to him.

'Mister Jackson, steer for the mouth of the estuary.'

'Will you board one of 'em, sir?'

'That I will. Does every man have a weapon?'

'Aye-aye,' they shouted back waving muskets, pistols,

tomahawks and cutlasses.

'This is our chance men. They won't see us until the last moment,' Lynton was shouting now. 'We'll board the nearest of them. See to your priming now.'

Men fumbled with their powder horns in the dark. Probably no more than half of them would fire, but Lynton didn't mind. It would be bright steel that would decide this battle. He could see the enemy more clearly now. The brig wasn't there, but there was a schooner that looked like the sister ship to his own, wrecked *Mohawk*, and a larger ship with ungainly square sails and the appearance of a fat merchantman, a troopship, perhaps. And what was that astern of them? Only now as the light poured onto the lake could he see the string of bateaux being towed by the troopship. There must be half a dozen of them, and they were all stuffed with men. Well, he couldn't do much about them; the schooner was closer and that was his target. A wild thought came into his head: a schooner for a schooner. He gripped his sword tightly.

***

'Put me alongside the schooner, Mister Jackson.'

'Aye-aye sir,' Jackson grinned fiercely in the gathering light.

They'd be at grips with the enemy in a minute and still they hadn't been seen. Was Haldimand aware of the approaching threat? A bugle sounded from the shore. Not the measured notes of the reveille, but the strident blare of the alert.

And still they hadn't been seen.

Pop, pop. Now they'd been spotted, and muskets were firing at them from the schooner.

'Pull for all you're worth, men!'

The troop ship had no cannon that Lynton could see, so if he could take the schooner, those hundreds of men would have to land without any support.

There was a regular crackle of musket fire from Fort Ontario now. They couldn't be wasting their powder and shot on the ships from that range! Then he saw the answering flashes from the shore to the east of the fort. The French must be attacking from the sea and the land.

'Steady, men!' Lynton shouted.

There were only yards to go now. One of the cannons in the schooner fired, but it couldn't depress low enough and the round shot hummed harmlessly overhead. They must have been loaded with ball to support the landing and they hadn't had time to change to grape or canister. So much the better.

Crash! The whaleboat's larboard bow smashed into the side of the schooner. They had no grapnel, but the boat's anchor was thrown by a mighty bateau-man and it caught in the capping of the gunwale.

'Follow me!' shouted Lynton, only to be trampled underfoot as the soldiers and bateau-men charged over the side.

They knew this schooner, it was identical to their old one, and they felt as though they deserved ownership. A hundred men in a sloop could hardly have resisted that rush of fierce fighting men, and the forty in the schooner had no chance at all. It was easier than the last time but now Frenchmen were leaping over the side rather than face these wild men who had appeared out of the dark, as though they were spewed forth from the nether regions of hell. Lynton was willing enough, but he found his enemies scattered before him, and it was with a clean sword that he reached the quarterdeck. He slashed at the ensign halyard, with a feeling of *déjà vu* and down floated the white flag of Bourbon.

'Herd them below, men, get the hatches on them!'

There was still some sporadic resistance, but only from Frenchmen who couldn't see their fellows throwing down their weapons. Lynton grabbed the abandoned tiller; the schooner had only yawed a little off its course.

'Mister Jackson! Man the larboard battery, it's probably loaded.'

This was too easy. The layout was identical to *Mohawk*, even down to the stowage for the rammers and worms. The men knew just where to lay their hands on all the implements.

'Larboard battery ready, sir,' he shouted back after a quick look at the priming, 'but I can't say what it's loaded with.'

'Never mind.' Ball probably, but grape or canister would do for the first broadside.

Lynton looked to larboard. The troop ship was still coming on, but he could see confusion on the quarterdeck. The captain over there couldn't know what was happening. He wouldn't have seen the whaleboat's wild attack, and it was too dark to see the detail of the action on deck. But he would have heard the musketry and the single cannon shot; he may even have noticed the lack of an ensign and he'd now be drawing his own conclusions.

Lynton pulled the tiller towards him, and the schooner came two points off the wind. He was converging with the troop ship, approaching at an acute angle while keeping his broadside arcs open.

The artillerymen were at the guns now, and he could see that the corporal was taking charge. Jackson was beside him, insistently taking charge of the tiller. It was amazing how quickly everyone sought their rightful place, even so soon after as sharp an action as Lynton had known.

'Stand by, Corporal.'

The muzzles were being heaved forward now, pointing squarely at the troop ship.

'Fire!' shouted Lynton.

The flashes of the three guns rent the blackness and assaulted the eyes of everyone on the schooner's deck. At that range they could hardly miss, and all three balls swept the deck of … what was it? A brig? A snow? A cat? Lynton had seen nothing like it before; that haphazard collection of sails had never graced anything larger than a lake, that was for certain.

They were sailing alongside the helpless Frenchman now, and the artillerymen were worming, sponging and reloading as fast as they could. With the rapidly increasing light, Lynton could see the appalled faces on the troop ship's quarterdeck. He saw the master give the order to bring up the helm, and he even saw the bows start to swing away, but it was too late. The corporal knew his business and he'd reloaded with grapeshot. At that range, the cluster of small iron balls was quite capable of bringing down a mast as well as cutting a bloody swathe through the crew, whereas three-pound shot would need a lot of luck to stop a ship of that size.

The grapeshot cleared the waist and the foredeck. Where there had been a dozen men now there were none. The sheets were in ruins and the lower sails hung in shreds, but the masts still stood. The ship continued its turn to larboard until its stern was squarely facing Oswego. Some of the boats cast off and started pulling for the shore – the bolder ones with a greater sense of duty – but most put their tillers over, clung hard to their painters, and followed the troop ship in its retreat to the north.

***

'We'll let them go, Jackson, they won't bother anyone else. Now let's see about those bateaux.'

The French bateaux were pulling lustily for the shore and the musketry around the ruined fort was intensifying. The dawn showed a stirring sight. A skirmishing line of men in the most fantastic uniforms was assaulting Fort Ontario from the east. They looked like a mix of French regulars, colonial troops and Canadian militia. They were being met by regular volleys of musketry from the higher ground. As Lynton watched he saw a surge as the French attacked, only to be beaten back by the disciplined fire. On the beach under the fort, a solid block of British infantry was drawn up facing the oncoming bateaux. He saw the boats pause, undecided, then they turned to port and pulled like devils to the nor'east, following the line of the coast. The attack was over. Without the bulk of the force landing from the sea, this smaller land-based contingent realised that they had no chance and were in full retreat. It looked like the bateaux were going to pick them up, perhaps at the Salmon River where the whaleboat had spent the previous day.

'Let them go,' said Lynton. 'We can always catch them after we've spoken to the colonel, if he wishes. He may have some more urgent task for us. Steer for the harbour if you please, Mister Jackson. What is Serviteur doing?'

Serviteur had more foresight than most and he'd saved the ensign from *Mohawk* when she sank. He was bending it on to the cut halyard where the white of France had so recently flown. And so it was that the sister ship of the *Mohawk*, built to the same lines at the same yard at Oswego, entered the little harbour beside the fort flying the red ensign, for all the world like a commissioned schooner under Admiralty orders.

***

CHAPTER SIXTEEN

A Captain's Folly

Friday, Sixth of July 1759.
Le Petit Marais, Lake Ontario.

Above the creek the land rose steadily and here it was dry and firm. Holbrooke and Chalmers strode along a path that skirted the reed beds. Their footsteps were guided by the flag that flew over the place to which Prideaux had summoned the commanders of his force, his temporary headquarters until it could be moved forward nearer where the first sap would be dug. All around them were working parties carrying the stores onto dry land, away from the damp of the marsh. The guns were also being landed and Captain Strachan saluted Holbrooke as he passed by. At another time it would have been interesting to see how the Royal Artillery handled the task, but for now Holbrooke's chief aim was to miss nothing of the discussions. He knew only too well that his absence wouldn't stop the brigadier and his colonels forming their plans, and they had a dangerous habit of forgetting the naval element, even when both of their flanks were bounded by water and when the link between the rear and forward areas stretched a hundred and thirty miles across a lake that the enemy still nominally commanded.

'Ah, here's Captain Holbrooke,' said Hervey. 'Make space if you please gentlemen.'

Prideaux had seconded William Hervey from Farquhar's Forty-Fourth to be his brigade major and chief-of-staff.

Holbrooke was the last to arrive and it was clear that the conference had indeed started without him. Eyre Massey gave him a friendly nod and Sir William shuffled aside to let him into the front rank of attendees. They were one fewer now that Haldimand had been left behind at Oswego, but Farquhar was there and Johnston of the New York

Provincials. Strachan was supervising the unloading of the artillery, but the two engineers, Captain-Lieutenant John Williams and Ensign George Demler were in attendance, displaying a mix of eagerness and trepidation at the imminent prospect of being the focus of attention.

'I have already sent out a reconnaissance, gentlemen, light infantry and grenadiers supported by a band of Sir William's Indians. I expect a report within the hour. If this were Europe, I'd have sent cavalry, but as it's the American wilderness I must make do with what I have...'

Prideaux paused as the faint sound of musketry came down on the westerly wind.

'Colonel Johnston, Colonel Massey, your pickets are in place, I trust?'

Both men nodded as their heads swivelled automatically to the sound of the musket fire.

'Our perimeter is secure half a mile towards the enemy, sir,' Johnston replied, 'and I've given orders to move it forward to two miles from the fortress before dark. My provincials are securing the eastern shore and the mouth of the creek.'

'Very well. It appears that the enemy is aware of our presence.'

Just then they heard the boom of a heavy gun. Just a single shot then a few more bursts of musketry, then nothing. The silence was eerie after the gunfire.

'I intend to look at the fortress myself as soon as the reconnaissance returns. Sir William, Captain Holbrooke, I hope you will join me.'

***

It was still light as the small party moved cautiously towards the edge of the cleared ground. The commander of the reconnaissance had reported that they'd surprised a small group of French soldiers, apparently shooting pigeons for the pot. The men had retired quickly to the fort and not twenty minutes later a regular sally had been sent out, perhaps half a company in strength. They'd sent them back with a couple of volleys of musketry, and the French had fired a cannon, but the shot fell wide of the mark. It appeared that the defenders now knew that regular troops were at their gates, but would they know that they faced a substantial army with engineers and a siege train?

The reconnaissance force was still there in the cover of the trees, protecting the command group and watching the fortress. This was one of the most dangerous phases of a siege, when the attackers were not yet established with proper defences against a counter-attack. According to best practice, the defender should send out a strong sally now, much stronger than the half company which was really no more than a reconnaissance itself. If they could disrupt the attackers now while they were establishing themselves, they could have a disproportionate and deadly effect on the siege. Prideaux and his senior officers knew all this and were aware of the danger, and yet it was vital that they should see for themselves the state of the fort's defences.

The men studied the fort in silence. Back in New York, Sir William had assured Amherst and Prideaux that Niagara would fall easily, that the defences had been allowed to crumble and that in any case it was merely a palisaded enclosure like most of the forts in the American wilderness. However, what they now saw would have gladdened the heart of Vauban himself. It may not have been as big and as strongly constructed as the vast European forts, but it was built on the correct scientific principles, and was perhaps the strongest fort in the whole of inland America. It was clear to the watchers that this fort would not fall to an impetuous rush; it would require a regular siege.

Well, if the French had thought that they were faced with nothing more than a raid, perhaps by a company of rangers, then they would soon know otherwise, Holbrooke thought. No less than half-a-dozen telescopes were trained on the fort and with the sun setting in the west, it was certain that their reflections would be seen. It would be a tempting target for the French gunners, but the range was long, and with a siege in prospect, a wise commander would conserve his ammunition.

While Prideaux and his staff scoured the fort's defences, Holbrooke looked beyond towards where he knew there was a small landing place and an anchorage. It would be just to the left of the fort. Ah, there! A glimpse of twin topmasts and a squared-off yard with its sail stowed in a bunt. That was either a brig or a tops'l schooner. He tried to estimate the height. It was certainly taller than Lynton's *Mohawk*, and that allayed his immediate concern that *Mohawk* had been recaptured. He looked more closely. The foremast was significantly shorter than the mainmast. A brig then, or a snow. He rubbed his eyes and looked again. The only tall masts in sight were the brig's; there was nothing else lofty enough to be seen from here. Then that was almost certainly the French brig *L'Iroquois,* and she was alone. If he had read the events of last Monday correctly, and Lynton had been successful in drawing *L'Iroquois* away to the east, then it was perfectly possible for it to have beaten back up the lake to be here at anchor off the fort. How long could Lynton have fooled the French? Evidently it had been long enough and then when the ruse was known, or the Frenchman decided he had chased too far, he would have hurried back to Niagara. At some point the brig would have passed the flotilla. If in daylight then it must have been far offshore, if in darkness then it was easier to see how the French captain had missed an invasion flotilla of five hundred boats.

Yet it was an extraordinary failure on the part of the French captain. It suggested a lack of enterprise, a lack of ability, or both. What would be the relationship between the commander of a brig – a lieutenant probably – and this Captain Pouchot who commanded the fort? If the brig was commanded by a lieutenant, then he was the same substantive rank as the fort's commander. Would he be under Pouchot's orders, or would he have to decide for himself how best to further King Louis' aims? It was a question of more than mere academic interest, as it would frame the brig's courses of action.

Whatever motivated the brig's captain, Prideaux' army had been lucky to avoid detection. But still, he'd have liked to know how Lynton had fared. The absence of the schooner riding at anchor alongside the brig suggested that he hadn't been taken, but there were many other disasters that could account for the schooner's absence. She could have been sunk or have foundered on one of the many shoals and reefs over towards Frontenac. Holbrooke remembered the paucity of the schooner's charts, little better than an outline of the lake's shore with a few notes about Frontenac.

Prideaux lowered his telescope and stared angrily at Sir William.

'I see that we'll be requiring the services of our engineers,' he said drily.

Sir William shrugged his shoulders; he had relied upon the reports of his Indians. He had never seen Fort Niagara before today, being far to the west of his own lands in the Mohawk Valley.

'It's rather more of a regular fort than my scouts suggested. Nevertheless, you have the means to invest it, I believe, sir,' he replied archly. 'Engineers, artillery and regular line battalions, stores and ammunition. I see nothing to cause concern for the success of the expedition.'

Prideaux made a non-committal sound and resumed his study.

'Mister Williams,' he called over his shoulder to his chief engineer. 'Are you taking notes? I will expect a plan for the first sap before the end of the day.'

***

They returned to the creek as the light was starting to fade. The French had not fired again and had not sent out another sally. All was quiet, but it was certain that Fort Niagara would be a hive of activity this night.

Armed with the information from his reconnaissance, Prideaux gathered his colonels together again. His dispositions appeared sound to Holbrooke. The regular battalions were to guard the southern flanks and provide fatigue parties when required. The provincials guarded the creek and the ground up to the first sap and, with the bateau-men, were to be the backbone of the labour force. Sir William's Indians were to scout the ground before the fort to deter a sally and form a screen deeper in the woods. There was no mention yet of Holbrooke's role, but he knew it was coming.

Prideaux finished disposing his army before the walls of Fort Niagara, then paused and turned to his naval adviser.

'We must deal with that brig, Captain Holbrooke, before it interferes with the sap. We can't get any guns close to her while she's under the protection of the fort. What do you suggest?'

The engineers had departed to start moving their equipment into place. Ideally the French commander would wake in the morning to find the first mortar battery in place and the first sap already inching towards the fort. He would see roving bands of Indians and, beyond range of his cannons, he would see the lines of tents for the infantry. Pouchot would be able to make a good guess of the size of the besieging force.

The brig was another matter entirely, peripheral to the work of the soldiers but an important factor in the army's ability to maintain the siege. It was Monsieur Pouchot's most versatile asset. Now that the army's presence was known, the brig's ten twelve-pounders were more than sufficient to mount a blockade of the British army and prevent supplies or orders reaching it from Oswego. It could use its guns to interfere with the siege, and with a little ingenuity it could enfilade the saps and draw out the siege by weeks. And finally, it ensured that Pouchot's communications with de Vaudreuil and Montcalm in Montreal and Quebec were secure. Yes, certainly something must be done. This would be a good moment for Lynton to arrive in *Mohawk*.

Holbrooke thought for a moment. Without Lynton's schooner – and he really couldn't wait for it to arrive, even if it was still afloat – there was really only one way to deal with the brig, and the sooner it was attempted, the better, before the French started taking precautions.

'I'll cut her out at first light tomorrow, sir,' he replied with more confidence than he felt.

'Why not tonight, in the dark?' Prideaux asked. 'Every cutting-out expedition that I've heard of happened at night.'

Prideaux had a habit of casting doubt on Holbrooke's proposals. He spoke to his colonels in a similar fashion, but with less acerbity. He appeared to work on the principle that the lower the rank, the more suspect the suggestions.

'That's true, sir, but in this case, I have no chart of the mouth of the river and I don't know how the brig lies in relation to the fort's guns. I must throw the whole force upon her decks in one attack and the boats will need some light to find her and to co-ordinate their approach, otherwise the attack will be defeated before it ever reaches its objective. We can pass the fort on the lake before dawn. The moon sets at two o'clock tonight and with the morning mist that we've seen in these parts, we have a good chance of being undetected.'

Prideaux looked unhappy with the plan, but this was a naval matter and with ill grace he bowed to Holbrooke's experience.

'Very well. Colonel Massey, perhaps you will provide your grenadiers for this enterprise. I'll leave the details to Captain Holbrooke. Make your arrangements and God speed, Captain Holbrooke, God speed.'

***

'Well, what do you need, Holbrooke?' Massey asked when they were alone. 'You can have as many men as you want, within reason. I expect there'll be no shortage of volunteers; they're all restless after that long journey.'

The brig probably had a crew of around a hundred, half of whom would be soldiers. It was a balance; too few men in the attacking force and they'd be beaten back, too many and the force would become unwieldy and require too many boats with a greater danger of being detected.

'Seventy men should do it,' Holbrooke replied.

Massey whistled softly.

'That many?' he asked.

Holbrooke nodded silently in reply.

'Then you'll need a company commander. I'll give you Charles Craddock, he's a good man, and you can have all his grenadiers. It will do them good to get off their arses. Do you find that in the navy? If the men have too little to do, they start causing trouble, and when you want them to fight, to shed their blood as they are paid to do, they become sullen. Constant activity is the only way to prepare for war!'

'Yes, the problem is similar, but we have a simple and in-built remedy. The very business of keeping a man-o'-war at sea occupies so much of the men's time that they have little opportunity to grow sullen. Any spare time we take up with exercises in sail handling and working the great guns.'

Massey laughed in reply. It was the age-old problem for the infantry; how do you employ hundreds or thousands of men when there is no enemy to fight?

'I'll take seven whaleboats. Eight oarsmen to each and ten grenadiers. The bateaux could hold more but their sluggishness and size are against them.'

'Won't you have a covering force? Some bateaux with those great four-pounders that seemed to come in so handy at Oswego.'

Holbrooke thought for a moment. He'd considered it, of course.

'The whaleboats, especially with sixteen men in each, will sit low in the water and will be able to move fast. The bateaux are much easier to see and would have to start ahead of the whaleboats. If this enterprise is to succeed it will be by stealth, and not by brute force. No, I'll take no gunboats. Either we will reach the brig undetected, in which case we have a good chance of success, or we'll be spotted along the way, in which case I will have to withdraw. There'll be no hope of approaching the brig once they know we are on the way, not with those twelve-pounders of hers.'

They walked in silence as each man thought about the carnage that a load of grapeshot or canister would make against a flimsy whaleboat full of men.

'Well, my grenadiers won't let you down, Holbrooke, that I can assure you. I wish you the best of fortune. You know, don't you, that this idea of standing tall to receive the enemy's fire is just a myth. We lie flat on the ground with our faces in the dirt whenever we can, then rise to give the enemy a dose of his own medicine when we can't miss. I commend this to you as sensible behaviour, Holbrooke. Keep your head down, and make sure the enemy does the bleeding, not you!'

***

CHAPTER SEVENTEEN

A Moonless Night

Saturday, Seventh of July 1759.
Whaleboat, off Fort Niagara, Lake Ontario.

The short summer night had barely allowed time to prepare for the cutting out expedition, but here they were in the full blackness of the night, loading the soldiers into the waiting whaleboats. Holbrooke was trying to appear confident and cheerful when he felt nothing of the sort. He'd been on cutting-out expeditions before, but always it had been with true saltwater sailors and they had at least some sort of understanding of the layout of the harbour and where the enemy vessel lay. This rushing into the unknown didn't feel right.

'I'd feel better if I were going with you,' said Chalmers.

He and Sutton had come to the mouth of the creek to see their captain on his way. Holbrooke had been firm; there was no place in the boats for anyone but oarsmen and soldiers. Chalmers was no fighter and Sutton with his shipwright skills was simply too valuable to the army. He had become the chief artificer and his responsibilities had grown beyond the maintenance of the boats to cover all the mechanical arts. It would have been irresponsible to take either of them, but still Holbrooke felt the wrench at being separated from his friends.

'You know that's not possible, David.'

'Then a blessing before you depart.'

The soldiers were nervous and keen to get started. Most bowed their heads as Chalmers said a few swift words, and one or two mouthed the appropriate responses, but they weren't concentrating, their minds were already prepared for battle. Kanatase stared to the northeast, where the sun would soon rise, and his lips moved in his own form of worship.

***

On board ships at that time seven bells would be ringing, and the middle watchmen would be looking forward to their reliefs. Here on Lake Ontario the gibbous moon had set an hour before and the starlight was extinguished by faint wisps of high cloud. It was dark, pitch-dark, and yet even now the first signs of the new day could be detected over the tree-line to the southeast. Not enough to illuminate the water, but just a hint that dawn was on its way.

One by one the whaleboats followed Holbrooke over the bar and out onto the lake. The wind had dropped overnight, and the water was glassy-smooth with barely a ripple to disturb its surface. It would have been a pretty sight in starlight, but as it was the face of the lake showed a sinister, uniform blackness that was never seen at sea, and was broken only by the whaleboats' trifling bow waves. Holbrooke led the little flotilla nor'west to make an offing then turned west-sou'west towards their destination. Five miles to his objective, or thereabouts, allowing for the need to keep a good distance from the fort and to row a short way up the river to where the brig was anchored. He'd estimated that the whaleboats could cover that distance in an hour-and-a-half, and he aimed to be alongside the brig at five o'clock. It was a good time for an attack. Concentration was at its lowest ebb in the hours before dawn and lookouts would be sleepy. He remembered morning watches at sea when he could barely keep his eyes open.

Massey had selected good men for this attack, the best of a company of grenadiers. The captain commanding the company was sitting alongside Holbrooke in the lead whaleboat. Eight rowers in each boat, all volunteers from the ranks of the bateau-men, and ten soldiers. Consequently, the boats were lightly loaded and rode high in the water. Holbrooke had to restrain the rowers; he didn't want to get ahead of the schedule that he'd planned. Nautical twilight, the first time at which they could expect to be able to see the brig, was at five o'clock. They mustn't be there earlier than that.

'Have you done this before, sir?'

Charles Craddock, the company commander, was perhaps a little older than Holbrooke but he was still young for his position, particularly in the grenadier company, and he was showing signs of tension.

'Yes.'

Holbrooke was in no mood for chat. He had severe misgivings about this cutting-out expedition. He hadn't had time to prepare the men properly, and none of them were seamen, not even the bateau-men. The British navy had a long history of taking ships from under the noses of shore batteries, and in most boat crews at least one man would have been able to draw on personal experience for what to expect, and the others would have a spoken tradition to draw upon. At sea, sailors had a lot of time for spinning yarns of past commissions where cutting out expeditions would have been discussed long into the dog watches. These soldiers couldn't possibly know what they were up against. Were they prepared for the brutality and the imperative for speed and initiative at the lowest level when boarding the enemy? Could these bateau-men be relied upon to cut the anchor cable quickly enough and loose the mains'l to give them steerage way to drop down the river into the lake? It would be a bloody business for certain. As soon as the gunners in the fort were alerted, they would turn their guns onto the brig, and if it was anchored where Holbrooke expected, then it would be within range of the fort's cannon for at least half an hour. Yes, this was a desperate venture, but it had to be attempted. The brig *L'Iroquois* could make the difference between success and failure for the army. They may even now be too late. If he were the captain of that brig, he would have weighed anchor when it became dark and he'd be off the mouth of the creek bombarding the enemy as soon as there was sufficient light to venture close enough.

Craddock fidgeted beside him, and Holbrooke realised that his silence was probably not helping.

'Yes, I've done this a few times before,' he said. 'The key thing is to get onto the deck as fast as possible. It's rare for a ship to repel a cutting-out party once they've made it onto the deck; the tide of the battle has already turned by that time.'

Holbrooke could just make out Craddock's expression. No doubt he would be brave enough assaulting a breach or standing in line to give and receive fire, but his face betrayed his anxiety in this unfamiliar element.

'Do you think they'll have boarding nets, sir?'

Now, that was a question. Holbrooke had a feeling about the brig's captain. The very fact that he'd missed his great opportunity to destroy the flotilla on the lake spoke volumes about his sense of enterprise. There were many plausible reasons for the brig being here at anchor when she should have been on the lake creating mayhem among the bateaux and whaleboats, but none of them would stand scrutiny among sea officers. Did that indicate that the captain was defensive, and would he therefore rig his boarding nets? Holbrooke didn't think so. His impression – and it was only that – was of a man who didn't know his business. A man who's fighting spirit had been dampened by two years of fruitless cruising on this French-owned lake.

'I don't believe so, Mister Craddock, but the men are prepared, I believe.'

Materially, yes, they were prepared. There were only four muskets for every section of ten men and they would stay in the boat when they boarded the brig. The grenadiers were armed with pistols and swords. Every man had a tomahawk of course. After four years of experience of wilderness fighting, the British army had come to recognise the utility of that simple weapon. Nevertheless, Holbrooke still had reservations about their mental readiness. He'd already decided that he'd start the yelling himself as soon as they were alongside, or when they were detected, to get the men pumped up for the assault.

***

They rowed steadily through the darkness. Holbrooke could only see the two boats immediately astern; the rest were lost in the night. He just had to have faith that they were there, each following the other. There was a definite pre-dawn glow now and the silhouette of the tree-line was becoming visible, although the shore was still in complete darkness. The fort should be on their larboard bow now, no more than a mile-and-a-half away. Ah, there it was. He could see the square outline of the great house within the fortified walls. He even thought he could see the flagpole on its roof. God, it was getting light early!

Now he could distinguish the individuals in his own boat; the oarsmen rowing easy, with little apparent effort, and the grenadiers sitting on the thwarts. He was so used to seeing them with their muskets pointing vertically, as they had done on the coast of Brittany the previous year, that it came as a surprise to see them crouching low and no muskets in sight. That was as he had ordered, of course, but it still looked odd. The boats flew no banners, and they would be invisible against the darkened lake, he hoped.

The lights of the British camp had been left behind and there were only a few lights in the fort, probably just the dozen lanterns that the watch would need. The space between the camp at the creek and the fort was in absolute blackness, but Holbrooke knew that the siege work had already started. Somewhere on their larboard beam, half a mile from the fort, beyond the cleared area and under cover of the forest, the first sap was being opened. They would be working entirely without light so that the surprise would be complete. If Monsieur Pouchot still had any doubts about what he was up against, the opening of the first sap, the harbinger of a regular siege, would make his situation clear.

'I can only see two boats, sir,' said Craddock, looking astern.

The lake was definitely lightening and now it was

possible to determine that the rear of the flotilla had become separated from the van. The first three boats were close together but of the last four nothing could be seen.

Damn! thought Holbrooke. He needed all seven boats to make the attack, three was just too few. They must all be together for the last dash at the anchored brig. This was no place to be dawdling, under the guns of Fort Niagara, but there was nothing for it but to wait for the other four to catch up. Still, it would take a particularly alert sentry to spot the boats on the dark, dark lake.

***

Jean Bonnet of the militia was seething with resentment. He'd been called to his company in the spring with the promise that he'd only serve three months, and then he'd be released to return to his family and his farm on La Belle Rivière in time for the harvest. Yet here he was in July, in this ridiculous hot uniform, staring at the water, looking for an enemy that had no ships on the lake, and had had none for the past two years. This talk of a besieging army was nonsense, of course. How could the British have marched from their colonies to Fort Niagara without being seen? They couldn't have come by water, the French navy owned the lake, and the friendly Indians would have known if they had come by land. Those pigeon hunters yesterday had just been surprised by a band of British rangers – the scum of the earth – and they'd move on in a day or so.

Private Bonnet walked sulkily along his beat, twenty yards of packed earth behind palisades, some of which had not been replaced and consequently were rotten to the point of uselessness. He could only see the lake at each end of his beat – it was hidden by the palisades between the bastions – and yet the sergeant insisted that he keep walking. What was the point of that? Probably the great oaf thought he'd fall asleep if he wasn't constantly moving. Sleep! He thought of sleep all the time when he wasn't thinking of food or his wife two hundred miles away. Since this Captain Pouchot had arrived at the fort two months before, sleep, and food, had been in short supply. He and his fellow militiamen had been harried from dawn 'til dusk to repair the fort's walls and their food ration had been cut to build up a reserve. Curse the man and curse the French army!

A minute to look through the loopholes on the bastion, that was all he was allowed. He leaned on the horizontal pine beam that held the palisades in place, determined to look anywhere but out onto the featureless lake. He studied the way that the rot had started to eat at the foot-wide section of tree that formed the right hand side of the loophole. Bored with that he let his eyes wander out beyond the fort. It was strange how the darkness wasn't quite even, there were two or three lumps – he couldn't think of a better word – of deeper darkness over there. As he looked at them the thought gradually seeped into his mind that he could be looking at something moving on the lake.

'Bonnet, get moving you laggard or you'll be before the lieutenant in the morning!' He'd overstayed his minute at the end of his beat.

Should he report what he'd seen? Bonnet rubbed his eyes and looked again, hoping that the dark lumps had disappeared, but they were still there. It was probably nothing, but at least it would make the sergeant move from his comfortable chair by the guardhouse.

'Sergeant, I think I see something out on the lake.'

The sergeant came. He was sure that Bonnet was just making this up to get some rest, but when he looked, he too could see something, or thought he could. He wasn't sure but he sent Bonnet to fetch the officer of the guard, who took one look and sent his messenger away to inform the artillery commander and Captain Pouchot. Within minutes the artillery commander was at his guns, but not before Captain Pouchot had rushed up from his quarters, stumbling over the last steps to the bastion as he buttoned his waistcoat.

'There are two groups of them. See how the first group is stopped, waiting for the others to catch up. They think we can't see them.'

Pierre Pouchot could see nothing. He'd been writing orders by the light of a candle and he hadn't yet got his night vision.

'Are you sure, Ensign?'

'I'm certain, sir. There are boats on the lake, six or seven of them at least.'

Pouchot said nothing. He just stared out onto the lake trying to acclimatise his eyes.

'We should wait until they are closer together to make a better target,' said the artillery captain. 'It's long range for these guns.'

He had three guns here on the north bastion, and another two on a smaller post along the wall. They were all twelve-pounders and due to the rottenness of the fortifications there were no embrasures. They had to fire *en barbette*, over the top of the palisades. They were the only guns that could command the northern face of the fort.

'Very well. But if they are not together before they come abreast your guns, open fire anyway.'

Now Pouchot could see something but only when he looked sideways, out of the corner of his eye. If he stared at the spot it was just an even blackness. Something was moving on the lake and it could only be the British. What were they doing? Could it be an attempt to take the fort by a *coup de main*? Or were they carrying guns across to the other side of the river. He had few spare men to fortify the west bank of the river and it was no good sending less than a company.

'No bugles or drums, Ensign. Send half the men in the ravelin to the northern wall.'

He blessed his decision to have a strong company spend the night in the ravelin. From there they could quickly move to reinforce the walls in case the British should attempt an overnight assault to save the need for a siege.

'They could be making for *L'Iroquois*, sir,' said the lieutenant.

Pouchot merely grunted in reply. He felt no love for the brig or her useless captain. He had returned yesterday with some tall story about following the schooner *Huron* all the way to Frontenac, only for her to disappear overnight, and no sign of the British ships she was supposed to be chasing. Then he'd reported that there was no enemy between Niagara and Oswego. Yet here they were, and Pouchot was becoming certain that they were in force, and they could only have come over the lake. The Iroquois had mostly changed their old allegiances and sided with the British, but there were enough Seneca who were still loyal to him. He would have heard if the British had marched through the wilderness to Niagara, wouldn't he?

***

Holbrooke felt uneasy. The new day was coming fast upon them, and he realised that he'd probably be seen before he reached the brig. The three whaleboats that were in sight were all resting on their oars, and he was staring into the darkness astern.

Ah, there they were. One by one the boats came into view; they were just a hundred yards away. He was glad to see them but if he could make out those black shapes from so low on the water, an alert sentry could see them from the fort.

'Give way,' he said quietly.

Now the boats were all close together and he could row faster. If he turned into the river closer to the fort than he had intended, then he had only half a mile to pull to where he hoped the brig would be. In less than ten minutes he'd be in action. His heart started to race faster.

Boom! He saw the flash an instant before he heard the gun, and then in rapid succession two more flashes and booms. They'd been seen!

'Pull for all you're worth, men!'

They'd lost the element of surprise, but still the brig would have only minutes to prepare.

Boom! The guns spoke again. They were reloading fast

over there on the fort. It looked like there were three guns to the left and two further to the right, and they were well handled. Nine-pounders at least, perhaps twelve-pounders.

There were splashes around the boats now, and a crash that was surely a hit. Holbrooke saw one of the boats astern of him slew aside and the next boat slowed down, backing water to assist.

'Keep Moving!' Holbrooke was standing now, shouting at the boats astern, waving urgently although they could hardly see him. They were too far away. He could feel the momentum slipping from him. Didn't they realise that they had to ignore casualties now, that their best chance of living through this was to take that brig?

Five boats were moving forward now, the other two were lost in the darkness. Holbrooke's eyes were hurting from the flashes that seemed so close on their beam. A shot fell close astern and soaked the rowers and grenadiers in his boat. He glanced at Craddock and saw nothing to reassure him.

'Another hit,' said Craddock, writhing in his seat.

Holbrooke looked astern again. The boat immediately behind them was in trouble; her four starboard oars had stopped pulling. Either the oarsmen had been incapacitated or the oars themselves had been smashed. The boats further astern of it were hesitating, not knowing whether to help their fellow or follow Holbrooke. His command was falling apart. Soon, he knew, only his boat would be pressing forward and that could only lead to disaster. He looked again at Craddock; the man's face was appalled; he had never experienced anything like this. Holbrooke saw the futility of pressing on with the attack, with too few boats and men whose hearts weren't in it. With a dead weight on his soul, Holbrooke ordered the boat about. It was a retreat, an ignominious failure and he struggled to keep the shame of it from showing on his face.

***

CHAPTER EIGHTEEN

Mohawk The Second

Saturday, Seventh of July 1759.
Schooner Mohawk, Off Frontenac.

Colonel Haldimand – a man who had not condescended to notice Lynton before – was full of praise for the way he'd broken up the attack on Oswego, was it only two days ago? It was a sobering thought that de Vaudreuil and Montcalm, facing determined attacks up the Saint Lawrence and Lake Champlain, attacks that were aimed at the still-beating heart of New France, could still scrape together enough vessels and men to counter-attack at Oswego. And they had done it as soon as rumour of a British army reached them. They were formidable opponents indeed, even now when their communications with France were severed, supplies of all kinds were short, and they were outnumbered by a vigorous and determined enemy.

That was why Haldimand had overruled Lynton's first instinct to sail west to join Holbrooke at Niagara. At the council of war, to which Lynton had – to his amazement – been invited, Haldimand had given all the arguments a fair hearing. Yes, he understood that the main point of effort was at Niagara, and he listened carefully as Lynton gave his opinion that the brig must have steered for the fort, since it wasn't at the attack on Oswego. He listened carefully as Lynton outlined the perils of the expedition being caught on the lake and destroyed by those twelve-pounders, and he nodded in agreement when Lynton described how even a small schooner could intervene to save the force.

'I hear all you say, Mister Lynton, and I acknowledge the danger to the striking force. Yet that danger hasn't changed. Brigadier Prideaux set out on the lake knowing that they were likely to be opposed by a brig. In fact, the immediate danger should have passed and he's probably starting his saps as we speak, safely ashore. Otherwise – God forbid – he's in retreat with his force in tatters. Either way, your schooner will be of less help to him than it will be to me. When those Frenchmen get back to Frontenac, their generals will know within a day that Oswego is in British hands and held by a strong force. They'll guess that it's a rear position to hold a supply line back to New York, and as Frontenac itself hasn't been attacked, they'll conclude that the only possible target is Fort Niagara. Now, I have no knowledge of the French force at Frontenac, but unless the gentlemen that we saw this morning are all that are available, we can expect another attack at any time. Legally speaking I have no right to give you orders, Mister Lynton, but my military judgement and my firm – extremely firm – recommendation is that you stay here under my command until the threat to Oswego is over.'

There was little that Lynton could say to counter those arguments. It was true that Haldimand couldn't give him direct orders, Holbrooke had made that clear, but a colonel ranked with a senior post-captain and his firm suggestions would be ignored at a naval lieutenant's peril. And there was another factor. Apart from Jackson and Serviteur, the entire crew of the schooner *did* fall under Haldimand's command. The colonel had been too polite to mention it, but Lynton had no doubt at all of what would happen if he defied the *firm recommendation*; he'd have a schooner with no crew.

He'd spent the rest of the Thursday, after the action with the French and the council-of-war, refitting the schooner and making up the complement. There had been no shortage of volunteers after the bateau-men and soldiers heard of his adventures, and now he had a crew to gladden any captain's heart. He'd made an everlasting friend of Chief Okwaho by renaming the schooner *Mohawk*, in place of the lost one, and there had been no argument from Haldimand. Friday had been spent patrolling this southeast corner of the lake and this morning, after nothing at all had been seen of the enemy, he'd been sent north on a reconnaissance to the head of the Saint Lawrence River.

***

Life doesn't get any better than this, Lynton thought, as he let the warm July evening sun penetrate to his very core. He had a command again – another perfect little schooner – and a crew who compensated in enthusiasm for what they lacked in seafaring experience. In fact, it needed little skill to sail a tops'l schooner like this, it was far less complex than the fully-rigged ships that he was used to, and simpler even than the brigs that were the largest vessels this lake had seen. And the tactical situation was clearer now, at least as far as the naval activity on the lake went. The French had started with two brigs – huge, powerful vessels for this lake – and two identical schooners. One of the brigs was in refit and the captain of the *Huron* had said that it would be at the yard at Pointe au Baril for at least a month. Even if the work was rushed through, the shipyard was fifty miles downstream from Frontenac and with this westerly wind it would take days to tow the brig back to the open lake. *Huron* had been captured then foundered off Duck Island, and the second schooner was in British hands. That left only the brig and as she wasn't present at the attack on Oswego, it was a near-certainty that she'd been sent to Fort Niagara. Lynton had a strong suspicion that he was master of this eastern side of the lake.

'That's Duck Island over on the larboard bow,' he said to Serviteur. 'We'll be passing close to where the old *Mohawk* lies.'

Strange to think that it was only four days ago that he'd lost his first command, and only two days ago that he'd captured his second. This one was identical to the first, built to the same lines by the British at Oswego. There was one important difference and it had nothing to do with the schooner's build. The former captain of this *Mohawk* had fancied himself as a surveyor – Lynton had discovered that much when they'd interrogated him – and his charts of the approaches to the Saint Lawrence River were superb examples of the cartographer's art, even down to comments on the currents to be expected where the lake emptied into the river. Now Lynton could see exactly where he had over-estimated the force of the current with such fateful results. He could see the shoal where he had struck and foundered, stretching far to the nor'east of Duck Island.

Serviteur was studying the chart now. He'd slipped easily into the role of master's mate while Jackson fulfilled the twin roles of first lieutenant and bosun. He had a competent crew in the bateau-men, excellent gunners in the artillerymen and soldiers for marines. He even had a cook who had volunteered from the provincials.

'If we'd had these charts, we would never have lost the first schooner, sir. We'd have sailed on for another half an hour before heading sou'east and we'd have passed that shoal easily.'

Lynton smiled. Serviteur was becoming a useful navigator but he was still no tactician.

'If we hadn't lost the schooner then, it's odds-on that the brig would have caught us. Even if we had escaped, the French could hardly have failed to spot us as we stood to the south. They'd have immediately realised that they'd been duped. As it was, we forced another forty-eight hours of uncertainty on them. That was worth the loss of a schooner.'

Serviteur nodded in reply. He often looked as though he hadn't quite followed these conversations, but Lynton knew by now that he was filing it away in that capacious brain of his.

'Ah, Mister Jackson. Have a look at this chart, would you?'

The three men gathered around the chart that Lynton had pinned to the grating. The quartering wind that had wafted them so quickly from Oswego hardly stirred the thick paper, and the sounds of a working vessel went unheard.

'Now, with this excellent chart and our schooner rig we

can dare to sail right up to Frontenac. The channel there is two miles wide and we can tack in our own length, so even in this sou'westerly we can beat out without any danger. I intend to look into the anchorage here behind the fort.'

The fort was set on the west bank of a river that flowed down from the north to join the Saint Lawrence. Perhaps it could even be called the true source of the mighty river, it was hard to tell. The anchorage and careenage for naval vessels and anything that traded on the lake was in that smaller river, just abreast the fort.

'You see, we'll have to come right up past the fort to look into the anchorage. It's too risky to do that in the daylight, so we'll go up at night. If the sky's clear,' he looked up at the pristine blue with a few high clouds over to the east, 'then the moon will give us sufficient light for navigation and any vessels will be easy to see.'

'It'll be dark about two bells, sir,' said Jackson.

'Aye, and the moon will set at four bells in the middle. We'll have five hours to do our work.'

***

They passed Duck Island in the dog watches and ran down the channel towards Frontenac with the last of the daylight astern. Lynton hoped that any watchers looking up the channel would fail to see their sails against the setting sun, but he wasn't too concerned if they did. There was no force at this end of the lake except perhaps a few gunboats at Frontenac, and the guns of the fort itself. That was the real unknown – the state of the fort – and he'd been unable to pry that information out of any of the prisoners. Frontenac had been captured and destroyed by Bradstreet only the previous year. Rumour suggested that the French had rebuilt the fort and brought up new guns, but the extent to which it now dominated the channel was unknown. We'll, he'd know soon enough.

'Wind's veering westerly, sir,' said Jackson. 'We'll be sailing by the lee soon. I'd like to wear and put us on the larboard tack.'

'Very well, Mister Jackson, make it so, and hand the tops'ls before you wear, there's no point in advertising our presence and we won't want them when we beat out of here.'

Lynton heard the pipe for all hands, and he saw the off-watch pour up onto the deck.

'Keep the men on deck now, Mister Jackson. Have the cook bring their supper to their quarters.'

The last gleam of the sun disappeared suddenly, as though some vast creature had cast its shadow over the lake, to be replaced by a silvery glow from the sou'west: the gibbous moon, just three days from its full. After a few moments as his eyes adjusted to the new light, Lynton saw that the islands and the mainland were still quite visible.

The schooner was sailing past the first of two substantial islands that flanked the approaches to Frontenac. This one was to larboard. He'd read the French name in the daylight, but it eluded him now and he wasn't going to open the dark lantern to read the chart. This was the only difficult part of the passage. There was a shoal in the middle of the channel that he must keep to the north of. That meant hugging the shore of the island until its easterly point was abeam, then steering directly for Frontenac.

'No bottom on this line.'

He had to remember that it was only a twenty-fathom line. The island was no more than half a mile to larboard, so they'd be right in the middle of the channel and could expect to strike soundings at any time.

'I can't see the fort yet,' said Jackson, looking out on the starboard bow. 'It's black as a curate's coat out there.'

'The fort's still eight miles away, Mister Jackson. I expect we won't see it for another half hour yet.'

Jackson glanced covertly at the half-hourglass. It had just been turned.

'Two points to starboard, helmsman.'

The bateau-man hauled the tiller towards him, and the schooner settled on the new course with the wind now just a point on the larboard quarter.

'By the mark, nineteen.'

That sounded about right. Lynton was happy that he could pinpoint his position on the chart if asked. They were in the middle of the channel with the smaller flanking island coming up to starboard. But the shoal was between them and the island, and he had to keep well to larboard.

There wasn't the least hint of daylight and the only illumination was from the moon. A shadow passed over the sea, a solitary cloud that briefly dimmed the moon and allowed the easterly stars to shine in all their brilliance. There was nothing to do for a few minutes, no decisions to make, and Lynton was able to indulge himself in contemplating the sheer beauty of it all. This was a country he could live in once British dominion had been established.

***

'I think I see it now, sir,' said Jackson. 'Right on the ship's head, there are a few dim lights.'

The steersman turned the glass. The fort had appeared exactly where Lynton had forecast it.

'Now Mister Jackson, I want four of the best men to do nothing but examine that anchorage, and I want independent reports from each of them. I'm going to bring the schooner in to half a mile from the fort, so we may expect a shot or two.'

He'd been pondering how close he should sail to the fort. Probably they had twelve-pounders, just possibly eighteens, but no more. On a dark night like this, the schooner would be hard to see and while the gunners would be able to point their weapons accurately, their estimation of range would necessarily be inaccurate, probably wildly so. He could risk a few shots for a better view of the anchorage and the careenage.

There had been no bottom on the twenty-fathom line for some time now. That meant that there was still shoal water to starboard. The northern shore seemed terribly close in the dark, less than five cables, perhaps just three, it was difficult to tell. The chart showed that there was sufficient water right up to a cable from the shore, so he wasn't concerned.

'Keep the lead going, Mister Jackson.'

'No bottom on this line,' came the reply from the leadsman.

Now they were in the deep water approaches to the fort.

He could see the fort clearly. It looked like a low, square structure from the lake, although he knew that it was built as a regular star-shaped fort. There were lights showing at each corner and some between, but beyond the fort, where the anchorage was marked on the chart, all was in darkness.

'No bottom on this line.'

'Come a point to starboard helmsman.'

That would put the wind right astern. Any more to starboard and they'd have to wear again.

Now the wooded hills on the other side of the smaller river came into sight. The anchorage would be between those hills and the fort. Nothing, the anchorage was a pit of blackness. Well, they haven't fired at us yet, so I'll push my luck, Lynton decided.

'Three points to larboard helmsman.'

That brought the wind further onto their quarter and he could feel the schooner's easier motion.

'Brail up the main.'

He felt the schooner slowing as the big mains'l was gathered up by its clews.

The anchorage was fine on the larboard bow now. Could he see anything? Yes, there were masts visible, outlined by the pale light of the moon that was shining right up the anchorage.

'I can see them now,' shouted Jackson. 'There's that tub of a troop ship and there are a few small gondolas and suchlike.'

'No sign of a brig?'

'Nothing that big at all, sir, not even another schooner. It looks like we cleared them out!'

A few of the soldiers laughed at that.

'Silence!' Lynton called in a voice calculated to reach the foredeck and no further.

They stood on as the details of the anchorage and the fort became clearer.

'We've seen enough, Mister Jackson, bring her about and sheet home the main.'

'Ready about,' called Jackson when the men had the sheets in hand.

'Down helm, bring her about.'

Boom! The first gun from the fort spoke, its flash momentarily illuminating the low walls.

Boom! A second gun. There was no saying where either ball landed.

'Keep her full and by, helmsman.'

The schooner was heading up the channel now with the lake ahead of them. The fort was fine on the starboard quarter and in ten minutes they'd be out of range.

Boom! Those were heavy guns, eighteen-pounders rather than twelves.

Boom! Lynton saw a splash where a ball had dropped short, although it was good for line. As he thought, in the meagre light of the moon the gunners were having difficulty determining the range of their target; they weren't elevating their guns enough.

'Ready about!'

He couldn't go too close to the southern shore; it was guarded by shoals.

'Mark eighteen,' called the leadsman.

That was all very well, but in this steep-sided lake he could be aground between two casts of the lead.

'Helm a-lee.'

The schooner came smoothly around and steadied on the new course. There were no more shots, the gunners must have given up. Probably they couldn't see to shoot now, with the moon so low and the schooner tacking away from them.

It was a tricky piece of navigation, bringing the schooner back out onto the lake, but when the sun rose in its glory, they had left Duck Island astern and were setting their tops'ls for the reach to the south.

The troop ship and six smaller vessels, none of them men-o'-war. That was the considered opinion of the watchers, and it agreed with the quick glances that Lynton stole while concentrating on keeping the schooner off the shoals. It appeared that he was master of the eastern end of the lake, at least until that brig came back from the west, or they could work her sister up from Pointe au Baril.

***

CHAPTER NINETEEN

Tweaking the Serpent's Tail

Wednesday, Eleventh of July 1759.
Before the Walls of Fort Niagara.

These soldiers had a strange attitude, Holbrooke found. They delighted in success and were utterly stoical in the face of failure. Prideaux had merely shrugged when Holbrooke had reported the debacle out on the moonlit lake. There was only one casualty – a soldier's leg had been taken clean off by an unlucky shot – and a trifling loss of material. In an army of this size, that was less – much less – than a day's normal wastage from accident and disease. Holbrooke appeared to be alone in blaming himself for the debacle.

'You see, Holbrooke,' said Massey some days after the event as they shared a breakfast, 'Prideaux saw your cutting-out expedition in the same light that he would have viewed a failed *coup de main*; there was no shame at all in being repulsed. Most sieges start with an attempt to rush the defences, and they are invariably complete and very costly disasters. However, on the rare occasion that they succeed, they save the time, expense and tedium of a regular siege, so they are generally worth trying. Consider that the main purpose of a fortress's resistance is to buy time. All else being equal, and if the siege is properly conducted, few fortresses can resist in the end, unless they are fortunate enough to be relieved. We all wondered that Prideaux didn't order an immediate attack while the defenders were still unsure of our force. Now we know; you were that forlorn hope.'

Holbrooke had heard of this curious aspect of siege warfare, the forlorn hope. Some zealous and fatalistic captain, wishing to make a name for himself and not concerned at the odds, makes an impetuous charge at the fort's walls with a band of volunteers. Usually the casualties are high and, as Massey pointed out, nothing is achieved, but at least it has been attempted and it looks well in the dispatches. The commander of the siege can say that he has tried everything to cut the siege short before settling down to the greater predictability of the scientific approach. Perhaps Prideaux would report on this naval alternative to the *coup de main* with approval if he mentioned it at all. Really, it was nothing more than a footnote in the story of the siege so far, and it was best forgotten.

***

Holbrooke was fascinated by the technical details of the siege. He studied the art of siege warfare, ranging far across the saps and batteries, to prevent himself worrying about Lynton. He had never experienced anything like this before: the steady buildup of men and materials, the slow, inexorable creeping forward of the trenches, the relentless bombardment that was intended as much to break the defenders' wills as it was to destroy the walls. There was something cold-blooded about its inevitability, and in its hard-nosed reliance on logistics. The quartermaster-general of the army was the most important person in a siege, far eclipsing the battalion commanders, the artillery officers and the engineers.

Two days after the failed attempt on the brig, he heard at last a garbled account of Lynton. It had come with a small group of boats from Oswego that brought provisions for the army. The truth was difficult to establish, but it did appear that the brig had been lured far away to the east by Lynton. More disturbing was the talk of a schooner lost and another taken, and there was some talk of a sea-fight off Oswego, a repulsed French attack. It was difficult to be certain, but it appeared that Lynton had survived and flourished. Why, then, had he not written to Holbrooke?

It was during the forenoon of a Wednesday, five days after the army had landed at Le Petit Marais, that Holbrooke had definite news, and it came in the form of a schooner – as alike to the lost *Mohawk* as was possible – heaving-to off the mouth of the creek, and a whaleboat pulling hastily across the bar. He hurried down to the creek to hear the news before it was known by the army.

'Serviteur, how good to see you,' said Holbrooke as his huge servant stepped over the bows of the boat clutching a package of dispatches for Prideaux. There was something different about him though; the bateau-men who pulled the whaleboat were deferring to him as though he were an officer. One of the New Englanders even held the bow and offered his shoulder for Serviteur to steady himself as he stepped over the gunwale.

'Is Mister Lynton well?'

'Mister Lynton is in perfect order, sir, and so is Mister Jackson,' Serviteur replied.

'I had heard that you had lost the schooner, but I see that the rumours were false,' Holbrooke continued, looking keenly at the vessel lying just a few cables offshore with its tops'ls backed.

'I believe Mister Lynton may wish to tell you the whole story, sir. However, that,' he pointed to the schooner with a smile, 'is not the schooner that you captured, but one that looks very much like it. That is the second *Mohawk*, sir. Mister Lynton is on board. He thought it better not to leave his command until he understood the situation ashore.'

'Quite right, Serviteur, quite right. Now, if you'll give me a moment while I collect Mister Chalmers and Kanatase, you can row me across.'

There was more than a hint of pride in the way that Serviteur spoke of this replacement schooner. It only took five minutes to row across, but in that time he had heard the essentials of Lynton's adventures during the ten days since he had last seen him. It was a fantastic tale, but the result was that now only two men-o'-war were cruising the lake, and one of them flew British colours. Holbrooke stared hard to the west where the bastions of Fort Niagara could be seen against the forested shore beyond. Lynton's schooner was no match for *L'Iroquois* out on the lake, but something may be attempted, something to give Prideaux' army a boost, to expunge the shame of his failed cutting-out expedition and to restore the navy's prestige. An idea started to form, but it must be done quickly.

***

Holbrooke bounded onto the schooner before the whaleboat was secured.

'You're cleared for action, Mister Lynton?' he asked as the last notes of Jackson's bosun's call faded away. 'The men are at their stations? Then get your schooner underway and we'll pay our old friend *L'Iroquois* a visit. You can leave your whaleboat behind this time. You'll find the brig under the fort's guns six cables or so from the river's mouth. Keep well clear of the fort, it has twelve-pounders mounted on the seaward walls, as I found to my cost. You can report your proceedings for the past couple of weeks when we are underway. Strike that ensign if you please,' he added pointing to British colours flying from the main gaff. 'Good morning to you, Mister Jackson.'

If Lynton was expecting the leisure to tell his story and bask in the glory of it, he was mistaken. Instead he was carried away on the wave of Holbrooke's enthusiasm. The schooner would certainly have been seen from the fort – it was only just over three miles away – and now was the time to show the French that their mastery of the lake was to be challenged. *L'Iroquois* had been seen occasionally since the siege started, but apart from some half-hearted bombardment of the camp – the French captain appeared reluctant to come close enough inshore to be effective – the brig had done nothing useful. There had been no attempt to sever the supply line back to Oswego, no enfilading fire against the saps and no persistent presence off the mouth of the creek that would have at least unnerved the army and made resupply difficult. It was a most lacklustre performance from the French captain and it confirmed Holbrooke's assessment of his character.

'Stand well out, Mister Lynton, until you can make the

anchorage in a single tack.'

These westerly and sou'westerly winds were becoming predictable. *Mohawk* made a bold board to the nor'west, and the watchers on the walls, if they weren't acquainted with the principles of sailing to windward, perhaps thought the familiar schooner was steering for Toronto. They wouldn't have seen the ensign before it was struck, and they'd be wondering at its movements.

***

'...and so, I named her *Mohawk*, in compliment to the first one, which I hope you approve, sir,' Lynton said, trying to interpose his story in the pauses between Holbrooke's orders. 'Chief Okwaho was happy when he heard, and he came aboard to inspect again. She's identical to the old *Mohawk*, except that she has better charts. Otherwise, you'd be excused for mistaking them.'

Holbrooke glanced at Kanatase who nodded gravely. Lynton had done well in renaming the schooner immediately, before speaking to his superior. It looked very well to the Mohawks, and they were the most important of Sir William's Indians. Holbrooke barely mentioned the cutting-out expedition; Lynton could hear about that from other sources, although the incident had been largely forgotten in the camp. Perhaps there would be another opportunity, now that he had a man-o'-war of some force, although still not enough to openly challenge the brig. Then why was he flaunting his prize in front of its far more powerful opponent? He couldn't really say, it was just a feeling that he was getting about the Frenchman. Morale was unlikely to be high in the brig; they had contributed nothing to the defence of the fort and they had received no news from the east for a week. Surely the French crew would recognise the second of the schooners and would distinguish it from the one that they chased across the lake. Possibly they suspected by now that one or both schooners had been taken by the British. There was no time for the fort to send a message to the brig, so the French captain wouldn't know that a schooner was approaching until he saw it standing into the river. What would he think? The lack of an ensign may give him pause for thought, but it was almost certain that ensigns were only flown on special occasions on this French-owned lake. He hoped that a bold approach would persuade the French captain that it was *Huron* or her sister coming in after being delayed at Frontenac.

'How goes the siege, sir?' asked Lynton, running out of his own narrative.

'Slowly, Mister Lynton. Only the mortars have been in action. The engineers don't seem to know their duty, and the artillery is waiting for them to establish the batteries before they can move the guns forward. I expect the French are not too much disturbed yet.'

Lynton grimaced. It was a sad tale and reflected badly on the army's leadership.

'The mortar battery is in range of the brig's guns if he cares to come close inshore. I want to tempt him to try, to shame him into it, perhaps. Don't risk the schooner, not yet, but the brig's bows will be upriver and with this wind you can sail close to the western shore and reach in under her stern and salute her. You'll have to suffer some long shots from the fort. Watch the brig closely. If you see her passing a spring to her cable, or weighing her anchor, then you're to feel no shame in retiring.'

Yes, it was a risk, but Holbrooke had a devil-may-care feeling today; this would make amends for the failed cutting-out.

***

Mohawk came about when they were four miles off the river's mouth, offering a comfortable close reach to fetch the brig in one tack. They could see her clearly now, anchored in her normal position in the bay to the south of the fort with her bows cast towards the flow of the river. It all looked peaceful and the brig showed no sign of moving, safe as she was under the guns of Fort Niagara. Holbrooke intended to give her a rude awakening.

He watched the fort through his telescope. Those twelve-pounders could reach the schooner even on the far side of the river, but *Mohawk* was moving fast, and a hit was unlikely at this range. Even if they were damaged, losing a topmast perhaps, the swift Niagara River would carry them out onto the lake, and it would be strange if they couldn't make repairs and be underway before the brig interfered. It was worth the risk in any case.

Holbrooke watched in approval as Jackson ordered the lead to be cast. It was a strange experience, acting the commodore when he felt himself barely proficient in the art of captaining a man-o'-war. Again, he had that recurring feeling that he was an imposter, posing in the uniform of a King's officer. He shook himself out of it; he had to remember that he should give directives for the mission and leave the handling of the schooner to Lynton.

'I'll hand the tops'ls, with your permission, sir,' Lynton said, formally removing his hat.

'Very well,' Holbrooke replied with a glance aloft.

That was a wise precaution. They'd have the wind forrard of the beam until they could make their escape back onto the lake, and the schooner was much handier under her fore-and-aft sails. By now, with his recent intensive experience, Lynton would know more about handling a schooner than Holbrooke did.

They were stemming the flow of the river now, but with this keen, steady wind they were still making four knots over the ground. They'd be a difficult target for the gunners on the fort, even if they were identified as the enemy.

'Deep six,' called the leadsman.

'No further to starboard, Mister Lynton,' said Holbrooke quietly. He didn't know what the bottom was like here, probably it shelved quite gradually, but this was no place to be risking a grounding.

Boom! The first ball from the fort sent up a fountain astern of the schooner. That answered the question. The

French defenders knew *Mohawk* for the enemy that she was. Now *L'Iroquois* would be alerted.

The second shot fared no better. The battery commander must be adjusting the aim of his guns collectively. That was the way to fire at the creeping saps and besiegers' batteries, but it was no way to fire at moving targets.

'Larboard battery standby,' shouted Lynton.

They were only three-pounders, but the brig was so close that they had a good chance of striking home. The corporal of artillery was dashing from gun to gun, adjusting the elevation and training. The guns were so small that a strong man could shift them without the need for a hand-spike, and that was just how they were being aimed.

'Ready, sir,' shouted the corporal.

Lynton looked at Holbrooke, who nodded.

'Fire!'

The smoke cleared quickly, whipped away to leeward by the steady breeze. Holbrooke saw one hit right aft on the brig's quarter, indicated by a spray of broken woodwork and glass from the quarter-light. One out of three wasn't bad, and not a gun could reply although the deck was a hive of activity as they made frantic efforts to train the guns far enough around. Evidently it had never occurred to the brig's captain that the enemy now had a man-o'-war on the lake and that it would dare to enter the river's mouth and fire at them. At least now they were in no doubt as to who owned the schooner.

'We've made our point, Mister Lynton, you may retire and give him the starboard battery if it will bear.'

The schooner turned to starboard, its bowsprit pointing briefly at the western shore before she came about to settle hard on the wind on the larboard tack.

'Fire!' shouted Lynton.

The starboard battery erupted in smoke and flame, but the guns were at the extreme limit of their traverse, the barrels hard against the sides of the gunports, and the balls fell harmlessly astern of the brig.

Boom, boom!

Holbrooke heard the unmistakable sound of a heavy shot passing overhead at the same time as a waterspout appeared off the starboard quarter. As if by magic, a hole appeared in the mainsail, right aft near the leach, splitting the sailcloth vertically for some six feet. That would keep Jackson busy, he thought. It would need a whole new cloth with the peak and clew cringles and the reefing points worked in, as well as the bolt-rope. A long day's work for a skilled sailmaker and a mate.

'There's a nice new sail in the forepeak, sir,' said Jackson, reading his mind. 'I'll have it bent on as soon as we're clear. I was hoping for an excuse to retire that old thing,' he added pointing aloft.

Holbrooke was pleased to see that this scratch crew of landsmen, soldiers and bateau-men didn't flinch under the fort's fire. They were a steady crew and they were becoming good seamen.

Holbrooke waited for another gun, but it didn't come. Then there were only two cannons in that battery, an inadequate number to cover the river estuary. Surely Monsieur Pouchot would have to reinforce this side of his fort now that the threat from the lake was a reality. That would reduce the guns facing the sap, another benefit of this raid. Holbrooke could see that the walls on this side of the fort were nothing more than low earthworks, and the guns were all mounted *en barbette* with no real protection for either the guns or their crews. That was information worth having and made this foray worthwhile regardless of the discomfort that he had caused to the brig.

Boom, boom!

The shot fell astern. By the time the battery had reloaded *Mohawk* was far out of range, the combined flow of the river and her speed through the water taking her out onto the lake at more than twice the rate that she'd entered.

'You may heave-to now, Mister Lynton, we're out of

range of the fort's guns. Watch that brig carefully, she may yet feel inclined to follow us. The mainsail can wait until we know their intentions.'

They watched in vain. There was plenty of activity and through the telescope Holbrooke and Lynton could see that a spring was being rigged to the anchor cable. Too late. That spring would have allowed the brig to turn its broadside to face its attacker and then *Mohawk* would have had to retreat ignominiously without ever bringing its guns into range. Activity there may have been, but it was all defensive; Holbrooke's impression of his opponent was hardening.

'That tweaked the serpent's tail,' Holbrooke declared as they ran back to the creek, with the wind at their stern and the leach of the mainsail flying in tatters like the trophies of a hard-fought victory.

The whole fort had seen their exploits; they'd seen the French navy humbled under their very eyes and they'd seen the schooner – *their* schooner – sail serenely back to safety out of reach of the guns on the walls. Pouchot must be fuming at the inactivity of his naval force. Surely now he would insist that the brig did something useful rather than swing around its anchor under the fort's guns. That was what Holbrooke wanted, a chance to meet the brig out on the lake on his own terms.

***

CHAPTER TWENTY

Kanatase's Decision

Wednesday, Eleventh of July 1759.
Schooner Mohawk, off Le Petit Marais, Lake Ontario.

The mortars were firing steadily, flinging their explosive shells into the crowded fort. This was the first night that the second battery was in use, and it must have felt like the end of the world to Pierre Pouchot and his mixed bag of defenders. A siege had a deadly predictability about it, and the men on the walls could only watch as the trenches and batteries crept closer and closer.

Yet it was strangely peaceful out on the lake. The wind had dropped an hour after sunset, and now there was only just enough breeze for a schooner to cut the water at a modest two knots or so. A bright moon, just a day past full and waning reluctantly, shone down with eager concentration on the smooth lake, quite extinguishing the stars and giving the blackness of the shadows an unearthly intensity.

Mohawk was waiting for the brig, backing and filling on the outer limit of the range of the fort's guns. There was no question of hiding on a night like this and the schooner could be easily seen from the French positions. It was only because every gun and gunner was employed in trying to beat down the attacker's batteries that they had no time or energy to spare to fire at this insolent vessel on the occasions that it looked as though it had come too close.

Holbrooke had calculated that the battery and the trenches would be an irresistible target for the brig. Even if its captain wasn't so keen, Pouchot would most certainly see the value of this flanking attack. For it was an immutable fact of the geometry of siege works that even if they were well protected against fire from the fort, a gun in an enfilading position could wreak havoc out of all proportion to its weight of shot. Normally, that was impossible for a defender to achieve, but with the lake so close to the siege lines and with the defenders owning the most powerful vessel on the lake, in this instance it cried out to be attempted. But Holbrooke had laid a trap.

'Don't you move a muscle, men,' said Holbrooke.

The bateau-men, all familiar faces now, and the light infantrymen, were sweating behind the covering of reeds that disguised their position. They had moved fast as soon as the sun had set, bringing the two bateaux that were still rigged as gunboats onto the lake shore immediately adjacent to the battery, then towing out rafts of tall reeds to disguise their position. It was rudimentary concealment and would have been spotted in an instant in daylight, but by the light of the moon it was invisible to the fort.

The conditions were ideal for *L'Iroquois* to come out. If not tonight, then she could probably be discounted as a fighting unit. Holbrooke and his men were ready and waiting for the brig to make its move.

***

'Here it comes,' said Kanatase who was peering through the reeds, watching for the brig to approach from the west. The Mohawk had asked to come on this expedition, and it seemed to Holbrooke that he had some particular reason to want to be away from the camp. He'd realised that it was futile to attempt to understand Kanatase's thought processes, and he'd probably never know what was motivating him to spend an uncomfortable night on the lake.

Holbrooke breathed a sigh of relief. He couldn't know for certain that the brig would come. It was logical, certainly, but there were a hundred reasons that may keep it swinging impotently around its anchor under the fort's guns. He poked his head through the screen of reeds. The brig's tops'ls were clearly visible in the moonlight as she sailed boldly past the fort. This was the critical point; would the brig choose to chase off the schooner, or would it merely ignore the nuisance and get into position to fire on the battery? The French navy was famed for the discipline of its captains. Typically, they would focus on completing their mission before engaging in the sort of ship-against-ship action that King George's navy so loved. It was possible that in this case the brig would be so incensed at the audacious schooner that its captain would disobey the fort commander's orders and engage it. If he did, there was a surprise awaiting him; fifty light infantrymen had been embarked and Lynton only had to bring *Mohawk* alongside the brig to end its career in the French navy.

'She's still coming, sir, straight for us,' said the bow oar.

Holbrooke could see that for himself. The brig's captain clearly knew these waters and knew that he could come close inshore here, which would give him a good chance of hitting the besiegers' battery. There was no difficulty in finding the battery; it was illuminated with a bright red-and-orange glow every half-minute or so as its mortars roared out. The gunners in the brig wouldn't be able to see their fall of shot, but an hour of solid firing should see at least some damage to the battery, perhaps enough to persuade the attackers to abandon it and build a new less effective one further inland. That would delay the siege for two or three days giving more time for Montcalm to organise a relief force. In a siege, as Holbrooke had come to understand, every hour of delay was a positive benefit for the defenders.

Holbrooke saw the brig furl its fore-tops'l; it was going to pass as slowly as it could. There was a flash and a bang from the brig, but from its larboard side. It was warning the schooner to keep out of range.

There was another flash and a bang, much louder this time, as the whole starboard broadside of the brig fired. With a sound like ripping canvas the first broadside of five twelve-pound solid shot whistled over Holbrooke's head.

'Ready men?'

There was an answering growl from the oarsmen, the

gunners and the light infantrymen.

'Give way!'

The bateau shot out from the shore, scattering the rafts of reeds as it went, and pulled hard for the brig. On his right Holbrooke could see Jackson's boat following him. There was a crash from forrard as the four-pounder opened fire, and higher-pitched howls as the two swivel guns followed.

'That's it men, fire as fast as you can.'

What the brig's people must have thought at this unexpected attack, Holbrooke could only guess. Out to seaward *Mohawk* would be moving in now, risking a broadside from the brig to get into a boarding position.

The two bateaux sped across the smooth water of the lake, scattering a phosphorescent glow from their bow wave and wake, firing furiously at the brig.

But there was no answering fire from the Frenchman. One by one the brig set its sails until under all plain canvas, and with its stuns'ls flashing out in the moonlight, it sped away eastwards, towards Frontenac and towards order and regularity. Anything rather than this chaos and uncertainty, fighting an enemy that never revealed itself until the last moment, and away from Pouchot and his impossible demands. Lynton didn't even try to chase. In this wind no schooner could catch an undamaged brig sailing large. The captain of *L'Iroquois* would never know his lucky escape.

Kanatase watched the brig retreating with a rare expression of satisfaction, and he nodded his head slowly, as though some scheme of his own had come to fruition. Holbrooke watched him. Now what was it about this little action that so pleased the otherwise imperturbable Indian?

***

'They'll be celebrating the Glorious Revolution and the Boyne back in England; there'll be no work done between dawn and dusk,' Chalmers said as he packed away his writing materials and folded his portable desk. 'Drunkenness and licentiousness, that will be the order of the day.'

'I'm sure that will be the case when they wake up,' Holbrooke replied, 'honest folk will be abed for at least another five or six hours. And that's where I should be. I feel unaccountably tired.'

He yawned loudly as he spoke.

'Perhaps it has something to do with spending the night in an open boat annoying our French friends, then insisting on writing to their Lordships before breakfast, don't you think?'

'Aye, in all probability, but there's a whaleboat going back to Oswego today and it's too good a chance to miss. My letter could reach Whitehall in two months if I'm lucky. September is a good time to approach their Lordships for promotions, just after the summer and while the campaign season is still running. I have high hopes that Lynton will get his step.'

Yes, and that your own efforts will be recognised, Chalmers thought. He knew very well how much his friend yearned to be posted, to achieve the reassurance that one day, if he lived, he would hoist his flag, even if only metaphorically from his retirement.

'Place your finger on this fold, would you, while I apply this wax.'

Holbrooke pressed down on the folded letter while Chalmers held the candle and the wax stick over the top. He let a large drop fall on the fold and watched as it spread to seal the dispatch from prying eyes. Later it would be covered in sailcloth and wrapped in twine, the normal means of securing a letter to the Admiralty secretary.

The naval headquarters on Lake Ontario consisted of a small tent that Holbrooke and Chalmers shared and three chairs that Sutton had made and that had to be guarded day and night against pilfering. There were very many land officers who coveted those chairs and they had unlimited numbers of unscrupulous soldiers at their command.

If any writing had to be done, then Chalmers' folding table was erected. There was nothing else beside the table and chairs. Of the crew that had followed Holbrooke from England, Lynton, Jackson and Serviteur were in the schooner and Sutton had been seconded into the engineers to work on apparatus for the siege. Only Holbrooke and Chalmers were left, and with no servant, they shifted for themselves. If he needed a messenger, then the Forty-Sixth provided one, by courtesy of Eyre Massey.

Holbrooke had considered moving into the schooner, but he was in constant demand for planning meetings, and Prideaux would not hear of him separating himself from the centre of decision-making. Yet it was satisfactory in its own way. A larger staff would have taken more of Holbrooke's time; now he was free to concentrate on thinking of ways that his small naval force could assist in the siege.

***

'Here's Kanatase,' said Chalmers.

The Mohawk was striding towards them through the busy camp. It was usually impossible to glean anything from the Mohawk's face, but today he had a grim look, as though he was bearing bad news.

They spoke for a moment about the previous night's action. Kanatase was interested in Holbrooke's thoughts about what the French navy would do next, and why they appeared reluctant to risk the brig in an all-out fight, but something was distracting him, and his mind was elsewhere. At length, Holbrooke had said all that could be said about the French and there was a pause that would have been awkward if they were all Europeans, but Holbrooke had learned that silences were a normal part of Indian discussions.

'I have news of my brother Iroquois,' Kanatase said, breaking the silence.

Holbrooke looked questioningly at him. Did he mean the members of the six nations that had come with them from Oswego, or was he referring to the Indians that had remained loyal to the French?

'My brothers have been restless since the digging

started.'

Then it was the Indians under Sir William's command, not the French Indians. Evidently they had been unhappy since the first sap had been opened and the slow, deadly work of the siege had commenced.

'This isn't the fighting that we are used to, we have no place in a siege and many are muttering at the danger of patrolling before the fort, under both the French and English guns.'

Now Holbrooke understood. The Indians had been brought into the army to act as the equivalent of light cavalry. It was a role that admirably suited their temperament and skills: scouting, ambushing, screening a larger force of regular troops, attacking small outposts, harrying a retreating enemy. He knew that it was futile to expect them to fight as European armies did; they wouldn't stand in line to be fired upon and they had no discipline in a charge. He nodded but kept an impassive face. Kanatase evidently had more to say.

'Not all of the Iroquois are friends of the English. It is well known that there are other Indians in the fort from lands further to the west, but there are also some of our own brothers, the Seneca, that have stayed with the French. You know that after Montcalm took the forts at Oswego three years ago, the Seneca and the Oneida changed their allegiance to the French. Many of them have never come back.'

Holbrooke didn't interrupt but listened carefully. So far Kanatase had told him what he knew already; evidently there was more to come.

'Yesterday there was a meeting with our brothers on the French side. I of course missed the meeting because I was with you in the boat, Holbrooke.'

That explained Kanatase's eagerness to take part in the night's action. Holbrooke nodded but made no comment.

'The Iroquois who are loyal to the French are led by Kaendaé, a Seneca who is well known to me. It was Kaendaé who attacked the bateau on the Mohawk River the day before you arrived at Fort Stanwix. He has seen the French victories and has fought alongside them in many battles. He does not believe, even now, that the English will win this war, and he has cast his lot with Captain Pouchot.'

Another silence. It was sometimes hard to remember that Kanatase had to think carefully to phrase his speech in English.

'Iroquois have no wish to fight with Iroquois, it would create bad blood between tribes and families for generations to come. I know this because I have a feud with Kaendaé that goes back to my grandfather's time. The leaders of the Iroquois on both sides have agreed to withdraw from the battle. They will make camp a mile south of the fort, alongside the river. The French call the place *La Belle Famille*.'

Holbrooke was familiar with La Belle Famille from his study of the maps. It was nothing more than a clearing in the woods a hundred yards from an escarpment that fell into the Niagara River. He assumed the name had a religious meaning, related to the Holy Family, but as far as he was aware, there was no building at the site, nothing to distinguish it except for the cleared space among the trees. It was close to the fort and on the left wing of the besieging army, although beyond the immediate siege works. From there the Indians could join the besiegers or the besieged as they saw the tide of battle turning one way or another. This was an important development, but he had learned to show no emotion in his dealings with Kanatase.

'Has Brigadier Prideaux been told, Kanatase?' he asked.

'Yes, Holbrooke, he knows. He is deploying his own soldiers where my brothers once stood.'

These were unusually short answers, even for Kanatase, and Holbrooke began to understand some of the emotion that lay behind them. Shame, principally. Unlike the other Iroquois, Kanatase and the Mohawks had forged personal relationships with the English. Not only with Holbrooke and his crew, but with Sir William, and Kanatase was well known among the colonels and majors. Then there was this feud with Kaendaé that he had mentioned but not elaborated. How was that affecting him?

'Then I wish you well, Kanatase, and I hope that I will see you again when the fort has fallen.'

'I also, Kanatase,' said Chalmers, speaking for the first time. 'I will miss your wise council.'

There was another silence, but this time Kanatese forced the ghost of a smile.

'I will not go with my Mohawk brothers,' he said. 'I will not dishonour my forefathers. I have pledged myself to fight with you, Holbrooke, and you, Chalmers. I stand by that pledge. Perhaps time will show that I have made the wrong decision, but I do not believe so. Kaendaé also will not go, he stays with *Sategariouan* in the fort.'

So that was what Kanatase looked so pleased about on the lake last night. He had been pondering whether to decamp or whether to stay with his English friends, and that minor naval skirmish had made up his mind.

***

'The damned savages have gone, then,' said Prideaux. 'Well good riddance to them, that's a thousand less mouths to feed. They're of no use in this siege in any case; any value that they had disappeared as soon as we opened the first sap.'

Prideaux clearly didn't miss his Iroquois allies. Sir William rolled his eyes when he knew that Prideaux couldn't see him, then he winked at Holbrooke.

'You know that they've been in communication with the fort since the day that we arrived here?' Prideaux continued, oblivious to the byplay.

'Yes, I had heard something to that effect,' Holbrooke replied.

'They've been coming and going at their own leisure and no doubt carrying our secrets to the French. I know for certain that they've carried news of the French to me, so I must assume it's gone the other way too. The greatest wonder to me is that our arrival here was an apparent surprise to Monsieur Pouchot.'

'I believe I can shed some light on that, sir…'

Prideaux raised his eyebrows. He had tended to discard anything that Holbrooke had to say about matters concerning the land.

'…that attack on the Mohawk River, just below Fort Stanwix; it was led by a Seneca named Kaendaé.'

'I know of him, although we've never met. Quite likely he was behind it,' said Sir William. 'He's well known for his personal allegiance to Pouchot and he suffered when Pouchot was relieved of his command of the fort. He'll stay with the French until we make a practicable breach, then the force of circumstances will move him to change sides. We'll see him waving the British flag before the month's out.'

Holbrooke ignored the interruption.

'Well, according to Kanatase, Kaendaé led the only scouting party that Pouchot sent out to the east. When he had taken his scalps he retired to Fort Niagara with word of some English soldiers on the Mohawk, but he didn't know the size of your force or where you were heading.'

'English soldiers on the Mohawk would be no surprise to Pouchot, there's been a steady flow between Schenectady and Fort Stanwix since last year. The sort of report that Kaendaé could have made wouldn't have rung any alarms,' Sir William interjected.

'Then that probably explains how we arrived so unexpectedly. Now, what's your assessment of this withdrawal of our allies, Sir William?'

'They're just doing what they have done for generations, sir, watching which way the wind blows while sitting on the fence. It's how they've survived so long in the face of the Dutch, the French and now the English. We have no great need of them for the moment but be prepared for them to return *en masse* when they see it is to their advantage.'

Prideaux looked as though he would say something

disparaging; he had no love for his Indian allies.

'It's no different to the way we behave,' said Sir William before Prideaux could speak. 'Here we are at war with the French who are allied with the Austrians and yet in the last war we fought alongside the Empress. We're spilling British blood and British treasure to defend Hanover which is of interest only to King George, and we'll be fighting the Spanish soon, if all the reports are true, and yet we have no real quarrel with them. European politics are just like Iroquois politics writ large.'

***

CHAPTER TWENTY-ONE

Master of the Lake

Saturday, Fourteenth of July 1759.
Point Montreal, Lake Ontario.

Holbrooke stood on the low hill that the French called Point Montreal, surveying the scene. Across the river, less than half a mile away, Fort Niagara was shrouded in smoke, some of it from the defenders' guns but an increasing amount came from the fires that were started by the mortar bombs that rained down upon the houses and storerooms within its walls. There was barely a moment without an explosion or the dull thud of the mortars bursting inside the fort.

That was interesting but it wasn't really Holbrooke's business. He turned his eyes to the north, to something much more important to him. There was the schooner *Mohawk* patrolling the mouth of the Niagara River just out of range of the fort's guns. There could be no better testament to the application of naval force. Until the brig returned from the east, he was master of the lake. More than that, unless the brig should come back with a fresh set of officers that knew their business and were prepared to act aggressively on their own initiative, he would still control the lake. Now Fort Niagara was truly cut off, with an army surrounding its landward side and its seaward side dominated by the most powerful vessel this side of Frontenac. Pouchot was forced back upon his own resources, without even the means to communicate with his superiors.

He looked to the south, two miles upstream from the fort, and saw the half-dozen bateaux that he had dragged across from Le Petit Marais on their Sutton carriages. They were ferrying across the river the guns, ammunition and supplies to establish a battery to play upon the exposed western walls of the fort. A week ago, Pouchot must have believed himself safe from attack on this side. After all, he had complete naval control of the lake, didn't he? When Holbrooke had reported the parlous state of the fort's defences facing the lake, Prideaux had authorised this depletion of his artillery to be able to bombard from this less-protected flank. A twelve-pound field gun, a mortar, a howitzer and a six-pounder were all that he could spare.

The battery was already under construction and the French must have seen what was happening by now. The guns had been embarked where a small stream ran through a gully to join the Niagara River. The gully was out of sight of French watchers, and they probably hadn't been able to see what the bateaux were carrying. However, the creation of a strong earthwork for the battery was plain to be seen, a harbinger of the defenders' doom.

Holbrooke had another cause for satisfaction. He had persuaded Prideaux to formalise the appointment of Lynton in command of the schooner, as far as his limited powers would allow. That was enough for Holbrooke to write to their Lordships requesting that Lynton's temporary commission be approved. It hardly mattered whether their Lordships were inclined to agree; by the time that the letter reached them and they replied, the siege would be over for better or for worse and Lynton would have had three or four months in command. It would be a strong argument for him to be made commander when he returned to England.

Nevertheless, Holbrooke was still in an anomalous position. His commission seconded him to the brigadier's staff, but with a schooner and five hundred boats under his command, his role was changing rapidly, and he was more concerned with the management and employment of his vessels than he was with the conduct of the siege. He rarely saw Prideaux, but when he did it was evident that the brigadier had at last seen the value of having a naval presence in his command. He went so far as to acknowledge that his army was unlikely to have come to the walls of Fort Niagara if the French brig had not been cleared out of the way, and he was delighted that Pouchot's communication with Montreal was cut. He had readily placed Holbrooke in charge of this outflanking manoeuvre, to command a substantial force of artillery, infantry and bateau-men until the battery was established and its supply of ammunition assured.

**

The first wagon came bumping along the makeshift road from the river to the battery. It carried the gabions and fascines, the vast baskets and the bundles of sticks that would be used to create the revetments for the guns. He saw Sutton running along beside the load, ducking and dodging to see how it stood up while staying clear of the bateau-men who were hauling on the traces. The wagons had been adapted from half a dozen of Sutton's boat carriages and although at first sight they appeared ill-adapted to carrying barrels of powder and nets of cannon balls, at least they weren't falling apart over the rough ground.

Holbrooke had to admit that he was thoroughly enjoying himself. Everything about this operation was interesting: the logistics, the force protection, construction of the wagons, siting the battery. All had been carried out to his orders, and now it was culminating in this first wagon rattling up the road. It was particularly gratifying to know that none of this would have been possible without naval supremacy in the waters around the fort. If *L'Iroquois* had still been at anchor in the river, they would never have dared to attempt it.

'I've marked out the lines for the earthworks, sir,' said the young artillery lieutenant.

'Very well, I'll see them before anyone cuts ground,' Holbrooke replied.

They walked further along the slight rise to the chosen place. It wasn't quite the nearest point to the fort, but it had the advantage of a fold of land in front of it that would prevent ricochets hitting the battery.

'You see there are two embrasures for the field guns, sir, and I've sited the mortar and the howitzer further behind.'

Holbrooke looked carefully at the view of the fort from each proposed embrasure. It was remarkable that he was being allowed to construct this battery so close to the forts soft underbelly without any sort of interference.

'Where will the ammunition be stored?' Holbrooke asked.

'The main store is eighty yards behind, just the other side of those trees,' the lieutenant replied. 'There'll be a forward store for immediate use protected by another earthwork just behind the battery.'

This was the only part of the plan that Holbrooke wasn't pleased with. He'd argued for two twelve-pounders and two mortars, so that the variety of ammunition would be halved, but the artillery commander had made a counter-argument based on the need for the heaviest guns to support the main attack, which would be against the Flag Bastion at the northeast corner of the fort. His battery looked odd, and he knew that it wouldn't work so efficiently with four different types of weapon.

Holbrooke stood and gazed north again, out to the lake. There was no threat from there now, but it may not always be so.

'I want another embrasure here,' he said, pointing to the left flank of the battery area. 'It must allow either of the field guns to cover the approaches to the river.'

The lieutenant was a sharp young man, and he could see what Holbrooke was thinking. He squatted and sighted down the slope towards the lake, then he hammered in a couple of pegs where the gabions should be placed to create the embrasure.

'You may start as soon as you have enough materials,' Holbrooke said.

Here was the captain who was commanding the security force. His report was what Holbrooke had expected to hear: the perimeter of the battery was secure in all directions but with the strongest force to the south. Pickets had been pushed out a further quarter mile and light infantry were patrolling a mile out. The battery was well protected.

'I do believe they've worked out our intention, sir,' said Chalmers, who was watching the fort through Holbrooke's big telescope.

Holbrooke smiled at his friend. As Holbrooke's nominal clerk, Chalmers was careful to use a deferential tone when any of the land officers were within hearing.

'There are at least six officers on that nearest bastion.'

Holbrooke took the telescope and looked himself. There were three batteries that could reasonably oppose his own, and he was familiar with their neglected state. The guns had no protection at all, even the simple parapets over which they would fire had been eroded during the years of the fort's neglect. That group of uniformed officers could presumably see that soon they would be under attack from the other side of this very river that they had thought of as a protection.

He closed the telescope with a snap and handed it back to Chalmers.

'You must be ready for Tuesday, Lieutenant.'

It would require a huge effort to bring everything that was need across the river in the next three days, and it would be dangerous to unmask the battery before the earthworks were complete and all the ammunition was stockpiled. On that Holbrooke agreed with Prideaux, and he had committed himself to the plan.

**

The battery at Point Montreal had been firing for two days now, and only at night did Holbrooke have any respite. When he had reported to Prideaux that the battery was complete and ready to engage the fort, the brigadier had promptly ordered him to take charge of the bombardment for at least the first few days. Holbrooke could see the logic. The most senior and experienced artillery officers were needed at the main point of effort, opposite the flag battery, and only the most junior officer of the Royal Artillery could be spared for the battery on Point Montreal, and he couldn't be expected to command the whole effort of force protection and logistics as well as manage the guns.

Holbrooke left the artillery to the lieutenant, while he concerned himself with security and supplies. It really was astonishing how fast a small battery used up shot, shell and powder, to say nothing of the need for fresh gabions and fascines where the counter-battery fire had destroyed parts of the earthworks. And then his whole force needed to be fed and watered, the light infantry patrols had to be directed and reports sent back to the army HQ. Yes, it was sensible for him to be there, but he would far rather have been out on the lake even in that tiny schooner.

He had decided on the first night that the battery would only fire by day, when there was enough light to see their targets. If they had continued through the night, they would have used twice the ammunition and would have needed twice the number of artillerymen to keep the guns firing. Over on the landward side of the fort, with a target that they could hardly miss and with the ammunition dump so close, it was worth firing around the clock, but not here at the end of a long and fragile supply line.

Holbrooke was just waking up now, having been shaken half an hour before dawn. His first duty was to be on hand at the battery to view the fort at the first hint of daylight. He pulled on his waistcoat, picked up his telescope and stepped over the still-sleeping Chalmers. In a few strides he was at the guns returning the compliments of the lieutenant who quite properly had given orders to be woken fifteen minutes before his commander.

'There's a bit of mist out on the lake, sir, and I can't see any movement on the fort yet.'

Holbrooke looked for himself. He could make out the outline of the great house in the centre of the fort, silhouetted against the faintest precursor to dawn. It would be ten minutes before there was enough light to distinguish their opposing batteries. In the meantime, Holbrooke scanned all around the horizon, just as he had done a thousand times at sea. He started by looking upstream, where there was always the possibility that a stray band of Frenchmen may try to make their way back to the fort. Nothing. And there was equally nothing in the forests at their back. He turned his attention to the lake, looking north. There the dawn was disputing with the early morning mist and there was nothing to see beyond a mile. He knew that *Mohawk* would be out there somewhere, probably hove-to and waiting for the dawn, rather like he was.

The rumble of artillery was an unnoticed background to his daily life, and he thought nothing of it. It was just the heavy guns battering away at the fort's walls, and the French cannon firing in return.

The lieutenant heard it first. A higher pitched gun, quite distinct from the deep roar of the siege guns.

'That's coming from the lake, sir,'

Holbrooke listened intently. That was a three-pounder, he'd heard enough of them to be certain, and therefore that was Lynton in his schooner. He must have a good reason to be firing at this time in the morning.

'Sound the stand-to, Lieutenant.'

They had no bugler, or a drummer, but they had an old hand-bell that served the purpose of an alarm, and soon the battery was a hive of activity as the sleepy gunners went through their checks and loaded the guns.

The three-pounders were being answered by something larger now, twelve-pounders almost certainly. Holbrooke cursed the mist that was preventing him seeing what was happening on the lake.

'Let's have the twelve-pounder shifted to cover the lake,' he said. 'When this mist lifts, we may have company.'

Holbrooke could imagine what was happening. De Vaudreuil or Montcalm would have had plenty of time to order the brig or its repaired sister back to Fort Niagara with orders and perhaps even reinforcements. The brig, even as poorly-commanded as it was, could easily brush aside *Mohawk* and return to its old anchorage under the fort's guns. What the French captain couldn't know was that the anchorage was no longer safe. Lynton would know what to do. He'd keep to windward using his more weatherly schooner rig and encourage the brig into the river mouth. Damn this mist!

'The gun's ready, sir,' said the lieutenant.

Holbrooke could see that for himself, but the formal report was still necessary. He had resolved never to interfere with the management of the guns, but now he was going to break that resolution. He just couldn't stand aside and watch his battery engaging a water-borne enemy without directing it himself.

'Are you loaded with ball?' he asked.

'Ball it is, sir,' the sergeant reported, grinning.

'Have you ever fired at a ship before, sergeant?'

The soldier scratched his head and looked puzzled.

'No, sir, that I haven't,' he admitted.

'Then I'll point the gun, sergeant. Your quadrant will do you no good against a moving target.'

The gunners looked doubtful. They were used to making an estimate of range and then using a quadrant to set the gun's elevation. They had never, ever, fired at a moving target and traversing the gun to keep it pointing had never been a matter of any importance.

'Get that spike under the train and be ready to heave left or right as I say. This screw adjusts the elevation, I believe.'

The sergeant demonstrated the screw's mechanism. It was stiff, and clearly only used very deliberately when the gun was found to be firing too high or too low. It was easy to see why firing at a ship from a fixed location was more difficult than it looked. Inevitably the range would be great and any sea officer worth his salt knew that keeping his ship moving under bombardment was of the utmost importance.

The firing behind the veil of mist continued. The sun rose and slowly, yard-by-yard the visibility improved. Then with startling suddenness the brig showed itself. It was *L'Iroquois* of course; Holbrooke knew it by the wide patch in the clew of the fore-tops'l. The brig was steering up the river and *Mohawk* was nowhere to be seen, although evidently Lynton was close behind the brig as the sharp crack of its guns could be distinctly heard.

Holbrooke squinted along the barrel of the twelve-pounder.

'A turn on the screw,' he muttered.

It was guesswork really, but guesswork based on a dozen actions at sea. He would take the turns out of the screw as the brig came closer until the point where they could open fire. Now, the important thing was to stop the brig sending a boat inshore, so he'd fire as soon as it was in range and hope to send it packing. Lynton was doing a good job of shepherding the brig into range of the guns.

'Stand by.'

The sergeant blew on his match, waiting for the word of command.

Holbrooke gave another quarter-turn on the elevation screw and motioned for the man on the hand-spike to shift the gun a fraction to the left to allow for the speed of the brig.

'Fire!'

The gun bellowed and narrowly missed Holbrooke on the recoil. He would have to remember that there was no preventer tackle on field guns, and they ran back less predictably.

By the time that Holbrooke had fanned the gunsmoke away, there was no sign of where the shot had fallen. The lieutenant who had been standing to one side shook his head, he hadn't seen it either.

'Gun ready, sir,' the sergeant reported.

They were a well-drilled crew and that was a commendable reload speed.

Holbrooke repeated the process, bringing the elevation down a bit further this time. He leaped to the side before ordering the gun to fire, both to be clear of the recoil and to see the fall of shot.

'In line and short,' the lieutenant reported. Holbrooke nodded in agreement; he would have to fire a little higher.

'She's coming about,'

That was Chalmers. The only man other than Holbrooke who could recognise the manoeuvre.

'Fire!' shouted Holbrooke.

A hit this time, amidships and between the gunwale and the waterline. That was a good shot.

The gun's crew was delighted, and they worked with a will to reload.

The gun fire twice more before the brig was out of range. *Mohawk* was in sight now, staying prudently to windward and firing at extreme range as the brig rounded the fort and headed east again, down the lake, Whatever they were carrying, dispatches, supplies or reinforcements, they had decided that it was too dangerous to complete the delivery. That was the fourth time that *L'Iroquois* had been bested, and deep in his bones Holbrooke knew that this time she wouldn't be back. If the brig couldn't contact the fort, couldn't interfere with the siege and evidently couldn't deal with the schooner, then there was no point in being at this end of the lake at all. De Vaudreuil and Montcalm had probably already written off Niagara and were concerned with protecting the upper Saint Lawrence, the heart of New France. Two brigs wouldn't be too many to patrol that maze of estuaries and islands and if properly handled they were still the arbiters of naval power on Lake Ontario.

'Well, sir,' said the sergeant grinning broadly, 'if that's how you do things in the navy, I must say you have more pleasure of it than is right and proper. Where do I sign on, sir?'

***

CHAPTER TWENTY-TWO

An Incautious Step

Friday, Twentieth July 1759.
Before the Walls of Fort Niagara.

The opening of the artillery barrage must have terrified the French defenders. Until then they had only suffered mortar fire, and although it was dangerous, there had been few casualties and life in the fort had not been unduly disturbed. Now, with eighteen-pounders firing at the walls from the east and the guns and mortars on Point Montreal across the river to the west, the siege must suddenly have seemed very real. The walls of the fort were being systematically demolished, and the focus of the British artillery's fury was the Flag Bastion on the right of the attack, close to the lake shore. There the walls were in the most decrepit condition and that was the point chosen for the eventual assault.

Prideaux' army had never been a close-knit band of brothers, and the strain of the siege was opening up the cracks. The engineers took the brunt of the criticism. Early in the siege the chief engineer, Captain-Lieutenant Williams, had been incapacitated when a French shell burst near him. He would take no further part in the siege, leaving his inexperienced deputy, Ensign Demler, to suffer Prideaux' anger when the saps moved forward slowly, sometimes in the wrong direction, and the batteries weren't made ready for the guns. In exasperation, Prideaux appointed Colonel Johnston of the New York Provincials to oversee the engineering work.

***

The sun had long gone and although the sky was clear, the quarter moon wouldn't rise for another five hours and the stars were obliterated by a thin, high layer of cloud. It was as dark as a night could be, and Holbrooke stumbled as he made his cautious way through the trenches.

'Mind that broken fascine, Holbrooke,' said Massey, then continued with his explanation of the engineering works. 'This is the approach trench; it's the first sap that was cut and you can see that it's directed well to the right of the fort.'

Holbrooke could see nothing of the sort, his whole concentration was on keeping his head below the top of the trench, and not walking into the surprising amount of debris that littered the walkway. Massey was taking over as the field officer on duty at the head of the sap. It wasn't strictly his turn, but earlier in the day, Lieutenant Colonel Thodey of the Provincials had been hit in the leg by a musket ball and the duty roster had been thrown into disarray. He was the second of the senior officers to be incapacitated, after the chief engineer, and it put a strain on those that remained.

'We're well out of range of musketry here, and the fort's guns are all concentrated on our batteries and on the head of the sap. They still throw a mortar or two in this direction, so keep your head down. It's no shame to duck and weave in the trenches!'

Massey was having fun at Holbrooke's expense. When they had started their journey through the trenches, Holbrooke had walked erect, as he had done under fire on the decks of ships since this war began. The land officers had a similar disregard for their own safety in the field, but Holbrooke soon realised that they behaved differently in the trenches. As Massey had pointed out, the life expectancy of a soldier that disdained to crouch below the edge of the trench could be measured in hours, at best. In the trenches everyone, from the general to the private soldier, moved around in a semi-crouching posture.

'This is where that fool Williams laid out the approach in the wrong direction,' Massey said as they passed a spot where the remains of a trench could be seen diverging to the left. 'His first attempt had the trench pointing directly at the Flag Bastion, where the French have sited most of their heavy guns. When daylight came, they started firing right down the length of the trench, enfilading fire. It was an act of self-murder to set foot in it. That set us back two days right at the start. It's no wonder that we're behind. Well, I shouldn't speak too much ill of him. I understand the surgeon couldn't save his eye and he may yet succumb to the wound.'

They shuffled along in silence for a few minutes. It was a strange experience being here in this dangerous stretch of land that the French had cleared for their artillery fire. The last of the trees were two hundred yards behind them, and Holbrooke felt exposed and naked, even in the friendly darkness. Yet there was intense activity in the approach. Relays of soldiers carried powder and shot forward, and barrels of water for the thirsty gunners and infantrymen. They had to step aside once as a wounded man was brought to the rear, and they passed a corpse that would have to wait until daylight to be recovered. They could see the glow, hear the noise and feel the vibrations of the mortar battery coming closer.

'Here's the first battery, this is what that brig tried to fire at when you chased him away.'

Holbrooke was used to artillery in ships, but there was a quite different feel to the activity in this first battery. The siege guns had already moved forward to the second battery, and back here it was just the mortars: the royals and coehorns. The mortar crews were loading and firing with a steady, almost leisurely, rhythm that would have called forth his scorn on the deck of his old command *Kestrel*. Of course, here in the battery they had to keep this up for days on end, while at sea if an engagement lasted an hour it would be counted as long. There was a pile of shells and cartridges at the rear of the battery while the four mortars occupied the front. Holbrooke could see that they were well protected from direct fire and he could almost stand upright – tall though he was—and still be below the parapet. They were safe from the guns, that was evident, but Holbrooke soon learned that there was another danger. A sharp crack overhead had all the gunners ducking for cover, and Massey pulled Holbrooke down.

'We have a regular mortar duel going on here,' said the artillery lieutenant, laughing. 'It's deadly in the daylight when they can see where their shells burst and can adjust their aim, but at night there's little danger. Still, it annoys us and slows down our rate of fire, and occasionally they send over a twenty-four pound ball to stop us becoming complacent.'

Holbrooke shook the dirt off his waistcoat. He could hardly imagine complacency in this hellish place.

'You don't adjust your own aim, then,' he asked.

'No, sir, not at night. In the daytime I would be peering over the parapet there and calling down the adjustments. But really, as long as our shells are bursting over the fort or falling into it, it's good enough. It's not our job to bring down the walls, that's for the cannon in the second battery.'

Massey was poking around at the earthworks and quizzing the working parties that laboured constantly to keep the parapets high enough and the trenches and batteries deep enough. Here a fascine had been thrown aside by a shot, there a gabion had burst sending its load of soil cascading into a trench, and in another place a heavy ball had torn through the earth of a parapet. Massey wasn't there to direct the repairs, but to confirm that the working parties were being actively led, and that the subalterns were directing them properly.

'Let's move forward, Holbrooke, I want to see how the second battery is faring.'

***

The next trench was more treacherous than the approach sap, and it was narrower. Here they were far closer to the fort, less than half a mile Holbrooke guessed. They were also near to the shore and when he cautiously peered over the top, he could see that the direction that the trench took was well out towards the lake. There was a working party here, constantly repairing the trench, their sweating faces illuminated by the periodic glow of a firing mortar.

'Good evening, sir,' said Massey as the lean figure of the brigadier came towards them out of the gloom.

'Ah, Colonel Massey, good evening to you. And Captain Holbrooke, I see. Stir up those laggards at the head of the sap, would you? They're overly concerned for their safety, and I must have that third battery in place as soon as possible. Then we'll bring those walls down around their ears!'

'How far has it progressed, sir?' Massey asked.

'Well, they can go no further right, the lake's in the way, so they've struck off at an acute angle to the left. Young Demler at least knows his geometry even if he lacks some of the other qualities I look for in my officers. They should be able to turn right before dawn, but that's the danger point and they need to reinforce the parapet where it turns. But I don't need to be telling you that, Massey, do I?'

The brigadier turned away and continued back towards the mortar battery.

'Keep your head down, Holbrooke!' he called over his shoulder. 'I can find another colonel, but I can't find another commodore, ha ha!'

Holbrooke was mildly irritated by this new title that Prideaux had given him. When the brigadier had signed the commission for Lynton to command *Mohawk*, he'd joked that Holbrooke must now be a commodore with a captain under him. A handful of officers had heard that, and it was fast becoming the normal way of referring to him. It wasn't even a joke anymore. After some initial scepticism, the colonels and majors had seen the value of naval command of the lake, and in their minds, if there was a captain in command of even a schooner, then the next rank up must be a commodore. Holbrooke just hoped that word of his unofficial title never reached their Lordships.

***

The second battery was a step up in intensity from the first. Here the twelve-pounders roared incessantly as they poured their fire into the Flag Bastion. They were in imminent danger and nobody showed his head above the parapets. The guns each fired between two gabions, and on closer inspection Holbrooke realised that they were doubled-up, with nine or ten feet of close packed earth on either side of the gun barrel. The embrasure between the gabions was no more than eighteen inches broad, just wide enough to allow the barrel to protrude but with minimal space for training. He realised that the point of aim would hardly change during the life of the battery. These guns had been hauled here at great cost in labour and blood with only a single purpose, to batter away at the same spot until a breach in the walls was established.

The walls of Fort Niagara appeared horribly close now, and this wasn't even the final battery. He could see the next trench arrowing away to the left, away from the lake, at an angle calculated so that no enfilading fire could reach it.

'This must be familiar to you,' shouted Massey in the short intervals between the thunder of the guns. 'These are naval cannons on siege mountings, you know.'

Holbrooke merely nodded and tried to look enthusiastic. He knew they were naval guns, after all he had arranged for them to be hauled up the Mohawk River, across the portage and Lake Oneida and down the Onondaga River. He didn't like to point out that all his service in this war had been in frigates and smaller vessels; these were big guns compared with the nine-pounders that were the largest that he had used at sea.

The gunners worked with the same economy of effort that he'd seen in the mortar battery. They would have to keep this up for six hours before they were relieved. Six hours of continually lifting those twelve pound balls, of wielding the spongers and rammers, and of shifting that ponderous weight that impressed itself deeper into the earth with each discharge.

There was a strange thud and the earth below them shook.

'That was a twenty-four-pounder hitting the gabions,' said the lieutenant. 'A single shot can't penetrate, not through a double thickness of earth and wicker, but if they hit often enough in the same place, then eventually they'll break through. Then we'll have to rest one of our guns while a working party repairs the damage.'

Holbrooke shivered involuntarily at the thought of sending soldiers out to replace a smashed gabion. In principle he knew that it could almost all be accomplished from behind the cover of the remaining earthworks. Nevertheless, at some point a soldier had to expose himself to the defenders' fire, and many a brave soul had been lost that way. The navy had its dangers, certainly, but he would take that over being a soldier any day.

'The sergeant will take you forward to the head of the trench.'

This was why Massey had come forward. He was here to stiffen the resolve of the party undergoing the most dangerous duty of carrying the sap forward towards the enemy. Pouchot's men knew very well what was happening. Before the light had been lost, they had seen the sap start out from the second battery, moving forward across the face of the fort. From the fort it would look like a series of quick movements with periods of inactivity, offering fleeting targets that were gone before a musket could be levelled at them. This was specialist work and was being supervised by Colonel Johnston in person. They were in time to witness the point where the trench would be turned right again. A space had been prepared, and a small group of men stood ready with an empty gabion. At a word of command, they rushed forward and placed the gabion, holding it with outstretched arms while half a dozen others worked feverishly to fill it with loose earth from a pile that had already been prepared. It looked extremely perilous, but in five minutes it was done, and a solid mass of soil encased in wicker stood between them and the enemy fire.

'Oh, they're fairly safe in the dark,' said Massey, 'The enemy is firing blind. They know roughly where the sap has progressed to, but their shot rarely comes close. The real danger is from their marksmen, Canadians, mostly, and deadly.'

Now that it was mentioned, Holbrooke could hear a constant sound of musketry. They must be no more than a hundred yards from the fort's advanced positions, and a marksman who jealously guarded his night vision could often find a target, even in this blackness.

Massey saluted Colonel Johnston. They weren't good friends, but old enmities didn't last long at the head of a sap. They were both in extreme danger.

'We'll be working on the last battery by dawn, Massey,' the colonel said. 'Oh, is that you, Holbrooke? Good evening to you.'

He turned back to give an instruction, but in doing so briefly exposed himself. There was a soft thud and a gasp, and Johnston fell to the bottom of the trench. It was over in an instant and there was nothing to be done for him. A musket ball had entered under his arm and passed right through his lungs. Prideaux came rushing up from the mortar battery, but by then Johnston was incapable of speech and each breath brought a froth of blood to his lips. He died withing twenty minutes of being hit.

***

Four soldiers dragged the colonel's body back through the trenches. There was no question of carrying it, that would have required the men to stand almost upright, and the French marksmen had already shown how deadly they could be. The men they passed showed genuine grief; Johnston had been a popular commander and his loss would be sorely felt. The New York Provincials had lost both of their senior officers in one day.

Prideaux, Massey and Holbrooke followed in respect for their fallen comrade. They passed through the second battery which briefly paused in its work of destruction, and on through the trenches to the first battery where the mortars also stopped firing. There they were in relative safety and they could attend to properly covering the colonel's lifeless body and moving it back to the camp.

'You'll go back with the body?' Prideaux asked, turning to Holbrooke. 'Colonel Massey, I need you at the head of the sap; this is no time to let the men ease off.'

That was true. Extending a sap was not only perilous, but it required constant work. If the attackers stopped moving forward and paused in the work of repairing the damage, then the defenders' fire would put the whole enterprise into retreat. If left alone until the morning, they wouldn't have just lost the work of a few hours, but a whole night.

'You can find your way back, Holbrooke?' asked Massey.

Holbrooke nodded in the dark, he hardly trusted himself to speak.

'Then I'll see you in the morning,' and Massey turned away to retrace his steps.

Holbrooke started arranging the bearer party. Now they were out of immediate danger they could carry the colonel's body with more decency. He wouldn't be dragged back to the camp; he would be borne decently between six soldiers of his own regiment.

'Ready? Then lift,' said Holbrooke in an interval in the mortar's firing. His bearer party was preparing to move off now, and even with effectively three men abreast, they could just squeeze through the approach trench which was deliberately wider than the trenches nearer the fort.

Prideaux watched the bearer party set off down the trench. He waved at the artillery lieutenant to recommence firing then stepped back to let a group of soldiers pass, exhausted from their work on the sap.

Crash! The left-hand four-and-a-half inch coehorn mortar fired just as Prideaux, distracted by the loss of his second-in-command, stepped backwards, right into the path of the missile. The bomb struck the side of the brigadier's head, removing a third of the skull; he died instantly. Holbrooke caught a glimpse of the tragedy out of the corner of his eye, and he knew that the image would stay with him forever. The orange glow from the mortar barrel illuminated the scene with the brigadier and the mortar in its centre. Prideaux' arched body looked as though it was etched into the bright background, frozen in silhouette for all eternity.

The crew of the mortar looked appalled, dropping their rammers and sponges and looking around as though they contemplated running for it. It was hard to blame them. Whether or not it was their fault – and they had been in the army long enough to know that innocence was an elastic concept – their weapon had killed the army commander. The corporal furtively wiped the blood and gore from his face and looked around for orders.

***

CHAPTER TWENTY-THREE

An Election

Friday, Twentieth July 1759.
The Camp at Le Petit Marais.

Prideaux' body had hardly been laid in his tent when Holbrooke was summoned to a command meeting, a council-of-war by any other name. It was Massey who had called the meeting. As soon as he'd heard of the tragedy in the battery, he'd abandoned the sap and left a major to see the work through the night. As the ranking regular officer, he knew how important it was to establish a succession before any cracks started appearing in the command of the army.

They had lost three senior officers in one day – Thodey, Johnston and Prideaux – and now only Massey and Farquhar remained as regular lieutenant colonels. Sir William was a full colonel but held his commission as a provincial. Haldimand was a regular lieutenant colonel – even though he was Swiss – and he was senior to Massey and Farquhar, but he was back in Oswego and couldn't be reasonably summoned in less than three days. The only others in the meeting were Holbrooke and William Hervey, the brigade major who had been Prideaux' right-hand man. That was a measure of how the day's casualties had thinned out the ranks of the army's senior officers.

It had occurred to Holbrooke to wonder why he had been summoned to this gathering. After all, it was really no concern of his, this was a purely army matter. He saw the interrogatory glances from Sir William and Farquhar, they also wondered at Holbrooke's presence. Probably Massey saw him as an ally in case there was any dissent to his assuming command.

Already the battle lines were being drawn. Sir William was clearly irked that Massey had called the meeting before he had even been informed of the brigadier's death, while Farquhar and Hervey stood close to Massey, almost shoulder-to-shoulder. Sir William looked isolated.

To Holbrooke's naval mind it was easy. If an admiral or commodore should be incapacitated, then the most senior of the post-captains would assume command without any discussion on the subject. There was never any doubt about seniority, every captain knew the date that his promotion had been posted in the London Gazette – the event was known as being *gazetted* – and also knew the dates of the other captains with similar seniority. Apparently, it was not quite so simple in this case. Haldimand was the senior regular lieutenant colonel, but he was three days away to the east. Farquhar had no claim because Massey was senior to him. Yet Sir William was a full colonel, and should outrank them all, but he was only a colonial and his commission bore that stigma. Those were the battle lines as Holbrooke saw them and they were reflected in the positions that each man took in the tent.

***

Massey had the good grace to let Sir William bring the meeting to order, and in any case, he was confident of the outcome, he could afford to be generous.

'Gentlemen, you all know the situation, we now need to agree who will carry this great enterprise forward and complete the work that Brigadier General Prideaux started.'

Sir William paused and scanned the faces around him. 'I will nail my colours to the mast and say now that I should lead…'

Massey looked startled and rose to intervene.

'You will have your say in a moment, Colonel Massey.'

Massey dropped back into his seat with a look of thunder on his face.

'Now, if Colonel Haldimand were here I would defer to him as the appointed second-in command. However, I'm sure you would all agree that this is no time for a lengthy *interregnum*. We could have a practicable breach in days and meanwhile who knows what relief force Montcalm is mustering? We cannot afford to waste any time in pressing forward the siege. In any case Haldimand is doing vital work in holding our supply route open.'

Massey could contain himself no more. He leapt to his feet.

'Forgive me, Sir William,' he said with a face that looked far from soliciting forgiveness. 'This is an operation of war that we are considering here. I'm a regular officer with twenty years in the colours. Provincial ranks are rightly measured on a different scale to regular ranks, and I am the senior regular officer. I don't need to remind you that Lieutenant Colonel Haldimand was selected by the brigadier to be second-in-command over the heads of two full colonels with provincial commissions. With all the good will in the world, you cannot equate a provincial commission with a regular commission.'

'And there is something in what you say, Colonel Massey,' Sir William replied calmly. 'But consider, we have only two regular battalions here and you command one of them. Can you say that it will be properly handled in the field without you? Storming the breach and engaging a relief column in the field are complicated acts of war and need strong leadership.'

Sir William knew of the rivalries in the Forty-Sixth and was playing on Massey's oft-spoken complaints about the qualities of his company commanders. Farquhar had similarly criticised his own officers. It was a shrewd argument and applied equally to both regular lieutenant colonels.

Massey hesitated, confused by this unexpectedly cogent argument.

'Furthermore, with our Indian allies sitting on the sidelines there is little to keep me from assuming this command. I can give the siege my full attention.'

Massey rose to speak with a determined look on his face. Holbrooke had the distinct impression that he was going to challenge Sir William's military experience. It would have been an unwise move as the provincial had distinguished himself in King George's War and again early in this present war when with the temporary rank of major-general he had led an army that forced the French from Lake George. He had been made a baronet in recognition of that campaign. He hadn't mentioned his military experience yet, probably he was reserving it as a last argument, in case all else failed.

Massey closed his mouth with an audible snap and sat again; his arguments were being beaten down one by one. He'd called the meeting expecting to roll over any objections from Sir William, but it wasn't turning out that way. Massey looked sulkily around the room, gauging the level of support for his candidacy. What he saw didn't encourage him. Was he trying to find a way of gracefully conceding the command? It certainly looked that way to Holbrooke.

The silence was broken by Hervey. In a way it was appropriate that, as Prideaux' brigade major – his chief-of-staff – he should be the one to break the impasse, to force a rapid decision, for they all knew that time was against them.

'Perhaps Captain Holbrooke has a view,' Hervey said, looking around at the colonels to judge their reactions.

From the moment that the succession was contested by Sir William, Holbrooke knew that he would be called upon. He'd heard the arguments and he had enough experience of military affairs to have formed his own opinion. He knew how he would vote. Just to be certain he looked swiftly at Massey, who with a long face nodded his head almost imperceptibly. Massey was at the opposite end of the command tent and only Holbrooke saw that gesture, everyone else was looking the other way, at him.

'I'm awed by so much military expertise, gentlemen,' he said, thinking fast, 'and I've heard the arguments from the two contenders.'

That sounded as though he was buying time to frame his

words. He needed to come to the point before someone else took the floor.

'First, I believe most strongly that the successor should come from among you gentlemen, and that we should not wait for Colonel Haldimand to arrive, for all the reasons that Sir William enumerated.'

Sir William bowed stiffly.

'Then we can eliminate that option,' Holbrooke said.

'Second, I take the point that there is a difference between a regular and a provincial commission. Nevertheless, I for one wouldn't want the line battalions to undergo a change of leadership at this point. If a breach is to be assaulted, or if a relief force arrives, they will need the leadership that can best be provided by their appointed colonels.'

He looked again at Massey who nodded again, very slightly, a gesture of encouragement. Anyone who saw that without the earlier exchange wouldn't have known what it meant.

'In my view, Sir William should take command of the army.'

Nobody moved, not a head turned from its fix gaze on Holbrooke. In the silence, he continued.

'Again, in my view, this army needs an appointed second-in-command who is here at the scene of the siege. We've all seen how perilous it is. That should certainly be Colonel Massey as the ranking lieutenant colonel. We should not recall Colonel Haldimand, the security of our rear area is just too important at this critical time.'

No soldier on campaign would argue with the principle of securing the army's lines of supply.

The room was still hushed as everyone thought of their positions. Farquhar spoke first.

'I agree with Captain Holbrooke,' he said tentatively, looking sideways at Massey. 'These are wise words from an officer with no personal interest in the outcome of these deliberations. The Forty-Fourth and the Forty-Sixth constitute the whole of our offensive power and the battalions need strong leadership.'

'Then I bow to the collective will, gentlemen,' said Massey, interrupting before anyone else had a chance to speak and ruin this perfect opportunity to retreat from an untenable position. 'I wish you all the fortune of war, Sir William. The Forty-Sixth of Foot is at your command.'

***

'Thank you for that,' Massey said as he and Holbrooke walked back towards his battalion's lines on the left flank of the army. 'I had wrongly assumed that all the regular officers would be with me, but Sir William's arguments were just too strong. I can't say that I'm disappointed now that it's over. This siege is dull work, but we've heard nothing of the French forces over towards the Ohio, and we know from the Indians that Pouchot ordered them to fall back on Niagara. They could be here any day and they surely must come down the escarpment from the falls. The Forty-Sixth stands between them and the fort and will have its day in the field. I certainly don't want to miss it; now that will be proper soldiering!'

'You think they'll come in force, not just a few men to reinforce the garrison?'

'Oh, they'll come in force, and they'll aim to raise the siege, not just scurry into the fort to fill the gaps on the parapets.'

Holbrooke racked his brain for all he'd heard of the French further west, on the Ohio and Lake Erie.

'I had understood that they could only muster perhaps a thousand *troupes de marine* and some militia. Prideaux' army – Sir William's now – is some five thousand strong, excluding bateau-men and our Indians. Would they risk a fight with those odds?'

'This isn't a battle at sea you know,' Massey replied. 'We cannot put all our ships in a line and oppose them force-to-force. We left nearly two thousand behind at Oswego, and they have already been in action protecting our rear. About a third of what remains is engaged in the saps and the batteries, and another third is protecting our base back at the creek. If the French gather all their force – abandoning their ambition to take back Fort Pitt – then they will be able to march sufficient strength to give us a good fight. If they win, or even look as though they are drawing away our own force from the sap, then Pouchot will come out with every last man that he has. It won't be like that half-hearted sally at the start of the siege. He'll sweep across the trenches, fill them in and destroy our artillery and batteries. There will be no recovering from that, the army will have to retire.'

Massey looked wistful as they strode across the cleared ground. They were in range of artillery fire from the fort, but both men knew that the defenders didn't have powder and ball to expend on two officers at the limit of the area that their guns commanded.

'I'm sure the politics in the navy are like those in the army, just look at what happened to Byng!'

Holbrooke remembered it well. He'd been at the battle of Minorca where Admiral Byng was beaten and withdrew. He'd been executed for *not doing his utmost*, the only British admiral to have suffered a judicial death. The reverberations of that example must have been felt in the army nearly as much as in the navy.

'No, on refection, it's no bad thing that Sir William has the command of the army. If we retire it will be Sir William who suffers, and it leaves me free to take my battalion into action. I can almost feel those Frenchmen advancing from the south. They'll be on Lake Erie by now, and on the portage around the falls in a day or two. Oh, how I long for a field action!'

'Is it such a great thing? I've been engaged on the land already, and it seemed rather chaotic.'

'Ah, the action at Saint-Cast! No, the battle that I anticipate will be nothing like that. It will be much more regular, and it will be the French that will be forced to withdraw. You must join me, Holbrooke! That's a definite invitation.'

Holbrooke laughed; it may be a definite invitation, but it didn't sound so appealing a prospect for a sea officer. Twenty years in the colours must make a man yearn for a regular action in the field – that defining action of a field officer – and probably he'd be unable to understand that not everyone shared his enthusiasm.

'I'm serious Holbrooke,' he said stopping to face his friend. 'You have a halo of good fortune surrounding you and I want you at my side. The men feel it too, ever since you took that schooner off Oswego.'

Massey looked down at Holbrooke's sword and pistols.

'However, you'll need something a little more substantial than that. I've been meaning to mention it to you, but a sword and two pistols has a decidedly piratical look about it, most irregular. Now, a long land pattern musket will be a little unwieldy, but my sergeant is jealously guarding some carbines, like the light infantry have. One of those will be much more suitable. I'll have him clean one up for you and then you can fire a few balls into the forest, just to get your eye in. Trust me, you'll thank me in the end.'

'I think we're running ahead of ourselves a little. I have my naval duties to perform, I can't abandon those and enlist in the Forty-Sixth…'

'No, certainly not, but if the opportunity arises, you'll come with us, won't you?'

***

Massey's enthusiasm and his certainty that a French relief force was on its way gave Holbrooke food for thought. He'd believed that the successful conclusion of the siege was only a matter of a week or so away. He could see how the fortifications were being beaten down by the relentless artillery barrage, and he had detected the slackening of the defenders' fire. He'd dismissed tales of a French relief force because he'd believed the distances were too great and the French forces on Lake Erie and the Ohio River were too small and too dispersed. Of course, he'd reckoned without the long experience that the French had in these northern forests and lakes. They'd been here far longer than the British and their relations with the Indians had deeper roots. Just as Prideaux' army had used bateaux to move quickly along Lake Ontario, so could the French row along the shores of Lake Erie. The Niagara River was passable as far as the falls, and from there it was a march of only twelve miles along a good portage road to the fort. They weren't so far away after all. Yes, he could feel their presence also, a growing dread, like a gathering thunderstorm.

'Kanatase, have you heard anything about a French relief force from the south?'

The Mohawk's face betrayed nothing, as usual.

'I tell Sir William everything I hear,' he said. 'There is no news yet, but beyond the great falls is another country. There are no Iroquois there, and I have no information.'

'Is it possible, though? Could the French and the Indians march so fast as to reach here before the fort falls?'

Kanatase thought for a moment. He had a native's feel for the country and knew almost instinctively what was possible and what wasn't.

'Yes, Holbrooke. They could be here today or tomorrow or the next day.'

***

CHAPTER TWENTY-FOUR

The Relief Column

Sunday, Twenty-Second of July 1759.
The Camp at Le Petit Marais.

As soon as he had assumed command, Sir William had moved his headquarters forward and now he operated entirely from the rear of the sap. The army could feel in its bones that the climax of the siege was approaching. There was a restlessness among the men; an eager desire to see the job finished. Pouchot couldn't hold out much longer and only a relief column could save him, from the Saint Lawrence in the east or from Lake Erie and the Ohio – *La Belle Rivière* – in the west. It was clear that the defenders were running short of powder and shot and that some of their guns had been destroyed by the British bombardment. It was dangerous on the bastions now, and it looked like most of the French defenders were sheltering in the covered way, awaiting the inevitable assault.

The British army had its own problems with supply, and balls for the eighteen and twelve-pounders were running short. There was a bounty offered for all French balls of the correct calibre brought into the artillery store, and many soldiers spent their precious spare time combing the sap, the cleared area and the forest hoping to find the precious ammunition.

Holbrooke had moved his tent into the lines of the Forty-Sixth. There was little point in remaining back at the creek. The camp that had originally been the headquarters of the army was now nothing more than the logistics base, deserted by all the staff of the fighting elements of the army.

He and Chalmers had been on the lake today, enjoying the crystal clarity of the sparkling morning and checking that all was well with Lynton. What astonished Holbrooke was that the mixed bag of bateau-men, infantry and artillery had been forged into a crew that wouldn't have disgraced a small regular sloop or a cutter of the British navy. Between them, Lynton, Jackson and Serviteur had somehow shared their years of seagoing experience with the men; now they looked and acted like sailors. There was nothing that Holbrooke needed to do, the schooner was in safe hands, and although he was delighted, he also felt a secret disappointment that he wasn't needed. He was reduced to the level of a visiting staff officer, telling Lynton about the latest tactical situation, about the tragedy of Prideaux' death and the resultant change of command. He should have felt on top of the world, but he returned to his tent depressed.

'Charles Lynton seems to have it all under control,' said Chalmers, tentatively. He could see his friend's black mood.

Holbrooke tried to shake of his foul humour but found it impossible. He couldn't fake happiness in front of Chalmers any more than he could fly.

'Yes, I'd stake that schooner against any other of its size. Unless that brig comes back, Lynton owns this end of the lake.'

He stared at the fading light outside the tent.

'I appear to be superfluous.'

Chalmers said nothing. He could have told Holbrooke what ailed him before he knew himself.

'Oh, this mood will pass. I need something to do, something more than merely reassuring Sir William each day that his right flank is secure.'

'Well, I understand a French relief force could be imminent, and if you really are resolved to go with the Forty-Sixth, then you may get all the activity that you could wish for. I've noticed, by the way, how you carry that carbine around with you. If I may say, it looks most un-seamanlike, rather like you are posing as a gamekeeper or – saints preserve us – a soldier.'

Holbrooke smiled at that. Often it just needed Chalmers to make fun of him gently to change his mood.

'You'll notice that all the land officers carry some sort of firearm. I was left with the choice of being labelled piratical with my brace of pistols, or of impersonating a soldier. I chose the latter as being less likely to end on a gibbet.'

Just then the curtain of the tent was drawn swiftly aside and there stood Kanatase looking as though he'd run far and fast.

'Holbrooke, I have news. The French are on the way from La Belle Rivière.'

Holbrooke jumped up and his head brushed against the canvas of the tent. Even in that mad moment a part of his mind once again noticed how much better Kanatase pronounced the French words than he did the English.

'How close? What force? Does Sir William know?' His questions came tumbling out in a disordered stream.

'I'm on my way to Sir William now, Holbrooke. I have just come from La Belle Famille where I met a scouting party of Mohawks returning from the falls.'

'Then let's go, without delay. You can tell me on the way. Chalmers, are you coming?'

***

They found Sir William at the second battery, just where Prideaux had died. Holbrooke shivered at the thought and took great care that he didn't step in front of the mortars.

'They are on the Niagara River, you say, Kanatase?'

'Their boats were on the lake when the scouts saw them, but they must be on the river by now.'

Sir William thought for a moment, staring absently at the fort glowering at them defiantly in the last light of the day.

'They'll need to store their boats and set a guard above the falls. They could be here in two days, don't you think, Kanatase?'

'Yes, two days. They will be on the portage tomorrow and here the next day. A thousand soldiers and a thousand warriors, the patrol estimated.'

Sir William knew better than to trust an estimate of numbers given to him by an Indian patrol. Nevertheless, even if they were only half that number, it was a formidable force.

'Sergeant!'

He turned to his orderly.

'Send for Colonel Massey and Captain De Lancey, I'd like to see them both immediately. Kanatase, would you go too, and tell the colonel what you told me?'

The sergeant saluted and hurried out of the battery, not unhappy to get away from the British mortars and the occasional French shell that was thrown in their direction.

'I'll send a force of light infantry to La Belle Famille,' he mused, half to himself. 'You know Holbrooke, one of the advantages in being the besieging army is that – generally speaking – you can choose your ground for a fight. I know now where they are, and I know that they must come to us. Either they will march straight for the fort and fight their way in, or they will attack the sap. Either way, unless they want to spend days cutting their way through the forest, they must come down the road from the falls. And they certainly don't have days to spare,' he added inclining his head towards the fort whose bastions and walls even in the fading light were showing signs of relentless attrition.

'The only decent place to meet them is at La Belle Famille. There's a clearing there and space to fight without giving the French room for any flanking manoeuvres, and it's close enough for mutual support. Yes, it's at La Belle Famille that we'll meet them.'

'Will you march the Forty-Sixth there tonight, Sir William?' asked Holbrooke, wondering how serious Massey's offer was.

'No… no. Certainly not tonight, and not tomorrow either. Once Pouchot sees our lines empty he'll be tempted to make a sally, and with my force spread out before the fort, that could be dangerous for us. And I've no faith in the numbers that Indians report. Counting is not their strong point, and an army on the march is notoriously difficult to estimate. It wouldn't surprise me if this was no more than a reconnaissance in force, so I don't want to show my hand too early. I'll send the light infantry tomorrow, all of them that aren't committed elsewhere. De Lancey should be able to muster about a hundred-and-fifty of them. They can prepare the ground tomorrow, and when I'm convinced that this is a serious relief attempt, then – and only then – I'll send Massey. You can sleep easy tonight Holbrooke.'

Then he'd heard about Massey's offer! Well, it sounded like he was committed now.

***

They watched the three companies of light infantry march to the south as soon as there was enough light to see the path. As Sir William had estimated, there were about a hundred-and-fifty of them, three half companies. They marched with a swagger, in less rigid lines than their fellows in the musketeer companies, and they were lightly loaded, with just their small packs and their weapons.

'Well, at least I know the ground,' said Massey. 'I had a good look at it as soon as we arrived here, and I don't suppose the Indians have changed it much.'

'It's a clearing, I understand,' Holbrooke remarked. 'I must admit that I'm surprised. I thought we would want to constrain the French, squeeze them so that they can't manoeuvre.'

'Just so. However, we need some space to fight so the clearing is important. But I take your point about constraining the enemy. I've advised De Lancey to set up a log breastwork just to the east of the road. With the steep buff going down to the river, they'll be forced into a column rather than attacking in a line.'

Holbrooke had also seen the ground. He'd dragged the bateaux and guns for Point Montreal through the clearing at La Belle Famille to reach the gully where the boats had been launched. He tried to imagine the ground as Massey described it. The French couldn't outflank the position without forcing a way through the forest with its necessary loss of cohesion and momentum, and they couldn't pass a significant body of men between the bluff and the river. It sounded like a good plan.

'The breastwork will be a good defensive position as well as channeling the enemy,' Holbrooke said.

Massey looked at him and grinned.

'If I command there there'll be no skulking behind a breastwork. I'll put a few men to hold it, but we need to be in the open otherwise we can't attack. It's all very well exchanging volley fire with each other, but at some stage, we'll need to advance at bayonet-point, and I don't want a breastwork to hinder that movement. It's critical, you know. A few seconds delay and the initiative will be lost, perhaps forever.'

***

'Will the Mohawks fight, Kanatase?'

Holbrooke had caught sight of Kanatase hurrying towards La Belle Famille. He knew the situation as well as anyone and Holbrooke guessed that he was going to try to persuade his brother warriors to stay loyal to the British.

'I cannot say yet, Holbrooke. We have had messages from the warriors who follow the French and they have decided to stay neutral in this fight. The Iroquois also will stay neutral, but the Mohawks may yet decide to fight.'

The politics of the Iroquois Federation were still a mystery to Holbrooke. It was hard to understand how they could claim the friendship of the British, be on such intimate terms with Sir William, and yet be undecided whether to fight on their behalf. The army had dragged tons of additional food from Schenectady to Fort Niagara, just to feed their Iroquois allies, and now that they were required to pay the reckoning, they chose to sit on the sideline.

'I will see you at La Belle Famille, Holbrooke. Tomorrow I will be able to tell you whether the Mohawks will fight. Kaendaé is with the French,' he said with wild gleam in his eye. 'He will fight, I am sure of it!'

With that he was gone, loping off through the woods in that curious stooping, long-legged gait that all the Indians seemed to use.

***

They were sitting in their tent on the right of the battalion lines with a glorious view of the fort with the sun setting behind it. Since they had moved from the camp at the creek, they'd been adopted by the officers of the Forty-Sixth, and today they had enjoyed a good meal, albeit in rather rustic surroundings. The battalion's officers dined together whenever they could and enjoyed a level of luxury that Holbrooke and Chalmers had thought they'd left far behind at New York. Dinner was served on makeshift tables with pewter plates and cutlery, with real glasses and a few scraps of linen tablecloth. It had all been produced from a variety of campaign chests that the servants carried wherever the battalion marched. They'd even had wine, almost the last few bottles of the battalion's store.

'When you get the call, I'll join you, of course,' said Chalmers.

Holbrooke wasn't surprised. Perhaps he should try to dissuade his friend, after all it could be a desperate fight with French Indians hunting down the survivors, if the British line should be broken. He knew, however, that it would do little good. He could insist of course, but although Chalmers was signed on as his clerk, they just didn't have that hierarchical relationship.

'I'll carry a pair of pistols, for self-defence of course. I have no martial character to be maintained, and if Massey wishes to brand me a pirate or a highwayman, he is very welcome to do so. Unless I'm mistaken there will be need of a chaplain after the battle – if indeed there is a battle – and I know that the Rhode Island parson with the New Yorkers has orders to stay at the camp.'

'I expect Massey will make you very welcome,' Holbrooke replied.

'And now, Captain Holbrooke, you should write any personal letters that you believe are appropriate. I'll set up my desk and bring my writing gear.'

Holbrooke knew very well that Chalmers had nobody to write to. He was alone in the world except for their friendship, so he was surprised when the chaplain said that he had his own letter to write.

'I shall write to your father and tell him about the siege. You can tell him about the actions on the lake. You look surprised. Well, my dear fellow, I have a desire to leave some memorial if it should go wrong for me tomorrow, and your father is my only friend beside you. The letter will reach him as the trout start to think about spawning and lose interest in feeding; he'll need some distraction.'

That was true enough, and Holbrooke recalled that when he was courting Ann, his father and Chalmers were either pursuing the trout on the Meon that ran past the family cottage or were discussing how they should do so. It was a very natural friendship in fact. Chalmers was of an age somewhere between he and his father, and he had never had the means to indulge his passion for fly-fishing. The beauty of the cottage just outside Wickham was that the owner – Holbrooke's father – held the fishing rights upstream of the mill for some distance past the cottage.

'Then I'll write to Captain Carlisle…'

Chalmers interrupted.

'You'll write to Ann of course.'

'I don't know; it seems somehow impertinent, with her father's attitude.'

'Nonsense. The poor young woman probably sits by the front door every day waiting for a letter from you. In fact, I would bet a substantial amount of money on it. I know that Martin won't keep the letters from her; he would hardly survive his next interview with his wife if he attempted anything of that sort.'

That was true enough. Martin Featherstone had expressed his opposition to Holbrooke's courting his daughter in no uncertain terms. His wife Sophie, Ann's stepmother, was of a more romantic frame of mind and thoroughly approved of the match. Sophie was a dutiful wife in many respects, but she loved her stepdaughter and maintained a constant opposition to her husband's attitude.

'Nothing mawkish, of course. You don't want to frighten the poor lady and remember that she almost certainly shows her letters to Sophie.'

Holbrooke smiled at that. No, this letter wouldn't be some sort of last will and testament, but an up-beat description of the campaign so far. Nothing that Martin Featherstone could object to, but enough for Ann to be able to read between the lines. Besides, in a small town like Wickham, information was as good as gold. An account of the campaign so far would give Ann material for discussion with her friends for weeks to come, and perhaps, just perhaps, as his name became more closely linked with Ann's, her father would feel the weight of local pressure and relent.

It was all ridiculous, of course. Holbrooke knew objectively that a naval commander with a healthy bank balance from successful cruising should be more than an acceptable match for a provincial corn-merchant's daughter. It was all the fault of that blasted captain in Soberton; that and Martin Featherstone's unreasonable ambition for his only child.

'Now, would you like to dictate to me,' Chalmers asked with a mischievous look on his face. He had never been allowed to write Holbrooke's personal letters, even though he was invariably invited to review them for errors and for style.

They lit a pair of candles and settled down to their tasks. Neither man had any need to consider a will before a battle, nobody was dependent upon either of them and the bank of Campbell and Coutts already held their simple wishes for the division of their estates in the event of their deaths. Chalmers found it easy to write to his friend William. He described the long journey from Schenectady to Fort Niagara and the tribulations along the way. He was a good writer and telling the story of the siege came easily to him.

He even knew the correct military engineering terms and could describe the steady advance on the fort in a way that brought it to life. He enquired about the fishing. Had it been a good season? Did that big old trout that lived in the bend of the river below the cottage still scurry to the shelter of the alder roots at the first vibration from a footstep on the bank? It was important to give no hint that they would probably be engaged with the French on the morrow. With possibly months until another letter should reach Wickham, it was the greatest folly to leave a friend unsure of one's fate.

Holbrooke wrote quickly and fluently to his friend Carlisle. There was no saying when the letter would reach him; the last that Holbrooke heard, he had joined the fleet assaulting New France from the northeast, up the mighty Saint Lawrence. Probably they were besieging Quebec now, perhaps the city had already fallen, or the fleet and army had been repulsed. He sealed the letter and addressed it to the frigate *Medina*, under the care of the office at Halifax.

Holbrooke's second letter called for much more careful thought, and by the time he had completed it, the lines of the Forty-Sixth were in darkness with only one or two candles burning in the tents of officers engaged in the same letter-writing task.

Miss Ann Featherstone
Bere Forest House
The Square
Wickham

My Dear Ann, I trust that this letter finds you well, and I hope that I am not being impertinent in writing to you…

***

CHAPTER TWENTY-FIVE

La Belle Famille

Tuesday, Twenty-Fourth of July 1759.
The Lines of the Forty-Sixth of Foot, Fort Niagara.

Sir William stared south across the siege lines, as though by his sheer determination he could penetrate the thick forest that obscured his view. He had sounded confident yesterday, and yet he felt no such thing. He had to put on an act, had to appear to have a clear view of situation and act decisively. Any weakness would be used by the regular soldiers as a reason to force another change in command. Apart from the personal insult, he knew very well that it would be disastrous for the campaign. This was the critical moment, he was sure. The French had one throw of the dice left, and that was the relief force that his Mohawks had told him was approaching from the falls. Yesterday he had deployed his light infantry and assumed the air of a man who was certain that there would be enough time to send the Forty-Sixth when definite word came of the French advance. Nevertheless, he was nervous. In this wilderness, the tactical situation had a way of developing quickly. These weren't the plains of Germany where an army could be seen approaching from miles away; in the northern forest, the enemy could be within touching range and not be seen.

'The pickets are ready to march, Hervey?'

'Yes sir.' Hervey was a good brigade major and had all the answers at his fingertips. 'They stood to at dawn with arms, ammunition and packs.'

Sir William took another look to the south. He could see nothing and yet he knew that De Lacey's light infantry had been busy preparing the ground for a defensive battle all the previous day, and they were only a mile away. It was as though they had been swallowed up by the forest. He had few options if he didn't want to deploy his line battalions too soon, and the pickets were his only remaining body of reserves.

He squared his shoulders and spun around; his decision made.

'Then the pickets are to march now to La Belle Famille to join the light infantry. That will double De Lacey's force. He may be able to hold a first assault if the French are in a hurry.'

The three pickets were drawn from the Forty-Fourth, the Forty-Sixth and the New Yorkers; fifty of the best men from each, selected to be kept at high readiness for emergencies. They'd been spared much of the hard work in the trenches, and now they had to repay that indulgence. In less than an hour three hundred soldiers would stand across the road from the falls to the fort.

***

Massey nodded in approval as he saw the pickets marching hard towards La Belle Famille.

'It'll be our turn soon, Holbrooke, mark my words.'

Holbrooke could read the signs as well as any man and he was accoutered for battle, complete with his borrowed carbine. Chalmers emerged from his tent. His black coat and breeches – he entirely lacked a recognisable uniform – and his short sword and two pistols made him look not so much piratical as decidedly sinister. He completed the look with a pair of black riding boots that he had borrowed, and a canvas bag slung over his shoulder, filled with bandages and a few instruments. He was no surgeon, but he'd helped enough at sea to be useful in an emergency.

'Ah! here's something!'

A sergeant of the Forty-Sixth – one of Massey's own – was running towards the saps from the direction of La Belle Famille. This must be a new development, because the pickets had been dispatched long before he came in sight.

'What news, sergeant?'

'I durst not stop sir. Captain De Lancey sent me to tell

Sir William; the French are approaching in force!'

Massey paused for no more than a second or two as the sergeant hurried on his way.

'Drummer! Drummer there! Sound the muster!'

The soldiers of the Forty-Sixth poured out of their tents, grabbing their muskets and shouldering their packs. Sergeants bellowed and the drum continued its insistent tattoo. Soon the muster was complete. They were far fewer in number than Holbrooke had expected. Massey had already sent the best part of two of his companies – the light infantry and the pickets – to La Belle Famille, and now there were only a hundred-and-twenty-five or so musketeers of the line and twenty-four grenadiers ready to march. It looked a pitiful force to oppose the thousand Frenchmen and thousand Indians that the scouts had reported. Chalmers glanced at Holbrooke, who smiled nervously. They were committed now.

'Which way should we march, Sir William?' Massey called as the army commander strode in their direction. Sir William merely pointed south, towards La Belle Famille.

***

The way to La Belle Famille was through the woods, but here the undergrowth had been plundered by the besieging army for the gabions and fascines, and the musketeers and grenadiers had easy going. Massey set the pace and they trotted the mile to the clearing in the woods. It was hot work even this early in the morning, and the soldiers were puffing as they fell back into line. There was no sign of the French, but some of the hostile Indians were already trying to work around to the British left flank.

'I'll take command now, Mister De Lacey,' said Massey as he drew up to the breastwork.

'Forty-Sixth will form a line to the right of the breastwork and down to the road. Hurry now!'

He looked appraisingly at the ground. There was a ridge to the right of the road beyond which the ground fell steeply to the river.

'Lieutenant! Take your grenadiers onto that ridge between the road and the river and stop the French or Indians infiltrating our right flank.' He looked again at the ridge. 'And you'll be in a good position to fire into their columns when they attack.'

There were only twenty-four grenadiers but from that position they could pour in a heavy fire onto the enemy's left wing.

'The picket of the Forty-Fourth is to form a line between the Forty-Sixth and the grenadiers, straddling the road.'

Holbrooke saw Kanatase loping towards them from the woods. He was a welcome sight.

'Massey, Holbrooke,' he said, 'Some of the French Indians have chosen to fight. The Mohawks and a few of the other Iroquois will fight for our friends the British now. They are in the woods.'

They looked to their left. Beyond the breastwork, beyond the pickets of the New York Regiment and the Forty-Fourth, they caught fleeting glimpses of bare-chested warriors slinking through the trees. The British and French Indians were close to each other, but they weren't shooting. They may have agreed to serve their respective European friends but that didn't mean that they had to fight other Indians, at least not until the outcome of the battle looked certain.

'Well, I suppose it's better to have them than not,' said Massey after Kanatase had hurried away again, 'but I confess that I don't trust 'em. They won't stand and fight and many of them are only good for scalping the wounded and plundering the dead.'

There was a continuous line of defenders now, stretching from deep in the woods, across the clearing and the road, to the bluff and the river. It was a near-complete line, but it was dreadfully thin. Massey observed it with an appraising eye.

'Mister De Lacey!' he shouted. 'Bring your men from behind that breastwork and form them to the left. The

Forty-Sixth will occupy the right end of the works.'

'Damn them,' he said to Holbrooke. 'See how tardy they are, they don't want to leave the cover that they built. Mister De Lacey!' he shouted, 'Get your men moving. I need them to the left of the breastwork. The Left!'

Holbrooke heard a beating of drums from the other side of the clearing and through the trees he saw glimpses of white uniforms advancing. Then a huge white flag came into view, then a second flag, the white of the Bourbon dynasty. The French were coming!

***

Massey looked in exasperation as the light infantry at last started to move more quickly.

'Scandalous!' he muttered aloud, 'that the light infantry should seek to hide behind a breastwork while the line companies stand in the open.'

His line wasn't going to be complete before the French were upon them.

'Halt!' shouted Massey at the captain commanding the left of the Sixty-Fourth, who was trying to occupy the end of the breastwork. 'Stay where you are, there's no time to move further. Form a line.'

'That's not so bad, Holbrooke,' he said. 'See how the left of my line can catch the French flank if they attack my centre? And I have the grenadiers on the right. It's not so bad at all.'

Holbrooke tried not to look appalled. Massey had less than five hundred soldiers and an unknown number of Iroquois with dubious loyalty to oppose what could be two thousand Frenchmen and Indians.

'Front rank, fix bayonets,' Massey shouted at his Forty-Sixth. The order was taken up by the sergeants. 'Now lie down, men, get low until they're closer.'

Massey climbed onto a fallen log to get a better view of the advancing French. If he was disheartened by what he saw, he gave no sign of it. Just then, three Iroquois came running towards them from the left. Holbrooke knew them, they were Oneidas and had been with the army since Fort Stanwix. Kanatase had introduced one of them but Holbrooke couldn't remember his name.

'Massey,' the first of them called in a voice that could be heard by the soldiers close by. 'The French have ten times your numbers. See how many they are.'

'Hold your tongue!' Massey replied, furious at this unhelpful report.

The three Indians walked off nonchalantly towards the forest. They may fight for the British, but it was clear that they would change sides the instant that the French gained an ascendancy.

The information was being passed from man to man along the British line. Massey saw what was happening.

'Men!' he shouted. 'I see the French and they have greater numbers than us, but if you'll obey my commands, we'll win the day. They must attack us, they have no choice, and when they do, they'll feel British lead and British steel.'

There was a ripple of low cheers along the line, stifled from the lying position of the men.

Holbrooke could see the plan now. Massey's strongest force, his beloved Forty-Sixth, would block the French while the pickets, the light infantry and the grenadiers would guard his wings and fire into the flanks of the advancing French. His Indian allies would prevent the French infiltrating through the woods to the left, while the river guarded his right. The French really had no option. They had to attack the line of the Forty-Sixth and they had to do it immediately before the defence could be better organised and before further troops could be sent to reinforce them.

***

Captain François-Marie Le Marchand de Lignery was confident that he could break through the British line. He was a veteran of the wars in America and had served in the *troupes de la marine* for forty years. His Indians had taken some prisoners earlier that day, and under the threat of being handed back for torture and death, they had told him that only De Lancey's light infantry stood between him and the fort. A hundred-and-fifty men – and only light infantry at that, not the solid men of the line companies with their formidable long muskets – against his eight hundred Canadian and Louisiana soldiers. He had a right to be optimistic. He'd lost his Indians except for the Osages and Chippewa, but that didn't overly concern him. This would be a simple if brutal confrontation that would be decided with the musket and bayonet.

The French columns burst through the forest into the clearing. Lignery spread his arms side to side and his officers relayed the order for the columns to deploy into line as they came into the clearing. His few Indians moved away to his right.

Lignery looked right and left. His men hadn't completed their movement into a line, but he must attack anyway, the clearing wasn't large enough for manoeuvres. The British had chosen their ground well. And he could see that there were more than a hundred-and fifty men in front of him, and the unmistakable uniforms of the line companies of a regular British battalion were facing him! They were still deploying so they must have just arrived. Now or never!

'En Avant! Chargez!' he shouted.

The two huge white flags waved from side to side and with a mighty cheer and whoops and war cries from the Indians on the right, the French relief force surged towards Massey's defenders. The experienced and battle-hardened *troupes de la marine* took the front ranks while the militia pressed on from behind. There was a sense among even the lowest of the French soldiery that this was the culminating battle for North America. If they failed this day, then Fort Niagara would fall and all the vast French lands to the south and west would be untenable. The British would cut them off decisively from the mother country and the long dream of New France would come to an end.

On they came, firing and reloading on the move, confident of smashing their way through the line in front of them.

**

Holbrooke had no time now to feel uneasy. He'd insisted that Chalmers wait in the rear of the defences; not that it would do him any good if the French should break through, but it kept him out of the first shock of the impact. Now the soldiers around him were all on their bellies, burrowing deep into the grass, but Massey was standing proud on his fallen log, watching the French advance with admirable *sang froid*. His example was irresistible, and with a brief thought as to how foolish it was for him to be here in the first place, he climbed up onto the log beside the colonel.

The French were in no good order. The columns that had been necessary for the narrow road through the forest were still emerging onto the clearing of La Belle Famille. However ridiculous it was for a sea officer to be standing there in full view of enemy soldiers, and with no command function, at least he would have a grandstand view of the battle. His friend Carlisle would certainly be interested.

It was a dreadful sight as the eight hundred soldiers burst out of the woods into the clearing. The drums, the bugles, the vast white flags and the blues and whites of the uniforms would have been exciting in any circumstances. Now they looked dangerous.

'You see,' said Massey, 'they're stopping for a volley. No French line regiment would do that, they'd have come right on at bayonet point. I do believe they've made a fatal mistake. Steady men!' he shouted, 'wait until they're closer.'

The French line came to a halt and the entire front rank fired a volley, briefly hiding the French force behind a cloud of grey powder smoke. Holbrooke heard the musket and carbine balls whizzing through the air beside him.

'Damn!' exclaimed Massey and he brought his right hand to the side of his chest where a stain of blood was starting to seep through the ripped wool of his waistcoat.

Holbrooke moved to help him.

'It's nothing, Holbrooke, get your carbine ready.'

Another volley, but much more ragged this time. The French firing was doing little damage to the British soldiers, most of whom they couldn't even see as they lay in the grass or crouched behind logs.

'They're fools,' Massey commented through gritted teeth. 'A determined charge would have done for us but now they'll never advance together. Once you allow the men to stop and fire and there's no moving them as a body.'

Chalmers came up on Massey's left side with a bandage to pass around his body.

'Much obliged, Mister Chalmers. Pull it tight now, I'll need to move soon.'

The French came closer. Their caution was evident and some of them were loading and firing as an excuse for not moving faster. Their fire was ragged and inaccurate as their view of the enemy was obscured by their own smoke. Lignery was in front, shouting and waving, but still his men stopped and fired. Nevertheless, the whole mass, not a line at all, moved inexorably forward.

Holbrooke saw to his horror that Massey had swooned and only the support of Chalmers had stopped him falling off the log. He waved feebly at Holbrooke.

'Get them up, get them up,' he said in a weak voice.

Holbrooke knew what he must do. 'Forty-Sixth will stand!' he shouted, waving his arms in an upward motion.

The company commanders all knew Holbrooke and they could see what had happened to their commander. All along the line of British defenders the men emerged from the grass and the breastworks; the light infantry, the pickets and the grenadiers taking their lead from the line companies. To the French they must have looked like malign spirits of the earth as they peered through the powder smoke looking for targets.

The fit seemed to have passed and Massey was on his feet again, staring hard at the approaching French.

'Take aim!'

Chalmers knotted the ends of the bandage as all along

the line sergeants and corporals adjusted the aim of the individual muskets. There was a breathless pause. It was unclear whether Massey was even aware that Chalmers had finished, certainly he gave no sign. This was the high-water mark of his regimental career – when he ordered his men to fire into an attacking enemy on the open field – and no trifling wound would be allowed to interfere.

'Fire!'

The devastating volley seemed to rock the French front line backwards. Over on the right the grenadiers had started firing into the French flank and either side of the Forty-Sixth, the light infantry and the picket of the Forty-Fourth added their own musketry.

'Fire by divisions!' shouted Massey.

That would allow each group of around forty men to fire independently. The French would be under a rolling but disciplined hail of musket and carbine bullets.

Holbrooke suddenly remembered his own carbine. Should he fire? He desperately wanted to see the battle and didn't want to be distracted by the need to fire and reload. No, he'd keep it until it may be needed.

***

It seemed like only seconds, but Holbrooke counted seven distinct volleys from the Forty-Sixth in front of him. Here and there a few intrepid Frenchmen under determined leadership were still trying to reach the British line, but most were stationary, exchanging fire with their enemy, while some had started to retire. It wasn't going so well on the British left, and through the powder smoke Holbrooke could see that the New Yorker's picket was in retreat; he could clearly see their knapsacks while the gleam of their bayonets was hidden. The picket of the Forty-Sixth at the extreme left of the line was moving to cover the gap. That was the difference between regular line infantry and provincial regiments, or even light infantry. They may be experts at irregular warfare in the forests and mountains of North America, but they didn't have the experience or discipline to stand in line with musket balls bringing down their friends to their right and left. They were in the same case as the French *Troupes de la Marine* and Militia. Formidable on their own ground but outclassed by the British line infantry in an open battle.

'The Forty-Sixth will advance!'

To the steady beat of the drum the British line moved forward, the bright steel of their bayonets glinting in the morning sun. The grenadiers on the right and the light infantry on the left continued pouring their lead bullets into the flanks of the French but otherwise the line moved forward without a musket being fired. The soldiers were shouting now, mustering their courage for the hard hand-to-hand fighting that was to come.

In the forests, the Iroquois had seen how the battle had turned and they were already in full pursuit of those Frenchmen who were fleeing the battlefield. Of the French Indians, the Osages and Chippewa, there was no sign; they had already withdrawn into the depths of the forest.

The advance quickly became a rout. Lignery fell gravely wounded in the first of Massey's volleys and most of the French leadership fell in the subsequent fire. It was a leaderless and disorganised rabble that fled the field of battle, plunging back into the woods in their haste to retreat towards the falls, twelve long miles to the south. And it was in the woods that the Iroquois harried them, killing mercilessly and taking scalps before the life had left the body. For it was not only the loyal Mohawks that pursued the beaten enemy but all the Iroquois who had sat on the sidelines.

Holbrooke still clutched his unused carbine as he climbed down from his log and walked forward following the advancing soldiers of the Forty-Sixth. He had long ago lost sight of Eyre Massey, who was joyfully leading his men in pursuit of the beaten French, the passing weakness from his wound forgotten. He didn't see the Seneca Kaendaé creeping up on him until he heard the savage war-whoop from behind. He tensed for the blow that he knew was to come, at the same time diving to the right and trying to raise his carbine, for a hostile Indian could only have come from the direction of the forest. He even felt the breath on his neck, so close was the warrior. Then he heard a thud, just like the sound of a butcher's cleaver splitting a pig's carcass. The hot breath ended with a wheeze and as he spun further to the right, he saw the body fall behind him, with a tomahawk embedded in the back of the man's neck.

'You must take more care, Holbrooke,' said the familiar voice of Kanatase, thickened by the joy of battle. The Mohawk pulled his tomahawk free – he must have thrown it with deadly accuracy from twenty yards – and casually took hold of his scalping knife. He knelt on the back of the still-breathing Seneca and with two deft, practiced movements he removed the scalp and held it aloft with a wild cry of triumph. Then he looked into the pained yet defiant eyes of his beaten foe, muttered a few words in his own language and with another stroke cut his throat, ending his adversary's life in an instant.

***

CHAPTER TWENTY-SIX

The Silent Fortress

Wednesday, Twenty-Fifth of July 1759.
Fort Niagara.

It had taken some time to persuade Pouchot that what had looked like a minor skirmish to him, as he watched the action at La Belle Famille from the walls of his fort, was really the decisive battle of the campaign. Through the remains of the day he steadfastly refused to believe what the British emissary told him under a flag of truce. It was only when one of his officers was taken into the British camp to see with his own eyes the captured French soldiers and the gravely wounded de Lignery, that he realised that all hope of relief was gone. All that remained was to negotiate the best terms that he could and that was not completed until late into the night. However, the guns had ceased their incessant roar as soon as the British emissary had walked across the shattered no-man's-land between the sap and the Gate of Five Nations in the southeast corner of the fort.

The grenadiers took possession of that same gate early the next morning and when it was secured the line regiments of the army marched in with their drums beating and their banners flying, followed by the provincial troops. Holbrooke walked in with Sir William, as one of his first line of staff officers. In a sheer act of showmanship, as the British flag was broken out at the flagstaff on top of the great house, Lynton's schooner *Mohawk* dropped its anchor in the Niagara River, close under the fort's walls, where *L'Iroquois* used to lie. The schooner's three-pounders didn't roar like the broadside of a first-rate ship-of-the-line, but as they fired a measured salute to the flag, they made an emphatic statement about the role that sea-power had played in the demise of New France.

One-hundred-and-fifty leagues to the northeast,

Admiral Saunders and General Wolfe were trying to lure Montcalm out of Quebec to do battle. Meanwhile, ninety leagues to the east General Amherst was cautiously positioning his guns to overlook Fort Carillon and force a French surrender. There would still be hard fighting on the Saint Lawrence and Lake Champlain, but here in the west the war was won. There was no French force that could besiege Fort Niagara now that it was in British hands. De Vaudreuil and Montcalm knew that and would now be forced to abandon La Belle Rivière and the western Great Lakes to British rule.

***

'You have dispatches, from the Admiralty, no less,' said Chalmers when he found Holbrooke in his new quarters in the great house. 'A whaleboat brought them from Oswego this morning.'

Chalmers turned the package over in his hands. There had been little communication from their Lordships since they left New York and none in response to Holbrooke's commissioning of two schooners and appointing a captain, stretching his authority perhaps to breaking point. And how could there be? It was not only the cold wastes of the North Atlantic that stood between them, but the long, long journey up the Hudson and the Mohawk, across the portage and Lake Oneida, and down the Onondaga to Lake Ontario. It was something of a miracle that dispatches arrived at all.

Holbrooke gazed at the package for a few moments. It wasn't just a communication from a world that seemed remote, in this far wilderness; it was a testament to the way that control of Lake Ontario had been wrested from the French navy. Although they still owned the two most powerful ships on the lake, they had failed to intercept the army when it was most vulnerable, they had taken only the most trivial role in defending the fort, and they hadn't been seen at all for over a week. An unarmed whaleboat could travel in confidence between Oswego and Niagara, keeping open that vital connection with the world outside.

New orders? a promotion? an admonition for exceeding his authority? It could hardly be the last; their Lordships wouldn't have heard of the affairs with the brigs and schooners yet, much less have had time to send their displeasure. Well, no use in speculating. He opened the letter.

There was silence in the room as he read it through once, then with a frown read it again more carefully.

'It would appear that their Lordships had more faith in the eventual reduction of Fort Niagara than anyone in Prideaux' army.'

'Had they indeed? They should have been with the Forty-Sixth yesterday, then they may have felt differently. When that horde of screaming Frenchmen appeared out of the woods, I thought it was all over. And the savages!'

Holbrooke read the last lines again.

'They're forming a squadron, based here at Niagara. And they're sending a post-captain to command it and to oversee the building of two brigs. They mention the desirability of destroying French naval power on the lake to complete the encirclement of Montreal.'

'Do they indeed? I thought Montreal was one of the objectives for *this* season.'

'Perhaps they don't have so much faith in the Saint Lawrence expedition as they do in ours. It's been an unlucky river for the British and the navigation is treacherous.'

'Isn't it a little late for this talk of destroying the French navy?' Chalmer's asked. 'We seem to have done that already.'

'Not while those two brigs are still in the enemy's hands. With a little enterprise they could sweep aside Lynton's schooner and make life exceedingly difficult for Sir William. However that may be, it's this talk of a post-captain that disturbs me, although you may remember that Prideaux mentioned the possibility last month.'

Holbrooke had a look that Chalmers recognised. If a post-captain was required at Niagara it should be him, not some newcomer taking the glory once the work had been done. This was like Emden all over again, where he had effectively negotiated the surrender of the town the day before a commodore arrived to take over.

'Captain Joshua Loring. I've heard that name before, I believe he's spent the war here in the colonies. I wonder whether he's American-born, like Captain Carlisle.'

Chalmers shook his head. The name was new to him.

'I'm to relinquish command of my naval party to Loring. He could be here any day now by the look of the date on this letter. Ah, here it is. He's expected in late July or early August. Yes, any day now. But here's the curious thing. He'll have in his gift commissions for a commander and warrants for a bosun, a master shipwright and a purser. That's just the start. He can make acting warrants as he pleases when ships become available, either through building or capture. These are expansive orders indeed!'

'Mister Lynton may yet have his opportunity, then,' Chalmers said.

'He may indeed, although whether he'll relish a command so far from the sea for what would probably be the rest of the war, remains to be seen. It's not just Lynton though. Jackson already has his warrant of course, but Sutton may be tempted. The title of master shipwright will appeal to him.'

'You're forgetting Serviteur, I do believe,' said Chalmers. 'He has the education to be a purser. Whether the colour of his skin is a bar to a warrant, I really don't know.'

'There are precedents, I believe, on the Jamaica Station and the Leeward Islands. The Navy Board takes a liberal view of these things when the warrants are issued on remote stations. I wonder what Serviteur would think to that.'

'Speaking parochially, I wonder whether this Captain

Loring will want me?' Chalmers mused. 'I suppose in principal I'll have no choice, but I don't relish staying here now that the job's done. The Meon trout are beckoning and we can be home long before the spring.'

'Oh, it would be quite normal for you to come home with me. Clerks are usually the core of any following and commanders take their clerks from commission to commission. It would be draconian for Loring to keep you here. In any case, I'm to return to England as soon as he arrives, and I shall do my utmost to bring you along. So long as that's your wish, of course,' he added hastily.

He scanned the letter again.

'There's no word of a ship in this letter, so perhaps I'll have some time to amuse myself ashore. I shall speak to the others. If I do get another ship it will feel strange to sail without Lynton and Jackson and Serviteur, and even Sutton is growing on me.'

'Speaking of amusing yourself ashore,' said Chalmers, 'there's a letter from Wickham, and it's not in your father's hand. I waited until you'd read your dispatches, as you always wish,' he added, handing Holbrooke the letter. 'I think I'll take a turn along the walls and see those batteries that so discomforted you out on the lake.'

***

What was it that he was so afraid of? He'd boarded enemy ships with less trepidation than when confronted with a letter from Ann. He looked around – a habitual gesture to ensure he wasn't being watched – and slipped his hand inside his shirt. Yes, his heart was racing, and the beat was erratic; it felt as though it would burst out of his shirt.

The address was certainly in Ann's hand. Did that mean that she was openly corresponding with him? Then either her father had relented, or her stepmother was covertly sending the letters for her. The latter most likely, he decided.

Using his pocketknife, he cut the seal and the twine that surrounded the package. Whoever had wrapped it had found some light canvas for the outer wrapper and had made a workmanlike job of sealing it against moisture. He thought of the letter's long and difficult journey from the little town in Hampshire; it was truly a wonder that it had arrived here at all.

Inside the canvas was a further brown paper wrapper and then the letter itself, written on the same cream-coloured paper that Ann had always used. One more wax seal to break then he carefully unfolded the letter and raised it to his face. Yes, there was still the faintest trace of perfume. Had Ann sprinkled the letter? Probably not, that would expose herself in the event that he had fixed his affection elsewhere. Then it must be the residue from whatever scent she was wearing when she wrote it. That was a more pleasant thought.

My Dear George, she wrote.

It was ridiculous how he was looking for meaning in every word. And yet, Ann had never used his Christian name in her previous letters; she had always used his rank. There was something intimate in this use of his name in a letter. Only his father, Carlisle, Chiara and Chalmers in all the world called him George.

He read on eagerly. There was the small talk of a small town, the interest in the expeditions in America and how people asked if she had received any news. Holbrooke was pleased to see that in his hometown his name was being linked with Ann's. Small steps but in the right direction. Then the tone changed, moved down an octave and into a minor key.

You will know that my father is against our correspondence. He hasn't outright forbidden me to write and in principle he doesn't know about this letter, but I'm sure he guesses. Sophie is my ally in this subterfuge. She encouraged me to write and asked your father to see the letter on its way. Apparently, he understands how to send letters to sea officers far from home.

That explained the canvas cover and the twine, that was just how his father wrapped letters and parcels. He would certainly know how to send it; he'd been a sailing master in King's ships since before his son was born. Otherwise, Sophie would have had to ask endless questions in the town, and certainly her husband would have heard.

I do feel bad about keeping secrets from my father, but I know that he will relent in the end. He's dropped hints about meeting eligible young men, but I politely ignore him and pretend not to understand. I just can't believe that he will still be intransigent when you come home. In any case, the King must make you a post-captain soon, and then his main objection will be lost.

Holbrooke had never had such a letter from Ann before. She was nailing her colours to the mast, committing herself to him in a way that could only be called incautious, in the face of her father's continued objection. Yes, he must get home and press his claim at the Admiralty, then he would be able to meet Martin Featherstone with an established naval career that would see him an admiral one day – if he lived.

Holbrooke paced the few steps of the tiny room, his brain racing faster than his feet would carry him. There was no sense in replying to Ann. If this Captain Loring arrived in the next week or so, then he would outpace any letter in his haste to get home. He started to calculate how long it would take. He would ask for the *Mohawk* to take him to Oswego, then a bateau or a whaleboat up the Onondaga and across Lake Oneida and up Wood Creek. A march over the portage then a boat down the Mohawk and the Hudson to New York. He would buy a passage on first packet if a frigate wasn't leaving for home immediately. It was just the Onondaga and Wood Creek that would be difficult; from the portage to the sea was all downstream, although the Mohawk had many awkward stretches and the water would be lower after this hot summer. Perhaps two weeks if he was lucky, three if he wasn't, then another four weeks for the Atlantic passage. Allowing for delays he could be home at the end of September!

He was already in a fever of impatience for Loring to arrive. Then he steadied himself. The prisoners would be shipped out along exactly the route that he was going to take. Sir William would be less than human if he resisted the temptation to put him in charge of the transport. That would never do. It was all down to Loring's timing; he couldn't leave until he was superseded. The prisoners would be gone in a day or two; after that Loring could arrive as soon as he liked.

***

CHAPTER TWENTY-SEVEN

The Niagara Squadron

Saturday, Twenty-Eighth of July 1759.
Fort Niagara.

Holbrooke and Chalmers had just finished the painstaking task of writing a report to the naval secretary outlining the naval activities on Lake Ontario. It required skill with words to convey just what had happened and to cast the loss of the first schooner in the best possible light. The news of the second schooner —now bravely flying the British ensign on the lake – had to come first, to soften the news of the foundering off Duck Island. Those were the headlines, the news that would win their Lordships' attention, but the report had to cover the whole expedition since leaving Schenectady. They found it hard to put the events in the proper sequence and both men referred continually to their personal notebooks. Still, it was complete, and four copies of the report were on the desk, waiting to be sealed: one for the Admiralty, one for Sir William, one for Captain Loring and the last as a personal copy for Holbrooke.

'Well, I'm glad that task is done,' said Holbrooke, sitting back with a deep sigh, 'now Loring can appear at any time that he likes.'

It was a tidying up of loose ends. He'd already told the rest of his crew what he knew of Loring and his commissions and warrants, and of his own imminent departure. Sutton had immediately said that he would take any permanent warrant that he was offered. He'd fallen for the county and wanted to make a new life in a new continent. Holbrooke suspected that he was running from something in England, and that almost certainly meant woman troubles, or debt. Privately, Holbrooke thought that a Navy Board warrant was just a means to an end for Sutton, and that he had his eye on setting up his own yard in Albany or Schenectady. Well good luck to him, there was plenty of opportunity to prosper in the American colonies.

Serviteur was more difficult. It was worth preparing him, but it could easily come to nothing. Loring could be the sort of person who wouldn't countenance a warrant for a black man. Serviteur understood all that, and yet he was excited at the prospect of making something of himself. He had spent the last few days quizzing Lynton, Jackson and Chalmers on the duties of a purser.

Jackson's was a different case. When Holbrooke had raised the subject, he had shaken his head immediately.

'I'll stay with you if you don't mind, sir, if you'll have me.'

'You understand that Captain Loring may insist on keeping you here. He has that power, you know.'

'I understand, sir, but if anything can be done to persuade him, I'll be right grateful. I won't stay willingly; I have a hankering to see the open ocean again, and even Portsmouth Point. There's nothing for me here, and I can't bear the thought of some other bosun looking after your next ship.'

That flat statement reminded Holbrooke of how much he would miss Jackson if he were taken from him. He suddenly realised that the small band of followers that he had so painstakingly collected was in grave danger of being broken up. Lynton must go, of course, if he was to advance in the navy, and Serviteur mustn't pass up this opportunity if it were to be offered. But for Jackson there was nothing on offer that he didn't already have, and Holbrooke would miss him desperately. He realised how much they had been through together and he had a sudden mental image of the deadly little affair in the backstreets of Kingston. If Jackson hadn't appeared in the nick of time, Holbrooke's career would have ended there and then, on the edge of an assassin's cutlass.

'I'll do all in my power for you, Mister Jackson, you can

be sure of that.'

Then there was Lynton, and Holbrooke could see his indecision. He was in a strong position with an Admiralty commission that appointed him to Holbrooke's naval party. If he insisted on leaving, then Loring would find it hard to demand that he stay and take the promotion. Lynton had a choice, then, at least a theoretical one. They had talked long into the night, but still he was uncertain. From the perspective of the ruins of Fort Niagara, it seemed that the French could not long continue the fight, and when the war ended the promotions would dry up. Lynton ran a real risk of being a lieutenant for many years to come if he refused Loring's commission. And then, he had noticed how Lynton was enjoying this new land, he seemed at home here. The tussle between his loyalty to Holbrooke and his ambition was plain to see, and it hurt Holbrooke inexpressibly to see his friend's anguish.

Massey had gone. As Holbrooke had forecast, the prisoners were sent immediately to Oswego, and Massey, his wound still weeping through its bandages, was sent away in command of the escort. There was more than a suspicion that Sir William had sent him home to remove the threat to his authority. His claim to command the army had only been strengthened by the victory at La Belle Famille, and all-in-all, it was better for everyone's peace of mind if he were sent away, with an important task to keep him busy. Holbrooke had been sad to see him go. Theirs was a real friendship based on mutual trust and esteem, and the memory of standing side by side to brave the first volleys of the advancing Frenchmen would stay with Holbrooke until the end of his days.

Yes, he'd lost his friend and an ally, but at least the prisoners were gone, and he wasn't responsible for them. He planned to make better time than them, and if Loring appeared soon, he'd overtake them somewhere on the journey. Friendship or no friendship, Holbrooke was impatient to get home. There was nothing more for him here, no more battles to fight until the next campaign season, and when he was superseded, he would be like a ghost at the party: an officer with nothing to command and no reason to be there.

***

A pounding on their door disturbed Holbrooke and Chalmers as they stowed away their writing materials.

'Sir William requests your presence, Captain Holbrooke,' said the subaltern respectfully. Holbrooke's reputation in the army had soared after the battle at La Belle Famille.

Holbrooke had cleaned himself since the fort had fallen, but everyone's clothes had suffered in the campaign and only the most senior officers had managed to hold back a decent outfit for the victory. The subaltern's rig would have turned heads in England, stained and torn as it was, but it raised not an eyebrow in this fallen fortress.

'Do you know why I'm summoned?' Holbrooke asked.

He knew the subaltern, he had shared a bateau with him at one point on the Mohawk River, and they had a fellow-feeling.

'A naval gentleman arrived in a bateau from Oswego, sir, just twenty minutes ago. A captain I believe, and he had some other officers with him.'

Holbrooke dressed in haste, digging out his last pair of decent stockings and rubbing the grime from his boots. He well knew the moral disadvantage of being ill-dressed, particularly when meeting a senior officer. This newcomer could only be Loring. He found that he was nervous, like a schoolboy meeting the headmaster.

It was easy to see how he had missed Loring's arrival; there were bateaux and whaleboats and canoes running under the walls of the fort in a constant stream. Nearly all of them came from Le Petit Marais, carrying the army's stores from the temporary camp to the greater security of the fort. They had to pass around the western end of the fort and a few hundred yards up the river, then they could use the jetty or run up the shingle bank. There were so many of them that an extra one coming from Oswego wouldn't have been noticed. Loring had quite rightly set off to meet the commander of the army before seeking out his predecessor.

***

'Ah! Captain Holbrooke. How good of you to join us. May I present Captain Loring? I know that you were aware of his imminent arrival. I've been telling Captain Loring all about your conveying us safely here and wresting command of the lake from the French.'

Even with that auspicious introduction Loring looked sceptical, but he greeted Holbrooke affably enough. He was a bulky officer with an old-fashioned half-wig, and he wore a uniform coat that owed little to the navy board's patterns and everything to the imagination of the Boston tailor who had cut and stitched it in blissful ignorance. Loring had come directly from Amherst's army on Lake Champlain, and he knew little more than Sir William and Holbrooke about happenings in the wider world. He did know that Quebec had not fallen, although that information was two weeks old, and that Saunders and Wolfe were concerned about the lateness of the year. There was talk of Quebec having to wait for the next summer with the army subsisting in camps on the banks of the Saint Lawrence through the Canadian winter, a horrifying thought. Amherst had also made slow progress, and was advancing slowly and deliberately down the lake, securing his lines of supply with rigorous determination at each point. By contrast, the expedition to Fort Niagara looked like an unqualified and rapidly achieved success, the one bright point in the American campaign so far.

'You will know something of my orders,' said Loring when the preliminaries had been completed. 'I intend to take command of the naval forces on this lake immediately.'

'So I understand, sir. Lieutenant Lynton who commands the *Mohawk* of six guns is anticipating you.'

'You chose not to command her yourself? I'm

surprised.'

'Captain Holbrooke has been indispensable on my staff, Captain Loring.' Sir William intervened with only the slightest emphasis on the twice-mentioned rank of captain. 'With the lake and river on two of our three flanks and our supply route exposed to the French navy, I really couldn't have done without expert naval advice. I'm sure you understand.'

Loring bowed to Sir William but made no other admission of error.

'Is Lynton a sound officer, Mister Holbrooke? You know that I have a commander's commission in my pocket. Strictly speaking it's intended for the first brig that we'll build, but I am on the wing and can only spend a week here before I must return to Amherst's army. I'll need to leave a good man behind, and he'll need the appropriate rank. He can have the brig in due course.'

'Yes, sir. Mister Lynton is an enterprising and experienced officer. He's served with me for a number of years, and he captured the schooner that he now commands by boarding it from a whaleboat.'

Loring gave him a sideways look.

'You won't mind if I offer him the promotion? Legally, he's not obliged to take it, but God only knows where I'll find anyone else in this wilderness. I may have to insist if he's not willing. I hope you'll back that up, Sir William.'

Johnson nodded slightly, not choosing to commit himself.

'Mister Lynton knows the situation perfectly,' Holbrooke replied, 'but I can't say how he will answer if you make the offer.'

Holbrooke knew very well how Lynton would reply, notwithstanding his indecision of yesterday. Personal loyalty would be set aside in the face of a firm offer of promotion, as it should be. He'd already decided that if Lynton should be so foolish as to refuse Loring's offer, he would join Loring in forcing the issue. He hoped it wouldn't come to that.

***

Of course, Lynton accepted the commission. In the end, there was no real decision to make. Loring had to build two brigs at Niagara, and he had to do it quickly. When the brigs were ready Lynton would have a command fit for his rank, a brig-sloop with a complement to match. Lynton would be the senior captain on the lake, under Loring, who would act in the capacity of a commodore. It was an opportunity that, when all had been considered, really was too good to reject.

Sutton accepted the warrant as master shipwright with the air of a man who wasn't being offered any great favour, as though he had better things to do but would stoop to this level out of courtesy. Even Serviteur was satisfied. Loring had grilled him on his understanding of the purser's duties and had watched him total a series of figures and write with a good hand. The post-captain was visibly relieved. He had nowhere else to find a purser this side of Albany, and with a shipyard being set up and the crew of a schooner needing to be fed, watered and paid, he counted himself lucky that Serviteur was willing to join him. After an initial startled glance from Loring when Serviteur entered the room, the question of his colour hadn't been mentioned.

That left Jackson. He smiled and said how honoured he was, but still he dug his heels in, standing on his dubious rights as a warrant officer to decide when and where he would serve.

'I've trained up two of the bateau-men, sir, and they'll make a right good bosun and bosun's mate for a schooner. By the time your brigs are built they'll be ready to move up and they'll have trained their reliefs. There are some good fellows among those New Englanders and a few of them have sailed with the whaling fleets and on the Guinea run.'

Loring looked hard at Jackson.

'I'll think on it,' he said, 'but when I've decided there will be no arguments.'

Jackson left with a look that said he would see about the

arguments when they were needed.

'I gather Jackson is a follower of yours, Holbrooke.'

'He is sir. All these men have been my followers for years,' he chose not to mention that Sutton had only been with him for eight months, 'but Mister Jackson feels a particular attachment. I negotiated his warrant for him in Port Royal and I know he wishes to stay with me.'

'The needs of the service must come first, Holbrooke.'

'Indeed they must, sir. I can't argue with that. And yet, you have already taken my first lieutenant, my carpenter and my servant. I believe the traditions of the service would support you leaving at least one of my followers…'

Holbrooke bit his lip. He'd forgotten about Chalmers. That was Loring's opportunity to say that he would, magnanimously, leave Holbrooke his clerk but that he must have the bosun. He threw caution to the winds.

'…Of course, Mister Chalmers is a man of the cloth, and with no official position,' Holbrooke threw in that mild untruth, 'he is not subject to your orders or mine and may come or go as he pleases. In effect, I'm only asking for one of my followers to be left to me.'

Holbrooke watched Loring as he thought it through. He now knew that Loring was a peculiar kind of sea officer who not only had been born in the colonies like his friend and mentor Carlisle, but unlike Carlisle had spent almost his entire career in the Americas. He was as remote from the niceties of the rules that governed the navy as any officer could be. Holbrooke could sense that Loring was out of his depth. He wasn't sure whether his authority stretched to demanding that a warrant officer should serve under him. As for the status of a chaplain, he had probably never come across such a creature in all his years of service. Loring must also know that an unwilling warrant officer could make his life difficult. The position of bosun so far from the rigging shops of the King's yards demanded trust both ways and retaining him against his will would not be a good start.

Loring opened his mouth to speak, then closed it. He

thought for a few moments more, then very deliberately stated his decision.

'Very well, Mister Holbrooke. Jackson may follow you if he chooses, and of course your chaplain.'

'Thank you, sir.'

Loring sighed.

'I'm relieved actually. I could see that Lynton is attached to you, and he is critical to my command. He's worth half a dozen bosuns and clerks and I wouldn't want to start by alienating him.'

He paused and looked out at the masts of the schooner that protruded above the fort's walls. She was riding happily to anchor, the visible manifestation of the command of at least this end of the lake.

'To tell you the truth, Holbrooke, I had expected to find nothing but a host of useless bateaux and whaleboats, but I find that you have done most of my work for me. I have a schooner; I have a crew of sorts and the French have learned to fear the British navy on Lake Ontario. In six months, I'll have a squadron here, and then next year we will own the lake. I believe I'll call it the Niagara Squadron, until their Lordships tell me otherwise.'

***

CHAPTER TWENTY-EIGHT

A Suitable Man

Saturday, Fourth of August 1759.
Bere House, Wickham.

Wickham was already a-bustle, with workers and businessmen, housewives and market traders striding, strolling and sauntering hither and thither. Soon it would grow warm and those whose business didn't require them to be out and about would retire to the relative cool of their houses and cottages, to wait out the heat of the day. For the next hour at least, the square would be a cheerful place, and yet a strange gloom hung over the substantial house near The King's Head at the northwest side. But that wasn't quite right; it wasn't exactly gloomy, it would be more accurate to say that the house and all in it were divided into two camps, and both awaited the events of the next hour with trepidation.

'Try not to look so serious, dear, anyone would think that you were nervous about our visitor today.'

Sophie tried not to laugh. She knew exactly why her husband was worried, but he'd brought it upon himself and she didn't feel inclined to be too accommodating.

'I'm not nervous,' Martin Featherstone replied, 'why should you think I'm nervous?'

He fiddled with the pot of strawberry jam from which he had been anointing his toast. He'd piled three teaspoons onto a single slice when normally he wasn't at all keen on sweet confections, and he didn't know how to fix the problem without drawing attention to his mistake. He considered putting the jam back in the pot, but Sophie had fixed ideas about that sort of thing and he already felt at a moral disadvantage.

'Polly,' he called. When the maidservant didn't immediately appear, he called louder, almost shouting.

'Polly!'

Polly appeared. She was nervous at the best of times and permanently frightened of the master of the house, although in truth he had never been particularly harsh with her. In fact, he normally left all dealings with the servants to his wife. The atmosphere in the house this morning had rattled what little composure Polly possessed, and now she was apt to stumble in her words and to drop things.

'I'll have two more slices of toast,' said Featherstone daring his wife to intervene.

'Two… two more slices,' Polly stammered, 'Yes sir,' and she fled to the kitchen.

Featherstone stared after her, following her progress by the sound of her tripping over the threshold and falling against the closed door of the drawing room. A muffled *Ouch* reached his ears.

'I could have taken some of that jam,' said Sophie, twisting the knife into his discomfort.

They sat in silence waiting for the toast. On any other morning, the sounds of the kitchen and the scullery would have provided a jolly background, but today the noises of the house were suppressed, as though nobody dared speak aloud. Even Featherstone's daughter, Ann, was silent, when normally she could be heard moving about the house. He found it depressing and was almost regretting the visitor that they were expecting in an hour.

'You know, dear, if the gentleman caller is disturbing you so, you really should consider whether it was wise to encourage him,' said Sophie, exactly paralleling her husband's thoughts. 'Ann doesn't wish to see him, I don't wish to see him, and you appear to be in some discomfort about the whole thing.'

'Dammit, Sophie. I wouldn't be in discomfort if the women in my house weren't so obstinate. Surely you can see the desirability of Ann receiving callers at her age, and there are so few eligible young men in this town that we must cast our net wider.'

Sophie didn't reply for a moment. Polly returned with the toast and Featherstone angrily pushed the plate away from him. He had no appetite. Sophie quietly took one of the slices and leaned across the table to scoop half of her husband's jam from his plate. Then she calmly spread the jam on the toast and took a bite. None of this did anything for Featherstone's temper. He felt – quite correctly as it happens – that he was being manipulated. From the very first moment – two days ago – that he had announced that James Carrington would be visiting, he had been made to feel like an ogre. He knew that he had been deliberately and systematically relegated to the moral low ground and he didn't enjoy the experience. He was Ann's father, after all, and yet her stepmother had manoeuvred herself into the position of her protector. It was infuriating.

Sophie wiped her lips with her napkin.

'But you know perfectly well that Ann already has a suitor. Captain Holbrooke will be home in a few months, and she can think of nothing else.'

Featherstone glared at his wife, then looked hastily away. He'd learned the hard way that confrontation with Sophie rarely turned out well for him. He took a deep breath.

'We've discussed this a hundred times, dear…'

'We certainly have,' she murmured, looking modestly down at the table and sighing heavily.

Featherstone chose to ignore her interruption.

'…your Captain Holbrooke is no captain at all, but a mere commander. I know from an unimpeachable source…'

Your retired post-captain in Soberton – God blast him – thought Sophie.

'…that the rank of commander is in no way the equivalent of a post-captain. Many commanders never make post and then they are doomed to a life on half pay. Half pay! Can you imagine it?'

'Yes, but from what I understand, *Captain* Holbrooke,' she laid heavy emphasis on the rank, 'is very likely to be promoted, possibly when he returns from America, and in any case he has made a great number of captures in this war, and his fortune from prize money is considerable.'

'Ah! But that assumes that he will even come home from America. That's one of my main objections to a sea officer, the hazards of his profession. We hear almost daily of officers being killed or maimed or thrown into captivity. Why, even your *Commander* Holbrooke has been wounded, and he's been a prisoner of the French. He was lucky to escape with his life from what I've heard. That kind of thing never happens to a solicitor in Alton. Certainly not to a solicitor who is the heir to a very substantial business, as Mister Carrington is. What can this Holbrooke show in the way of prospects? Granted, his father is a respectable man, but he has no fortune, no business to pass to his son. Then Holbrooke faces a future of unemployed half pay or, even worse, full pay with all the dangers and separation from his family that go with it.'

Featherstone leaned back in his chair, satisfied that by his own standards he had made an indisputable case. He had made that same case time and time again and, on every occasion, he had believed it indisputable.

'And Ann's feelings have no part in this?' Sophie replied softly, disputing the indisputable.

'Certainly Ann's feelings are to be considered. But she has met so few suitable young men. She may not like Carrington, but she may.'

He looked archly at his wife.

'She may, if we encourage her and point out the advantages of marriage to a man with prospects and with his feet solidly on *terra firma*.'

Featherstone looked triumphant, as though he had just won the point.

Sophie sighed again. There was nothing to be gained now that her husband had started quoting in Latin. Soon he'd be displaying his sketchy knowledge of Homer and then all hope of a sensible discussion would be lost. She folded her napkin and left the table with a barely polite curtsy, calling for Polly to clear the breakfast things before their visitor arrived.

***

Ann refused to cry. This had been the worst year of her life, with George away on the far side of the Atlantic and with her father determined to undermine their relationship. She understood his motives and knew that he was acting for her own good; at least, he thought he was. She rehearsed his arguments again in her mind and still could not find that they outweighed her love for George. The thought of meeting another man – more less marrying him – was almost more than she could bear. She stared miserably at the window where the bright morning sun was pouring in, until she heard a knock at the door, and her stepmother's soft voice. She smiled wanly as Sophie came in.

'You'll need to get ready, you know, Ann. However much you don't want to meet Mister Carrington, you must at least look like the gentlewoman that you are.'

'Father won't relent, then?' she asked.

'There was never any hope, Ann, you know that. But remember, however much your father may encourage you to be amiable to his eligible young men, he would never go so far as coercion.'

She tried to give her stepdaughter encouragement. They had a close relationship, more like sisters with a decade or so between them than mother and daughter.

'No, no there wasn't, no hope at all, and I know that he means well. I'll make myself up and meet Mister Carrington and be amiable, but I'll give him no encouragement. Oh, do you think George has my letter by now?'

Sophie looked guiltily at the door.

'Shush now, speak quietly.'

Ann nodded. As far as they knew Martin Featherstone had no idea that Ann had been corresponding with Holbrooke, against his firmly expressed advice. Sophie had paid a visit to William Holbrooke while her husband was out of town on business, and the retired sailing master had taken her letter and sent it on its way from Portsmouth. Sophie alone would never have been able to solve the mystery of sending a letter to a sea officer at an unknown location in the wilderness of North America.

The clock struck the half hour, a single silvery ting.

'He'll be here in no time Ann; come, let's get you ready. Your hair needs some work and then we can look at some rouge. You're not planning to wear those shoes with that dress, are you? No, no, the grey and white leather will set of the colours so much better. Now, where are they?'

That made Ann smile. Just about the only time that Sophie acted like a mother was when she was criticizing her dress sense.

Sophie stepped back and looked at Ann.

'Now, give me a twirl. That's right. This Mister Carrington must be sent away knowing what a beauty he has lost. It's all about pride, my dear. Now, chin up, shoulders back and let's await the call.'

***

The problem was, as Ann had to admit, that were it not for her existing attachment, James Carrington would have been a most suitable man. She had to admit it to herself and even to Sophie, but not by word or gesture to her father. He was perhaps five years or so older than her, handsome – some would say *very* handsome – and he was polite and interesting to converse with. He had great prospects as a solicitor in his own right and would inherit his father's law business in due course. Ironically, James' career was the one that George had wanted before he achieved success as a sea officer; he had revealed as much to Ann on one of their long walks beside the Meon. It was only a lack of family funding that had prevented him continuing his education at a university to acquire the necessary qualification.

Ann wondered what had moved James to call on her. What had drawn him to this little town and to a corn merchant's daughter? As always, it was Sophie who had ferreted out the information. Apparently, she was spoken of for some miles around as a potential wife. She would inherit a modest fortune when her father died and there would be a substantial dowry in the meantime. A daughter of the nobility was beyond the aspiration of an Alton solicitor, but Ann, with her looks, her fortune and a good temperament, was an achievable prize.

They had talked politely, but not intimately. Ann had given little away about herself, and in the end James must have realised that however affable Ann was being, she really was not interested in him as a suitor. He left a disappointed man and made no promises of a return visit.

***

Martin Featherstone strode out of the house. He'd lost a morning at work and he now knew that it was utterly wasted, and to a man so dedicated to making money as he was, that was an irredeemable sin. It had been futile from the start. In the face of his daughter's doggedness and his wife's collusion, he was powerless. Well, he had one card left to play. He was damned if he would agree to a match until this Holbrooke should be made a real captain. That would take away one of his objections. The sheer unsuitability of a sea officer as a husband would still presumably remain, and he couldn't reasonably use that as a reason to withhold his consent, but until he saw Holbrooke's name in the Gazette, there would be no marriage.

Sophie and Ann sat quietly in the garden, shaded from the fierce midday sun by the tall house at their back. They could hear snatchers of laughter from the inn just a few yards away as the apprentices and working men celebrated their half-day holiday.

'Well, I don't believe we'll see him again,' said Sophie, reaching for Ann's hand. She was worried about her stepdaughter, she looked pale and strained after the meeting, as though she had used all her emotional energy to both appear pleasant and yet leave the caller in no doubt of his prospects.

'I hope I'll never have to endure such a meeting again,' Ann replied, 'and yet I don't believe father has given up hope, has he?'

'Oh, he's discouraged for now, but in a few weeks, he'll try again, I don't doubt. You must just remain as resolute as you were today. It really was a most admirable performance. You should have seen Mister Carrington's face when he left, he was thoroughly confused! He couldn't understand why you didn't fall for his charms'

'He is a very pleasant man, any girl would be lucky to have him call on her,' Ann replied. 'Just not me.'

'You are truly determined to wait for George, aren't you?' asked Sophie looking earnestly into Ann's face.

'Yes. Yes, I am. Oh, I don't want to appear overly romantic, like a character in one of those new novels, but I truly believe that George is the man for me. George and no other.'

Sophie paused, carefully phrasing her response.

'You know, don't you, that you will be getting a reputation for being – how can I put this? – unattainable. You know what I mean, don't you?'

'I'm burning my bridges. Yes, I know that. But still I'll wait for George.'

Neither woman mentioned the obvious fact of Ann's age; Sophie out of sensitivity and Ann out of a refusal to heap up objections to her determination. In three months, she would be twenty.

'And you know the hazards of the life of a sea officer? I don't want to alarm you, but Captain Holbrooke is in one of the most dangerous parts of the world, and you must be prepared in case he doesn't come back.'

Ann stared blankly across the garden. On the brick wall at the end she had encouraged a particularly beautiful purple wisteria to climb up a trellis and then horizontally along the top. It survived each winter and every year it became stronger with a tighter grip on the trellis and wall. A metaphor for her devotion.

'I know,' said Ann squeezing Sophie's hand, 'I know.'

***

CHAPTER TWENTY-NINE

The Admiralty

Monday, Twenty-Fourth of September 1759.
The Admiralty, London.

It was clear that Holbrooke's party would travel swifter than the fastest messenger and so he was entrusted with dispatches from both the army and the navy. That was the excuse for using *Mohawk* to take them as far as Oswego. It was one of the most pleasant passages that Holbrooke could remember and yet it was bitter-sweet. He and his five companions had left England together; they had endured the wilderness, the lakes, the rivers, the forests and the enemy together, and now they were parting. They had much to talk about as they sped with the wind along the southern shore of the lake. At Oswego Holbrooke, Chalmers, Jackson and Kanatase said their farewells and took a bateau with a crew of New Englanders up the Onondaga River. They crossed again the beautiful Lake Oneida, struggled up Wood Creek and so to the portage and Fort Stanwix.

The parting with Lynton and Serviteur had been hard, but at least there was a probability of their paths crossing again, either in the Americas or at home. Kanatase was a different case. Holbrooke was itching to move on, but he spent a night at Fort Stanwix – a night he could ill-afford – to speak with the proud Mohawk warrior. They had become friends, and it was unlikely that they would meet again. The moon had set with the sun, yet they talked until the last light of the stars was extinguished by a band of cloud from the west which brought with it a brisk shower.

***

The bateau had pushed off into the flow of the Mohawk River before the sun had appeared above the forest, and yet Kanatase was there, standing on an outcrop of rock solemnly watching their departure and sending them on their way with a loud whoop.

They had caught up with Massey and the French prisoners at Fort Stanwix but soon left them far behind as they sped down the Mohawk River to Schenectady. From there a small schooner not unlike *Mohawk* took them down the mighty Hudson to New York.

There were no frigates or sloops sailing for England. Everything was still going north to Halifax and beyond to the Saint Lawrence where General Wolfe was trying to persuade Montcalm to meet him in the field. Holbrooke used the time to have his uniforms overhauled by a tailor; they had suffered badly in the forests and were in no fit state to be seen on the steps of the Admiralty in London. Despairing of a King's ship, after five days they took a regular packet to Falmouth and then a coasting sloop to Portsmouth.

It was raining as they worked through the Spithead anchorage – it was always raining in Portsmouth – and by the time Holbrooke reached the port admiral's office he was soaked through. There was some bemusement when he told his tale. Few had heard of the Niagara campaign, overshadowed as it was by Quebec, and nobody seemed aware that a sea officer had accompanied the army on that expedition through the wilderness. Nevertheless, a post chaise was summoned and within two hours of landing Holbrooke was speeding up the London Road, having left Chalmers and Jackson to find lodgings in Portsmouth.

***

It may have been raining in Portsmouth, but that was nothing to the downpour in London. It reminded Holbrooke of the afternoon rain in the tropics: the streets were like streams and the smell of warm, liquified horse dung filled the air. The day had grown late when Holbrooke paid the driver at the steps of the admiralty, but it was still daylight and he could see that there was activity in the building. He left his trunk with one of the porters, and having sent up a note, he waited to see whether he would be admitted, clutching his package of dispatches to his chest.

He'd only been there five minutes but through the malign influence of fatigue and nervous exhaustion he was already falling asleep. He dimly noticed a porter looking around at the half dozen unknown sea officers, each of whom sat up expectantly, but not Holbrooke who had convinced himself that he was in for a long wait. He was startled to see the porter approach him.

'The first secretary will see you now, sir,' said the porter.

Holbrooke shook himself awake. It would never do to march into the first secretary's office looking as though he'd been caught napping. And as all sea officers knew, the first secretary was the gate-guard for their Lordships, he could find himself in front of Anson within minutes. That thought brought him back to reality with a start.

'Captain Holbrooke, how good to see you! You've returned unscathed I see. What news from Niagara?'

Well, at least he'd heard of the damned campaign. Holbrooke had been starting to think that it was all a dream and that no sea officer had fought with the army at that furthest outpost of civilisation.

'Fort Niagara is ours, sir. I have Sir William's dispatches here as well as my own and Captain Loring's. Would it be possible to send Sir William's package over to Horse Guards?'

'Sir William?' Clevland looked surprised. 'We heard that Prideaux was killed, that must be Sir William Johnson, the Mohawk Baronet.'

'That's correct and I believe these are the first dispatches since the fall of Niagara,' he said offering the heavy packages.

Clevland rang a bell beside his desk and a porter appeared before the last tinkle had faded.

'They'll be glad to read these, Holbrooke. You must walk over there tomorrow and present yourself, it's too late now. The army doesn't keep navy time you know. I'm sure they'll have something amiable to say to you.'

Cleveland looked at the clock.

'The first lord isn't here this evening, but we can see Admiral Forbes in fifteen minutes. Now, how did the navy acquit itself in the campaign?'

***

Admiral Forbes greeted Holbrooke warmly. He looked as though he hadn't moved since the last time that Holbrooke met him. He was still the same gruff, formidable old sea-dog, but as Holbrooke studied him, he thought he could detect a new avuncular attitude. He'd always believed that Forbes had a partiality for him, even when his promotion hadn't happened, and even when he was cast into the outer darkness of the Niagara campaign.

'You're back sooner than I'd expected, Commander Holbrooke, bringing news from the wilderness, I trust?' he asked without any hint of a smile. Perhaps he was expecting the worst.

'Fort Niagara has fallen, sir. The French have withdrawn to Frontenac and we have a schooner on Lake Ontario.'

It was best to get the main points out first, then he could fill in the details at leisure. Forbes cracked a thin smile.

'Now, I must say that is good news and we haven't had much recently. The latest from Admiral Saunders isn't encouraging. The army is taking altogether too long to get ashore and deal with Quebec, and Amherst is moving as slowly as he dare. Hawke is hoping to lure out the Brest fleet, of course, but so far, they're consulting their ease and probably waiting for the season to be over so that they can decently give up the enterprise. Are you the first to bring the news?'

'I was certainly the first to reach New York. Possibly the news came from there faster, but I took the first packet and came straight here.'

Forbes paused in thought.

'Well, I've heard nothing at all. Let's get this to the King immediately, before some damned soldier beats us to it.

Clevland, would you draft a note? You know the form, just tell him the minimum: great victory, the road to the west has been opened, the navy secured the army's passage across the lake, Sir William is in residence at Fort Niagara. And request an audience tomorrow. Lord Anson must know, of course. He's at his town house now, so send a copy of the note to him.'

Clevland bowed and left the room, calling for the duty clerk as he did so.

'Now Holbrooke, tell me the details. Is that your best coat? I expect you've been dragging that through rivers and swamps. Still, it lends an air of authenticity.'

Holbrooke looked down at his coat. The tailor in New York had done is best in the short time that he was allowed, but the coat had certainly seen better days; he would need a new outfit if he was given another ship. He took a deep breath and told his tale. He'd determined that it was best to be perfectly frank about the circumstances of the loss of the first schooner *Mohawk*, and he watched carefully for Forbes' response, but the admiral just brushed it aside.

'You've done your duty in telling me, Holbrooke, but let's not dwell upon it. The schooner was never formally commissioned so there's no loss to the service. This Lieutenant Lynton did well, I remember he was your first in Kestrel.'

'He did, sir, and he's an acting commander now, Captain Loring gave him his commission before I left.'

'Ah yes. Captain Loring. We had to give him *carte blanche* to make promotions otherwise there'd have been no progress before the next campaign season. I'm relieved to hear that he's using his powers wisely; let's hope he continues to do so.'

Now, was there some hint of doubt about Loring's judgement? Holbrooke had barely heard the name before the man himself appeared at Niagara, perhaps it was just his imagination.

'We'll confirm Mister Lynton's rank of course, but he

may have to stay on the lakes for some time. Next year should see a whole squadron of our own brigs and schooners sailing from Niagara, then the French will feel the pinch.'

This is the moment that Forbes could at least allude to the possibility of Holbrooke's gazetting. It would be perfectly normal, after his first lieutenant was promoted, but the admiral said nothing.

'It's late, Captain Holbrooke, and you'll need your wits about you tomorrow. Meet me here at eight o'clock and when we have heard from the palace, I'll take you over to Horse Guards. It's of the utmost importance that we don't give the army a chance to bring the news before we do.'

***

His lodgings were noisy and hot, and Holbrooke slept fitfully, tossing and turning with dreams – nightmares almost – of being presented to the King. He had no idea of the protocol, or even whether he was likely to see the King himself. Wasn't it more probable that he'd tell his story to some equerry? He woke with the dawn and spent the remains of the morning watch working on his coat. How he missed Serviteur! His servant would have worked his magic and had him turned out spotlessly, for the honour of the ship and the service. But there was no servant and there was no ship, and Holbrooke felt like a vagabond when he stepped out towards the admiralty. New York's outfitters could provide shoes, breeches, stockings, shirts and even a hat, but not even the fastest tailor could work up a uniform coat and waistcoat in less than a week, not even if they owned a Navy Board pattern, and none had yet been sent to the colonies.

The porter had clearly been waiting for him.

'The first lord will see you now, Captain Holbrooke,' he said in a dry, toneless voice, turning to lead the way without any sign of human feelings.

Lord Anson was in his office talking earnestly to Admiral Forbes over a small table, untidy with coffee cups and papers. Evidently Anson stood on no ceremony on this his home ground and Holbrooke was ushered in without formality. This was a significant moment in his career. Sea officers went a lifetime without meeting the first lord in person, and he was deeply conscious of the sense of occasion. Holbrooke had only a moment to form an impression before he was pointed to the third seat around the table.

George Anson was in his sixties. He'd guided the navy for the past eight years, right through the present war, and he was at the peak of his abilities. He wore the imposing dress uniform of an admiral and a short wig that had become popular in recent years. He inspected Holbrooke with an appraising eye.

'This is the man who gave Emden to Holmes as a free gift,' Anson said, smiling. 'I regret that I haven't had the pleasure of meeting you before, Commander Holbrooke, but Admiral Forbes has told me about your career. Minorca, Cape Francois, Emden and Saint-Cast! You have had an eventful war for a commander.'

Holbrooke nodded cautiously. He didn't like this emphasis on the rank of commander, it sounded too permanent. Anson must know that each commander he spoke to was analysing his every word for some hint of his prospects of promotion. Or had he forgotten the sinking, powerless feeling of time slipping by and watching others being promoted, while he waited in growing despair?

'Now, we don't have much time so tell me briefly about Niagara, and your part in its downfall. You already know the importance of describing the navy's role, but I want to be sure that you say the right things in the War Office and when we meet the King.'

It was a trying half hour. Either Anson or Forbes interrupted at almost every sentence, offering advice on how to present the campaign in the best light for the navy. Holbrooke was increasingly aware of the poverty of his uniform, of his general appearance of personal neglect. This was the summit of his career so far, and he felt emotionally unprepared. He clasped his hands firmly to prevent himself from fidgeting as he spoke. But all torments come to an end, and a knock at the door reminded Anson that he must leave soon if he was to visit Horse Guards before his audience.

***

It was ridiculous to take a carriage the few steps down Whitehall, but it would have been even more ridiculous for the three of them to walk, so it was by carriage that Holbrooke first visited Horse Guards. It was a whirlwind visit. Anson had orchestrated it so that they had only a brief half hour to spare before they had to leave for their audience with the King.

Field Marshall Viscount Ligonier made a poor attempt at hiding his chagrin at being told of the victory at Niagara in this way. He came close to demanding that he join Anson when he visited the King but bit his lip before risking a damaging rebuff. He had to be content with Sir William's dispatches and Holbrooke's brief account. It all passed in a blur for Holbrooke and then they were back in the carriage and bowling along Pall Mall to St James Palace.

'Well, that went rather well, Holbrooke,' said Anson. 'Ligonier can't possibly get to the King before we do, and in any case, he wasn't there, and you were. You can't imagine the importance of being the first to bring news of a victory to the King. The army had all the glory with Minden last month, but since then Boscawen's victory at Lagos has set the bells ringing. This will put us ahead, and there is still a hope that Hawke will catch the French fleet before the year's end.'

The carriage swung off the road in front of St James Palace, rattling on the paving stones and sending up bright sprays where the rainwater hadn't yet drained away. The palace was an imposing if rather old-fashioned building that dominated this end of the wide Pall Mall. It was built of red brick in stark contrast to the Portland stone that was the current London fashion. Two tall octagonal towers flanked a wide arched gate with a large clock face above it. Hawkers and shoe-shine boys, flower sellers and sedan chairs all jostled for space in front of the palace. I seemed a most unlikely place for the King and titular ruler of a vast empire to be residing, more like a busy and prosperous market square.

The carriage continued through the gate without pausing and the soldiers on sentry duty slapped their hands to their muskets in salute as the officer in charge removed his hat. Evidently the first lord's carriage was well known.

Holbrooke had seen the palace from outside on a previous visit to London, but he hadn't been through the gates into the inner courtyard. Ordinary members of the public never came this close to the reigning monarch's official residence. He looked around with interest. Here the flagstones had been dried and where the water had refused to drain away, rushes had been placed so that visitors might arrive dry-shod. Noisy London was left behind and there was an air of ordered calm that was lacking in the bustling street outside.

They were ushered into a large room where small groups of people were gathered seemingly awaiting an audience with the King. Anson stared intently around, nodding here and there to acquaintances and bowing to one enormously fat person in bright court garments.

'I had half expected Ligonier to have sent one of his staffers to hold a place, but it appears that we have stolen a march on him,' Anson said, still inspecting the company. 'I don't expect we'll have long to wait; His Majesty usually makes time to hear about victories.'

Holbrooke noticed how the first lord's conversation had become more formal now that he was away from the Admiralty. Now it was *His Majesty*, rather than *the King*. Even he had to mind his manners at the Court of St James.

There was no refreshment on offer and the groups of people chatted together while they waited. Some had a confident and assured manner, while others looked uneasy, as though they were unfamiliar with the protocol. Just like Holbrooke in fact. Anson glanced sideways at him as though reading his mind.

'It's quite simple, Holbrooke, you don't have a hat to worry about and all that's required is a low bow. And remember, never to turn your back on the monarch. Showing the rump is His Majesty's prerogative and it's unlikely to happen to us, not today at least.'

Holbrooke had heard something of this manner of showing the King's disapproval but had hardly believed it to be true. It seemed like such a gross breach of normal everyday good manners to turn one's back on a visitor.

A plainly dressed man in a black suit with just a very few discreet gold trimmings approached them, a chamberlain or something, Holbrooke guessed.

'His Majesty will speak with your Lordship first,' he said, bowing solemnly.

'And when may I retire?' Anson replied.

'His Majesty is aware of the duties of his First Lord of the Admiralty and would be pleased if you would remain in the hall until he has spoken to two further groups,' the chamberlain replied. 'I will indicate when you may leave.'

Anson grunted in reply. Holbrooke would have been interested to know how long he had expected to be detained. Was this a longer period or a shorter period? Would all these others have to remain until the audience was finished?

Holbrooke didn't have long to wait. A pair of great polished doors at the end of the hall were swung open by two liveried footmen who then stood perfectly still. The chatter ended abruptly as King George the Second entered and walked straight towards them.

Holbrooke watched Anson out of the corner of his eye. When the first lord bowed, he did likewise, and when he straightened up Holbrooke waited two further seconds and followed him.

'Now then my Lord, what is this you have to tell me

about Fort Niagara? I'm intrigued that a sea officer should be bringing the news.'

'Victory, your Majesty. The army was carried across Lake Ontario by Commander Holbrooke's boats. Fort Niagara is in our hands and the French navy has retreated to the far end of the lake.'

Holbrooke noticed how cleverly Anson kept the navy in the forefront of the report. No doubt if Ligonier had come here first, he would have emphasised the army's role. More than that, the navy probably wouldn't have been mentioned at all.

'That's excellent news. If Amherst and Wolfe can show similar progress, we'll have the French out of America by next year. Now, Commander Holbrooke, please describe the expedition as succinctly as you can.'

Holbrooke felt strangely at ease now that the first shock at being presented to the King had passed. He had rehearsed his story and told it well and fluently. The King only interrupted at a few key points. He was interested in the taking of the French schooners and in the death of Prideaux and showed a keen understanding of the battle at La Belle Famille. He was after all a soldier himself and had led an army to victory at Dettingen.

'A most creditable affair, Commander Holbrooke, and I understand there is a post-captain at Niagara now, isn't that so my Lord?'

Now, did he look meaningfully at Anson while he emphasised Holbrooke's rank and the rank of his successor. That may not be a good thing, Anson was known for his refusal to be influenced by political considerations or family interest in naval promotions.

'Yes sir, Captain Loring will supervise the building of a squadron and then we can rid the lake of the French navy.'

'Well, as I said, most creditable and I'm pleased to see the navy and the army cooperating so harmoniously. Ah, there's Ligonier, I wonder what he has to tell me? Well, he'll have to wait,' he said glancing at his chamberlain.

The audience was over, and Anson and Holbrooke bowed low as the King passed on to the next group. They didn't speak to Ligonier and after ten minutes the chamberlain nodded significantly in their direction.

'We can go now, Holbrooke,' Anson said turning carefully to avoid rumping the King. 'Now, let's get back to Whitehall. I have something more to discuss with you.'

***

CHAPTER THIRTY

An Unfinished Sentence

Saturday, Twenty-Ninth of September 1759.
Bere House, Wickham.

Martin Featherstone held the calling card in his hand and turned it over as if attempting to glean additional information from the few sparse words, glaring at it all the while.

Captain Holbrooke requests the honour of calling on Mister Featherstone on Saturday at twelve o'clock.

Now what the devil was this all about? He'd made clear his objections and had hoped to hear nothing more from this persistent young man. His first instinct was to send a flat refusal, but then he thought again. Holbrooke had become something of a local hero in Wickham and people spoke of him as someone who would become important when the war was over. Some even spoke of a seat in parliament, although that was preposterous. Was it wise to dismiss his request? And then again, he had always described himself as *Commander Holbrooke*, it was only others who gave him the courtesy rank of captain. Had he been promoted? Featherstone had heard nothing and if it were known in London and Portsmouth then the town would have heard, and he would certainly have been aware. Perhaps Holbrooke was just taking on airs and graces. On balance he decided that he must see the man, but it was irritating, and with only an hour before he arrived there was no time for enquiries.

'Polly, Polly! Where's the damned girl?'

Polly appeared before Featherstone's voice had ceased ringing through the corridors and rooms. She had heard about the note – it wasn't covered or sealed – and she was already dressed for outdoors.

Featherstone finished his reply. It was as terse as he dared without being rude. It offered Holbrooke the favour of a call but contrived to appear that Featherstone's time on a Saturday was precious. That was of course untrue. As Holbrooke well knew, he was in the habit of completing his work by 11 o'clock and taking his ease for the rest of the day.

'Take this to the Holbrooke cottage,' he said. 'Don't run, it's not important. You do know the Holbrooke cottage?'

'Yes, sir,' Polly replied with a curtsy.

She had known where Holbrooke's father lived from the first time that Ann had mentioned him. Polly lived for gossip, and the romantic liaisons of the daughter of the house offered a rich seam of interesting material. Yes, she would hurry to the cottage, but not before she'd quickly told Ann about her errand.

***

'You've heard, then, Ann,' said Sophie.

She'd found her stepdaughter in the garden, seated on a bench in the warmth of the late summer sun. From there she had no chance of being seen by a visitor, she could think her own thoughts and brood on her unhappy state.

'Yes,' Ann replied in a distracted way twirling the stalk of a nondescript flower – a weed perhaps – between her fingers.

'And will you not make yourself presentable? You still have forty-five minutes, and you know how punctual these navy people are.'

'Oh, what's the point?' Ann replied despondently. 'Father will just refuse to let him see me; he's made that clear. I'm beginning to believe that for George's sake I must break off our letter-writing and forget about him.'

'But think, Ann. George knows your father's position very well. I can only believe that something has changed. Perhaps he is leaving the navy and coming ashore. You know that he has sufficient fortune now to live as a gentleman should…'

'But that won't be enough for Father,' Ann interrupted, 'You know that he's holding out for something more substantial…'

'I know. He and I have discussed it until we grew hoarse with talking. There's another possibility, of course. He could have been promoted. That would answer your father's principal objection.'

'It can't be so. Father read the gazette only two days ago; I read it myself and his name wasn't there.'

'Nevertheless, Ann, I must insist that you put on a clean dress and allow me to brush your hair again, for the honour of the household if nothing else. If you don't see George then nothing is lost, but if you do see him you really must look your best. Come, Polly won't be back for a while,' she refrained from pointing out that Polly would be busily spreading the gossip around the town, 'so I'll help you.'

***

Dressed in her best, her hair brushed and with a hint of rouge to hide her pallor, Ann once again found the bench in the garden. She heard the bustle of a visitor arriving at the same moment as the clock in the square chimed the hour. She heard her father's loud voice and the more moderate tones of the visitor. Try as she might, she couldn't recognise Holbrooke's voice; it could have been anybody, one of the tenant farmers haggling over the price for his crop or the pastor looking for a subscription for the poor. Time passed; she heard the half-hour struck. Now she could hear her mother's voice. Had the visitor left without her knowing? Her heart missed a beat then skipped erratically through the next three or four. She tried to look composed, as though the result of the interview was of no concern to her.

'Mister Featherstone wishes to see you, Miss,' said Polly who had timed her return to the house to a nicety so that she missed nothing of the unfolding drama. She had crept into the garden so quietly that Ann hadn't been aware of her presence.

'Captain Holbrooke is with him,' she added in a conspiratorial whisper.

Ann ignored her. Normally they shared intimacies quite freely, but Ann had used up all the emotional strength that she had, and it was all she could do to walk without staggering like a drunk.

'Shoulders back, Miss. Captain Holbrooke won't want to see you looking unhappy.'

That shook Ann. She realised that she was acting like a nervous child, and if even Polly was emboldened to correct her, she must be sadly astray in her wits. She stopped so abruptly that Polly bumped into her.

'Beg pardon, Miss,' she said.

Ann paused for a half-dozen heartbeats. She straightened herself, tucked a stray whisp of her behind her ear and marched boldly forward. If this was the end, then she would face it with fortitude.

'Miss Featherstone, sir,' said Polly in a formal tone, holding open the door and offering a curtsey to the master of the house.

The image of that scene in the drawing room would be seared inro Ann's memory. The first thing she saw was her father seated in the big leather chair looking stern. Then she saw Holbrooke, standing, smiling confidently, and then there was a blur of movement as Sophie left her seat and clasped her hand.

Then her father forced a smile.

'Captain Holbrooke has done me the honour, Ann, of being the first person in Wickham to know that he has been promoted to post-captain. His appointment will appear in today's Gazette. I am happy to say that...'

But poor Martin Featherstone never did finish his sentence. He was firmly and swiftly guided from the room by his wife as Ann flung herself sobbing into her sailor's arms.

***

HISTORICAL EPILOGUE

Fort Niagara

One has only to scan a map of North America then stand on the parapets of the restored Fort Niagara and look across the river to the Canadian side to understand why the French attached such importance to this lonely outpost. Canada had been occupied and claimed by France for a hundred-and-fifty years at the start of the seven years war, but the vast majority of French settlements were in the lands surrounding the Saint Lawrence River and Lake Ontario. Beyond Lake Ontario movement had necessarily to be by boat, and that meant passing up the Niagara River, portaging around the falls and eventually coming to Lake Erie, from where the western Great Lakes and the Ohio Valley were open to exploration and settlement. In the eighteenth century, whoever owned the estuary of the Niagara River owned the hinterland of the American continent. The loss of Fort Niagara really was the death-knell of the centuries-old dream of New France.

I have faithfully retold the story of the siege of Fort Niagara, except where I have introduced Holbrooke and his followers, and the Mohawk Kanatase. The siege is true to the historical record; Prideaux did die after incautiously stepping in front of a mortar and the battle of La Belle Famille happened much as I have reported.

***

The Dream of New France

With Fort Oswego re-occupied and Fort Niagara secured, the French were forced to withdraw to the headwaters of the Saint Lawrence, ceding control of the lake to the British. Quebec would fall a bare three weeks after Fort Niagara and the brilliant general the Marquis de Montcalm would fall with it, effectively isolating New

France from the mother country across the Atlantic. New France could only communicate with Versailles by the most arduous and uncertain means, and there was no question of material support reaching the colony.

The French in Montreal, with their supply line to France severed and their best general dead, could have been forgiven for thinking it was all over for New France. Yet, with commanders such as the Marquis de Vaudreuil, the Chevalier de Lévis and the Chevalier de Bougainville, and the remains of an army in Montreal, there was still hope. As the Saint Lawrence thawed in the spring of 1760, it would be a race between a British relief force and the advance of the French downriver from Montreal.

***

Annus Mirabilis

1759 became known in Britain as the *Annus Mirabilis*, the Wonderful Year. In North America, the French had been defeated at Quebec and Fort Niagara. In Europe, the Battle of Minden had secured Hanover for another year. In the West Indies, the important sugar island of Guadeloupe had been captured. While at sea, the Battles of Lagos Bay and Quiberon Bay had ended French plans of invasion of England and had reduced the French navy to a hollow shell. The sea routes of the world were in the hands of the British navy. The seemingly endless succession of triumphs led to the famous remark: *Our bells are worn threadbare with ringing for victories.*

***

French Despair

The future of New France hung by a thread at the end of 1759, and it proved to be a financial disaster for Versailles, with the government cancelling its debts and the merchants losing heavily. In response to the financial crisis, the budget for the French army fighting in Europe was cut by more than a third. Pitt's grand strategy was vindicated, and its success in faraway North America produced tangible results on the battlefields of Germany and Flanders.

***

Where Fact Meets Fiction

One of the well-established strategies for developing the plot for a period novel is to look for gaps in the historical narrative and fill them with the exploits of one's own characters. Most of what we know of the defenders' perspective of the siege of Fort Niagara comes from Pierre Pouchot's *Memoir Upon the Late War in North America*. His is an exhaustive and partisan account, and it's hard to resist the impression that it was written principally to justify Monsieur Pouchot's actions. Clearly inter-service rivalry was not (and is still not) confined to the British forces.

The gap in the narrative that I exploited is the barely-credible failure of the French brigs on Lake Ontario to spot the British invasion flotilla as it coasted along from Oswego to Niagara. A determined attack while the bateaux and whaleboats were vulnerable and defenceless on the lake would surely have caused the destruction of Brigadier General Prideaux' army before it ever appeared before the walls of the fort. This was compounded by a near-complete absence of an attempt to interfere with the siege when the French navy still had mastery of the lake and could enfilade the right flank of the siege lines.

Then there is the apparent disregard of the French naval threat by the British planners. I spent a year with the British army learning the staff work of military operations and I am convinced that Prideaux would have made some plans to neutralise those brigs before committing his army to the lake. To do otherwise would have been to court disaster.

These were my gaps in the historical narrative; and what handy gaps for a writer of naval adventures! The principle of a sea officer supporting a land advance was already well-established. In the early years of the war Lieutenant Charles Spendlow and thirty-two seamen accompanied Braddock's expedition to Fort Duquesne. Evidently the fort on the forks of the Ohio was only the initial objective because Spendlow carried ironwork, cordage and sails to build a sixty-ton armed vessel on the lakes. However, he lost his life at some point during or after the disastrous defeat at Monongahela and the fate of his seamen is not recorded.

That is how George Holbrooke and his followers came to accompany the expedition to Fort Niagara. I hope you'll agree that it is a more plausible story than the uncharacteristic ineptitude of the French navy that Pierre Pouchot left for us. They're better than that.

***

OTHER CARLISLE & HOLBROOKE NAVAL ADVENTURES

Book 1: The Colonial Post-Captain

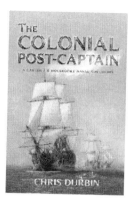

Captain Carlisle of His Britannic Majesty's frigate *Fury* hails from Virginia, a loyal colony of the British Crown. In 1756, as the clouds of war gather in Europe, *Fury* is ordered to Toulon to investigate a French naval and military build-up.

While battling the winter weather, Carlisle must also juggle with delicate diplomatic issues in this period of phoney war and contend with an increasingly belligerent French frigate.

And then there is the beautiful Chiara Angelini, pursued across the Mediterranean by a Tunisian corsair who appears determined to abduct her, yet strangely reluctant to shed blood.

Carlisle and his young master's mate, George Holbrooke, are witnesses to the inconclusive sea-battle that leads to the loss of Minorca. They engage in a thrilling and bloody encounter with the French frigate and a final confrontation with the enigmatic corsair.

***

Chris Durbin

Book 2: The Leeward Islands Squadron

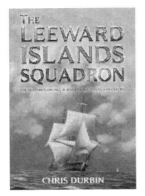

In late 1756, as the British government collapses in the aftermath of the loss of Minorca and the country and navy are thrown into political chaos, a small force of ships is sent to the West Indies to reinforce the Leeward Islands Squadron.

Captain Edward Carlisle, a native of Virginia, and his first lieutenant George Holbrooke are fresh from the Mediterranean and their capture of a powerful French man-of-war. Their new frigate *Medina* has orders to join a squadron commanded by a terminally ill commodore. Their mission: a near-suicidal assault on a strong Caribbean island fortress. Carlisle must confront the challenges of higher command as he leads the squadron back into battle to accomplish the Admiralty's orders.

Join Carlisle and Holbrooke as they attack shore fortifications, engage in ship-on-ship duels and deal with mutiny in the West Indies.

***

310

Book 3: The Jamaica Station

It is 1757, and the British navy is regrouping from a slow start to the seven years war.

A Spanish colonial governor and his family are pursued through the Caribbean by a pair of mysterious ships from the Dutch island of St. Eustatius. The British frigate *Medina* rescues the governor from his hurricane-wrecked ship, leading Captain Edward Carlisle and his first lieutenant George Holbrooke into a web of intrigue and half-truths. Are the Dutchmen operating under a letter of marque or are they pirates, and why are they hunting the Spaniard? Only the diplomatic skills of Carlisle's aristocratic wife, Lady Chiara, can solve the puzzle.

When Carlisle is injured, the young Holbrooke must grow up quickly. Under his leadership, *Medina* takes part in a one-sided battle with the French that will influence a young Horatio Nelson to choose the navy as a career.

***

Book 4: Holbrooke's Tide

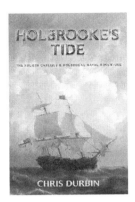

It is 1758, and the Seven Years War is at its height. The Duke of Cumberland's Hanoverian army has been pushed back to the River Elbe while the French are using the medieval fortified city of Emden to resupply their army and to anchor its left flank.

George Holbrooke has recently returned from the Jamaica Station in command of a sloop-of-war. He is under orders to survey and blockade the approaches to Emden in advance of the arrival of a British squadron. The French garrison and their Austrian allies are nervous. With their supply line cut, they are in danger of being isolated when the French army is forced to retreat in the face of the new Prussian-led army that is gathering on the Elbe. Can the French be bluffed out of Emden? Is this Holbrooke's flood tide that will lead to his next promotion?

Holbrooke's Tide is the fourth of the Carlisle & Holbrooke naval adventures. The series follows the exploits of the two men through the Seven Years War and into the period of turbulent relations between Britain and her American colonies in the 1760s.

***

Book 5: The Cursed Fortress

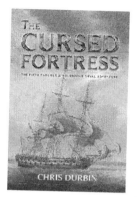

The French called it *La Forteresse Maudite*, the Cursed Fortress.

Louisbourg stood at the mouth of the Gulf of St. Lawrence, massive and impregnable, a permanent provocation to the British colonies. It was Canada's first line of defence, guarding the approaches to Quebec, from where all New France lay open to invasion. It had to fall before a British fleet could be sent up the St. Lawrence. Otherwise, there would be no resupply and no line of retreat; Canada would become the graveyard of George II's navy.

A failed attempt on Louisbourg in 1757 had only stiffened the government's resolve; the Cursed Fortress must fall in 1758.

Captain Carlisle's frigate joins the blockade of Louisbourg before winter's icy grip has eased. Battling fog, hail, rain, frost and snow, suffering scurvy and fevers, and with a constant worry about the wife he left behind in Virginia, Carlisle will face his greatest test of leadership and character yet.

The Cursed Fortress is the fifth of the Carlisle & Holbrooke naval adventures. The series follows the two men through the Seven Years War and into the period of turbulent relations between Britain and her American colonies in the 1760s.

***

Book 6: Perilous Shore

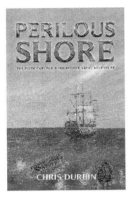

Amphibious warfare was in its infancy in the mid-eighteenth century – it was the poor relation of the great fleet actions that the navy so loved.

That all changed in 1758 when the British government demanded a campaign of raids on the French Channel ports. Command arrangements were hastily devised, and a whole new class of vessels was produced at breakneck speed: flatboats, the ancestors of the landing craft that put the allied forces ashore on D-Day.

Commander George Holbrooke's sloop *Kestrel* is in the thick of the action: scouting landing beaches, duelling with shore batteries and battling the French Navy.

In a twist of fate, Holbrooke finds himself unexpectedly committed to this new style of amphibious warfare as he is ordered to lead a division of flatboats onto the beaches of Normandy and Brittany. He meets his greatest test yet when a weary and beaten British army retreats from a second failed attempt at Saint Malo with the French close on their heels.

Perilous Shore is the sixth of the Carlisle & Holbrooke naval adventures. The series follows Holbrooke and his mentor, Captain Carlisle, through the Seven Years War and into the period of turbulent relations between Britain and her American colonies in the 1760s.

***

Book 7: Rocks and Shoal

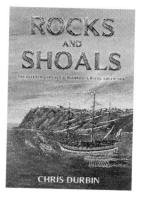

With the fall of Louisbourg in 1758 the French in North America were firmly on the back foot. Pitt's grand strategy for 1759 was to launch a three-pronged attack on Canada. One army would move north from Lake Champlain, and another smaller force would strike across the wilderness to Lake Ontario and French-held Fort Niagara. A third, under Admiral Saunders and General Wolfe, would sail up the Saint Lawrence, where no battle fleet had ever been, and capture Quebec.

Captain Edward Carlisle sails ahead of the battle fleet to find a way through the legendary dangers of the Saint Lawrence River. An unknown sailing master assists him; James Cook has a talent for surveying and cartography and will achieve immortality in later years.

There are rocks and shoals aplenty before Carlisle and his frigate *Medina* are caught up in the near-fatal indecision of the summer when General Wolfe tastes the bitterness of early setbacks.

Rocks and Shoals is the seventh of the Carlisle & Holbrooke naval adventures. The series follows Carlisle and his protégé George Holbrooke, through the Seven Years War and into the period of turbulent relations between Britain and her American colonies in the 1760s.

***

BIBLIOGRAPHY

The following is a selection of the many books that I consulted in researching the Carlisle & Holbrooke series:

Definitive Text

Sir Julian Corbett wrote the original, definitive text on the Seven Years War. Most later writers use his work as a steppingstone to launch their own.

Corbett, LLM., Sir Julian Stafford. *England in the Seven Years War – Vol. I: A Study in Combined Strategy*. Normandy Press. Kindle Edition.

Strategy and Naval Operations

Three very accessible modern books cover the strategic context and naval operations of the Seven Years War. Daniel Baugh addresses the whole war on land and sea, while Martin Robson concentrates on maritime activities. Jonathan Dull has produced a very readable account from the French perspective.

Baugh, Daniel. *The Global Seven Years War 1754-1763*. Pearson Education, 2011. Print.

Robson, Martin. *A History of the Royal Navy, The Seven Years War*. I.B. Taurus, 2016. Print.

Dull, Jonathan, R. *The French Navy and the Seven Years' War*. University of Nebraska Press, 2005. Print.

Sea Officers

For an interesting perspective on the life of sea officers of the mid-eighteenth century, I'd read Augustus Hervey's Journal, with the cautionary note that while Hervey was by no means typical of the breed, he's very entertaining and devastatingly honest. For a more balanced view, I'd read British Naval Captains of the Seven Years War.

Erskine, David (editor). *Augustus Hervey's Journal, The Adventures Afloat and Ashore of a Naval Casanova*. Chatham Publishing, 2002. Print.

McLeod, A.B. *British Naval Captains of the Seven Years War, The View from the Quarterdeck*. The Boydell Press, 2012. Print.

Life at Sea

I recommend The Wooden World for an overview of shipboard life and administration during the Seven Years War.

N.A.M Rodger. *The Wooden World, An Anatomy of the Georgian Navy*. Fontana Press, 1986. Print.

The Niagara Campaign

There is a paucity of sources for the Niagara campaign. I found the following to be most useful:

Brian Leigh Dunnigan. *Siege 1759, The Campaign Against Niagara*. Old Fort Niagara Association, 1996. Print.

M. Pouchot & Franklin B. Hough, *Memoir Upon the Late War in North America, between the French and English 1755-60. Vol 1*. Leopold Classic Library. Print.

***

THE AUTHOR

Chris Durbin grew up in the seaside town of Porthcawl in South Wales. His first experience of sailing was as a sea cadet in the treacherous tideway of the Bristol Channel, and at the age of sixteen, he spent a week in a tops'l schooner in the Southwest Approaches. He was a crew member on the Porthcawl lifeboat before joining the navy.

Chris spent twenty-four years as a warfare officer in the Royal Navy, serving in all classes of ships from aircraft carriers through destroyers and frigates to the smallest minesweepers. He took part in operational campaigns in the Falkland Islands, the Middle East and the Adriatic and he spent two years teaching tactics at a US Navy training centre in San Diego.

On his retirement from the Royal Navy, Chris joined a large American company and spent eighteen years in the aerospace, defence and security industry, including two years on the design team for the Queen Elizabeth class aircraft carriers.

Chris is a graduate of the Britannia Royal Naval College at *Dartmouth*, the British Army Command and Staff College, the United States Navy War College (where he gained a postgraduate diploma in national security decision-making) and Cambridge University (where he was awarded an MPhil in International Relations).

With a lifelong interest in naval history and a long-standing ambition to write historical fiction, Chris has completed the first eight novels in the Carlisle & Holbrooke series, in which a colonial Virginian commands a British navy frigate during the middle years of the eighteenth century.

The series will follow its principal characters through the Seven Years War and into the period of turbulent relations between Britain and her American Colonies in the 1760s. They'll negotiate some thought-provoking loyalty issues when British policy and colonial restlessness lead inexorably to the American Revolution.

Chris lives on the south coast of England, surrounded by hundreds of years of naval history. His three children are all busy growing their own families and careers while Chris and his wife (US Navy, retired) of thirty-eight years enjoy sailing their classic dayboat.

**

Fun Fact:

Chris shares his garden with a tortoise named Aubrey. If you've read Patrick O'Brian's *HMS Surprise*, or have seen the 2003 film *Master and Commander: The Far Side of the World*, you'll recognise the modest act of homage that Chris has paid to that great writer. Rest assured that Aubrey has not yet grown to the gigantic proportions of *Testudo Aubreii*.

**

FEEDBACK

If you've enjoyed *Niagara Squadron*, please consider leaving a review on Amazon.

This is the latest of a series of books that will follow Carlisle and Holbrooke through the Seven Years War and into the 1760s when relations between Britain and her restless American Colonies are tested to breaking point.

Look out for the ninth in the Carlisle & Holbrooke series, coming soon.

You can follow my blog at:

www.chris-durbin.com

***

SEYÐISFJORÐUR
ICELAND.

Printed in Great Britain
by Amazon

52179635R00199